SONG OF THE DEMON COURT

DAKOTAH GUMM

ISBN 979-8-9860157-7-4 (paperback)

Library of Congress Control Number: 2023920586

dakotahgumm.com

Andrew
To new beginnings

CONTENTS

FEVER

ANNIKA

H e was burning up.

I wrung out the cloth and placed it back on my son's head. *Please, God, let him recover.*

Falk wasn't the only child who'd come down with the illness. Most of the town's children had been confined to their beds with horrid lesions and skin like fire. A few adults had developed the fever, as well, but unlike the children, they recovered quickly.

Most of them, at least.

I looked up as the door opened and my sister entered our small cabin, carried on a freezing wind.

"Brigid." No sign of the doctor with her. Where was the man?

"How is he?" Brigid removed her scarf and cloak, coming to place a hand on Falk's head.

"The same." I frowned. "The doctor?"

She shook her head. "Busy with the Weiss family. They've all caught it."

My heart sank. If he didn't come...

I didn't let myself finish the thought. "Go fill a bucket with snow." We'd have to drive the fever down ourselves. When he was a baby, Falk had gotten sick in the middle of a snowstorm. With the doctor unreachable, I'd brought his fever down myself. It had been eight years since we'd faced such a horrible sickness, but I could do it again. I had to.

I rubbed some more ointment on his lesions as Brigid stepped outside. The wounds were an angry red, seeping pus. Still not healing.

The door opened and closed again,

"Annika." Brigid set the bucket down, her voice tense. "I ran into Dietrich on the way home. He was going to a council meeting. He said—" She faltered and began again. "He said the council's calling a piper."

A stone formed in my stomach. "No." We'd all heard the stories. The brutality of the pipers, the high price they demanded. The ruin they wrought on those who couldn't pay. "They can't." The town had no money. The pipers would kill us all.

She filled a cloth with snow and settled it on Falk's brow. "Maybe we can pay in installments."

"Have you ever heard of the pipers taking a payment plan?" Even if they agreed, it wouldn't matter. The price the pipers were sure to demand would be astronomical. Generations from now, the town would still owe. "Someone has to talk to them. Make them see sense. They haven't called them yet?"

"I don't know. They're meeting now."

I stood, reaching for my cloak. "Stay here. Try to bring his fever down." I hated to leave Falk like this, but healing him wouldn't matter if the pipers murdered us all in our beds.

As I moved toward the door, Brigid grabbed my hand. "Isn't it worth it? If the pipers really can drive out the plague, isn't it worth whatever price they ask?"

I shook my head. "Not if we can't pay. You know what happens if they don't get paid." An unpaid piper could call the plague back, or send a pack of wolves to terrorize the town. He could draw out our livestock, leaving us to starve. Or he could play a death tune, killing everyone who heard it. "I'll be back soon." I pulled my hand from hers and stepped out into the snow.

The council met in the main room of the town's only in. I shook half-melted snowflakes from my coat as I entered.

A number of people stood around the small room, though not as many as usually attended council meetings. Most of the town's inhabitants were at home, recovering from the plague or tending the ill.

I squared my shoulders and strode to the head of the room, where the council sat at a long table. Mathys Kiefer, the town weaver, was addressing the men. He fell silent at my approach.

I met the gaze of the council head, an old man named Elmar Beck. "You plan to call a piper?"

A murmur went through the room. They hadn't announced it, then. Elmar scowled at me. "Mrs. Brandt, this council operates on order. If you have a matter you wish to bring before us, you must wait your turn." He looked back at the weaver.

Mathys shook his head. "I yield my time to Mrs. Brandt. Answer the question, councilman."

He let out a long breath before saying through gritted teeth, "Yes. We have called a piper."

Have called. A pit yawned in my stomach. They'd already called him. The murmur that swept the room was louder this time, distressed.

"Take back the call." I slammed my hand on the table. "You'll get us all killed!"

Elmar stood, his gray mustache trembling with the force of his breath. "We're already being killed! Whatever the price, we'll pay it. We'll make an agreement with the pipers, pay them in installments."

"And if they don't allow that?" someone called from the back of the room. Dietrich, I thought.

The room erupted in argument. I rubbed my temples as frustration, worry, and lack of sleep combined in a pounding headache. Fools, the lot of them.

The door burst open, cutting through the clamor. Everyone fell silent. Snow swirled into the room as a tall figure strode in.

The piper.

He dressed like a king. White fur trimmed his black cloak, the hood hiding his face in shadow. He glanced around the room and stepped up to the council table.

I didn't dare to breathe as he stopped next to me and took off his hood.

He was beautiful. That was the danger of pipers; they lured you in, not just with their music, but with their appearance, their voice, their very *scent,* if the tales could be believed.

He looked at each of the council members, giving me a chance to observe him unnoticed. His skin was tawny, his hair short and dark, with two small black horns peeking up through his curls. A spattering of scruff covered his chin, not enough to be called a beard. Apart from his horns and ears—his large, pointed ears that twitched toward every sound—he could have been human. A beautiful human.

Until he turned his gaze on me. There was nothing human in those hazel eyes. They were cold, the pupils vertical slits. My heart skipped a beat as he scanned my face.

Then he turned back to the council. I shivered, a breath escaping my lips.

"You summoned a piper." His voice was as cold as it was melodious.

Elmar trembled, rising to his feet to bow. "We did not expect you so soon."

The piper didn't respond.

Elmar tugged at his collar and coughed. "Yes. Our town is overrun by plague. We wish you to remove both the disease and its source."

Silence hung in the air for a moment. The piper drew a pan flute from beneath his cloak, watching Elmar. "Are you prepared to pay?"

No, I begged him with my eyes. *Don't do it.*

"Name your price."

The piper scanned the room again before listing a sum. I gasped, and those cold eyes flicked to me again. It was outrageous, more money than I could imagine. More money than a dozen generations would have been able to pay.

"We are prepared."

The piper raised a dark brow. "You have the means?"

He was offering us a way out. *Take it. Please, take it.*

Elmar straightened his shoulders, looking offended at the mere suggestion. "I said we would pay."

The piper watched him, face unreadable. Then he nodded once. "The deal is made."

My chest tightened. Stupid, stupid men. They'd doomed us all.

I took a step back, then another. I had to get out, had to take Brigid and Falk and leave, before it was too late.

The piper put his flute to his mouth, and I froze mid-step.

The tune he played was like nothing I'd heard before. Low and mournful, it reached into the corners of my mind, demanding attention, calling out my darkest depths. I couldn't move. Couldn't do anything but listen, as my fingers tingled and my chest tightened and the room around me faded away.

Somewhere in the distance, I heard a scratching, like tiny claws. Hundreds of them. Part of the music? Or something else?

The music grew louder, the mournful tones giving way to a sweeter, more cheerful melody. I wanted to laugh and weep and dance all at once.

With one final, exhilarating note, it ended.

I blinked as the room came back into focus. A metallic taste filled my mouth. The piper still stood next to me, flute at his lips. I looked around; everyone wore dazed expressions that matched how I felt.

The piper tucked the flute back under his cloak. "It is done."

Done. My heart thudded against my ribs, and I took another step back. I had to get out, had to go, now. Before he discovered the truth.

Before he found out we couldn't pay.

Those animal eyes flicked to me again as I backed toward the door, but I didn't stop.

I couldn't.

The door slammed into the wall as I flew into the house. "We have to go."

"Mama?"

I stopped mid-step, my gaze drawn to the bed. Falk sat up, looking better than he had in days.

"How do you feel, *liebling?*" I took a seat on the bed and drew him into my arms, pressing a kiss to his brow. His skin was cool, no sign of fever.

The piper had done it. He'd driven out the plague.

"Good." He wriggled out of my embrace. "What's wrong?"

"Nothing!" I scanned his bare chest and stomach. The lesions were gone as well, not even scars remaining. "Nothing. We're going on a little trip. Just for a few days. Do you feel up to it?"

Questions burned behind his eyes, but he could tell this wasn't the time to ask. He nodded, a wrinkle forming on his forehead as he frowned.

I stroked his blond head. "Good. Can you get dressed? I need to talk to your *Tante* Brigid for a minute."

I watched as he clambered out of bed and reached into the trunk for a clean set of clothes. His ribs stuck out from malnutrition—it had been a long winter—but he moved with his usual energy, no weakness left over from the illness that had confined him to bed for the past three days. No remnant of his brush with death.

Brigid's hand on my shoulder jolted me from my musing. "What happened?" she asked in a low voice.

I swallowed. "A piper came. He asked for...more than we could ever pay. The council agreed." I stood and began stuffing supplies into a bag. "Obviously the piper fulfilled his end of the bargain. I left before he found out we couldn't pay ours."

Brigid reached for a sack. Taking the braid of onions from the ceiling, she asked, "Where are we going?"

Somewhere. Anywhere. "I hadn't gotten that far." Augsburg, maybe We didn't have much money, but we could get help at one of the *kirchen* until I found work or we could return home.

If there was a home to return to.

We packed in silence. Even Falk seemed to sense the need for urgency, not complaining as I helped him layer on all his clothing. He'd need the added warmth, and whatever he wore he wouldn't have to carry.

Brigid and I did the same, finishing with our cloaks and strapping a pack to each of our backs.

Had the piper discovered the council's lie yet? What would his revenge be? I shuddered to think what he might do.

What if he played a death tune? Wild animals we could flee from or fight, but how could we fight a song?

I turned to Brigid. "We need to stuff our ears." The stories all said that blocking out the noise would do little to help, but we had to do *something*. I scanned the room for something to use. Rags. I had rags near the stove. We could tear off pieces to use as stuffing.

As I reached for the cloth, a sound swept into the room. Furious and frantic, it surrounded us.

"Block it out!" I clapped my hands over my ears as the call of the piper rose over the fire crackling in the hearth, over the howl of wind against the windows.

Eyes wide, I looked for Falk. He stood frozen, staring at the door.

The song pounded through my body, the ascending notes setting my teeth on edge. A sob caught in my throat as I reached for Falk, but he pushed the door open and ran outside, a puppet pulled by invisible strings.

"Falk!" I tore after him. Where was he going? Other children were outside as well, their parents behind them. There were the Weiss children, all three of them running hand-in-hand with the same blank stare Falk wore.

The piper was calling the children, but why? What did he want with them? Was he going to lead them into the river or over a cliff?

I slipped on a spot of ice, barely keeping my feet as I ran after Falk. If I could catch him, get him out of the piper's spell, we could still escape.

The music stopped its climb, holding on a shrill, frantic note. It pierced my skull like a knife. I dropped to my knees, clutching my head and screaming.

At last the sound stopped. In its place remained a hollow, ringing silence. Head still aching, I scrambled to my feet. My son. Where was my son? Tears threatened to blind me. I wiped them away as I ran down the street. It wasn't too late. It couldn't be.

Darkness surrounded the town. I peered into the shadows, but nothing moved. There was no sign of the children or the piper anywhere.

I whirled around, heart in my throat. Brigid. Had Brigid been taken, too?

No. She was there in front of our house, kneeling with her head in her hands. I ran back to her and pulled her to her feet. "Are you hurt? Did you see where they went?"

She shook her head, half-frozen tears streaking her face. "I didn't—I didn't see. Falk?"

A vice closed around my heart. "He's gone."

Not one child under the age of twelve remained. The entire town spent all night searching for them, but they'd left no trace behind.

Near dawn we returned to the inn. Cold numbness burned my fingers and nose, but the worst was the ache in my heart.

I'd told them not to do this. Why hadn't they listened? If they'd just listened to me, Falk would still be here.

Elmar took his seat at the front of the room. Running one hand through his mussed gray hair, he raised the other for silence. "This is a dark day for our town," he began. "Though our search efforts were ineffective, I can assure you, we will make it through. Perhaps our children will return to us."

"They won't," I snapped. "You know they won't." The pipers were demons. Once they punished someone, they never mitigated that punishment with mercy.

He went on, ignoring me. "Or perhaps they will not return. Whatever happens, we cannot allow this tragedy to tear us apart. We need each other, now more than ever"

Tragedy. The only tragedy here was the council's stupidity. They were as much to blame for this as the piper.

I pointed at Elmar. "You did this. You brought him here. You agreed to pay him. We'd all heard the stories; we knew what could happen. But you lied to him. You let him take our children." I took a deep, shuddering breath that did nothing to calm me. "You lost three grandchildren tonight. Do you still think it was worth it?"

His wrinkled mouth turned down at the corners. "Mrs. Brandt, I understand that you're grieving. We all are. But I can assure you that we did everything possible to pay the piper's price."

I scoffed. "Pay him with what? We couldn't have paid that in ten generations. And now we've paid a price higher than any gold or silver." I spat on the floor. "You disgust me."

"It's been a long night. We'll all feel better once we've gotten some rest." He tugged at his bushy mustache. "Go home, everyone. We'll reconvene this evening."

As if rest would bring back our children.

Brigid and I walked home in the gray pre-morning light. She clung to me for support. I didn't stumble, exhaustion turning my steps to clockwork.

We reached the house and peeled off our outer garments as we stepped inside. I didn't bother to lock the door. Not out of any misplaced hope that Falk would come home—no, my mother had told me endless stories about the pipers, and Pater Huber, the parish priest, loved to delineate their evils at every opportunity. I knew the pipers wouldn't release my son. I didn't bother to lock the door because the worst had already happened. What more could be done to me?

Brigid and I crawled into bed. We held each other tight as our tears lulled us into blessed oblivion.

KING EDRIC

LOIC

My stomach soured as I stepped into the silent hall. My father watched me cross the packed room. His tawny face, marked with spots of white, contorted in a scowl more severe than usual. He'd called a special meeting of the court on my return. To *deal with* me.

This wouldn't end well.

"Loic." King Edric's voice was deathly calm.

I stopped at the throne and bowed low, sweeping my travel cloak backward. "Your majesty."

"Do our laws mean nothing to you?"

I'd spent the entire journey home thinking about how to respond, but still I faltered. If I feigned ignorance, that would only make things worse.

I raised my chin. "I hold our laws in the highest regard, Father."

The king's cold umber eyes narrowed. "And yet here you are, with a whole passel of human brats in tow. Am I to assume you took them for slaves, as payment?"

"Not at all." I kept my face cool, impassive. An armored mask against his anger. "I was not paid."

"Then *why* do you have the children?"

I allowed myself a cocky grin, one I knew would infuriate my father. "What better way to punish those that try to cheat us than to take their children?"

Silence reigned. At last the king spoke again. "You expect me to believe that you acted in accordance with our laws? That your idiocy was not out of some misguided sympathy for the humans, but a desire to punish them?"

Rage turned my vision red, though I kept my mask firmly in place. It was one thing for him to berate me in private, but in front of the whole court?

The last time he'd called me an idiot in this room, I'd been only six. I'd found a litter of kittens in the stables. One was a runt, shunned by the mother, and I'd taken it into my room and tried to nurse it back to health. A servant had found it and informed my father, who used the opportunity to teach me about the futility of sentiment in rulers.

"The weak have no place in our society," he'd said. "Keeping them alive draws resources away from the more valuable members of the kingdom. Sentiment for them is worthless."

Then he'd made me snap the beast's neck.

I'd learned the lesson well. Sentiment and mercy were foreign concepts to me now.

I hadn't answered my father's question yet, and fury was building on his pied face like a rising storm.

"I followed our laws to the letter, your majesty," I said finally. "We are required to take lives equal to those we saved. I did take those lives, and I took them in a manner that will punish the village more than anything else I could have done. Not one child remains, and knowing their children are alive but forever separated from them is far worse than any death. Learning that their children are being raised as pipers would be paramount to damnation in their minds." I allowed a smirk to slip out. "There is nothing worse than the loss of a child, Father." Not that the king had ever felt such a fear. For one to fear the loss of a child, one had to care for that child, and my father despised me.

A low murmur went through the hall, but the king raised a hand for silence. He met my gaze. "Very well," he said, his words deceptively cool despite the anger still simmering behind his eyes. "I have determined that your actions break none of our laws. The children may stay."

I bowed. "I thank you for your wisdom."

The king waved a hand, indicating that I should join him on the dais. As I climbed the steps, I kept my expression neutral. I may have won the battle, but I would have to be the idiot my father believed I was to think this was the last I would hear on the topic. My father was never one to accept defeat, and I'd made him look ridiculous in front of the court. If the children were to survive living among the pipers, I'd have to keep them far from him.

Teta, the closest thing I had to a friend, grinned at me from across the room. *Well done,* she signed. I nodded, not allowing myself the indulgence of signing back. I had to be more vigilant than ever after my mistake of lenience—and that's what it had been. No matter what I told my father about the cruelty of my decision, vindictiveness had not been my goal. I hadn't been able to bring myself to kill those people, not even the fools who had made the choice to call me, knowing they could never pay the price.

It had been clear the village was impoverished, even by the usual human standards. Maybe two dozen huts and rundown byre-dwellings centered around an inn, the only building that hadn't appeared on the verge of collapse. The inhabitants had been lean and gaunt, many on the verge of starvation. I'd known they wouldn't be able to pay me. I'd even given them the chance to back out, asking if they were certain they could pay.

But they'd lied to me. Not until after I'd driven out the plague had they told me they couldn't pay my price—my father's price—in full. They had wanted to pay it off in installments, gradually.

It would have taken them centuries.

Fools they were, the whole town. The council had risked not only their own lives, but the lives of all the people under them, by lying to me. Taking the children had been an act of mercy in more ways than one; no child should be raised by such reckless oafs.

And yet not everyone had agreed with the council's decision. My thoughts lingered on the woman who had stood next to me when I'd approached the high table. She'd looked at me with such fear and hatred in her eyes. She could never have condoned calling a piper. No, she hated me and everything I stood for.

Good for her. At least she, alone in the world, knew what the risks were. The rest of her people might be stupid enough to risk their lives with the pipers, but she would know better. She knew to fear me.

In truth, it was hard not to fear myself.

BRING HIM·HOME

ANNIKA

I didn't sleep long. When I woke to the shining sun, I had one brief moment of peace before the events of the previous night came crashing back. Despair threatened to smother me, but I disentangled myself from Brigid's arms and reached for the pack of food she'd tossed on the floor. I pulled out yesterday's bread and tore off a chunk, popping it into my mouth. I barely tasted it. I took another bite anyway, staring at the cold fireplace. Our small house was freezing; we needed the fire built back up, but I couldn't bring myself to move. Couldn't bring myself to do anything but keep eating.

At last Brigid stirred. She blinked blearily at me as she sat up, then her face crumpled.

"Any news?" she whispered, as though afraid to break the silence.

I shook my head and tossed the rest of the bread to her. A poor breakfast, but she ate it as I had, not seeming to notice the taste.

A knock sounded at the door, sending my stomach tumbling down to my feet. Had someone found a trace of the children?

I opened the door to see the ruddy face of Dietrich, the sheep farmer who'd been courting Brigid since childhood.

"Annika." He took off his hat and inclined his head. "I'm so sorry for your loss."

He's not dead! I wanted to scream. Instead I gave a tight nod and let him into the house.

Brigid bowled into him with a gasping sob. He held her tight, and I turned away, a lump in my throat. I didn't begrudge her this small comfort. Just the opposite. If it wasn't for me and Falk, she'd have already married Dietrich. Our parents had died in the fire that destroyed their apothecary, leaving Brigid without a dowry—not that Dietrich cared, but when my husband had died of illness a year later, she'd refused to leave us.

After a few long minutes, he gently guided her to a seat at the table. Holding her on his lap like a child, he looked over her head at me. "How are you doing?"

I took a seat as well. "Still trying to understand."

"I can't believe they did it. They knew the stories."

We all did. I clutched my stomach, the yawning pit threatening to swallow me whole.

Dietrich reached out with his free hand and squeezed mine. "Anything you need, Annika. I'm here for you. Both of you."

The only thing I needed was my son back, but I forced myself to say, "Thank you."

"Have you thought about what you'll do next?" he asked quietly.

Bring him home. Bring him home. Bring him home.

The words pounded through my head. But what could I do? I didn't know where he'd been taken, and even if I did, I couldn't hope to force the pipers to free him.

That didn't matter, though. He was my son. A stray tear trickled down my cheek. "I have to find him."

Brigid's head lifted from Dietrich's chest. "You're not going after him."

"I have to." I didn't know where the piper's land was, didn't know where much of anything was beyond our village and Augsburg, but I could find directions or a guide in the city. If the demon had taken the children back to his court, I'd find him and beg him to let them go. Even if I had to trade myself for Falk's freedom.

If he hadn't taken them to his court...

That was a problem for the future. *Sufficient unto the day is the evil thereof.*

Brigid wiped her nose on her sleeve. "I'm coming with you."

"Absolutely not." I didn't need to worry about her, too. "You'll stay here and keep things ready for us to come home." If we came home. I looked at Dietrich. "You'll take care of her?"

His eyes widened, but he dipped his head. "Always."

I reached for the bags we'd packed the night before and began repacking them. I'd need only what I could carry, and if I was going to find the piper, there was no time to waste.

"Where will you go?" Brigid asked.

"Augsburg, first. From there, Laute." City of the pipers. The demon court.

She shuddered, but she knew me too well to try to stop me. "Be careful," she whispered.

I put on my cloak and slung the pack over my shoulder before drawing her into an embrace. Tears sprang to my eyes, but I blinked them away. I didn't have time to waste crying. It would take several hours to reach Augsburg on foot, and I wanted to be inside the walls before dark.

I patted Brigid's back and turned to go, nodding to Dietrich, but he pulled me in for a brotherly hug. I stiffened in surprise before hugging him back.

As he let go, he took my hand and pressed something into it. I looked down at the object—no, objects. A small handful of coins.

"I can't accept this," I said, trying to give them back.

He shook his head, closing my hand around the money. "We've got enough. Take it."

My throat threatened to close up. I slipped my hand into my pocket and choked out, "Thank you."

Brigid threw her arms around me again and kissed my cheek. "Bring him home."

"I will," I swore, and I stepped out into the cold.

I arrived at Augsburg just before dusk. As I passed into the city, I looked around. The spires of *kirchen* reached up into the clouds, too many to count, and unlike my small village home, the buildings here towered over me.

I'd been here before. My husband, Nikolaus, used to bring me to the city for Holy Week during the years we could afford it. I hadn't been since his death two years past, but the city was still familiar. Fewer people filled the streets than at Easter. I didn't have to elbow past anyone as I made my way to the nearest *kirche*.

I stopped in front of it, looking up at the two towers. It was a beautiful building, much larger than our tiny village chapel. Its only flaw was a sculpture on the church's facade, a vile image of pipers playing their flutes as they followed behind a goat-headed devil.

I shuddered at the sight. These were the demons that had stolen my son from me. They were damned, receiving their unholy magic from Satan himself. But was it necessary to depict their evils next to the door to God's house?

I shook my head and walked past the foul image, stepping into the blessed relief of the *kirche*.

Vespers was just ending. I slipped into the backmost pew, taking a deep breath of the incense-filled air. The scent calmed my soul, and I drew my medallion of St. Anne from my pocket.

The pewter medallion, large enough to fill my hand, had been a gift from my father. It depicted St. Anne reading with a young girl—the Virgin Mary. I'd been born on the Feast of St. Anne, and I'd had the medallion most of my life, but it took on special meaning now. I held it by the cord as I prayed to the patron saint of mothers and her daughter, the Queen of Heaven.

St. Anne, pray for me. Holy Mother Mary, pray for me. A demon has stolen my child, and I fear for both his body and his immortal soul. Please, guard and guide my son in my absence, and I will— What could I possibly offer the saints? I had nothing.

I scanned the sanctuary. Vespers had finished, and the few con-gregants had already made their way to the door. A skinny priest approached me; our eyes met, and he glanced down at my medallion and smiled.

"St. Anne?" he said. "A personal favorite of mine."

"Mine as well, Father."

He took a seat in the pew next to me. "What brings you here, child?"

"I—" The words stuck in my throat. I swallowed and started again. "I need help. It's my son."

In halting words, I related the events of the past few days, from the beginning of the plague to the piper's disappearance with the children. When I finished, tears drenched my cheeks, and the cord from the medallion bit into my skin where I held it.

The priest's face was solemn as he asked, "You intend to travel to Laute?"

"I have to find my son." I rubbed my thumb over St. Anne's face. "Is it wrong to go among demons, Father? Even if I'm doing it to save my son?"

He frowned. "What makes you think the pipers are demons?"

That was what the Church taught, wasn't it? That pipers were demons made flesh.

Weren't they?

"I was taught about their evils my whole life. Even my priest..." I faltered when his look darkened.

"Yes, there are some within the Church that preach hatred from the pulpit. My predecessor here did the same. But I believe pipers are human."

Surely this was heresy. I stared at him, open-mouthed.

He gave me a wry smile. "I see I've stunned you, but allow me to explain. You've heard of the indigenous people of the Americas, or Africa, or the Far East, yes?" At my hesitant nod, he went on. "They look different from us, with different skin and hair, different body shapes. And yet no one denies that they are as human as we are. How is it that the pipers, with their large ears and horns, are any less human than they?"

He had to be wrong. No human would be so cruel as the pipers. They were barbaric, like animals. "But they're pagans," I argued.

"As are many of the peoples I just mentioned. But Christ came for the pagans, did He not?" He gestured toward the altar. "Why should salvation be denied to these people?"

"They use pagan magics to murder people." I threw my hands up. "They stole my son!"

"They've committed many atrocities," he agreed, his voice soft. "But remember, even St. Paul did atrocious things before Christ found him on the road to Damascus. Pipers have the capacity for great evil, but they also have the capacity for great love." He sighed. "No, I don't believe pipers are demons. They're souls created by God, and like many souls in this world, they're lost."

I couldn't believe that. Not when I'd seen what their unholy magic could do. I'd felt the evil in the piper's music, felt it in my bones. Such wickedness couldn't be natural.

"To answer your original question, no. I don't believe it's wrong to go among the pipers. Just the opposite. I think your influence, as a believer, could be instrumental in drawing them from their pagan darkness to the light of the Gospel."

He wanted me to be a missionary to the pipers. The idea made me sick. Telling those monsters, those demons about the mysteries of the

Church. No, I couldn't do it. I wouldn't. I was going to find my son and take him home.

The priest stood, thankfully not choosing to press the issue. "I shouldn't keep you here discussing the particulars of theology. You must be exhausted. We have a room set aside for those in need. You're welcome to stay there tonight. Tomorrow morning you can go to the apothecary up the street. The owner, Gisela Volk, might have some insight for you as you prepare for your journey. She's had some dealings with the pipers herself."

I stood as well. "Thank you, Pater—"

"Trost. Ehrhart Trost."

"Thank you, Pater Trost."

I spent a restless night in the whitewashed room off of the sanctuary. At dawn, I finally rose and splashed water on my face to combat the heavy bags beneath my eyes. I'd just finished dressing when Pater Trost knocked at the door.

"I'm sure you're anxious to be on your way," he said when I opened it. "I have to prepare for service, but Mrs. Volk should be at the apothecary this morning. It's just three buildings down, next to the inn." He held out a small bag. "Some breakfast for you."

"Thank you, Pater," I said softly, taking the food.

"The Lord will be with you, child." He made the sign of the cross over me. "May the angels guard you on your journey."

I nibbled on the bread in the bag as I walked down the slush-covered street to the apothecary. The wooden sign above the door read *Volk's Apothecary.* A bell tinkled at my entrance, and a variety of scents barraged me, from the familiar notes of lanolin and comfrey to more exotic ones I couldn't place.

The woman behind the counter wasn't much older than me. She couldn't have been more than thirty, probably the shop owner's daughter. She wore a black dress with a white apron and cap. Despite the early hour, she greeted me warmly. "Good morning. How can I help you?"

"I'm looking for Gisela Volk," I said. "Is she here?"

"That would be me."

I blinked in surprise before schooling my features into an expression of polite interest. "I'm sorry. I was expecting someone—"

"Older?" She smiled, the severe nature of her appearance softening with the gesture. "Yes, I hear that often. My husband owned the shop before me. I took it over on his passing."

"I'm sorry for your loss." She was like me, then, widowed young. *Or not like me,* I thought, glancing around the shop. She'd obviously had far more success maintaining her husband's work after his death.

"Thank you. What can I do for you?"

"I'm traveling to Laute."

She stiffened, features turning to ice. "Can you pay however much they ask?"

I shook my head and opened my mouth to speak, but she cut me off.

"Then it's not worth it. Whatever you think you need from them, I promise, it's not worth the consequences."

"No, I…" My eyes burned. I swallowed the lump in my throat and went on. "They have my son."

"Ah." Her face crinkled in sympathy. She gestured to the door behind the counter. "Please, come with me."

She led me to a cozy sitting room warmed by a small fire. "Have a seat."

I sank into a chair next to the fire, and she sat across from me. "What's your name?" she asked.

"Annika Brandt."

"I wish we were meeting under better circumstances, Annika," she said. "So, you've come across the pipers."

"One of them. He—" My throat closed, and I shook my head.

"Took your son?" Gisela patted my hand. "Mine as well. My husband and son, actually. A death tune."

I shuddered, seeing the depths of grief in her eyes. At least Falk was still alive.

"It's been three years. He would have been six next month." She pulled a handkerchief from her pocket and dabbed at the corner of her eye. "How old is your son?"

"Eight. The piper took him, and all the children from our village." I clenched my hands in my skirts to keep the tears at bay. "I want to find them. To bring my son home."

"I understand." She didn't meet my eyes. "I don't wish to upset you, but are you sure—"

I cut her off. "They're alive." They had to be. The piper wouldn't have taken them away only to kill them. We would have found them by now if he had. An image flashed into my mind—Falk, lying half-covered in snow, his lips blue and his eyes open, sightless. "He's alive," I said again, more to myself than to my companion.

Gisela nodded. "You believe the piper took them back to their court?"

"He must have." *Please, God, keep him safe.* "Do you know where I can find a map, or a guide?"

"You won't find a guide in Augsburg willing to take you there." She rose and went to a shelf in the corner, shuffling through papers. "You can read?"

"Yes." My parents had worked hard to improve our lot in life. They'd taught me and my sister to work in their apothecary, but every spare bit of money had gone to paying for our education, with the hopes that we might someday be able to use that education to get out of our village and into a better life.

I doubted this was what they had imagined when they thought of me leaving the village.

"Good." She dragged over a stool and spread a map on it as she took her seat again. "Take this road from the city, and take the first fork on the left. It's unmarked, but it will lead you directly to their mountains. The pass into the valley is here." She pointed. "It will be guarded, but if you ask for an audience with the king, you might get it."

We both knew what she didn't say. *You might get your audience, or you might be killed on the spot.* It was a risk I couldn't avoid. I peered at the map. A small ring of mountains surrounded a small valley. It wasn't far; if I left immediately, I could make it there by nightfall. Tomorrow morning at the latest.

I could be with Falk again within a day.

"Thank you," I murmured as she folded up the map.

"What's your plan?"

Find the pipers. Bring Falk home. "I hadn't thought that far."

Gisela pursed her lips. "I'm sure I don't need to tell you how dangerous the pipers can be." She pushed the map toward me. "If you make it into the city, killing you isn't the worst they could do to you."

I nodded, tucking the paper into my pocket. Everyone knew that pipers could enchant a person, force someone to be their thrall.

"I've been working on something," she said, going back to the shelf. This time she took a small box and opened it, bringing out two small lumps of fabric. "I've not had a chance to test them, but I've soaked these in a—a substance. If you keep them in your ears, they might help you withstand the pipers' magic."

A substance. I hesitated, considering the pieces. A potion? Was she dabbling in magic? Scripture explicitly forbade such things.

"It's not magic," she said quickly, seeing the hesitation on my face. "Not really. It's more like anti-magic. Battling the forces of Satan with the means God has given us."

What she said made sense. It was no different from using medicine to treat a wound or illness. I accepted them and drew out my purse to pay her.

"Free of charge. If you have a chance to bring your son home, do it. I—" She made a choking sound and shook her head. "Good luck."

"My sister," I said. "I left my sister, Brigid, back in the village south of here. Can you get in touch with her if I don't come back?"

"Of course."

On impulse, I stood and wrapped my arms around her. If things had gone just a little bit differently, I could have been like her, mourning not just my husband, but also my son. Instead, thanks to her, I had a chance to bring Falk home. A chance she'd never have.

She embraced me as well. "Be careful, Annika." She pulled back and looked into my eyes. "And find me if—when you return. I'd love to meet your son."

"I will. Thank you, Gisela."

LAUTE

ANNIKA

I hadn't reached the pipers' city by nightfall, but I did find an inn along the road to spend the night. Again, I woke before dawn, and by midday I reached the ring of mountains I sought.

Cold seeped into my bones, and my feet and back ached. Up ahead, I saw the dark, rocky mountain pass, devoid of life. Just wide enough for a single wagon to pass through. I scanned it warily. Would there be guards? Would they kill me on sight, or take me prisoner for trespassing?

I took out the earplugs Gisela had given me and stuffed my ears with them. She hadn't promised they would work against the pipers' sorcery, but their presence comforted me nonetheless.

As I took a cautious step into the shadowy pass, a voice came from behind me, muffled but not entirely muted.

"Looking for something?"

I whirled around, heart in my throat, and met the cold eyes of the piper who'd stolen the children. Too close. He was far too close, only steps away. How had I not heard him approach? I pressed a hand to my chest and took a step back, further into the dark path between the mountains.

He matched my step, keeping the distance between us even. "What brings you here?"

Dangerous. This man—this demon—was dangerous. Every instinct urged me to run, to flee.

But he had Falk.

I squared my shoulders. "I want my son back."

He quirked a brow. "What makes you think I have him?"

Cold fear rushed through my veins at the words, but I forced myself to remain still. He wouldn't have taken the children only to leave them stranded somewhere. We would have found them if he had. "I saw you take him."

The piper circled me. "Ah, yes. I remember you. The one from my latest call. The one who hated me." He tsked. "All the others feared me, but they respected my power. You, on the other hand...I saw no respect from you. Nothing but fear and hatred."

I turned with him, keeping him in sight. "My son did nothing to you. You have to return him."

"You're right. *He* did nothing to me." He stopped circling, looking down at me with a scowl. "I was well within my rights to take him, though."

"According to whose law?" Anger burned through my fear. "No laws of God or man allow you to take a child for a debt he doesn't owe. A debt his family doesn't owe."

"I'm glad to say I'm neither god nor man, nor subject to their laws. My own laws, however, allow me to take your child."

"Why?" Hot tears, tears of fury, not sadness, filled my eyes. "Why him? He did you no wrong. I did you no wrong."

"Your people did." His voice was flat, almost bored. "At any rate, it's not my place to cancel a debt. That right belongs to the Pied Piper."

The Pied Piper. King of the pipers. My blood froze in my veins. Beelzebub incarnate, the cruelest of all the pipers, held my son for ransom.

"Please," I whispered. "I just want my son back."

He surveyed me with empty, cat-like eyes. "If you want to take him home, you'll have to petition the king. I warn you, though, he's not a forgiving man."

Anything. I'd do anything to save Falk. "I'll go."

The piper stepped further into the mountain pass. "Then follow me."

Stone cliffs seemed to swallow me up as I followed him, barely breathing. What would the city look like? Would its appearance reflect the hell it was? I pictured a wasteland, cold and desolate, with a pile of riches reaching to the sky. With each step, my feet grew heavier. I couldn't do this.

I had to do this. For Falk.

At last, the light ahead of us grew until we stepped out of the darkness and into the valley.

A castle rose up in the middle of it, larger than I could have imagined. The towers glinted in the sunlight—glinted because gold lined the surface. My eyes widened, and I stopped walking, fear temporarily forgotten in my awe. The opulence astounded me. I'd never seen such a gross display of wealth. Beyond the castle, the city stretched across the valley. Each house could have been a castle in its own right, large enough to fit at least four of the homes in my village. People—pipers—moved through the streets, their horns and long, pointed ears bared to the sky.

The piper turned back to me, his scowl deepening. "Keep up."

We hiked down into the snow-covered valley, nearing the giant castle. Two guards stood at the top of the castle steps, swords at their hips. They opened the doors for me and the piper who led me, not giving us a second look. I peered at the doors, so well-crafted as to have been carved from a single piece of wood. Rubies encrusted the gilded handles.

Were the pipers so rich that they could just throw away wealth like this? It soured my stomach. So much excess, and yet they committed such atrocities when they weren't paid. They didn't need the money; that much was obvious. But they'd stolen my son for money.

I looked around as we entered the castle—every bit as opulent inside as out—hoping to catch a glimpse of Falk. Would the piper let me see him first, or would he take me straight to his king? I opened my mouth to ask, but he halted suddenly. I crashed into his back.

He turned to glare at me before opening the door before us and ushering me inside.

A fire blazed on one end of the large room, filling it with warmth and light. Shelves lined the far wall, filled with books, more books than I'd ever seen in my life. Sitting on a couch near the fire was a piper woman, her skin golden brown, sharp black horns peeking up through her tight curls. Her ears twitched, and she looked up at our entrance.

She raised a brow at the sight of me before turning to my escort. "Good afternoon, Loic," she said. "Who's your friend?" Her voice came out loud and somewhat nasally, not as melodic as the piper next to me.

"She wants to speak to the king." As he spoke, he made strange gestures with his hands. "I need you to keep an eye on her until Hall."

She gestured back at him without speaking, her face animated. He responded in kind, his movements becoming more agitated by the moment.

What were they doing? Clearly this was some form of silent communication, but why? Were they deciding my fate? My chest tightened, breath coming short as I looked between them. Maybe he wanted to have me killed. Maybe *she* wanted me killed.

After a moment, she glanced at me and held up a hand. "I'm sorry," she said, rubbing her chest. "We're being rude. I'm Teta." She brushed a fist near her eye.

I stared at her, wary, and she turned back to the man and sighed. "You really are an ass." She made horns with her fingers. "You've terrified the poor thing. Did you even bother to introduce yourself?"

He rolled his eyes. "No, I didn't bother to introduce myself to the human the king will probably have killed by morning." His words dripped with sarcasm. "Why do you ask?"

She made a face at him before turning back to me. "I'm Teta, and this is Loic." She swiped her fist next to her eyes again—her thumb tucked between her first two fingers—and then made an L shape with both of her hands and held it over her head, as though putting on a crown. "What's your name?"

I touched the wall behind me, the wood a solid, comforting presence. It wouldn't help me if they decided to attack, but I felt better nonetheless. "I'm Annika Brandt."

She frowned and glanced at the man, who repeated, "Annika Brandt."

She smiled warmly at me. "It's lovely to meet you, Annika Brandt." She stopped gesturing as she spoke my name, but otherwise her hands moved in conjunction with her mouth. "I'm sorry Loic was your first introduction to our court. For a prince, he's incredibly lacking in interpersonal skills."

Prince. The piper who stole my son was a prince? My cheeks flushed, and I dropped down into a clumsy bow.

Teta let out a barking laugh. "I like her," she said. "Go ahead. I'll stay with her until tonight."

"Keep her in the room," he said before turning to me. "I can't vouch for your safety if the king finds out you're here before Hall." He gave the woman a sharp nod and left.

The most immediate danger gone, I turned a wary eye on the piper woman.

She gave me a brilliant smile. "Annika. Am I saying that right?"

I nodded.

Her smile widened. "Good. I'm deaf, so it's hard to know sometimes. I can read lips, but it's not always clear if it's not a word I'm familiar with."

A deaf piper. That explained her silent communication with the prince. How did she live in a city where music was magic, where sound was everything? I felt a flash of sympathy before remembering what she was. A demon. Even a disabled demon was deadly.

She gestured to the couch. "Please, have a seat."

I shook my head. "I'd rather stand," I said slowly, exaggerating the movements of my mouth so she could understand me.

She laughed. "No need to do that. I can understand you just fine as long as I'm looking at you." She motioned to the couch again. "But you should have a seat. Hall won't start for hours, and you don't want to meet the Pied Piper exhausted."

I glanced at the available seats. The couch would put me too close to her, but there was a stiff-backed wooden chair not far from the door. I perched on the edge of it. If I needed to run, that distance could help.

As if those few extra feet would make a difference if she attacked.

Her smile flickered for a moment, but she sat on the couch, tucking her feet underneath her fine silk dress. "What brings you to the court?"

I raised my chin. "I want my son back."

This time her smile disappeared entirely. "I see."

Fear coursed through me. Did she know something? "I want to see him. Please. Before I meet the king—"

"I would," she said, "but Loic's right. The king won't be pleased that you're here. It's best if you're not seen by anyone else until Hall."

What about the guards who'd seen me? Didn't they report to the king? *She's lying,* a voice inside me whispered. *She's trying to lure you into a false sense of security.* Falk could already be dead, or languishing in some dungeon below the castle.

I clutched my skirts. Falk was safe. He had to be. I'd see him as soon as I faced the Pied Piper.

In the meantime, anything I could learn about this terrifying place would help. Even if the piper was lying to me. "What is Hall?" I asked her.

She leapt at the opportunity for conversation. "It's the weekly meeting of the court. King Edric hears petitions from his subjects and dispenses justice or mediates disputes. Occasionally someone will come to demonstrate their new abilities for the court."

"Abilities? Like, their magic?" Why would they need to demonstrate that? If all of the pipers could perform magic, there would be no need for demonstration.

"Yes, exactly!" She nodded encouragement, looking pleased at the question. "Our abilities don't manifest until late childhood, once we've shown a proclivity for a particular instrument."

"Instrument? Can't you use anything?" In the stories my mother had told me, pipers could use anything around them to make music, and every tune they made was enchanted. She'd told tales of imprisoned pipers who had played songs on their prison bars to force the guards to set them free.

She laughed. "No, of course not. We've each got our own talents. You don't think enchantment is easy, do you?" She didn't wait for me to answer before going on. "No, most of us can only use a single instrument—for enchantment, I mean, not for music. Occasionally someone will develop the ability to use a second, but it's rare."

It wasn't true. She was trying to convince me that pipers had a weakness, that they couldn't enchant with the very sound of their voice. But why would she lie to me about this? I was no threat. Outnumbered and alone, I would only survive this place by a miracle. What benefit did her misinformation bring the pipers?

Unless she wasn't lying, and what I'd always been told about the pipers was wrong.

I couldn't accept that possibility. If I planned to rescue Falk, I had to trust everything I'd been taught, not listen to this demon's pernicious lies.

PETITIONING THE PIED PIPER

LOIC

Idiotic woman.

What could have possessed her to come after the children? No one else had bothered. I'd taken a dozen children, from at least six sets of parents, and yet only one woman came for them. The rest weren't foolish enough to try.

When I'd seen her in her village—if such a hovel of shacks could be called a village—I'd thought that she had enough sense to stay far away from my kind. Apparently I'd been wrong.

She was lucky she'd survived this far, trying to sneak into Laute to rescue her son. If the guards on duty had been more loyal to my father than to me, or if they'd been more inclined to attack first and ask questions later, she'd be dead.

She was a little slip of a thing, malnourished and desperate. Her cheeks were gaunt, like humans so often were in the winter, and small enough to snap in half with my bare hands. No match for even the weakest of the pipers. In a way, she reminded me of a little bird, a songbird, frantically trying to protect her nest and her young. Even a child could kill her, but still she fought.

My father would eat her alive.

That was none of my business. If the fool wanted to go up against the Pied Piper, why should I stand in her way? Like as not, my father would kill her for trespassing on our lands, for having the audacity to try to reclaim her child. The matter of the children had left him in a foul mood already; her arrival wouldn't do them any favors.

I stalked toward the council chamber. My rendezvous with the little songbird had made me late for a meeting, an infraction my father wouldn't fail to note. Then again, he might appreciate my absence. I'd contradicted him at the last council meeting, for which infraction he'd sent me to the village. Responding to a call from an impoverished community was beneath me, as we usually reserved such calls for the untested, but he'd wanted to humiliate me.

He wouldn't try the same thing again, not after I'd managed to humiliate him in turn by bringing home a dozen human children with me.

I slipped into the back of the chamber. Despite my silent entrance, several people glanced up, my father included. He scowled, his usual expression for me, but he didn't interrupt the speaker as I took my seat at the foot of the table.

"...need to consider an alliance with a stronger kingdom, one we can trust to protect us." The words came from my father's latest appointment to the council, a gold-horned young man named Alois. The bumbling youth had only been appointed to appease his mother, the king's latest conquest. "Rome already hates us. Who's to say the pope won't begin another crusade, this time against us?"

I rolled my eyes. This child had nothing new to add to an old, tired subject. "Who, might I ask, do you suggest we approach?"

The question caught him by surprise. He stammered out his answer. "I—perhaps France?"

I snorted. "Louis is terrified of us."

He frowned, displeased at my criticism. "Well, what about someone nearer? Frederick is Catholic, but he's no papal fanatic."

The Elector of Saxony. Another bad decision. "Frederick follows the whims of his people, and his people hate us. He's no more likely than Louis."

He crossed his arms like a petulant child. "Then what do you suggest?"

"I?" I shrugged. "I suggest nothing. Unless, by some miracle, you can convince the Church to change its stance on our damnation, we are alone in Europe, and likely to stay that way."

"Enough." My father had finally grown tired of the bickering. He stood. "This topic has been discussed at length, Alois, by older and wiser men than you. If you have nothing new to add, hold your tongue." Looking around the table, he met each council member's eye. "Does anyone have any *new* business to bring before the council?"

Everyone remained silent.

"Then you are dismissed."

I stood with the rest, but the king called me back. "Not you, Loic."

Retaking my seat opposite him at the long table, I leaned back and crossed my arms.

Once we were alone, he folded his hands in front of him. "Do you have an excuse for your tardiness, or do you do it just to gall me?"

If I'd intended to provoke him, I would have skipped the meeting entirely. "A pressing matter required my attention."

His nostrils flared with anger. "What, pray tell, was so important that you missed the entire council meeting?"

I hadn't missed the entire meeting, but I didn't bother to correct him. I flicked a hand in dismissal. "Nothing to warrant the king's attention. It's taken care of."

Irritation twisted his features, but he didn't reply.

"If there's nothing else, I have other obligations before Hall." I'd spend the rest of the afternoon on the training grounds. I needed to burn off some of this frustration.

I stood and turned to go, and he didn't call me back.

ANNIKA

The hours passed slowly. Teta offered me food, but despite the growling of my empty stomach, I refused. If they wanted to kill me, they could do it without poison. I wouldn't give them more opportunities. Who knew what they would put in my food?

Finally, she looked at the clock and rose. "It's time."

Time to meet the Pied Piper. I stood, brushing the wrinkles from my dress. "Is the prince coming?"

"He'll meet us there. Just stay with me. As he said, it's not safe for you to be here. Most of our court are tolerant of...your kind, but there are some who won't be pleased to see you."

My kind. Humans. "Like the Pied Piper?"

Her lips formed a tight line. "Yes." She opened the door and peered out. "Let's go."

We walked through empty halls, my heart pounding in my throat. Where was everyone? Were we late? Teta didn't seem concerned; she walked at a brisk pace, but not so fast that I couldn't keep up. At last we reached the main hall. Two large doors, flanked by guards, stood open, revealing a huge crowd.

Cold sweat formed on the back of my neck. What was I thinking, coming here? In this city, demons outnumbered me by hundreds. Thousands.

Falk. I came here for Falk. I lifted my chin as we entered the room.

I looked around the room, observing my enemies. They seemed so...normal. I'd always been told that demons masquerade as angels of light, with a predatory beauty that drew in the unwary soul, but I didn't see that here. They didn't look entirely human, but they weren't as preternaturally alluring as I'd expected.

I glanced at Teta, standing next to me. She was beautiful, but only in the way a human woman raised in luxury might be. The prince's beauty seemed unnatural, but perhaps seeing him in my village had warped my perception.

The other thing that struck me about the pipers was the variety in skin tones. I'd never seen such colors on human skin, from creamy white like my own, to golden-brown like the prince and Teta, to dark as night. Their horns, brown or white or black or gold, glinted in the torchlight, and their ears twitched as they milled around, greeting each other.

They dressed much like I imagined nobles would dress—rich silks and velvets, lined in fur—although they wore nothing on their heads, displaying their ornate hairstyles and lavish jewels. A scarf covered my own head for modesty, and next to the wealth before me, my clothes were nothing but rags, but despite my appearance, few paid me any notice. Those that did glance my way eyed me with more curiosity than hostility.

Windows lined the enormous room on both sides. Incredible paintings covered the ceiling, hedonistic scenes of drunken festivities or nude human-like creatures. I eyed one image, a nixe. With the torso of a woman and the golden tail of a fish, she lay naked on a river rock, singing to a fisherman on the shore. The painting drew me and disgusted me at the same time. Such brazen nudity, and the fisherman watched her with flagrant lust. But despite the heathen image, the craftsmanship was incomparable, the figures lifelike.

I tore my gaze away, looking around the hall again. On the far end, two thrones set atop a dais. As I watched, the door behind the dais opened, and the room fell silent. I held my breath.

A tall piper strode in, his green velvet robe billowing behind him. A crown of gold and emerald encircled his twisted black horns, and his skin...his brown skin was pied, spattered with spots of white.

The Pied Piper. King of the pipers.

The prince, Loic, trailed behind him. He wore simpler clothes than the king's, though no less fine. A red tunic topped black stockings, and he'd combed down his dark curls to display more of his black horns. I'd seen similar pictures of the devil, and the sight made me shiver.

The king stopped in front of his throne and waved a hand as he took his seat. The chatter in the room resumed.

I kept my gaze fixed on the prince. He bent down to speak in the king's ear. The Pied Piper pursed his lips, but he nodded. The prince turned, eyes meeting mine across the crowded room. His mouth twisted in a cruel smile.

I raised my chin, determined not to let him see my fear, as he stepped off the dais and walked toward me. The crowd parted for him. Someone laid a hand on his arm, stopping his advance, but his eyes didn't leave mine, even as he responded to the interruption.

When he reached me, he gave a sweeping bow, that cruel smile still playing on his lips, mockery in his eyes. "Annika Brandt. I bid you welcome to my father's court." He turned to Teta. "Give us a moment," he said, signing his words as well.

She melted into the crowd, and he turned to me.

I'd waited long enough. "Where is my son?" I demanded before he could speak.

"He's fine. Safe."

Teta had said the same, but she'd refused to tell me where they kept the children. I grew more anxious by the moment. "How do I know you're telling the truth?"

His eyes narrowed, and his smile vanished. "Are you calling me a liar?"

I quailed before the thunder on his face. "I just want to see him, your highness."

"It's not up to me." He looked around the room as though bored. "You broke your agreement. The law demanded lives as restitution. Be grateful I let them live; I could just as easily have killed them to fulfill the terms of the law."

"I made no such agreement," I hissed.

He turned a cool gaze on me. "No. You didn't. Your leaders made it on your behalf. But you did benefit from the arrangement, did you not?"

"I—"

He cut me off before I could answer. "As I understand it, your son was ill. Dying, even. I saved his life, and I wasn't paid for my services. The law demanded lives, so I took them. What else would you have had me do?"

"I—" My tongue stuck to the roof of my mouth. "I just want to take my son home."

The prince shook his head. "Your song grows tiresome, little bird. As I've said, it's not up to me." He nodded toward his father, sitting on his throne. "You'll have an opportunity to plead your case. The king hears petitions tonight. Convince him that you don't owe this debt, and you and your son can return home."

My chest tightened. He said it so simply. Convincing the prince was hard enough, but the Pied Piper himself?

For Falk, I reminded myself. For Falk, I could do anything. I nodded sharply.

"I'll call you when he's ready," he said. "He's not fond of your kind, so you should grovel. Bow low when you approach the throne, and don't rise until he bids you to. Refer to him only as 'your majesty' or 'King Edric.' And don't show any sign of weakness." He flashed his teeth in a grin. "I'm sure that will be difficult for you, little thing that you are, but do try."

With that, he left me standing alone in the crowd.

No, not alone. As though his departure had summoned her, Teta stood at my elbow. "Is everything alright?"

"Fine," I said, watching the prince's retreating back.

Ages later, the king raised his hands for silence.

"It appears that my son has brought another novelty to court," he said. He wore a cruel smile, the twin to his son's, although somehow colder, crueler. "A human petitioner. Why don't we start off the evening with that little bit of entertainment?"

Loic gestured for me to approach. I walked on trembling legs toward the thrones. Had the room always been so warm? I stopped at the foot of the dais and made my best bow, my head nearly touching the ground.

"Rise." The Pied Piper's voice held cold amusement. I forced myself to meet his gaze. "I'm told you wish to reclaim a life we took as payment."

"I do, your majesty." I spoke more confidently than I felt. "I want—I'm here to reclaim my son."

"Was he taken by mistake?" He addressed the question, not to me, but to the prince.

The prince didn't blink. "He was not."

I clenched my fists at my sides. "I did not agree to sell my son. I did not agree to call a piper. Why should my child suffer for a deal neither he nor his family made?"

The prince scowled at me. "I hardly think he's suffering. He's being treated as one of our own. Raised as a piper. He's been well-treated here."

"He's a *human*," I said, fear forgotten in my anger. "He should be with his own people, not here with you *demons*."

"Enough." Though he didn't raise his voice, the Pied Piper's words sliced through the silent room. "With whom did you make the deal?"

"Her village council."

"'Her village council.'" The king sneered. "Someone who, according to both your laws and our own, has the right to enter into agreements on your behalf. Yes?"

"Yes, but—"

He spoke over me. "Then what grounds do you have for challenging the payment?"

"My son is not *payment!*" I shouted.

He bolted to his feet, fury contorting his features, and I faltered. This was no human lord. Beelzebub glared down at me. I reached into my pocket for my medallion. *Christ, protect me. St. Anne, pray for me.*

I took a deep breath and bowed again. "Forgive me, your majesty. My distress got the better of me. I meant no offense. I just want to take my son home."

I held my breath as the king seated himself and waved a hand.

"I'm not in the habit of leaving debts unpaid," he said. "The children will stay. All of them."

Hot tears filled my eyes. "That's not— You can't—"

"Enough. You're dismissed." The king nodded to his guards, and one stepped forward to take my arm.

"No, wait!" Tears spilled down my cheeks, and I jerked against the guard's grip. "At least let me see him. Please."

The prince, who had watched his exchange impassively, leaned toward his father and whispered in his ear. The king scowled again, but he waved the guard off.

"It seems my son is in need of a new pet." The Pied Piper looked down his nose at me before turning to him. "Any trouble she causes is on your head."

Pet? Wiping at my eyes, I looked between the king and the prince, who bowed to his father and stepped down from the dais. He jerked his head at me to follow. Heart thundering and face still wet from crying, I bowed to the king and hurried after the prince.

He led me out of the hall. Whispers followed us. We passed Teta near the back of the room, and she gave me a sympathetic smile.

The prince's pet. What did that mean? Had I become a prisoner as well? Would he let me see Falk? I opened my mouth to ask one of the questions racing through my mind, but the words caught in my throat. I could only imagine the sick, twisted games this demon had planned for me.

He led me up a flight of stairs, into another wing of the castle. I barely noticed my surroundings, absorbed in my thoughts.

At the end of the corridor, before a closed door, he stopped and turned to me.

"You may stay," he said. "As long as you obey me and the rules of the court, you will have my protection."

"My heart leapt. "You'll let me see Falk? And the other children?" I hardly dared to hope.

"The minute you try to steal away with them, you become my prisoner, and the children lose all their rights as guests of the court. Is that clear?"

Anything, so long as he'd let me see my son. "We won't try to escape."

He jerked his chin toward the door. Brow furrowed, I turned the handle and pushed it open.

NEW PET

ANNIKA

A low fire lit the room. I spotted a small, white-haired child curled up in a chair, his eyes closed and his thumb in his mouth. Little Johann Weiss. My heart leapt, and I scanned the room for Falk.

He sat next to the fire, playing at marbles with another boy. A choked sob escaped me, and I clutched the doorframe for support.

The oldest child from the village, Peter Beck, looked up from his seat near the window. "Mrs. Brandt?"

His words set off a flurry of commotion. All the kids turned to see. Falk scrambled off the ground, scattering marbles, and ran to me, shouting, "Mama!"

Tears choked me as I drew my son into my arms. He was safe, and whole, and healthy. I pulled back and gazed into his eyes, brushing his cheek. No injuries, no remnant of his illness. He was safe.

The rest of the children surrounded me, all trying to speak at once. The sleeping Weiss boy sat up, wailing, his eyes still closed.

"Hush, hush, it's alright." Keeping an arm around Falk, I picked up the crying child.

"Are you here to take us home?" Marta Weiss, Johann's eldest sister, asked.

The rest of the children looked at me with hopeful eyes. A lump formed in my throat, but before I could answer, the prince spoke.

"She's here to stay with you."

At the sound of his voice, little Johann, who had settled in my arms, gave a shriek of terror. I patted his back, frowning at the prince.

"We're not going home right now, no," I told them. "But you're all safe? Healthy?"

Thea, a curly-haired nine-year-old, plucked at my sleeve. "I want to go home."

The prince flopped down into the chair where Johann had been sleeping. He crossed his arms. "They've been well-treated. As I told you before."

"They shouldn't be in here alone. And where have they been sleeping?" I looked around the room. "In here, I suppose. A whole castle, and you couldn't even spare a couple bedrooms?" With the children around me, my fear had faded, replaced with anger at the pipers.

The prince rolled his eyes. "We gave them each their own rooms. They didn't want them. As to supervision, someone checks in on them twice a day, to bring them food and such, but that one," he indicated Peter, "won't let us near them."

Good. At least Peter, at twelve, was old enough to care for the rest of the children. His grandfather, Elmar, headed the town council, and it seemed Peter had inherited some of those leadership skills.

Hopefully he had more sense than his grandfather.

"What do you expect?" I asked the prince, nodding my approval at Peter. "You kidnapped them!"

He flicked a hand in dismissal. "'Kidnapped them.' From poverty. From a town with no honor. From parents who would risk their lives by making deals with—what did you call us? Oh, yes. Demons." He tsked. "Yes, I see why you would cast me as the villain in this story."

"Enough." I looked around at the frightened faces of the children. "Don't mind the prince. He's just grumpy because it's past his bedtime." I met his gaze, daring him to contradict me. "It's past your bedtime, as well," I said, shifting Johann so I could tap Falk on the nose. "Let's get you all settled in beds tonight, shall we? We'll all feel better in the morning."

"I don't want to be alone," Marta sniffed, grabbing her sister's hand. "Don't make us."

"Of course not. We'll set it up so we're all three or four to a bedroom. That'll be nice and snug, won't it?"

The prince raised a brow, but he didn't object. He stood. "I'll send someone to show you to your rooms, then."

Finally, I finished settling all the children into their beds. Even Falk lay sleeping peacefully in the room we'd been given.

I rubbed my neck. Taking care of one child was exhausting, but twelve? Not to mention the emotional strain of the day. Tired as I felt, I couldn't seem to settle. I stepped out of the room, closing the door gently so as not to wake Falk.

I wandered the empty halls until I found a door leading to a balcony. Stepping outside, I shivered in the sudden onslaught of frigid air. The half-moon lit up the city below me. Firelight flickered in the windows of the houses. The beauty took my breath away, almost made me forget where I was. Why I was here.

I leaned against the railing and let out a shaky breath. I'd put on a brave face for the children, but now a few tears trickled down my face.

"I don't recall giving you permission to wander the castle."

The sound of the prince's voice made me flinch. Wiping my tears away, I replied without turning. "I didn't realize I needed permission."

He snorted, leaning on the wall next to me and looking out over the valley. "What sort of pet is allowed to wander wherever it will?"

My stomach clenched, and I inched away from him. I didn't want to be his pet. "Are you often in the habit of making women your pets?"

He eyed me, an inscrutable look on his face. "Not human women, no."

So I was to be his first. Was that good or bad? I shivered, once again imagining what he might expect of me. Would he lock me in a cage? Put a rope around my neck and make me follow him everywhere?

"I'm not going to lock you up, if that's what you're thinking." Scorn filled his voice.

I flinched again. "I wasn't—"

He turned to face me fully, eyes narrowed in distaste. "Don't lie to me, little songbird, and I won't lie to you. You're here at my pleasure, and I'm the only thing standing between you and my father's wrath. If you want to stay with your son, you'll do what I say. Whatever I say."

I closed my eyes and slid my hand into my pocket, feeling the cold pewter of my medallion. *Pater noster, qui est in coelis...* I squared my shoulders and met his gaze. Demon or no, I wouldn't allow him to stand between me and my son. No matter what he made me do. "And what do you say?"

He leaned closer, eyes locked on mine. I could smell him, something sweet and spicy and exotic. *...et ne nos inducas in tentationem, sed libera nos a malo.* Which face of the demon was worse, the tantalizing angel or the terrifying monster?

"Right now," he breathed, "I want you in bed."

I let out a gasp. Though no worse than I'd expected, his words sent shards of ice through my heart. *St. Anne, pray for me.* I should have asked for guidance, asked the priest what to do if the demons demanded this price of me.

I hadn't, though, and I couldn't let this demon with the angel's face keep me from Falk. I gave a clipped nod.

Scowling, he took my arm, his grip painfully tight, and pulled me back inside. I struggled to keep pace with him, focused on keeping my breathing even.

What would he be like? Nikolaus had been gentle with me—or as gentle as he could be—and had tried not to draw the unpleasant experience out. This piper held no affection for me, nor even respect. Would he hurt me while taking his pleasure? Worse, would he do it intentionally?

Lost in my fears, I stumbled when he stopped. He let go of my arm. "Bed," he said, waving at the door.

He'd brought me back to the room Falk and I shared. Did he intend to take me in the room where my son slept? I'd thought he would at least have the decency to take me to his own room.

When I didn't move, he let out a long-suffering sigh and reached for the door. "To bed, songbird. Unless you mean to spend the whole night singing."

When I still didn't move, he shook his head. "Fine. Sleep in the hallway, for all I care. But you'll be safer behind closed doors. I'm not staying all night to protect you."

Frowning at me, he went to the next door—his own rooms, the girl who'd shown me my room had said—and let himself in, leaving me alone in the hall.

He didn't mean to force himself on me? I pressed a hand to my racing heart and leaned against the wall. Had I misunderstood? Maybe he'd changed his mind.

Or maybe he'd given me a brief reprieve, and he would insist on taking his payment tomorrow. I couldn't let my guard down. As he'd said, I was here at his pleasure.

I let myself into my own room. Two rooms, actually. The first held a fireplace, a desk, and several chairs. It could have held my entire house with space to spare. A door on one wall led to the prince's quarters. It was locked on this side, not that a lock would keep him out if he wanted to get me. On the other wall, a door led to the bedroom where Falk slept.

Before going to the bedroom, I took a seat at the desk and lit the lamp. I didn't know if I would be allowed to write to anyone, but I needed to let Brigid know that Falk was safe. We wouldn't be returning any time soon.

I found paper, quill, and ink in the desk.

Brigid,

Falk is safe, as are the other children. I am here with them in Laute, but do not be concerned. They have been well treated, and I have been invited to stay here with them. I will continue to work for their release, but I do not know when I will be successful.

I didn't know *if* I would be successful, but there was no need to worry her. I went on.

I hope you and Dietrich are married by now. I know he does not worry about your lack of dowry, but please sell the house, if you can, and keep the money for your family. I will have no need of it.

She wouldn't want to sell it, but I knew they would need the money, especially if God blessed them with children. I doubted I would return to the village for years. Not unless I could change the Pied Piper's mind, and I'd seen the hatred on his face. He would never free the children.

I swallowed the lump in my throat at the thought. I'd cried enough today. Dietrich would take care of Brigid, and I could remain with Falk. That was all that mattered.

I signed and folded the letter without bothering to seal it. The prince didn't trust me; even if, by some miracle, he let me send it, he would want to read it first.

He was right not to trust me. If I thought I could get the children away safely, I would do it, no matter what threats he made.

I paused for a moment, then took out another sheet of paper.

Gisela,

Thank you for your kindness and generosity in helping me reach Laute. I have been reunited with my son, who is safe and whole. I will remain here in the city until they allow him to leave, which does not seem likely in the foreseeable future. Until then, your gift, which I have not had opportunity to use, gives me comfort.

I had taken out the earplugs she'd given me, placing them in my pocket before the meeting with the Pied Piper. The imminent danger of enchantment had passed, and I hadn't wanted to risk angering the king if he discovered them. I would keep them with me in case I needed them, but I couldn't wear them everywhere I went.

I signed and folded that letter, as well, tucking it under the first. Dousing the lamp, I went into the bedroom and propped a chair against the door, a precaution against any nighttime visitors. Then I climbed into the bed next to Falk.

As I lay down, he rolled over, cuddling closer to me. I took a deep breath, relishing the moment. I'd thought I'd lost him forever, but he was here, safe with me. I pressed a kiss to his soft blond curls and closed my eyes.

LOIC

I was a damned idiot.

It was bad enough that I'd shown weakness in front of my father, asking to keep the woman as a companion. But that, my father could understand. The Pied Piper kept doxies, women intended to entertain him and warm his bed.

If I had stuck to that plan, reckless and half-cocked as it was, we would be fine. If I'd taken her back to my room, ignoring the chords of sympathy playing in my frozen heart, she would have been safer.

Instead, I'd seen the terror she tried to hide behind those large brown eyes. Her bony shoulders had trembled even as she'd met my gaze and nodded, agreeing to give herself to me no matter what twisted ways I would use her. I saw what she refused to admit, her fears that I would chain her to my bed and abuse her. No matter what the court might think of me, I couldn't be the monster she believed I was.

If I was wise, I'd let myself into her room, drag her from her bed, and take her against the door. She'd hate me for it, but she already hated me. At least I'd be protecting her. If my father, my father's circle of companions, believed that I held any affection for the woman, they wouldn't hesitate to use her against me. Sentiment was weakness here, and even the shreds of sympathy in my hardened heart could risk her and her child.

She thought I was a demon, but she had no idea. If I was what she expected, she might be safer. Instead, my leniency just might get her killed.

SETTLING INTO COURT

ANNIKA

I woke the next morning to see Falk at the table across the room, chewing on a large chunk of bread. Safe, whole, and with me. Tears sprang to my eyes.

Thank you, God.

I sat up, looking around the room. Someone had moved the chair away from the door and placed a dressing gown at the foot of the bed. A chill went through me at the thought of an unknown piper—possibly the prince himself—coming into the room while we slept.

Falk followed my gaze. "A girl brought that in this morning with the breakfast tray."

A girl. A servant. That made sense. There was no reason for the prince to lower himself to such tasks as fetching breakfast and dressing gowns for his...guests.

I turned my attention to the tray of food on the table before Falk. On it sat two glasses of milk, a tray full of bread, and a bowl of preserved fruit. Next to the bread was a hefty pat of butter, and two plates each held a piece of salt pork. My eyes widened at the abundance. In winter, even the workers in the lords' castles didn't eat so well.

I pressed a kiss to the top of Falk's head before I sat down. "How are you feeling, *liebling?*"

"Hungry." He reached for another piece of bread, spreading a liberal spoonful of preserves on top of it.

Nothing new there. I laughed, feeling lighter than I had in weeks. I sat down next to him, and after blessing the food, I broke my own fast.

We'd hardly finished eating when a knock sounded at the outer door. My cheerful mood evaporated. Had the prince come to claim me already? Or had the Pied Piper changed his mind and sent his guards to throw me out of the castle? Heart in my throat, I put on the dressing robe and went to the door, Falk on my heels.

The deaf piper I'd met the previous day stood in the hall. Teta. "I haven't woken you, have I?" she asked, scanning my attire.

What was she doing here? "No, I was awake. We've just broken our fast. Come in." Curiosity and trepidation battled in my breast as I stepped back to allow her into the room.

Falk clutched my hand, but he held his head high as he watched the piper woman.

"Good morning," Teta said. "Did you sleep well?"

When he didn't answer, I gave his hand a squeeze. We'd need all the allies we could get in this place; provoking her would get us nowhere. He nodded once.

"I'm glad." She gave him a bright smile. "I'd like to talk to your mother for a bit, but afterwards, if it's alright with you, maybe I could show you and the rest of the children the grounds? Your mother would come, too, of course."

He frowned. I could see the battle going on in his mind. On one hand, he loved being outdoors, especially in the snow, but on the other hand, this stranger was a piper. He couldn't be sure she was safe, even for something as mundane as showing us the courtyard.

I knew how he felt.

He glanced up at me, though, and I gave him an encouraging smile. He looked back at Teta with narrowed eyes. "That would be...fine."

"Wonderful!" She clapped her hands. "I took the liberty of having the servants set out winter gear outside each of the rooms for you."

"Go let the others know to get ready," I said.

He hesitated, casting a wary glance at her, but I patted his shoulder. "I'll be right here when you get back."

He scowled at Teta once more, then scampered out the door.

I shook my head affectionately as I watched him leave, then turned back to the other woman, who looked around the room.

"Do you read?" she asked.

"Yes." Pride swelled my chest. At least I wouldn't appear as a complete rustic.

"I'll have some books sent over. This room is so sparse. You need something to do."

"You don't have to do that." I'd never held a book. Not a real, bound book. I'd read tracts and pamphlets, and my mother had tied scraps of paper together with yarn to form our lesson books, but we'd never been able to afford a real one. Tears threatened in the corner of my eyes at her offer.

"It's nothing." She waved her hand in the air, as if the idea of giving someone a book was inconsequential. And for someone from such wealth, it probably was. "Have you thought about what you'd like to do while you're here?"

I hadn't had time to think about much of anything. "I expected the prince would have...duties for me." I flushed, my thoughts lingering on what he might require. Serving him daily, sexual depravity, things too terrible to name.

"He'll let you do what you like, I'm sure, as long as you stay out of the way of the king and his faction. Loic's not a slaver."

"I didn't mean to imply—"

"He is an ass, though," she continued, interrupting me. "It's his father's fault. Edric thinks he's 'too soft.' Uses every opportunity to try to 'toughen him up.' It's why the king allowed you to stay. I think he hoped that if Loic wanted to keep a—well, a whore—then maybe Loic might be taking after him, at least in one way. But don't worry." She winked at me. "Your virtue is safe with the prince."

I made a noncommittal noise. The prince's expression on the balcony last night had seemed to bely that. Though he had left me untouched, at least for the night.

"We should come up with something to keep you busy, though." Teta walked to the fireplace and took a seat in a large blue armchair. "What did you do before?"

"Before I came here?" She nodded, playing with one of her long, twisted braids. "My husband was a weaver, and I worked with him until he died." Falk was still too young to apprentice, but I'd done my best to take over Nikolaus's practice. I hadn't been able to keep up with the village's needs. A year after my husband's death, the council had called a new weaver. The sale of the practice had afforded us a little money to live on, but not much. "Since then, I've just been trying to survive."

"I'm sorry for your loss. How long ago was it?"

"Three years ago this summer." I smiled sadly. Nikolaus had been a good husband, a good father. "I live—lived with my sister. We did what we could to get by."

"That must have been difficult."

I shrugged. I didn't need anyone's pity, not the least this stranger. She was kind, though, despite the unfortunate circumstance of her birth. She hadn't asked to be born a demon.

"We've done better than some," I said.

"You have a lot of heart." Teta touched her heart. "And you're not afraid to speak your mind. I like that." She frowned and made a fist, tapping first her lips and then her heart. "Annika. Yes?"

"Yes?" Had she forgotten my name?

"You need a sign. A name—a deaf name. It's easier than spelling your name every time I talk about you." She made the sign again. "Do you like it?"

A sudden feeling of warmth spread through me, and I copied the movement. "I do."

Teta grinned. "Well, then. Pleased to meet you, *Annika.*" She signed my name as she said it. "I'm *Teta.*" She swiped a fist upward from her eyes in a sign I recognized from the previous day. "This is a T," she said, showing me the fist, her thumb tucked between her first two fingers. "Teta, see?" She made the sign again.

"Teta." I repeated the motion.

"Wonderful!" She clapped her hands together. "Would you like to learn? I've never had another woman to sign with. Loic is the only person who's fluent. Other than my parents, I mean."

"I'd like that," I said honestly. "The prince learned it just to speak to you?"

Teta wrinkled her nose. "To pester me, more like. When we were children, he used to sign to me whenever we were supposed to be quiet, trying to get me in trouble. It worked, more often than not."

I couldn't picture the prince as a child, much less a mischievous one. He was too cold-hearted. I'd pictured him as having sprung from the ground—or the depths of hell—fully formed and cruel.

The door opened, and Falk leaned inside. He cast a wary glance at Teta before looking at me. "Are you ready?"

Caught up in the conversation, I'd forgotten the children were waiting for us. "Give me a moment to get dressed." I turned to Teta. "Thank you, *Teta.*" I signed her name. "I appreciate the welcome."

Outside, the children huddled together, staying as close to me and as far from Teta as possible, but it wasn't long before little Johann forgot the danger and tumbled face-first into a snowdrift, giggling madly. The rest of the children soon realized they were safe, at least for the moment, and began to wander away from me. Falk formed a snowball and lobbed it at Peter's head. In an instant, snow flew all around us, intermingled with shrieks and laughter.

Teta and I dodged a few snowballs and found refuge on a bench next to the castle wall.

"It's good to see them smiling," she said. "I've been worried. I tried to check on them, but the oldest boy wouldn't let me past the door."

I smiled. "That's Peter. His grandfather is the head of the town council. I think he feels responsible for them."

"That's good. It's good that they have someone to protect them. Besides you, I mean." She bumped her knee against mine with an affectionate grin."

It would be easy to become friends with this woman. She wasn't the monster I'd expected. Part of me rebelled at the thought—after all, I'd been told my whole life to fear her. She was nothing like I'd envisioned. The Pied Piper and his son, they were what I'd thought pipers would be like. But not Teta.

A shadow broke into my thoughts, and I looked up to see the prince himself, his face grim. My heart plunged into my stomach.

"I see you let my songbird out of her cage," he said to Teta, his gaze fixed on me.

Teta made a vulgar gesture. "Go sit in a nettle patch."

The audacity of this woman astounded me. I watched the prince, waiting for him to order her immediate execution, but he just rolled his eyes.

The children had formed a tight huddle again, their laughter subsiding at the appearance of the prince. Peter stood at the front, watching us, ready to protect the younger ones from whatever danger Loic represented.

Teta waved at them. "It's alright. Go on and play."

Peter looked at me for confirmation. When I nodded, he shooed the rest back to their game, though he kept a wary eye on the prince.

Loic scowled at the boy, but Teta spoke before he could say anything. "We were talking about what Annika," she signed my name, "could do while she's here. I'm going to teach her to sign, so I have someone to talk to besides you, but I was also thinking she could teach the children." She glanced at me and bit her lip.

It was a good idea. They would have more time to learn here, not being overwhelmed with chores like they so often were at home. If they ever got out of Laute, the extra education would go a long way toward improving their fortunes. Some of the boys might even be able to go to university one day. I looked up at the prince, waiting for his answer.

"Why should she teach them?" He scanned me. "Can she even read?"

My blood boiled, emboldened by the proximity of my new ally. "Yes, *she* can, thank you."

He scoffed. "Our teachers are far superior to any they would have in your world, and I didn't bring the children here to have them form their own little bubble inside the court. They'll join the rest of the students in the city school. There's no need to have a barely-literate human teaching anyone."

"You expect them to sit in a room all day with people they're terrified of?" Teta snorted. Her hands flew as she spoke, so fast I couldn't make out individual signs. "They'll learn better if they're with someone they can trust. Maybe in time they'll be more comfortable, but until they are, Annika should be with them. Besides," she added, "the school is clear on the other side of the valley. They shouldn't have to travel all that way. Wouldn't it be nice to have a school on this side of the city?"

He glanced at the children. "Yes, it would be a pity to interrupt their busy schedule to send them to school." He shook his head. "I'll allow it, if only to keep her from being idle. I'll be monitoring their progress, though. If I find they're not learning at an appropriate pace, they'll be walking across the valley every morning to attend a *real* school."

Turning to leave, he stopped and looked back at me. "You'll dine with me tonight. Alone."

I shivered, hearing the threat in his words. Tonight. Tonight he'd take my virtue, make me pay for protecting my son. I watched as he stomped off through the snow, skirting the snow-castle the children had started to build.

"Annika?"

I blinked at Teta, trying to focus. "I'm sorry. Did you say something?"

"I said, what do you think? I know I should have asked you first, but it only just occurred to me. You can manage it, can't you?"

With the prince watching over my shoulder the whole time, waiting for me to make a mistake? He wasn't wrong; compared to some, I was *barely literate.* I'd never even read a real book. But Teta was right, too. The children wouldn't learn anything from pipers, not when they were terrified. Better to have me teaching them than to have them learning nothing at all. And it would give me something to think about while I suffered through the prince's touch tonight.

"I'll do it."

DINNER

ANNIKA

That afternoon, warm, dry, and full from a hearty lunch, we gathered in my room to rest. Teta remained with us—whether she'd been ordered by the prince to keep an eye on me or genuinely enjoyed my company, I didn't know. She took a seat on the couch, and little Johann climbed up next to her, rested his head on her lap, and promptly fell asleep. Peter stood nearby, eyeing her in case she posed any threat to his young friend.

Teta saw him watching and gave him a warm smile. Peter's face darkened at the gesture.

"I had the servants bring some books over while we were out, Annika," Teta said, pretending not to notice Peter's mistrust. "They're on the shelf over there."

The bookshelf in the corner held five books of various sizes. I hardly dared to breathe as I picked them up. Homer's *Odyssey,* translated into German. *Le Morte Darthur* by Sir Thomas Malory, bound in vivid blue fabric embossed with green vines. A simple black book labeled *Romance of the Three Kingdoms: a translation of the Chinese novel.* A rose-covered manuscript titled *Der Rosengarten zu Worms.* All beautiful treasures beyond any I'd ever dreamed of holding, but the last book brought me to tears.

The simple leather cover bore no markings, but the first page, in large gold letters flanked by angels, read *The Holy Bible.*

I traced each word with my fingers. I held the holy Scriptures in my hands. Turning away from the book, I wiped my face. A single stray tear could mar these priceless pages, and I couldn't bear to allow any harm to come to them.

"Children," I called, my voice trembling with barely suppressed emotion. "Sit down by the fire. I'm going to read to you."

The rest of the afternoon, we lost ourselves in the stories of the Bible. The children crowded around to look at the bright illustrations. Around the time Cain killed Abel, a young piper woman brought in a light supper for the children, and by the time Noah and his ark landed on the mountain, the light outside was fading. I finished the story and closed the book to a chorus of groans. "It's time for bed," I told them.

Teta helped shepherd them out of the room. "You should go," she said as the door closed behind Marta. "Loic will be waiting."

The knot in my stomach returned, so tight I couldn't breathe. I jerked my chin in acknowledgment.

"He won't hurt you, Annika. You'll be fine."

I wanted to believe her, but how could the man who'd kidnapped a dozen children be anything but evil?

"I'll come find you after breakfast tomorrow, and we can set up a classroom." She waved. "Good night."

The click of the door shutting echoed loudly through the room. I could have locked it, barricaded myself in the bedroom with Falk and maintained my virtue for a brief time. But that wouldn't save me, and more importantly, it wouldn't save the children. So I left the door open when I went in to kiss Falk goodnight.

He was almost asleep already, but he opened his eyes when I entered. "I'm glad you're here, Mama," he said, his voice sleepy.

My heart clenched, and I bent down to kiss his brow. "Me, too, *liebling.* Now get some rest."

"I love you," he slurred.

I doused the lamp next to the bed and tucked the blankets up to his chin. "I love you. More than anything." Which was why I wouldn't deny the prince's demands.

I crept out, closing both doors behind me. In the hallway to my right, behind the nearby doors, I could hear the low murmur of voices as the rest of the children readied themselves for bed. To my left, the prince's room was silent.

Jaw set, I knocked on the door.

"Come in."

Yea, though I walk through the valley of the shadow of death, I will fear no evil, for thou art with me; thy rod and thy staff they comfort me.

I could do this.

His quarters were simpler than I'd expected, no more ornate than the rooms I'd been given. The far wall contained a door, a shelf full of books, and an empty desk. The left wall held another door, and a suit of armor stood in one corner, with a sword hanging on the wall on either side. A low table and two large chairs sat by the fireplace, and in one, the prince sat watching me.

"Don't just stand in the doorway." The prince's voice dripped with scorn. "Come sit down."

I walked across the room on wooden legs. As I sank into the chair opposite him, the door opened, and a servant came in carrying a large tray, which he set on the table.

"That will be all, Josef," the prince said. "See that we aren't disturbed."

Josef left, and the prince removed the silver lid from the tray to reveal four plates. The larger two held stewed turnips, fresh bread, and slices of roasted beef slathered in brown gravy. The smaller plates held slices of fried, battered apples drenched in honey.

My stomach growled at the sight.

"Well?" The prince settled back in his chair with his plate on his lap. "Eat."

The knowledge of what would come next made me physically ill, but my fears couldn't quell my hunger. The meat melted in my mouth, wine and exotic spices bursting on my tongue. Even the stewed turnips, a staple in my childhood home, tasted richer than ever before. The bread felt like a buttery cloud, and the sweetness of the fried apples made me want to cry. I ate every bite with my head bowed over the plate, ignoring the heavy feeling of the prince's eyes on me.

Finally, stomach full to bursting, I set the plate back on the tray.

"Are you satisfied?" he asked.

A fresh wave of nausea rose in me, and I wished I hadn't eaten so much. "Thank you, your highness," I murmured.

He stood, going to the desk. "You said you can read?"

"I can." Why was he asking? There was no need to make conversation. If he wanted to use me, why not just get it over with? I twisted my hands into my skirts to stop them from shaking.

"Any other hidden talents?"

I parsed the question, searching for hidden meaning. There was no need for him to have an exhaustive list of my skills. "None to speak of, your highness."

"Drop the 'your highness' act, little songbird." He glanced at me as he drew a leatherbound book from a drawer in the desk. "It's just the two of us here, and your false obsequiousness grates on me."

"Yes, your—" I cut myself off. "Yes."

"My sources tell me your parents were apothecarists, and your husband a weaver. Is that true?"

"Yes." I bit my tongue to forestall the questions burning in my throat.

The prince pulled out several papers, a quill, and an inkwell and placed them on the desk. "Did you learn either of those trades?"

"I did. Both." Before I could stop myself, I asked, "Why?"

"You belong to me now. I need to know what you are."

What you are. Like I was an object, an exotic creature for him to study. The implication chafed, but I breathed deeply. I couldn't respond to his insults. I couldn't anger him. He held my son's life in his hands.

He tossed me the book he'd taken out. I caught it before the in-valuable object could crash to the ground. Such carelessness, and for something that most of the world could never dream of owning. Were all pipers so negligent with their belongings? Judging by their wealth, I thought it likely.

"Read," he said, taking a seat at the table. "Out loud."

I opened it and read the title. *Das Narrenschiff. The Ship of Fools.*

The book contained a series of verses on the fools Brant had en-countered, each verse emphasized with a woodcut illustration. I read through the scathing indictments of clergy and educated men as the prince seemed to ignore me. My throat ached, but I didn't dare stop reading; if I stopped, I would draw his attention.

Finally, he stood and stretched. "Stop."

I closed the book and set it on the table, at once grateful for the reprieve and terrified of what came next.

"Come here."

Holy Mother, pray for me. Whatever he did to me, I would survive it. For Falk and the other children.

"Take off that ridiculous scarf," he demanded.

Face hot enough to ignite, I did, revealing my brown hair braided in a coronet.

He huffed in displeasure. My appearance offended him. Why claim me, then? If he disliked me so much, what was the purpose of keeping me here?

If he decided I wasn't attractive enough, would he send me home? I didn't want to be his mistress, but I couldn't bear being separated from Falk. Not again. Not like this.

My lip trembled as I watched the prince's face. He shook his head. "It will have to come down."

"Your highness?" I didn't understand.

"The braid." He drew a circle with his finger. "Take it out."

He wasn't sending me away, then. Not yet. I hurried to do as he commanded. If I pleased him, he would allow me to stay.

As my hair fell down in mussed waves, I kept my eyes on the prince, and he watched me, impassive, calculating. I'd never felt so exposed.

"That won't do," he said. He stepped closer, ignoring my involuntary flinch away from his touch. Combing my hair out with his fingers, he arranged it where he wanted, draped over my shoulders. Too intimate. His touch was too intimate, and yet cold. Emotionless. Disgust and unwelcome desire battled within me. Disgust at the touch of a demon, and desire brought on my his satanic wiles.

He reached for the top of my dress, and I gasped.

His lips pressed together, his irritation evident. "Stand still." Grabbing my collar in both hands, he pulled, and the fabric split down the middle.

Tears filled my eyes. This was it. The top of my chest, bared to him, rose and fell with uncontrollable gasps. I closed my eyes, skin aflame in anticipation of his touch.

It never came. I peeked through my lashes to find him a step away, considering me with a clinical air. "Not enough," he muttered.

Stepping closer again, he gathered my skirts in his hands and scrunched them. Was this some piper mating ritual, the destruction of a woman's clothing? Or was he attempting to confuse me?

If confusion was his goal, he'd succeeded. I forgot to cry, too focused on his strange actions.

"Your stocking. Take it off and give it to me."

I slipped off my shoes, feeling the woven carpet beneath my feet. Bending down, I untied my stockings and removed one.

"Just the one." He held out a hand.

What did he want with it? I gave him the stocking he requested, then stood waiting for his next order. Humiliation burned through me.

"You can go."

I stared at him, shifting from stockinged to bare foot and back. Go? Did he mean back to Falk, or out of the valley? I'd done everything he ordered. I couldn't have displeased him already.

He sighed loudly and waved at the door. "You'll join me for dinner again tomorrow, but you'll sleep on your own. Go to bed."

Not waiting for him to change his mind, I rushed out the door. In the hallway, I crashed into someone, but I didn't stop to see who it was. I had to get back to my room before the prince decided to follow me.

Slamming the door, I locked it and leaned against it, breathing hard. I was safe tonight, again.

Tomorrow, he'd said. We'd do this again tomorrow. But what did he want to do? We'd eaten in silence, I'd read to him, and then he'd ruined my clothing and sent me away. There was nothing in his actions tonight to imply pleasure or gratification. So why bother?

It didn't matter. Whatever his deranged motivation, I would endure. Perhaps this was God's mercy. Maybe God had struck the prince with impotence to protect my virtue while allowing me to remain with my son.

I slid to the floor, bowing my head in prayer. I would thank God for this reprieve, however brief it might last.

LOIC

This was a dangerous game.

I tossed the little human's stocking into the corner of my bedroom. It would have been easier to just bed the woman, but I couldn't bring myself to do it.

It wasn't lack of attraction that prevented me. I'd had more beautiful women, certainly, but she wasn't unappealing, despite her malnutrition and ridiculous attire. But something in me, some tiny piece my father had failed to snuff out, refused to force a woman to have sex with me.

Which was why the king could never find out about this.

I pulled my cock from my pants and grasped it tight. Josef was loyal to me, but servants gossiped. If he found my bed clean of fluids, he would know I hadn't bedded the woman, and the news would be back to the king within a day.

I'd arranged her clothing to look like she'd been ravished, and her missing stocking—now hiding beneath the chair in the corner—would add to that impression. All that remained was to dirty the bedclothes.

I closed my eyes, trying to draw up an image that would speed the process. Nothing came to mind. It had been months since I'd last enjoyed a woman's touch. No, years. Not since Eva.

I frowned. Had it been so long? No wonder I'd been angrier than usual lately. I needed to find an outlet for my tension.

Later.

Sighing, I focused on the task at hand. A bead of moisture gathered at the tip of my half-hard cock. I wiped it away with my thumb and pumped myself, relishing the tight grip.

The little songbird's face flashed in my mind as I brought myself closer to release. Fragile as she was, she had a strange sort of beauty. The flush in her cheeks as she tried to hide her hatred for me... She thought she was afraid, but she wasn't. Not really. She feared what I could take from her, but she didn't fear me. The little fool.

My breath came shorter. I pictured her on her knees, looking up at me with that wide-eyed stare. Her ridiculous clothes gone, replaced with something smooth and soft that hugged every curve.

I wanted her.

My climax struck me like lightning. The thrill of release traveled down my spine as I spilled onto the blankets. I reached for the bedpost, holding myself up as tremors shook me. Once I finished, I wiped my cock clean with a handkerchief and tucked it back into my pants.

I tossed the blankets on the floor and went to the chair by the fire. An empty pit remained in my chest, despite my release. What was wrong with me? I hadn't been myself since Eva. She and my father had taught me never to trust anyone, never to allow any weakness, but here I was, leaving myself vulnerable for the sake of some fragile human woman. I didn't want her. I couldn't.

I needed to fortify my defenses, protect myself. For the sake of everyone who depended on me, I couldn't allow her to get under my skin.

If I did, she could ruin everything.

FRIGHTENED LITLE BIRD

LOIC

Armed with my newfound determination to remain emotionally uninvested, I stood outside the classroom the next morning. My new pet had settled in quickly. I watched from the shadows of the doorway as she flitted from desk to desk, instructing each of the children in turn. A white-haired little girl scrunched her face up, asking a question, and the woman—Annika, as Teta had reminded me—bent down to reply.

I didn't understand how she could move in those cumbersome clothes she wore. Voluminous, drab-colored skirts, a collar that stretched up to her chin, and a scarf that she kept tucked tight around her head, even indoors. Such a ridiculous ensemble. I couldn't allow her to continue dressing like that; she looked more like a nun than my mistress, and the more virtuous she seemed, the more likely it was that my father would see through my ruse.

I caught the eye of Teta, who sat in the corner observing the class. *I need the woman this afternoon,* I signed. *Can you keep the children busy?*

Teta frowned at me, disapproval clear on her face. *Her name is Annika,* she signed back, using the sign she had given the woman. *Not "woman."*

I rolled my eyes. *Same thing. I'll give you an hour. Send her to my rooms.* Under normal circumstances, I wouldn't relegate Teta to nursemaid, but she'd managed to breach the children's defenses in the brief time since Annika had arrived. The eldest boy still refused to let anyone else near them.

Why do you need her? Teta asked, raising a brow in question.

I plan to make her undress for me, I replied with a dry expression. I looked over at the woman.

As though she felt my eyes on her, Annika stiffened, then glanced toward the door where I stood.

I inclined my head in a bow, and her lips tightened at the gesture.

One hour, I signed to Teta.

Returning to my rooms, I took a seat at my desk and pulled a large stack of papers to me. In all the distractions of the last few days, I had been neglecting my correspondence, something which I could not afford to do. Few things prevented the destruction of Laute; our detailed knowledge of the goings-on in the other courts in Europe was one of the most vital.

My spy in England had little to report, save for the old news that Queen Catherine had lost another child, a boy. The queen of England had lost four children since her marriage to Henry, this being the third stillbirth. A few years earlier, she'd birthed a living son, but the boy died less than two months later. Both Henry and his queen were growing desperate. Important news for England, I was sure, but it had little relevance for my people.

France had more interesting news. Their king, Louis XII, had died of a case of gout, leaving as successor his cousin Francis. Francis was said to be more intrigued than frightened by our abilities—perhaps this would be an opportunity for Laute. If we could persuade Francis to take a piper into his court, we might be able to take steps toward forming a treaty between our two kingdoms.

I set aside the letter from my French contact and made a mental note to send the new king my congratulations, along with an expensive gift. Perhaps a rare painting; the man was a patron of the arts.

As I moved on to the letter from Rome, there was a knock at my door.

"Enter," I said. The seamstress, a tall, middle-aged woman, stepped into the room, followed by her red-haired assistant. They both bowed.

"Your highness. I understand you have need of my services?"

"Wina, yes." I set the papers down, lacing my hands behind my head. "As I'm sure you've heard, I recently acquired a new...pet." I gave a lascivious grin, daring them to show disapproval, but neither so much as blinked. "Her wardrobe is severely lacking. She'll need everything made new."

Wina had fulfilled similar orders in the past, though not for me. My father chose a new mistress almost annually, searching for novelty to sate his frequent boredom. For all his eclectic tastes, though, he'd never yet brought someone as unusual as the woman I'd claimed. He'd never chosen a human at all.

"Of course, your highness. Do you have anything in mind?" She began pulling papers from the satchel she carried.

I waved a hand. "I'll leave the designs to your discretion. There's no need for her day clothes to be particularly scandalous." My father preferred his women to be dressed in wisps of fabric at all times. While I would need to dress my new pet similarly for any court events, there was no need to dress her like a whore while she taught the children. "Her evening clothes should make a statement." That statement being her status as my possession. "She'll need something to wear to dinner tomorrow, if you can have something ready on such short notice." My father was holding a dinner for his council members and their wives, and he expected my presence. The dinners, frightfully boring as they were, provided a good opportunity to show Annika off and stake my claim in front of anyone who might want to threaten her. If I could convince the council that she was my whore, it wouldn't matter what happened between us behind closed doors.

"That won't be a problem, your highness. Is there anything else?"

The woman in question knocked at the open door and stepped inside, closing it behind her. I held Annika's gaze but continued speaking to the seamstress. "Some new nightclothes, as well. Something sheer, perhaps? With plenty of laces. I like to unwrap my gifts."

The little songbird flushed crimson at my words. Turning her face to the ground, she bowed clumsily. "You wanted to see me, your highness?"

"These women are here to take your measurements for a new wardrobe." I turned back to Wina. "She's a little ragged, but I'm sure with your expertise she'll be worth something." I was being unnecessarily cruel, I knew, but things would be better for both of us if I showed no softness. And besides, this slip of a woman had caused so much disruption in my life. She could suffer through a little humiliation.

"I don't need—" she began, but I scowled, cutting her off.

"I won't have you parading around court in those ridiculous rags you call clothing."

Her face contorted with anger, but she didn't speak. She tucked her hand into her pocket, fiddling with something. A weapon? I dismissed the thought. She wasn't so foolish as to think she could fight me. Probably a bauble of some sort, or a memento from home.

She took a deep breath, lowering her head. "Of course, your highness. Thank you."

Wina led my trembling songbird to the center of the room, where Josef had earlier placed a stool for this purpose. "If you'll step up here, please."

"I—" she began, but I narrowed my eyes at her. She closed her mouth and stepped up onto the stool.

I turned my attention back to my papers as they began removing Annika's numerous layers. Austria was next in my correspondence; my contact informed me that Maximilian was making arrangements to meet with the kings of Hungary and Poland. The Holy Roman Emperor had also issued a decree expelling the Jews from the city of Laibach.

I made a note to send aid to the exiles from my personal funds. At the next council meeting with my father, I would bring up the possibility of accepting refugees into Laute. He would refuse, I was certain, but the proposal had to be made. Of all the populations across Europe, Jews were the humans with which I bore the most sympathy. Renounced by the Church and shunned by their neighbors, their plight bore striking similarities to that of my own people. The pope called both our peoples heretics, and in many regions, working with both Jews and pipers was forbidden by law, owing to our transgressions. Jews had committed the grievous sin of crucifying the savior; my own people had made the mistake of being descended from demons.

While I read, the room had gone silent. I glanced at the women in the center of the room, and my gaze snagged on Annika. The seamstress and her assistant had stripped her down to her shift, and the body they had revealed—I paused. There was a strange quality about her that I couldn't look away from.

I'd seen beautiful women. The women of my father's court dripped with gold and jewels, their bodies carefully curated to please the eye. Next to them, Annika was like a tiny sparrow entering a court of clockwork songbirds; she was completely mundane, but the life inside her made her all the more striking.

She noticed me watching and jutted her chin out, as though daring me to judge her body. The motion only served to enforce my earlier impression. This small, ordinary woman was more vibrant than anyone I'd ever met before.

I smirked at her, letting my gaze travel down over her exposed skin. She bristled at that, crossing her arms and disrupting the seamstress, who was in the midst of measuring her waist.

Her attempt to cover herself didn't stop me from noticing how underfed she was. Through the sheer fabric of her shift, I could almost count her ribs. If a strong wind passed through the room, it would knock her over. It was no wonder she'd scarfed down every crumb from dinner last night.

I watched as Wina finished taking her measurements and helped her to dress. At last the seamstress turned to me. "Everything will be delivered to the palace as soon as it's done, your highness," she said.

"I'll have her first dress delivered tomorrow afternoon." She bowed to me, nodded at Annika, and swept out the door, her assistant behind her.

Annika mumbled something incomprehensible and moved to follow them. Her headscarf was askew, the ties on her skirt untucked and loose.

I stood, moving between her and the door. "Where are you flying off to, little songbird?"

"Back to my room." She tugged at her headscarf, trying to adjust it. "The children—"

"Are otherwise occupied. Teta will keep them busy for the rest of the evening." I gestured toward the couch. "As I told you yesterday, your nights are mine. You have other responsibilities here." The foremost of which being to eat a full meal.

ANNIKA

Dread filled my stomach at the prince's words. Last night, his strange behavior as he ruined my clothes, had been an assessment of sorts. He'd been testing me to see if I would obey his orders, if my clothes would suit his desires. Now my reprieve was over, and he would take me to his bed.

St. Anne, pray for me.

"Sit." His voice, almost gentle, was a pretty lie meant to lull me into complacency. I did as he commanded, perching on the edge of the couch. He rang a bell on the wall.

The servant from last night came to the door.

"You can bring in our dinner now, Josef."

The door closed, leaving us alone once more. I watched him like a rabbit watching a hawk. What would he do to me?

It didn't matter. Whatever he required, I would comply. If giving him access to my body was the price I had to pay to keep my son, I would do it.

But the prince didn't move toward me. He leaned against the wall and crossed his arms.

"Annika Brandt," he said quietly. "Age twenty-seven. Widow of the weaver Nikolaus Brandt. Mother to Falk, age nine. Sister to Brigid." He paused. "What brings you to Laute?"

I glowered. He knew perfectly well what brought me here. "I came for my son, your highness."

"Yes." His expression was unreadable. "You did. Out of all the families I stole children from, you were the only one foolish enough to follow me. Why is that?"

Because I had nothing left to lose. The words rose, unbidden, to my lips, but I swallowed them back down.

When I didn't respond, he unfolded his arms and stalked toward me, bending down so our faces were inches apart. I forced myself not to flinch away from him. Showing fear would only make things worse for me.

"When I ask a question, little songbird, I expect an answer," he murmured. "Why did you come after me?"

"What sort of mother would I be if I left my son in the hands of a demon?" The words escaped before I could stop them, and my eyes widened in horror. I didn't know what he would do to me if I angered him.

Unlike his father, the prince didn't seem upset by my outburst. His eyes widened, lips quirking up in the corner.

He opened his mouth to respond, but a knock sounded at the door. He straightened and called out, "Enter."

Josef came in bearing a covered silver tray in each hand.

"Just set them down," the prince said, waving at the low table before the fire. "And see that we're not disturbed for the rest of the night."

Josef glanced at me, and I flushed. It was bad enough that I had to suffer through this, but to have others know that it was happening? It was almost unbearable. I stared at my hands, folded in my lap, as he left.

The prince removed the lids from each tray, revealing a wide assortment of food, at least twice as much as last night. Various tantalizing scents reached me, and my mouth began to water.

The prince filled two plates with the contents of the trays, then took a seat on the couch and passed one to me. "Eat," he said, nodding to the food.

I scanned what he'd given me. Some, like the chunk of yellow cheese and the slices of smoked meat, I recognized, but others were less familiar. I picked up a round, black thing and sniffed it. It smelled salty and sour, like pickled cabbage.

"I said, 'eat,'" the prince said, watching me. "Not 'smell.'"

I popped the object into my mouth and gagged. *Not* like pickled cabbage. It was bitter and far too salty. I pulled my handkerchief from my pocket and tried to discreetly spit it out.

The prince's whole body radiated disapproval. "Eat," he said for the third time. "Or I'll feed you myself."

"Sorry," I muttered, picking up a piece of cheese and taking a bite. I could feel his eyes on me as I chewed and swallowed.

I finished the cheese and poked tentatively at a wrinkled, brown thing. What was it? Some sort of strange nut? Last night's supper had been delicious, but these strange foods bewildered me. I longed for something more familiar.

"It's not going to bite you." The prince sighed. "It's a fruit. Here." He picked it up and held it out toward me. I stared at him, and he placed it in my open mouth, fingers brushing my lips as he did.

"I can't chew it for you," he said.

The fruit was chewy and sweet, like a dried plum or a raisin. My eyebrows rose.

"It's good, isn't it?" He picked up a tart from my plate and held it up to my mouth. "Try this one."

Why was he feeding me? Was he trying to make me accustomed to his touch, so I wouldn't resist when he took me to his bed? I leaned back, away from the proffered food. "Thank you, but I can feed myself."

"Can you?" He set the tart back on the plate. "Judging by the bones under your shift, it doesn't appear so."

Blood rushed to my face. He'd lived in excess his entire life. He'd never once gone without. How dare he judge my body? He had no idea what my life was like, the poverty I'd been through once my husband died.

He can judge your body because he bought it, an insidious voice whispered in the back of my mind. That was the agreement I'd made. The prince could do whatever he wanted with me, as long as he let me stay with my son.

We ate in silence after that. I avoided the more exotic foods, nibbling at the meat and cheese and doing my best not to gorge myself on sugared almonds and sweet grape pudding.

Finally, I set my plate aside.

The prince frowned at me. "You can't be finished already."

I'd eaten more tonight than I'd ever eaten in my life. My stomach was full to bursting, and if I ate another bite, I would be sick. "I am." Besides, it was late. I needed to get back to Falk, and I couldn't do that until the prince was finished with me. "I'd like to get th—get back to my son."

I twisted my hands into my skirt. I'd nearly said "get this over with," and I didn't think the prince would appreciate the implication of those words.

He stood and reached out a hand.

I squared my shoulders and took it, letting him help me to my feet.

He pulled the scarf from my head and draped it over the back of the couch, then began unbraiding my hair.

"You mended your clothing quickly," he commented as he combed out my braids with gentle fingers. I pinched my leg through my dress, trying to keep myself from succumbing to the pleasure of his touch. Nikolaus had brushed my hair for me on occasion during our marriage, but to have this demon prince touching me in such a tender, intimate way? It was a mockery of love, no matter how enjoyable it felt.

"I had nothing else to wear." I'd woken early this morning, before Falk, to fix the tear he'd left down the front of my collar. Even if the entire kingdom knew of my shame, I wouldn't allow my son to see.

"You'll have more suitable clothing soon."

No doubt scraps of fabric meant to humiliate me. I'd have to take special care of my clothing from home if I wanted to preserve my modesty in front of the children.

The prince stepped back and surveyed me. "Almost," he muttered. He tousled my hair a bit, then snatched my headscarf and handed it to me with a flourish and a mocking bow. "Goodnight, little songbird."

I took the scarf, my thoughts in a whirl as I backed toward the door. He'd left me untouched yet again. What game was the prince playing?

Compared to the rich, beautiful women of his court, I was nothing. He'd seen my body, barely concealed beneath the sheer fabric of my shift. He didn't want me; his actions proved it. If he wanted me, he would have claimed me already.

But he hadn't sent me away. He'd taken the time to feed me, to sit with me, even to take my braids down. Was he playing with me? Trying to coax me into a false sense of security before ripping it all away? Or did he have some other objective, one that wasn't clear to me?

The prince was a terrifying enigma. In these games of demons, I was no more than a pawn to him, no matter what his goals.

I slipped out the door with a backward glance. He still watched me, the ghost of a cruel smile playing on his lips.

In the hallway, two young maids stood whispering to each other. Their eyes widened at the sight of me, but they inclined their heads and hurried past.

My face heated. No matter that the prince had hardly touched me. I was irreparably branded as his mistress now. I'd dressed in haste when the seamstress had left, and the prince had tousled my hair. I probably looked as though I'd been to a bacchanal, not a quiet supper.

But what did it matter what these pipers thought of me? I still maintained my chastity, if not my dignity. God knew my heart.

I straightened my shoulders, raised my chin, and walked down the hall back to my room.

SONGBIRD CLAIMED

ANNIKA

Teta joined us for lessons again the next day, ostensibly out of an interest in what the children were learning, though I suspected the prince had assigned her to watch us and ensure I didn't try to escape with the children. Whatever the reason, I appreciated her presence. With Teta, I felt as though we were safe from harassment by other, less friendly pipers.

The morning passed as the children learned to write their letters and recite their prayers. Peter and Falk, the oldest boys, could read a little, so I worked with them on reading from a small set of books Teta lent us. We ate dinner in the schoolroom, and Teta taught us all some signs. The children, despite their initial reticence around her, took to the subject with zeal, their fascination with the new language evident in their enthusiasm. My own movements were timid and awkward, but Teta gave me a dazzling smile each time I copied her correctly.

After the afternoon lessons of arithmetic for the boys and sewing for the girls, I released the children to their rooms to play. Falk raced off with Peter to play marbles in the room Peter shared with his two cousins. Teta excused herself, saying she had business, so I walked back to my room alone.

As I stepped into the bedroom, my gaze went to the dress hanging on the privacy screen. It was breathtaking, made from a red fabric so deep it could have been woven from wine. Gold thread and rubies decorated the black stomacher. I couldn't imagine how much it had cost.

Calling it a dress was being generous, though. It was thin, practically a shift, and the square neckline was so low I doubted it would even cover the wearer's breasts.

It had obviously been placed in my room by mistake. I rang for a servant.

A freckled young girl with pale skin answered my summons. "Yes, mistress?"

I gestured at the dress with a sheepish smile. "I think this was left in the wrong room."

"The prince sent it to you, Mrs. Brandt. He says you're to accompany him to dinner with the king this evening."

My cheeks blazed. He expected me to wear *that?* In front of the king? "Please thank him for me, but I can't accept it." I knew the clothes he'd ordered for me would be unseemly, but this was worse than I'd expected. What if all of the clothes were the same?? I couldn't teach the children dressed like a Jezebel!

She cleared her throat. "He said you might say that, and he asked me to remind you..." Shifting on her feet, she stared at the ground. "He said I'm to remind you of the agreement you made with him. He owns you."

The threat was clear. If I didn't comply with his wishes, he would send me home without my son.

Heat rose in my cheeks again, this time from anger as much as embarrassment. My choices were to be paraded around in front of this court of demons dressed as a harlot, or to leave Falk and the other children here alone.

The prince was a monster.

The servant girl—her name was Silvia, she told me—prepared me for dinner. I wasn't permitted a headscarf, so she curled my long brown hair, wrapping it around a heated iron rod until it formed ringlets which she artfully arranged on my shoulders. After that, she took pots of colored powders and applied them to my face, turning my lips and cheeks redder and lining my eyes with black kohl.

Then she removed my shift—another indulgence I wasn't to be allowed—and helped me into the dress. The fabric was silk, something

I'd seen in the markets of Augsburg but never dared to touch. It slipped over my skin like water, cool and smooth.

Silvia brought me to the mirror, an indulgence I'd never had. I didn't recognize the woman staring back. The woman in the reflection was desire incarnate, lips a deep red and eyes dark. The rise of her small breasts were visible, as was the valley between them. The skirt clung to her legs, showing every line of her body.

My face turned scarlet beneath the rouge. It couldn't be me in the mirror, dressed as a royal courtesan. My brown eyes were large and seductive, my lips sinfully full.

I looked like a temptress. Which was undoubtedly the prince's intention.

As Silvia finished tying the last strings of the dress, the door opened, and the prince came in.

He looked me up and down, one brow raised in consideration. "I'm impressed. You look almost presentable."

I'd never felt so exposed. I cast a glance around the room, searching for a rescuer, but Silvia had already slipped out the door, leaving me alone with the demon prince.

He offered me his arm. "Come. We wouldn't want to make the king wait."

The king. Cold dread seeped down my spine. I hadn't seen the Pied Piper since my arrival. He hated me. How would he react to my presence tonight?

"What about the children?" I asked, stalling for time. "I didn't tell them I was going to be gone tonight."

"We have a bowling hall on the other side of the castle. Teta is planning on taking them bowling."

When I still hesitated, the prince huffed a sigh. "You can walk in on my arm, little songbird, or you can crawl."

I squared my shoulders and took the proffered arm, allowing him to lead me from the room. The children would be safe with Teta. They were settling in quickly, more secure now that I'd arrived, and Teta's warm personality was charming them despite the stories they'd been told about the pipers.

I was grateful that she would keep them distracted. None of the children would see me in this shameful state.

As we walked through the castle, pipers stopped, staring wide-eyed at the two of us. Were they scandalized by my appearance? Or merely by the fact that the prince was claiming a human as his concubine? I stared at the ground, humiliation burning through me. It was almost a relief when we reached the dining hall.

The doors were open, the room—small, but no less ornate than the rest of the castle—already full. Two enormous golden chandeliers illuminated a long table full of food. The Pied Piper sat at the head of the table, drinking from a silver goblet encrusted with emeralds. Behind him hung a barbaric painting of a curly-haired man surrounded by half-dressed women, all vying to feed the man grapes.

My heart skipped a beat, and I stumbled. I was walking into a room full of the highest members of the Pied Piper's court, dressed no more modestly than the drunken heathen women in the painting.

I should never have come here.

The prince took no notice of my faltering courage. He pulled me along by my arm, guiding me to the table.

The king spotted us and scowled, the promise of violence in his eyes. I tugged on the prince's sleeve.

"What?" He frowned down at me.

"I don't think I should be here." I glanced at his father, who hadn't removed his gaze from us.

"It's too late for that, little songbird." The prince bared his teeth in a mockery of a grin. "Unless you're trying to break our agreement?"

And leave my son in this hellish court? I gritted my teeth, but I didn't resist as he led me toward the Pied Piper.

"Good evening, Father," the prince said, taking a seat next to the king. He gestured for me to sit as well.

"I see you brought your human whore." The Pied Piper's voice held as much venom as his gaze, and I shrank into myself.

The prince let out a laugh. "You could hardly expect me to miss this opportunity to dress her up and show her off." He draped his arm over my shoulders, trailing his fingers along the bare skin of my bosom. I stiffened but didn't pull away. I didn't want to anger him. "I seem to recall you doing the same with your own women on occasion." He lifted the silver goblet before him, raising it for a servant to fill. "Speaking of, where is Lady Helene this evening?"

"Otherwise occupied." The king's response was clipped.

"Shame." The prince took a sip of his wine. "She makes an excellent conversation partner." Judging by his dry tone, I suspected he had a less than ideal opinion of the noblewoman.

The servant moved to fill my goblet, but I covered it. I couldn't risk clouding my thoughts with wine.

The prince, noticing my hesitation to drink, raised a brow. "Come, now, little songbird. You must taste the wine. It's from the king's own vineyards. You won't find a finer vintage anywhere on the continent." Eyes sparkling with a dangerous light, he raised his own cup to my lips. "Drink."

I didn't dare refuse. Red wine trickled into my mouth, dark and earthy. When he pulled the goblet back, a droplet of wine remained in the corner of my mouth. I moved to wipe it away, but the prince trapped my hand with his. Setting the goblet down, he used his thumb to capture the droplet, then lifted it to his mouth to lick it away. Shame coiled in my chest, along with something low in my stomach that I couldn't name. I stared into the prince's face, my eyes wide with fear.

The strum of an instrument broke my trance, and I flinched. In the corner of the room, a brown-skinned minstrel with straight black horns had brought out a lute.

"Relax." The prince's breath tickled my ear. "No one would dare try to enchant my property, and I don't require magic to bend you to my will."

I fought the urge to shudder at the possessive words. My whole life, I'd been warned about the dangers of the pipers' music. Now, as the beautifully menacing strains filled the room, music was the least of my worries.

The biggest threat in the room was sitting right next to me.

Servants entered the room with enormous golden platters full of food. They sat a roast bird, displayed with its exotic blue and green feathers, before the Pied Piper, who took a hearty slice before waving the tray further down the table.

I watched, mouth watering, as the prince heaped his plate with delicacies. He waved the servants past when they offered to fill my plate. Did he mean to make me sit here the whole evening without eating? I'd suffered longer periods of far worse hunger, but the idea chafed at me. I took a drink of my wine to hide my frown.

With the cup at my lips, I paused. Maybe his intention was to intoxicate me. If he filled me with wine and denied me food, no doubt I'd be less inclined to fight him when he took me back to his rooms after dinner. Not that I had any intention of fighting him. I was doing this for my son, and I wouldn't risk him for anything. Not even my eternal soul.

But once the prince's plate was full, he didn't start eating. Instead, he turned to me, the corner of his mouth twitching upward. He plucked a small rose-shaped object from the plate and held it up to my lips.

I didn't bother to resist his offering. It melted on my tongue, sweet and nutty. The prince didn't remove his fingers until I'd closed my lips around them, and the salty taste of his skin mingled with the flavor of the food. He leaned in close, murmuring against my ear, "It's called marzipan. Good, isn't it?"

I nodded as I swallowed. It was delicious.

He popped one into his own mouth, then picked up a piece of meat that had come from the green- and blue-feathered bird. "This one is peacock," he said. "Beautiful birds, but far too noisy. I much prefer them like this." He slipped the morsel into my mouth, brushing my bottom lip as he did.

Surely he didn't mean to feed me like this throughout the whole meal?

From the look on his face, I gathered that was exactly his intention.

I glanced around the room. Most of the dinner guests were ignoring us, although I spotted one, a young man with golden horns, glaring at me as though I had murdered his only child. I shivered, looking quickly away. Best to pretend no one could see me. It was the only way I would make it through this dinner without losing all my dignity.

The meal continued in that manner, the prince alternating bites between me and himself. Occasionally, he would lean closer, whispering the name of the food or some interesting fact about it into my ear. I did my best to ignore the room around us, but I could feel the golden-horned man's glare, the king's scowl, and the disapproval radiating from everyone else, though they didn't stare.

Finally, the interminable meal ended. The prince helped me to my feet, then placed a hand on the small of my back to guide me to the door.

The man with the golden horns blocked our way. Up close, he looked even younger. He couldn't have been older than twenty.

"Your highness," he said with a bow just short of irreverence. "I see you brought your whore to dinner."

I bristled at the word, but the prince just laughed. "Jealous, Alois? I'm certain if you asked my father, he would find you your own pet to play with. That is, if he's not too busy." He glanced back over his shoulder at the king, who had caught the wrist of a serving girl and was tracing her horns with a finger. "You may want to hurry, though. It seems like your mother's charms are fading fast."

The boy—Alois—bunched up his fists, but the prince pushed past him, pulling me along.

Back upstairs, he led me to his own room. Would he send me away again, letting everyone think he'd bedded me? Or had he been waiting for this, making me accustomed to his touch? He'd branded me publicly as his, dressing me as a courtesan and feeding me with his own hands at his father's formal dinner. Maybe now he would take what he'd paid for.

My insides quivered, but I held my head high as he guided me into the main room of his suite. He waved a hand toward the door adjoining our rooms.

"It's late."

Relief filled me. I rushed to it and threw it open.

"You'll attend Hall with me tomorrow evening," he called after me.

I closed the door between us and sank into the chair next to the fireplace. From the bedroom, I could hear Falk's soft snores rise and fall. I drew closer to the fire, letting the flames drive away the winter chill.

Did the prince not want me? Not that I wanted him to want me, but his motivations made no sense. He allowed—no, encouraged—everyone to think that I was his concubine, but in private he hardly touched me. Was he protecting himself from something? Maybe he was expected to marry and was pretending to take me as his mistress in order to drive away potential wives. Or maybe he wasn't as cruel as he appeared, and this was the only excuse he could come up with to allow me to stay at court.

Considering he'd stolen my son for an unpaid debt, I was more inclined to believe the former.

Even with the heat from the fire, the wispy dress I wore left me cold. My stomach grumbled as I rose and put on a real dress, covering my carefully curated curls with a headscarf. I wasn't hungry—I hadn't been truly hungry since my arrival at the court—but the pit of loneliness in my stomach gnawed at me. I needed something to fill it.

I left the room, closing the door quietly so as not to wake Falk. I wandered through the castle until I caught sight of a servant girl carrying an empty tray, and I followed her down to the kitchen, a cavernous room with a fireplace large enough to stand in. It smelled of fresh bread and exotic spices, and despite the winter wind whipping outside, it was warm, the heat of the cooking fire filling the whole room.

Given the late hour, the kitchen was almost empty. The girl deposited her tray on a table and hurried off, ignoring the old man kneading a massive pile of dough. The old man was portly with a large purple nose. Gray hairs speckled his black hair, and his black horns curved upward like a goat's.

He glanced up as I came into the room.

"Something I can do for you, miss?"

"I…" I looked around, tears coming to my eyes. The stress of the evening was catching up to me. "I'm just looking for something to eat."

He frowned, coming out from behind the large trestle table. "You alright? You look ill."

I swallowed the lump in my throat. "It's been a long day."

He pulled out a stool and patted it with a floury hand. "Take a seat. I'll find you something."

He left the room and came back a few moments later with a tart and a cup of warm spiced wine. Setting them down before me, he pulled out another stool and took a seat next to me.

"Now, then," he said. "Eat, and tell old Hugo all your troubles."

My mouth watered at the sight of the tart. It was still warm, and it smelled sweet and sharp, filled with apple and exotic spices. I picked it up and took a bite. Chunks of apples in a flavorful syrup filled my mouth. I let out a groan, and the cook laughed.

"I'm glad you like it."

I flushed, setting the tart back on the plate. "It's very good. Thank you." I took a drink of wine to clear my throat.

"So, what's bothering you?" He reached out and patted my hand. "Tell me everything."

I knew better than to vent my fears and frustrations about the prince to this man. He was a servant in the castle, subject to the rule of the prince and the king both. Anything I said could get back to them.

I shook my head. "It's just been a long day, as I said."

"You're Annika Brandt, aren't you? The girl who faced down the Pied Piper to save your son." He gave me a sympathetic smile. "I'm sorry Edric didn't let you go. It was a brave thing you did."

"Thank you." Was he genuine, or trying to lull me into complacency?

"I imagine it was hard to leave your home. Did you leave anyone behind?"

I considered him for a moment. What harm could it do to tell him about my family? The prince already knew about me. "A sister. She's...probably married by now, or will be soon."

He tutted. "And you had to miss her wedding to come serve the prince."

I nodded, not trusting myself to speak through the lump in my throat. My eyes burned. It had only been three days, but I missed my sister and my home. I missed the familiar cadence of Mass and the comforting lullaby of sheep bleating.

A tear trickled down my cheek, followed by another.

"There, now, don't cry." He picked up a towel from the table and handed it to me. "It'll be alright. I'm sure you'll find a way out of this."

There was no way out of this. The king would never let my son go, and the prince would never let me go. He didn't even want me, but he wouldn't let me go. More tears came, blurring the room.

The cook, Hugo, put an arm around my shoulders. "I know it seems hopeless right now, but you're a brave girl. You'll figure things out. They can't keep you here forever."

I wiped my face. "They can. I won't leave without my son, and they won't free him."

"Not now, maybe, but someday." He squeezed me in a fatherly hug. "Does your sister know you're safe? Have you heard from her?"

I shook my head. I hadn't even bothered to ask. "I'm sure the prince won't let me write to her."

He frowned. "Keeping you here is one thing, but he can't expect to cut you off from your loved ones." He cast a surreptitious glance around the room and lowered his voice. "I can't promise anything, but I have a friend in Augsburg. She might be able to get word to your family, if you pass your letter on through me."

I considered him through tear-soaked lashes. It could be a trap, someone placed by the prince to trick me into betraying him so he could send me away. But then again, if the prince wanted me gone, he didn't have to keep me. He could send me away on a whim. "Couldn't you get in trouble for helping me?"

He laughed. "I've been working here since the king was still in diaper-clothes. Edric doesn't scare me, nor does his little boy."

I darted a look around the room. Still empty. I shuddered to think what the prince would do if he heard someone call him *little boy*.

I reached into my pocket, where I'd hidden my letters to Brigid and Gisela. "You're sure it's safe?" I looked up into his eyes, dark brown with the vertical pupils of pipers, but wrinkled with age and kindness around the edges.

"Your secrets are safe with me. Any girl as brave as you deserves to have someone on her side."

A fresh rush of tears filled my eyes, this time from gratitude and relief. I pulled the letters from my pocket and pressed them into his hand. "One of these is for Gisela Volk, a shop-owner in Augsburg. She'll know how to get the other letter to my sister."

His eyebrows rose. "Aye, I can get word to Gisela Volk for you."

I smiled through my tears. "Thank you, Hugo." Another unlikely ally. Maybe the pipers weren't as terrifying as I thought.

Some of them, at least.

MONSTER

Annika

"So if a third of your men are killed or imprisoned, how many men do you have left?"

Falk furrowed his brow, counting on his fingers. Peter scribbled on a piece of paper, chewing on his lower lip.

Finally, Falk looked up at me. "Fifty?"

"Exactly," I said.

His chest swelled. "I knew it!"

He'd always been a quick learner, but he'd done so well in the fortnight at court, he was going to surpass me soon. I'd have to find some other way to occupy his mind. If I couldn't, I'd find myself obligated to do as the prince had wanted, sending both boys to school across the valley with the piper children. They'd settled in well, but they weren't ready for that yet.

I set my quill and paper down. "Well done, both of you. You can go on outside."

The two boys didn't wait for me to change my mind before rushing out the door.

"Don't forget your coats!" I called after them. The rest of the children were already in the courtyard playing. They were now comfortable enough to roam the castle without supervision. They avoided most of the pipers but Teta, although they'd found a few friends among the younger servants.

As the sound of Peter and Falk's footprints faded, the prince appeared in the doorway. I stiffened.

I'd seen him almost every night since I arrived at court. We shared a meal, after which he mussed my clothes and sent me back to my room. Our dinners were silent affairs; the prince usually worked at his desk while we ate, and I sat by the fire. Despite the time we'd spent together, I was no closer to understanding him than I had been two weeks ago.

"Already done for the day?" he asked, his tone mocking. "I'd expected you to put in more effort."

"They've done plenty of work. They need to use some energy."

"Hm."

Dressed in my comfortable, relatively modest day clothes and emboldened by the daylight streaming in through the windows, I raised my chin at the prince. "Did you need something, or did you just come to criticize? I've done nothing wrong, and the children are learning at an excellent pace, so unless you have something else to say—"

"As a matter of fact, I do." He drew something small from his pocket and held it up.

My breath caught in my throat. It was the protection Gisela had given me, the small pieces of cloth she'd warded against the piper magic. "What were you doing in my room?"

Loic raised his brow. "Why would I be in your room? A servant brought these to me." He considered them. "Now, I know you can't be foolish enough to believe that something as simple as stuffing your ears would protect you from my magic. So I can't help but wonder why you bothered to bring these at all."

"They...help me sleep." I met his gaze, daring him to contradict me. "Falk snores."

He sniffed them. "Is that so? Then why do they smell of laurel leaves and ashes?" He strode across the room and deposited them on my desk, lowering his voice as he leaned in. "Do you know what I think? I think you're lying to me. You've been experimenting with magics, haven't you, little songbird? These are doused in a potion."

The tips of my ears heated.

"Shall we see how they work?" He drew his flute from beneath his shirt and gestured to the pieces of fabric.

My eyes widened. He meant to enchant me, to use his magic on me. I scrambled for the earplugs and stuffed them into my ears. *Please, God, let them work.*

He put the flute to his mouth and began to play.

The fabric muffled the sound but didn't obliterate it. Unlike the night he'd taken Falk, this music was gentler. It didn't fill me with the same buzzing feeling. It didn't set my teeth on edge.

Gisela's creation had worked.

The tune was sweet, and despite the lack of magic, it seemed to make the whole world brighter. I looked up at the prince, a smile spreading across my face. He hadn't managed to enchant me, but he was still a masterful musician.

Eyes closed, he swayed gently, caught up in the music. He really was beautiful, wasn't he? I stepped around the desk, drawing nearer as I watched him. The tune softened him. I wished he could play forever. I wished—I wished those beautiful lips were on mine. I wished he would touch me.

I reached out to him. So beautiful. How did anyone like this come from the earth? He had to be an angel. As I brushed his cheek with my fingers, his eyes opened. He leaned into my touch and let the flute fall. Then his mouth met mine.

The touch brought me back to reality, and I jerked back, crashing into the desk.

"Wh—what—" I yanked the earplugs out and tossed them on the desk. A thick, metallic taste coated my tongue.

He raised a brow. "Is something wrong?"

"You—you—"

"Me? No, you're mistaken. *You* touched *me.*" He caressed my cheek, and I flinched. "Did you not enjoy yourself?"

"You *enchanted* me!"

"I did warn you. It's not my fault your little experiment didn't work."

I glared at him. "You're a—a—"

"Angel, I believe, was the term you used."

I flushed. I hadn't even realized I'd spoken aloud during the enchantment. Boiling with rage and shame, I pushed past him and ran from the room.

My steps led me to Teta's quarters. She was on her way out, but she stopped when she saw the look on my face.

"What's wrong?" she asked, opening the door to let me into her sitting room.

I took a seat on the plush green couch. *Loic,* I signed.

She raised a brow as she sat down next to me. "What about him?"

She signed the words for me, and I repeated them, clumsily. All of our conversations were like this. I would say something, and then she would repeat it, signing it for me. It took a long time to say anything, but I was learning quickly.

"He's just..." I sighed. "How are you and the prince so different?"

Teta repeated the words, slower, signing as she did. *"How are you and the prince so different?"*

I frowned, trying to imitate the movement of her hands. *How are you and the prince so different?*

Excellent!" She clapped, a wide grin splitting her face. "What do you mean by 'different?'"

"Loic is cruel. You're...well, you're nothing like him. You're not what I expected from a piper."

Her smile faded slightly. "Loic isn't cruel." She demonstrated the sign for cruel, then shook her head and made another sign, dragging her open hands through the air in front of her face. "He's sad."

Sad. I repeated the sign. "I don't think I've ever seen anyone who looks less 'sad.'"

"It's a mask." She covered and uncovered her face with her hands. "He—well, it's hard for him to let people get close to him. You've seen his father."

I shivered. I'd never seen anyone look at me with such scorn as the Pied Piper. At the weekly Hall meetings, I stayed as far away from the king as possible. "Yes, I see where Loic gets his personality from."

"He's nothing like his father," Teta bit out.

I jerked back at the vehemence in her voice. "I'm sorry."

She took a breath. "No, it's okay. You have every reason to see him as the villain. But you have to understand, he did it out of mercy."

"He kissed me out of mercy?"

She looked sharply at me. "He did what?!"

My face heated. Teta was, as far as I knew, the only one aware of the true state of my relationship with the prince, though she wouldn't explain his motivations to me. "He kissed me. Or rather, he made me kiss him." I told her what had happened in the schoolroom.

When I finished, she made a face. "That was...ill-advised."

I snorted at the vast understatement.

"You have to understand, though. He did need to test them to see if they worked. If someone managed to create something that blocks our magic, that could be a threat to the court."

"He didn't need to do *that.*"

"I know." She reached out and took my hand. "But he's trying to protect our people, and he was raised to do that by whatever means necessary. For him, doing that was...well, a mercy. I know that doesn't excuse it," she said, seeing I was about to speak, "but that's why he did it."

"What was his excuse for stealing the children, then? Was that *mercy,* too?" My voice was bitter.

Teta frowned. "You'd prefer he kill people instead?"

"I'd prefer he left us alone!" I threw up my hands. "He didn't *have* to take them!"

She remained quiet. After a moment, she said, "Didn't he explain the law to you?"

"That he had a right to take them? That he was being 'merciful' for kidnapping them, rather than killing them? Yes, he explained that quite well." Monster. I could think of worse names, but a Christian woman didn't use such language, even in her own mind.

"The right? Annika, he didn't have a choice."

I cocked my head, furrowing my brow at her. "What are you saying?"

"I'm saying that the law—the *king*—requires any piper who performs a service to take payment for it. If we're not paid for saving a life, we're forced to take a life instead." She sighed. "Loic was expected to kill the same number of people he healed in your village. He chose not to. He found a loophole in the law, and he 'took' those lives by bringing the children back here instead."

My mind raced. When he'd told me he did it to be merciful, I hadn't believed him, but he hadn't exactly tried to convince me. Why? Did he *want* to be seen as the villain?

"The king was furious, but Loic managed to convince him he hadn't broken the law." Teta scanned my face. "He didn't tell you?"

"No," I said. "No, he didn't."

LOIC

She'd looked at me like I was a monster.

I probably deserved it. That enchantment was the least of what I'd done to her. I'd stolen her son, after all, and done my best to humiliate her in front of the entire court. No matter why I'd done those things. Maybe I was no better than my father.

Maybe I shouldn't try to be.

I should have learned this lesson with Eva. Kindness, gentleness, *emotion*—those traits had no place in a prince's life. Not for the prince of the pipers. The future Pied Piper should be formidable, driven. His very name should strike fear into the hearts of his enemies. He shouldn't care for the opinion of some fleeting songbird who chirped in his ear when he stole the egg from her nest.

You're not even half the man your father is. The last words Eva had said to me when I'd banished her from the court. She wasn't wrong; if my father had caught his lover with another man, he'd have killed them both on sight. *He* wouldn't have spared her over some misguided sentiment.

Small wonder my father hadn't remarried after my mother's death.

My fingers brushed my flute, hanging on a cord around my neck. The look in Annika's eyes earlier this evening had done something to me. She'd looked at me with something other than hatred or fear. A fleeting victory, I knew, but still. It had been nice to have that crumb of affection, false though it was. I hadn't meant to kiss her, but the temptation had been too much.

I shouldn't have done it. Any chance I might have had at earning her trust—and that chance was small already, given the way we met—was gone, vanished like the chords I'd played to enchant her. Any sentiment between us would be as false as my relationship with Eva, bought by title and wealth or by magic.

I brought the flute to my lips. A wave of magic rose in my lungs, but I banked it. I didn't want to charm anything. I just wanted to let out this insidious tide of feelings inside me. To channel it into something before it destroyed me.

The notes rose and fell all on their own, a magic independent of my blood. The pipers' ability to enchant living things might come from the core of magic in my father, but this, this was mine alone.

Some would deny that music held a natural magic. They were boors who wouldn't know Obrecht from a drunken tavern performer. They would never know the agonizing beauty or the heady thrill of pouring one's heart into one's music. How one could get lost in the sound, swept away on the melody until the messy emotions that filled them were gone, floating away on the air, and one could be at peace. *I could be at peace.*

I poured my soul into the music, and it came alive for me.

As Evil As You Seem

Annika

I brushed a lock of hair off Falk's face. He looked so sweet when he slept. Peaceful.

I hadn't expected it, but our time here in Laute was having a positive effect on him. He was happier here. Here, he had the freedom to study and learn, and hours of play and exertion. He'd even made new friends. He didn't have to spend all his time carting wheat and flour for the miller, working dawn to dusk just to keep us from starving.

No child should have to bear that burden.

And if what Teta had said was true, Loic had been ordered to kill him. Falk and every other person his magic had healed. I shuddered at the thought.

He'd been ordered to, but he hadn't.

Why, though? He wanted everyone to believe he was cruel, but then he spared the lives of a dozen people. Went up against his father and faced the consequences to save their lives.

And why hadn't he taken everyone he'd saved? Why take the children? Falk and the Weiss children had been sick, yes, but Peter hadn't been. Nor had Brida, the blacksmith's daughter. If the prince was following the letter of the law, why did he take the children and not the adults?

I shook my head. It was all too confusing. I needed sleep, but I'd never be able to with my thoughts all in an uproar.

I pressed a kiss to Falk's forehead and slipped out the bedroom door. For the first time since I arrived at court, the prince hadn't summoned me to his rooms for supper. I'd eaten with Falk instead. Now it was late enough that the kitchens would be empty, but if Hugo was still working, he might have something to settle my stomach and mind. At the very least, he would let me share my thoughts.

As I stepped into the hallway, the faint sound of music drifted to my ears. I froze, ready to flee, before realizing there was no magic in it. Even the prince's enchantment earlier had left me with a bad taste in my mouth, once the charm faded and I realized what had happened. This didn't have the same effect.

The music came through the crack in the prince's door. It was melancholy, a song of loneliness and mourning, but magical in the way only something God-given could be. It brought a tear into my eye as I peeked into the room.

The prince sat by the fire, staring into it as he played his flute. The expression on his face reflected the song he played. Empty. Alone.

This moment was private. I wasn't meant to see it. I took a step back, hoping to slip away unnoticed.

The music stopped, and the prince looked up. "It's not polite to linger at doors," he said.

Mouth dry, I pushed the door open and stepped into the room. "I didn't mean to intrude."

No trace of the emotion I'd seen remained on his face. He raised a brow and waved me closer. "And yet, here you are. What do you want? Have you come to sing me a song?"

"I—" I walked toward him, stopping in front of him. The warmth of the fire bolstered my resolve. "Why did you take the children?"

He looked into the flames, his expression unreadable. "I believe I already answered that. It was my right."

"Your right? Or were you forced to take them?" I squeezed my hands in the folds of my skirts to stop them from shaking.

His mouth formed a line as he scanned my face. "Does it matter?"

"Yes, of course it matters!"

"Why? Because Teta told you I'm lonely? Because you want to find the good in me?" He stood, forcing me to crane my neck to meet his eyes. "I'm not the hero, songbird. Yes, I was required to take lives—one for each life I had saved. But I *chose* to take the children, and do you know why?"

I shook my head, eyes wide.

He leaned down to whisper in my ear. "Because I knew that would hurt worse than any deaths."

I shivered at the cruelty in his voice. Why was he like this? Did he enjoy hurting people?

But that expression he'd worn, that song he'd been playing...he knew pain. He'd experienced it. Maybe Teta was right. Maybe he didn't enjoy hurting people. Maybe he did it to protect himself from being hurt again.

I took a step back and raised my chin, meeting his gaze again. "I don't believe you, your highness."

"Oh?"

"If that was the only reason you took them, you would have killed them. It would have saved you a lot of trouble." I put a hand on his arm. "You may not be the hero, but I don't believe you're the villain, either."

He looked down at my hand and blinked, as though surprised I'd dared to touch him. My boldness surprised even me, but I didn't remove it.

He did, though, picking up my hand between two fingers and dropping it. "I thought my demonstration earlier cured you of any such misconceptions. Was that insufficient?" He picked up his flute from where it lay on the chair. "I would be happy to show you again."

My eyes narrowed. His kiss had been unwelcome, but Teta's reasoning made sense. He had to protect his people, and what he'd done, while distasteful, was hardly the worst thing he could have done to me. I'd seen his abilities. Limiting himself to just a kiss was, in a strange way, almost a kindness.

I shook my head. "I don't believe you're as evil as you seem."

"Believe what you will." He stepped back and gave a mocking bow. "Goodnight, Mrs. Brandt." He turned and went into his bedroom, closing the door behind him.

HALL

LOIC

I drummed my fingers on the arm of my throne, scanning the growing crowd. My little songbird was late. Was she ignoring me after my experiment yesterday? Unlikely. She'd come to my room afterwards of her own free will.

I caught a flash of violet silk in the back of the room. Not late. Hiding in the back, hoping no one would notice. Unfortunately for her, *notice* was exactly what I needed everyone to do.

Standing, I stepped off the dais. The crowd parted before me like reeds in the wind, and I approached my prey unnoticed.

"Going somewhere?" I murmured in her ear.

She flinched. Turning to look up into my eyes, she opened her mouth to speak. "I—"

I brushed a thumb over her lips, cutting her off. "At least you look decent tonight." A lie. She was beautiful. Two weeks of regular meals had caused her to lose the haunted look of malnourishment, and the vivid purple dress with its plunging neckline revealed the perfect amount of skin.

She jerked away from my touch. My eyes narrowed, and I leaned down to whisper in her ear. "Unless you wish to suffer the consequences, little songbird, you will not push me away." I had no intention of forcing her into my bed, but I couldn't allow her to reject my touch in public. Not with the eyes of my father and his supporters all around us. "Am I understood?"

She shivered. "Yes."

"Good." I took her arm and led her into the fray. My goal for tonight was to show her off to as many people as possible. I'd staked my claim in front of the council; tonight was for the rest of the court.

A baker and his wife stood nearby. I made a beeline for them. "Mr and Mrs. Klepper, congratulations." Their oldest son, Gerhard, was making his debut before the court today after discovering his musical gift. He would demonstrate his control over the magic, and the king would declare him a Delegate of the Pied Piper.

"Thank you, your highness." Mrs. Klepper dipped into a bow, eyeing Annika. "And how kind of you to bring your new friend to watch, as well."

The little songbird flushed. I could practically see her thoughts; she wanted to be anywhere but here. I stroked her cheek. "Yes, Mrs. Brandt is overjoyed to have this opportunity to observe our culture up close. Isn't that right, songbird?"

Her wide, innocent eyes flashed to my face. "What?"

"I was telling Mrs. Klepper how excited you are to see a claiming ceremony."

"Oh." She worried her lip. "Yes."

"If you'll excuse us." I nodded to the baker and his wife and swept the little human back into the crowd.

Lady Helene scowled at us from across the room, her dark mouth twisting with displeasure. She tucked her arm into Alois' and whispered something in his ear. They moved closer to the dais.

The noblewoman didn't know it, but her time as my father's mistress was quickly drawing to a close. Already, the king's eye was wandering. He didn't have a replacement chosen yet—he never abandoned a mistress without another woman to take her place—but as soon as he found one, Lady Helene and Alois would be forgotten. I allowed myself a small smile at the thought. I'd never liked Lady Helene, and I liked her son even less.

Next to me, my songbird had gone pale. Something had frightened her. I looked around and saw an old man with long, curved horns leering at her. Lord Pepin, one of my father's most ardent supporters. I bared my teeth at him in a snarl. The old man quailed at the sight. He was a favorite of the king, but even he knew not to cross the crown prince.

The blast of trumpets announced my father's arrival, and Annika cringed. Some part of her knew that the worst was yet to come.

ANNIKA

As the Pied Piper entered the room, I expected the prince to release me so he could sit next to his father on the dais in the front of the room. He did move toward the dais, but he didn't release me. We walked up the steps, and the king gave me a cold glare as Loic took a seat in the ornate golden chair next to his father's throne.

What did he want me to do? Was I supposed to stand there the whole time?

The prince raised a brow and pointed at the ground in front of him. He wanted me to sit at his feet. Like a dog.

I clenched my teeth as I sank to the ground, my back straight as a fencepost. He rested his hand on my head, and it was all I could do not to flinch away.

I barely heard the king as he welcomed everyone. A stream of petitioners followed. I watched as they bowed to the king and brought him their complaints and requests, but my attention was fixed on the man behind me.

At first, the prince's hand remained on my head. As the petitioners came, he took a curl and twisted it absently around his finger, then trailed it over the skin of my neck. I shivered.

When he dropped the curl and brushed his finger over my collarbone, then lower, I bit my cheek to keep from moving. This was no more humiliating than dinner with the king. I could do this. For Falk.

His finger dipped between my breasts, and I shifted. Not by much; just enough that he couldn't touch me like that. I didn't dare to look back and see his reaction. He placed his hand on my shoulder and squeezed—not hard enough to hurt, but enough to show his displeasure.

I kept my gaze fixed on the next petitioner, a young man carrying an enormous stringed instrument. A small white goat followed him on a short leash. A goatherd, perhaps; but then why did he bring an instrument as tall as he was?

"Gerhard Klepper," the herald announced, "demonstrating his proficiency for king and court."

The king waved a bored hand at Gerhard Klepper and his goat. "Begin."

The young man drew the bow across the strings with a screech. Cringing, he looked up at the king, whose jaw tightened. He started again.

This time, a beautiful melody poured out of the instrument. Slow and graceful, it sounded like the melting of snow in spring, like the joy of a mother holding her child for the first time. With the music, the goat rose up on two legs and began a stately, processional dance before the throne. The contrast between the beauty of the music and the ridiculous sight of a dancing goat made me want to laugh, but I didn't dare. Not with the king sitting so near.

When the song drew to a close, the prince gave a slow, deliberate clap. "Well done," he said, his voice lacking all emotion. "Your goat can dance a pavane. But can he do a galliard?"

A hysterical laugh bubbled up in my throat, and I covered it with a cough, turning my head so no one saw. The musician bowed his head back over the instrument and began a fast-paced tune. The goat performed a series of leaps and kicks.

The Pied Piper waved again. "Enough." The music stopped at once, and the goat dropped back down to four legs. "Gerhard Klepper," he intoned, sounding bored. But how could he be bored? I knew these magics came from the devil, but I couldn't look away.

"We hereby instate you as a Delegate of the Pied Piper. Report in the morning for training."

The man, Klepper, bowed and faded back into the crowd, goat trailing after him. A woman with night-black skin and white horns took his place. She carried a golden trumpet and a tiny potted seedling.

"Cerise Wimmer, demonstrating her proficiency for king and court," the herald called. Cerise Wimmer placed her plant on the ground before the king, bowed, and raised the trumpet to her lips.

A loud, regal blast sounded, and the plant shot up, sprouting dozens of lilies. As the march of a royal army played from the woman's trumpet, the lilies multiplied, spreading out across the floor and twining together. The assembled court staggered out of the way of the swelling plants. Sweet perfume filled the air, almost thick enough to see.

As the final notes of the song faded, the lilies trembled and fell still. Stretched out on the ground before the dais, the plant had formed into words: *King Edric of Laute, long may he reign.*

The king's permanent scowl slipped away, and the ghost of a smile took its place. He trailed his eyes over her body. "Well done, Cerise Wimmer. We hereby instate you as a Delegate of the Pied Piper. I will speak to you after Hall regarding your first assignment."

Speak to her after Hall? He'd told the other musician to report for training. A quick glance up at the prince showed a slight narrowing of his eyes, the only hint of a reaction. It seemed Loic didn't appreciate his father's special attention toward this woman.

The musician bowed and stepped to the side as another young man came forward carrying a pan flute. His large brown ears twitched with nerves as he gave the Pied Piper a shaky bow.

"Alfred Balzer, demonstrating his proficiency for king and court," the herald called.

The anxious young man looked around at the flowers from the previous demonstration. Lifting the flute to his lips, he blew softly. A dark, haunting melody filled the air. An ache grew in my chest as the lilies wilted and turned black. The song went on, and the lilies decayed before our eyes. Tiny mushrooms of purple and blue sprang up from the rot.

The mushrooms grew with the music, rising up until they towered over the man and hid his face from our view. Still, the song went on. The mushrooms swayed beneath their own weight as one low note lingered in the air...

And the caps burst into a million spores.

Shrieks rang out as the spores filled the room. I fell backward, blinded by purple powder. Loic grabbed my arms and pulled me onto his lap, as if he thought I would run away in the chaos.

"ENOUGH." The king's voice cut through the cacophony "Guards, take him."

I wiped my eyes and squinted through the fog of settling spores. The young man with the flute knelt amid the ruined mushrooms, hands clasped in petition. "They're not dangerous, your majesty! It was an accident!"

He thrashed and kicked as two men grabbed him and dragged him from the room.

"Hall is dismissed." The king stormed off the dais and out the door.

"Are you hurt?" the prince murmured in my ear.

"I'm fine." I stared out at the near-empty room. The few remaining attendees picked their way through the mushroom debris. "What will happen to him?"

"Balzer?" Loic shrugged. He set me on my feet and stood. "There will be an inquiry. If it's found that he tried to kill the Pied Piper, he'll be executed. If it was an accident, he'll be whipped and fined, but the king will release him."

Whipped? Executed? The thought sickened me. "But he didn't do anything wrong."

"He humiliated the king. He'll be lucky to get away with his life." He held out his hand. "Worry about yourself, little songbird. Alfred Balzer is none of your concern."

"Is Hall always like this?" I asked as we left the scene of the disaster behind.

He chuckled. "No, tonight was the most interesting night we've had in a long time. I expected your presence to make it more enjoyable, but I hadn't realized there would be so much...excitement."

My stomach did a funny flip at the look he gave me. His proximity should appall me, but I couldn't find it in myself to hate him like I had when he first stole the children.

"Don't anticipate a spectacle every week," he went on.

"Every week?"

"Yes." He raised a brow at me. "As long as you remain here, you'll attend Hall and any other court functions I require."

Dressed like a harlot and paraded around as his mistress. A question burned on my tongue: *If you want everyone to think I'm your whore, why don't you bed me and get it over with?* But I didn't want to provoke him. He'd allowed me to maintain my integrity before God, if not before his pagan court. I had to be content with that.

"And dinner in your rooms?" I asked instead.

"Those will continue as well." He stopped outside the door to my rooms. "Go bathe, songbird. Get that mushroom filth off of you."

A strange cord of connection hung in the air between us, and our eyes locked. He opened his mouth to say something, then shook his head.

I put one hand on the door. "Goodnight, your highness."

"Goodnight, Mrs. Brandt."

RELIGIOUS CONVICTIONS

ANNIKA

"A ve Maria, gratia plena. Dominus tecum, benedicta—"

The door crashed open, interrupting my prayers. The prince strode in, his brow knit together with anger.

I bowed my head and continued. "Benedicta tu in mulieribus, et benedictus fructus ventris tui, Iesus."

He stopped in front of me, his boots near my forehead as I knelt. "Are you intentionally trying to rile me?"

My heart raced, but I ignored him as I finished my prayer. "Sancta Maria, Mater Dei, ora pro nobis peccatoribus nunc et in hora mortis nostrae. Amen." I made the sign of the cross and kissed my rosary before rising to my feet, taking care to shake the wrinkles from my skirt. "Good afternoon, your highness."

He glared at me. "What are you doing?"

"I was praying."

"And you're not in the classroom because…"

"Today is a holiday." I took a seat next to the fire and pulled a stocking from the mending basket. Truly, I didn't know how Falk managed to put holes in every piece of clothing he owned. Silvia had offered to mend them for me, but I needed something to occupy myself when I wasn't attending to the children or the prince. "I gave them the afternoon off."

"And what holiday is that?"

"Ash Wednesday." I threaded my needle and set to work. "It marks the beginning of Lent, the forty days before Christ's Resurrection on Easter. Normally we would spend the day in Mass, but as that isn't an option here, I chose to let the children have the afternoon to themselves." Some of the boys had gone exploring the woods, and the rest of the children had gone to the bowling hall.

He scowled at me. "I suppose the holiday is your excuse for starving yourself, as well."

"I did speak to Hugo about the children and myself fasting during Lent, yes." The sweet old cook had frowned disapprovingly at my request, but I hadn't thought he would go to the prince about it.

"Is it your intention to make me look like a fool in front of the court, or do you just enjoy the effects of malnutrition?"

I sat my needle down and leveled my gaze at him. "I'm following the mandates of the Church." Believers were exhorted to fast, subsisting on bread and vegetables, during the penitential season of Lent. On Ash Wednesday and Good Friday, the first and second-to-last days of the season, the fasting was even stricter—nothing but water, watered wine, or beer before sundown. I couldn't attend Mass here in Laute, as was required on holy days, but that wouldn't stop me from following the Church in whatever ways I could.

He rolled his eyes, the motion making him seem more like a petulant child than a prince. "I hardly think your priest would begrudge you eating enough to survive."

"I'm not starving myself. And anyway, what would you know about the Church? All you pipers are pagans." Pater Trost may have been right; they weren't demons, as I'd feared, but I wasn't going to accept theological guidance from a pagan.

He pursed his lips, then jerked his head toward the door. "Come with me," he said. "And grab a cloak."

Confused, I did as he said, slipping on the sumptuous ermine cloak I'd been given. It felt wrong, dressing in such lavish clothing, but I had nothing else. As soon as my new clothes had arrived, the dress I'd come to court in had disappeared with the dirty laundry, and it hadn't been returned. At least my new wardrobe consisted of relatively modest garments for day usage. The eveningwear, which the prince paraded me around in after the children were in bed, filled me with shame.

The ermine cloak did its job of keeping me warm as he led me out of the castle and through the city. Snowflakes bit at my face, whirling around at the whim of the winter wind. I had to run to keep up with the prince's unhesitating long strides.

I hadn't walked through the city, preferring to keep myself and the children isolated in the castle as much as possible. In the prince's wake, I didn't have time to notice details, but what I saw of the city was magnificent. Pine trees and houses the size of castles lined the snow-covered streets.

At last, the prince stopped in front of a large white house. Glass windows looked down onto the street, candles shining in every one. It was no more ornate than any of the other houses, but even after two months at court, the opulence of Laute still overwhelmed me. If I'd seen this house in Augsburg, I would have assumed it belonged to a nobleman or a foreign dignitary. Here, it could have been the baker's house, for all I knew.

The prince knocked sharply. After a moment, the door opened, and a middle-aged man peered out at us. His skin was light, like mine, and his hair, eyes, and horns were all brown. He wore a set of wire spectacles on his nose.

"Your highness!" He bowed and waved us into the house. "What an unexpected honor. What brings you here?"

"Konrad." The prince nodded. "This is Annika Brandt. Annika, meet Konrad Bach."

"A pleasure to meet you, Mrs. Brandt. I've heard your name, of course."

"Pleasure," I said, casting a questioning glance at the prince.

His expression was smug. "Konrad is a Catholic. As you can see, we're not all pagans."

I flushed in shame, but Konrad smiled wryly. "I was baptized, yes, but I believe the Church still considers us demons, your highness. Calling us pagans would be a generous interpretation of canon law."

A baptized demon. What did that make him? Was the baptism even valid? My world tilted on its axis.

Konrad led us down the hall. "We were just about to eat a late dinner. You'll join us?"

The prince glanced at me. "Unfortunately, Mrs. Brandt is fasting for the next six weeks."

"You'll still join us, though, won't you?" His eyes were wide and earnest. "I can have watered wine brought out for you, or some fresh bread. I know my wife, Ilse, would love to meet another Catholic."

"I would appreciate some watered wine, thank you." I could smell something fragrant—roast chicken, perhaps—and my stomach rumbled. Fasting was always the hardest part of Lent, and though the rest of the season wasn't so strict as Ash Wednesday, the forty days were still akin to torture. Watered wine dulled the ache a little.

He guided us into the dining room. "Please, make yourselves comfortable. I'll be right back."

The prince gestured for me to sit first, then took the chair to my left. He didn't speak, but I felt his eyes on me as I looked around the room.

A small chandelier hung over the dark wooden dining table, and a painting of Christ in the Garden took up most of the wall opposite us. My eyes lingered on the painting, Jesus' face twisted with agony as his disciples slept in the foreground.

At last I turned to the prince. "I'm sorry for what I said, your highness. I shouldn't have called your people pagans."

"So you admit that your way of practicing your faith is not the only way?"

I frowned. "Of course. I never said otherwise."

"Good. Then I expect this ridiculous fasting concept is at an end. I won't have you starving yourself or the children."

My mouth dropped open. "I—that's not what I meant!"

Before I could collect my thoughts, Konrad walked back into the room, followed by a younger woman, heavily pregnant. "Mrs. Brandt, this is my wife, Ilse."

She was a tall, plump woman. Short, red-brown horns peeked up above her two brown braids. She dipped her head in a bow. "Welcome to our home, Mrs. Brandt. Prince Loic, it's an honor to have you in our home."

"Thank you for having me, Mrs. Bach," I said. "I didn't mean to intrude."

"Not at all." She took a seat at the foot of the table as her husband sat at the head. "I love having guests."

A pair of servants came in, each with a tray. They filled the table with a spread of food—roast chicken, boiled potatoes, a loaf of warm bread, and a dish of butter. My mouth watered, and I forced myself to look down at the table as someone placed a cup of wine in front of me.

"May I bless the food?" Konrad asked. When the prince nodded, he folded his hands and said, "Gracious Lord, we give you thanks for the loving kindness you have given us through your Son, Jesus Christ, and we ask that this food before us may bless our bodies and the company around this table may bless our souls. For Yours is the kingdom, and the power, and the glory. Amen."

"Amen," I echoed through a tight throat. The simple prayer brought tears to my eyes. It had been so long since I'd been among fellow Catholics. Even such strange ones as these.

As the servants filled the plates, Konrad turned to me. "May I ask why you're fasting, Mrs. Brandt?"

"I—" I paused. Was he unaware of the holiday? Maybe they didn't know the holy days of the Church, separated as they were from a congregation. "Today is Ash Wednesday."

"Yes, but what are you fasting for?" He shook his head. "Forgive me. That must seem like a rude question. I only meant that, as I understand it, fasting is to be done in combination with prayer and repentance. I wondered if you were fasting for a specific reason, or only because of Church tradition."

I'd never thought about why I fasted. I'd just always done it. "I...don't know," I admitted.

"I see." He leaned forward, gazing earnestly at me through his spectacles. "I know I'm no priest, but I would caution you against undertaking something so serious without examining your spirit."

The prince gave me a pointed look. I ignored him; he'd probably arranged this whole conversation, though why, I couldn't fathom. Why did it matter to him if I fasted?

"I appreciate your concern," I said, reaching for my drink. "I don't believe anything good for the spirit can be harmful, though." If it was, the Church wouldn't encourage it.

"Yes, as we all know, starvation loses its dangers when one does it for the right reasons," the prince said in a dry tone.

Konrad's mouth twitched in what might have been a smile as his wife said, "Are you opposed to fasting in general, then, your highness, or merely for Mrs. Brandt?"

"I have no objection to whatever spiritual disciplines anyone chooses to take, so long as they do not deliberately harm themselves while under my protection." He met her gaze, but the words were meant for me.

"As I said earlier, *your highness,*" I said, my ears heating, "I'm not harming myself."

"You've barely begun to look like a woman, rather than a pile of sticks in a dress. Six weeks of fasting will undo all that, and the entire court will think I can't control you."

Of course, that's what this was all about. His reputation in court. I felt a twinge of disappointment and quickly tamped it down. I'd let

Teta's view of him influence my perception overmuch; he might not be the demon I'd originally thought, but he was no saint.

"I hardly think your...companion's religious convictions could reflect poorly on you, your highness," Ilse said in a soft voice, glancing at me. She'd hesitated on the word *companion,* as though unsure of a polite term for me. *She* didn't know I wasn't the prince's bedmate. None of the city did. I picked up my drink and took a large swallow to hide my flaming cheeks.

When the prince looked at her, she shrank back, dropping her gaze to her plate. "I hardly think my *companion* appearing half-starved reflects well on me, Mrs. Bach, regardless of her reasons," he said coldly.

"Fasting is prescribed in Scripture," Konrad said, "but not so specifically as the Church dictates today. Given that you were so recently underfed, and you're not fasting for a specific reason, I'm inclined to agree with the prince on this matter."

My stomach twisted, and I wasn't sure if it was from hunger or moral quandary.

The prince nodded as though he'd won. "It's settled, then." He waved for a plate. "You'll eat."

"How did you come to be baptized?" I asked.

Ilse Bach and I sat together in her parlor, sewing on opposite ends of a tapestry she intended to give the king for his birthday celebration next month. During the six weeks since our impromptu Ash Wednesday dinner, she'd taken it upon herself to extend me the hand of friendship, coming to the castle to see me or inviting me to her home at least once a week. When her husband was home—he was a merchant, I'd discovered, and was often away—the children and I joined them on Sundays for prayer services.

During our weekly service, Konrad read from the Bible. He often followed the Scripture passage with a reading from one of the innumerable theological texts they owned—the shelf of these spanned ceiling to floor in the parlor—and then invited us to discuss it with him. I always declined, having heard my village priest, Pater Huber, speak on innumerable occasions about the dangers of women teaching men. The children enjoyed this form of Sunday service, and the older ones would offer their thoughts, swelling with pride whenever Konrad complimented them on a particularly insightful comment.

Ilse looked up from the tapestry at my question. "It was Konrad's doing. He met a priest during one of his travels and was so taken with the man's message that he convinced him to come back to Laute. He preached in the city for a month and offered to baptize anyone who was willing. Konrad and I were the only two in the city who wished it. We were already betrothed, and the pater baptized and married us on the same day." She grimaced. "The king wasn't pleased. He sees the Church as a threat to his throne, and not without reason. But Konrad has enough sway in the city that he couldn't afford to banish us. He gave us a hefty fine and ordered us not to bring clergy into Laute again."

I hadn't thought about how the Pied Piper might react to some of his subjects joining the Church that called him Beelzebub. "It must be difficult for you, being so isolated here."

"We've been incredibly blessed. I won't deny that I wish to attend Mass, to confess my sins and do penance and take the Lord's Supper, but this is where God has placed us. I try not to wallow."

I shifted in my seat. Was that what I'd been doing? Wallowing? This was where God had put me. Pater Trost, the priest in Augsburg, had told me my journey to Laute could be an opportunity. That I could be a positive influence on the pipers. I'd been blinded by my prejudice and too focused on my own misery to realize the opportunity I had here. I might not be able to take the children home as I had hoped, but God could still use me. I could have some influence for good in this court, however small.

Have You Been Poisoned?

Annika

A week later, I found myself confined to bed with an unusually painful monthly cycle, and my resolve to keep from wallowing fled.

I lay there, clutching my stomach and biting my lip to keep from crying out. Why did a woman's lot have to be so painful?

At least Falk wasn't here to see me. After he ate breakfast, I sent him with a note for Teta, letting her know that I was ill and asking her to take over class. She already joined us most mornings, and the children adored her; they would be thrilled to have her teaching them for the day. Although I doubted much would get done, given her tendency to indulge them in whatever they asked.

A knock sounded on the outer door, but I ignored it, grinding my teeth against a fresh wave of cramps. The knock sounded again, insistent this time. After a few moments, I heard the outer door open, followed by the door to the bedroom. The prince's scowling face appeared.

"What's wrong with you?"

I clutched the blankets higher and glared at him. I was in no mood to deal with his criticism. "What's wrong with *you?* You should know better than to barge into someone's private—" I gasped, doubling over with another cramp.

When I straightened back up, breathing hard, he was watching me with a quirked brow. "Have you been poisoned?"

What I wouldn't give to throw something at his face. Preferably something heavy. Attacking the prince would be enough to have me removed from court without my son, though. In as calm a voice as I could manage, I said, "I doubt anyone would consider me of enough import to poison."

"Hm." He stepped toward the bed, looking down at me impassively. "You don't appear to be faking your illness, as I thought."

Faking? Blood rushed to my cheeks. How dare he? I opened my mouth to respond, but he grabbed the covers and yanked them from me.

Rage boiled up as he scanned my body. Mortification quickly followed, as I realized the shift I wore was nearly transparent with sweat. He could see everything, from my uneven breasts to the dark patch of hair between my thighs. And slightly further down...

He wrinkled his nose at the patch of red staining the lower part of my shirt. "Did you intend to ruin the mattress, or was this a happy accident?"

I didn't approve of swearing, but if anyone could make me, it would be him. Horrid man. "I'm sorry I didn't bring my rags with me, your highness, when I was hunting down the man who stole my son."

Was it my imagination, or did I see the hint of a grin flash across his face at that?

"I'll have fresh rags brought to your room, then." He turned toward the door. "I suppose you may be excused from your duties for today, and I'll inform my father that you are too ill to attend tonight's hall. I'll expect you back to work as soon as you're...recovered." With that, he strode out of the room, closing the door behind him.

I let out a small shriek and chucked the pillow at the door. Not as satisfying as hitting his head with a rock, but it would have to suffice. Another cramp dragged me onto my side, and I clutched my stomach. If only I could transfer some of my pain to the prince. That would teach him to taunt me.

I woke a while later to more knocking, and Silvia, the young servant girl, came into the room. "Your bath is ready."

I sat up, rubbing the sleep from my eyes. "I didn't ask for a bath."

"Prince's orders. I have a basket of menstrual cloths for you, as well, and a cup of hot chamomile."

Loic did this? Why? I puzzled over it as I climbed out of bed, moving slowly in consideration of my tender abdomen. Maybe he was trying to ensure that I didn't waste castle resources by remaining unwell. Or perhaps it reflected poorly on him in court to have his "pet" ill.

As I stood, I cast a guilty look at the stained mattress.

"Don't worry," Silvia said, following my gaze. "We'll get you a fresh one."

"Thank you." Face hot with shame, I stepped into the bathroom—I'd been surprised, at first, to find that each suite in the castle was equipped with a room specifically for bathing, but now I found it quite practical—and stripped off my shift, making my way to the large silver tub.

The water was near-scalding, and I sank into it with a sigh. Near the tub sat a tray with a mug of chamomile, a cloth for washing, and several bottles of what I assumed were different soaps. I sniffed at the contents of one—sweet and floral. There was no sign of the bar of lye soap I'd been given for previous baths.

I reached for the mug and sank back into the water, moaning at the heat on my aching muscles. I'd never been this pampered. My courses were infrequent, but when they arrived they were painful. Nikolaus had always insisted I spend the first day in bed, but hot baths and expensive soaps had been beyond our means.

I never knew what I'd been missing.

I sipped my drink, thinking about the prince. I couldn't understand him. Around the king, he was every bit his father's son, cold and calculating, not a drop of kindness in him. In private, he ignored me, and yet he'd shown disproportionate concern for my health by taking care to see that I was eating properly and sending me this.

I didn't delude myself into thinking his motives were entirely noble. He'd made it clear he never did anything without considering how it would reflect on him. Still, there was little reason for him to be so solicitous. I couldn't imagine how it would improve his reputation to send me a bath when I was confined to my room.

The door opened, and the subject of my thoughts walked in. He wore a self-satisfied smirk, and his eyes traveled the length of my body, my knees and the swell of my breasts visible above the water. I flushed and sank lower into the tub.

"You're looking better." His voice was lower than usual. Seductive. He'd changed clothes, now wearing nothing but a loose white shirt and breeches. His feet were bare, and his hair was tousled, as though he'd just come from bed.

"The bath helps. Thank you." I should tell him to leave. It wasn't appropriate for him to be here. Especially not with both of us in such a state of undress. I could see a slight spattering of hair rising above the collar of his shirt. The water grew uncomfortably warm, and I looked away.

"I didn't just mean today." He stopped next to the tub and knelt, considering me with his head cocked to one side. "You've gained weight. Added curves." I hadn't realized he'd noticed. "It's...appealing." He leaned against the tub and draped his hand over the edge. Ripples formed where he touched the water. The rings grew until they brushed against my skin, causing goosebumps to form. "Lean back."

I frowned, but he moved behind me and gently tugged my head back, down into the water. Once my hair was wet, he picked up a bottle of soap and poured some into his hands, then worked it through my hair, massaging my scalp. I shuddered with pleasure as his hands trailed down my neck and then my shoulders, working out the knots of tension.

A nagging sense tickled the corner of my mind, but I ignored it, too caught up in the sensation of his touch. "No one's ever done this for me," I said.

"I've wanted to touch you for weeks," he admitted, leaning down so his lips nearly brushed my ear. "That's why I had the bath sent up." He slid both hands down my back, tracing my waist.

"You have touched me." I twisted around to look at him. His hazel eyes were hooded. "You touch me all the time at Hall."

"Not like I want to." His thumb brushed my nipple, and my breath caught. "I'd like to do more than that, songbird."

I couldn't believe he would say those things to me. Couldn't believe he was touching me. "Like what?"

His eyes dropped to my mouth. "I can think of a few things."

I nodded slowly, my heart racing. My core tightened in a way it hadn't before. He gave a predatory smile, leaning closer...

Something splashed, sending water all over my face. My eyes flew open. My cup of chamomile had slipped from my hands into the bath.

I picked it up and glanced around furtively, but I was alone in the room. I'd been dreaming. Just dreaming, lulled to sleep by the bath and whatever had been in that cup. I'd never have dreamed something like that if Loic hadn't slipped something else into my drink. It had *tasted* like chamomile, but there must have been something else, some sort of tasteless herb designed to cause wicked thoughts.

I set the offending vessel next to the tub and quickly washed myself, desperate to get out of the bath he'd sent me. If the prince thought to rile me with his bath and his potions, he wouldn't find me so willing a target.

DRUDEN

Anika

"Please, Mama?" Falk clasped his hands together and put on his best pleading face. "We won't be far, only a day away."

Konrad Bach had offered to take Falk and Peter with him on his upcoming journey to Augsburg. If we'd still been at home, I wouldn't have hesitated, but the thought of being separated from him again, even for a couple days, caused a knot to form in my stomach. "I'd feel better if I were going with you."

"Out of the question." The prince's voice came from behind me, in the doorway to the sitting room.

My cheeks heated as I turned to look at him. "You won't let me go with my son?" I couldn't meet his eyes. Not after the mortifying dream he'd caused me to have.

"And risk you fleeing with him? Not a chance. I may be fool enough to let you fly free in my city, songbird, but the two of you will not leave the borders of Laute together." He looked at Falk. "I haven't yet decided if I'll even let the boy make the journey."

I jerked my chin up, staring fixedly at a point above his head. "I resent your implication. I would never leave the rest of the children here alone."

Falk stepped forward. "Please, your highness. I'll be with Mr. Bach the whole time. Peter and I won't try to run away, honest."

"What surety do I have of that?" Loic asked.

He straightened his shoulders and met the prince's gaze, unflinching. "My word of honor."

My heart swelled with pride. He'd grown so much in the few short months we'd been at court. I glanced at Loic. If he laughed, if he dared to mock Falk's sweet attempt to speak to him like a man, I would never forgive him.

But he didn't say anything to damage Falk's fragile pride. Instead, he paused, then asked, "Can you speak for your companion, as well?"

Falk raised his chin defiantly. "He can speak for himself."

"Good. If you'd said yes, I wouldn't have believed you." He narrowed his eyes. "Your mother remains here. You give me your word you will return, and I give you mine she will be safe under my protection. Do you agree?"

Falk gave me a quick glance, as though unsure, but he didn't wait for me to respond before sticking out his hand. "I agree."

Loic took the offered hand and shook it, his expression solemn. "It's settled, then." He turned to me. "Unless you have any objections?"

As if I could say no after that exchange. I shook my head.

A huge grin split Falk's face, and he threw his arms around me. "Thank you!"

"You'd better go let Konrad know," I said, ruffling his hair.

He bowed to the prince and rushed out the door.

Too late, I realized I was now alone with the prince. I fiddled with my skirts, not looking at him.

"Have I done something to offend you?" he asked, a hint of amusement tingeing his voice.

I forced myself to meet his gaze. "Not at all." I wasn't going to give him the satisfaction of knowing his tea had worked.

"You're red. You've been avoiding me since you were ill, and you never even thanked me for the bath." He sat on the couch and leaned back. "You're acting strange, little songbird, and I want to know why."

He was taunting me. I glared at him. "It's nothing."

"Are you embarrassed that I saw you while you were indisposed?"

"As if you don't know what you did," I snapped. "Was it your idea or your father's to put something in my drink?"

He gave me a blank look. "I'm afraid I don't know what you're talking about."

"The chamomile you had sent with the bath. What did you do to it?"

"Nothing." His brow knit together. "Did it harm you in some way?"

"No. Not at all. It was nothing." My cheeks blazed. I shouldn't have said anything.

He stood and stalked toward me. His voice lowered as he said, "I don't like being lied to. You're under my protection. If someone gave you a drink that caused you harm, I need to know. What happened?"

I took a step back, glancing around the room for a way out. He didn't mean to make me tell him, did he?

A stupid question. Of course he did.

"I think there was some sort of...herb added to it. Something to cause...dreams. Disturbing ones." I swallowed, trying not to dwell on the dream in question. He was too close, and I could almost feel his hands on me.

"Disturbing dreams. I can't say I've heard of such an herb. What exactly did you dream about?"

I pressed my lips together and shook my head. "Nothing important."

He considered me for a moment, then a wicked grin came over his face. "I see. You were dreaming of me, weren't you?"

No. No no no. This couldn't be happening. I clenched my fists, nails digging into my skin.

"What did you dream about, songbird?" He stepped closer, backing me into the wall.

I closed my eyes, waiting for fear to come crashing down over me, but it never came. Instead, the sweet and spicy smell of him overwhelmed me. I could feel his breath on my neck as he leaned in.

"Did I touch you in your dream?" he whispered. "Is that why you can't look at me?"

I didn't dare to open my eyes as I nodded. He traced my collar with a finger, and I shuddered. *Strange,* I thought with detachment. Nikolaus's touch had never made me feel like this.

"Did I kiss you?"

I shook my head. He shouldn't be this close to me. Shouldn't be saying these things to me. Allowing him such liberties was a sin, but my head felt light, and my core ached. I couldn't think enough to tell him to stop.

"No?" Teeth nipped at my ear, sending ripples of pleasure through me. "Allow me to remedy that oversight."

My breath caught as he wrapped his hand around the back of my neck. I should say no. He wasn't enchanting me, wasn't forcing me. I ought to push him away and tell him to leave me alone.

I opened my mouth—to make him leave or beg him to kiss me, I wasn't sure—and his lips met mine.

His kiss was soft and demanding, his face scratchy with stubble. His free arm snaked around my waist, pulling me close.

Was this what kissing was supposed to be like? Nikolaus had kept our kissing, like our sexual encounters, brief and to the point. Nothing like this. Heady and overpowering, it threatened to sweep me away. His hand pressed into my lower back, and against my stomach I could feel—saints, was that what I thought it was? Heat pooled low in my abdomen. He wanted me.

My hands rested on his chest, feeling the powerful muscles beneath his shirt. His tongue swept into my mouth, tangling with mine. He was surprisingly gentle, and he tasted of spiced wine and...and...I couldn't think past his touch.

His mouth left mine, and I gasped at the sudden loss of sensation.

"What did you dream about?" he murmured.

My head still spun. I leaned against him, breathing hard. "I was in the bath, and you came in."

"Mm?" The sound rumbled in his chest.

"You washed my hair, and you were going to kiss me."

"And then?"

"And then I woke up." My heart had begun to slow, allowing me to think a little more clearly. I raised my head, pressing a hand to my burning cheeks. I would regret this later.

"You..." He made a choking sound that might have been a laugh. *"That* was the dream that mortified you so much you couldn't look at me for days?" He took a step back and looked at my face, his own expression contorted with suppressed laughter. "If I didn't know better, I'd think you were a virgin, little songbird. Are you the Virgin Mary?"

I scowled at the blasphemy, but my stomach twisted into knots. *Blessed Virgin, pray for me.* I was guilty of the sin of lust, and likely to become guilty of worse if he kept standing so close to me.

Racing footsteps sounded in the hall, and I jumped sideways, putting as much space between me and Loic as I could. Falk rushed into the room, oblivious to the tension.

"He wants to leave at dawn so we can make it to the city before dark." Noticing the prince, he bowed. "Sorry. I didn't know you were still here."

The prince had slipped back on his mask of disinterest. "I had some things I needed to discuss with your mother," he said. "We can continue our conversation later."

I swallowed. "I thought we were finished."

"No, I hadn't finished."

My eyes widened at the crude implication, but before I could respond, he swept out the door, brushing my cheek with his hand as he passed.

"What was that about?" Falk asked.

I shook my head. "Nothing." I turned to him with a bright smile. "We should pack. You need to get to bed if you want to be up on time tomorrow."

LOIC

I sank onto my bed with a sigh, kicking my boots onto the floor. It had been a long day. My father was in rare form; he'd threatened to exile two of his council members for suggesting an alliance with Spain. Alois, the upstart son of my father's mistress, was one of them. Come to think of it, I hadn't seen Lady Helene lately. The king's mood today didn't bode well for her. I doubted she'd remain his mistress for long. Not if her son kept making stupid proposals in council.

I closed my eyes, putting the meeting out of my mind. I had more pleasant things to think about, like the conversation I'd had with my songbird yesterday. A smile slipped out at the memory of her embarrassment. "A disturbing dream," she'd said, and yet when I'd taken her in my arms, she hadn't looked disturbed. Her eyes had closed, her head tilting back and her mouth opening ever so slightly. She'd beckoned me to kiss her. I'd obliged, naturally.

She was unskilled but eager, and the redness of her face when the high of the kiss had faded was like the sweetest wine. Even better had been her expression when she'd divined the meaning of my parting words. Teaching her the art of the bedroom was a task I would relish.

Despite the show I put on for the court, I'd given up the thought of making her my mistress. But when she'd admitted to her dream, when she'd melted in my arms, a new plan had formed in my mind. I'd break down her already-cracking virginal facade and see what passion she kept hidden behind it.

It was more than passion that I wanted to reveal. She hid her body beneath layers of clothing, and though the clothes I'd ordered for her were more flattering than those ridiculous Bavarian skirts she'd worn when she arrived, I wanted more. During Hall, I could see the swell of her breasts and the sway of her hips. Both had filled out nicely now that she was eating regularly. Her skin was a lovely cream color that turned brilliant pink from embarrassment, and I found my own body responding to hers whenever I caught a glimpse.

A scream came from the direction of her room. I jolted upright. Someone was attacking her.

I grabbed my lamp and dagger from the bedside table. Rushing through our adjoining suites, I threw open the door to her bedroom.

She was alone.

I scanned the room, heart pounding, but there was no threat in sight. She lay frozen in her bed, whimpering.

I almost didn't notice the horned creature clinging to her neck. The size of a small mouse, its deep purple skin and black-furred legs blended in with the shadows.

A drude.

I set the lamp and dagger down and crept toward the bed, trying not to spook the beast. Once in reach, I grabbed it and wrung its neck, tossing the body to the floor.

Threat eliminated, I turned to my songbird, who remained trapped in the claws of her nightmare. "Annika!" I said in a firm voice. She didn't respond, so I took her by the shoulders and shook her gently. "Annika!"

Her eyes flew open. "Falk," she gasped. "Where is my son?"

"He's safe." She was fine. I took a seat on the bed next to her. "He's in Augsburg. It was just a drude."

"A drude?" Her voice was shaky, but she sat up, following my gaze to the vile creature.

I nudged it with my foot. "Demonic little pests. They steal into houses at night and cause nightmares. They feed off of fear." I considered her. "I thought you'd been raised on fairy-stories about Laute. Didn't anyone tell you about druden?"

She shook her head. "My mother always told me I didn't have to worry about demon creatures, because we were washed in Christ's Blood. Demons can't harm the saved."

What a ridiculous concept. I laughed. "Does your baptism protect you from bears and wolves, as well?"

She scowled, and the contrast of her prim expression and her disheveled appearance only made me laugh more.

"I'll thank you not to mock the Sacraments," she sniffed.

"Druden are no more demons than rats or mice," I said. "They're just pests."

She stared at the blankets, trying to hide her embarrassment. "Well, thank you for killing it, whatever it was."

"I couldn't have you waking the entire court with your screams." I paused, scanning her body. The tops of her breasts were visible over the collar of her shift. They rose and fell with each breath. "Well, I could, but I'd much prefer to be the source of those screams."

It took her a moment to parse out the meaning of my words. When she did, she ducked her head, pulling the blankets higher. "Yes, well, thank you again. I'll just dispose of the body and go back to sleep."

"No need." I kicked it into a corner, then leaned back against the wall. "The servants will deal with it in the morning."

She shifted, obviously uncomfortable. "It's late. We should be in bed."

"We are." I flashed a grin. The lamplight dancing across her skin and the beautiful pink blush on her face were hard to resist.

"Alone."

"Ah, but where's the fun in that?" I trailed a finger down her leg, over the blanket. Her breath caught, and I could see by the way her eyes fluttered closed that it wasn't from fear. She wanted me as much as I wanted her, even if she wasn't willing to acknowledge it yet.

"I don't believe sleeping is supposed to be fun," she said.

"You haven't been doing the right kind of sleeping." I would have continued to tease her, but I caught sight of her neck. A mark remained where the drude had bitten her, and blood trickled from it. "You're bleeding."

She slapped her hand over the wound. "I'll bandage it."

I stood and rang for a servant, then wetted a cloth in the washbasin.

"That's not necessary," she began, but I sat down next to her and began sponging away the blood. She didn't fight me.

As I finished cleaning off her neck and collar, a young woman entered the room. Showing no surprise at my presence, she bowed.

"Mrs. Brandt was bitten by a drude," I said. "Bring me something for the wound."

"Right away, your highness."

Annika shifted, twisting the blankets in her fists. "There's no need for all this fuss," she said. "I'm not even bleeding anymore."

"Yes, you are." Barely. I wiped another small trickle and cocked my head. "Are you ashamed to be seen with me?"

"She's going to assume I'm—" She cut herself off, looking away.

"Sleeping with me? The entire court already thinks that. What does one servant's opinion matter?"

She pressed her lips together. "It doesn't. Nevermind."

She was embarrassed by the rumors that protected her. Strange creature. I lowered my voice. "If you're afraid of people believing lies about you, I'd be happy to make it true."

Her breath caught. "What do you mean?"

I brushed my mouth over her collarbone. "I think you know what I mean."

"I—"

"Your highness?" Annika stiffened and pulled away at the sound of the servant girl's voice. "I have what you asked for."

The bleeding had stopped by now, but I took the bandages from the girl and dismissed her.

I patched up the tiny cut on my songbird's neck and stood. She wasn't ready to admit her attraction to me yet, and if I stayed here much longer, I wouldn't be able to resist. We had time. She'd come to me soon enough.

"It's late," I said. "I'll see you at Hall tomorrow evening."

Disappointment flashed across her face, so brief I almost missed it. "Good night, your highness."

I turned to go, then turned back on a whim. "Loic."

"Loic," she repeated, as if testing the word out. "Good night."

"Good night, songbird."

Worm in Your Apple

Annika

Despite Loic's assurance that Falk was safe, I couldn't breathe easy until he came back from Augsburg. He and Peter returned with a newfound confidence, a swagger in their step from being allowed to accompany Konrad. According to Falk, the merchant had shown them how to read people's expressions in order to judge the right moment to make a sale, and how to apply arithmetic to ensure they weren't being cheated. Both boys had a newfound appreciation for their lessons, and their first morning back, at least, was going well.

On our way from morning lessons out to the gardens, the children and I passed Loic in the corridor. He gave me a curt nod as he moved past us.

Falk waved. "Your highness!" Before I could stop him, he ran down the hall after the prince.

Loic turned, raising a brow at my son. "Do you need something?"

Please, God, don't let him be offended. I'd sensed some softening between us in the past few weeks, but I wasn't sure it would last. I didn't want Falk to be caught up in the prince's displeasure if his mood shifted back to the colder, crueler version of him I'd met when I first arrived in Laute.

Falk dug into his pocket. "I have something for you." He drew out a shiny red apple and held it out. "I got this for you in Augsburg. As thanks for letting us go."

A strange expression crossed the prince's face. He took the apple. "It...looks good. Thank you." The words were stiff, as though he didn't often say them.

Falk bowed. "You're welcome." He turned to come back to me, then paused. Looking back at the prince, he gave a sly smile, one I was only too familiar with. "Hey, do you know what's worse than finding a worm in your apple?"

I froze as Loic frowned down at him. I'd heard this question many times before—Falk asked it at least once a week—but I didn't know how the prince would react. He didn't seem the type to appreciate jokes. Unless, perhaps, the jokes were sexual in nature.

After a moment, Loic shook his head. "What?"

Falk's face split in a huge grin. "Finding half a worm."

I held my breath, watching the prince.

A deep belly laugh burst from him, and his eyebrows lifted like the joke had caught him off guard. "I believe you're right. That would be worse." He glanced at me, and our eyes locked.

I gave him a tentative smile. *Thank you,* I signed. He nodded back.

"Your mother's waiting," Loic said. "You should go. But thank you—for the apple and the joke."

LOIC

I rounded the corner, tucking the apple into my pocket. A smile still played on my face from the foolish joke the boy had told me.

I'd heard better jokes before. I'd received better gifts. Certainly more expensive gifts. But the boy didn't have any money of his own. Whatever coin he'd managed to save for the trip to Augsburg had to have been given to him, either by his mother or by Konrad. And he'd used it, not for himself, but for me. To thank me for letting him leave, as though it wasn't my fault he was here in the first place.

His mother had been pleased, too, at either the gift or my response to it. She'd smiled at me for the first time when our eyes met over the boy's head.

I knew she desired me, but I'd not looked for anything beyond that. It seemed that, along with her weakening resolve toward me physically, she was beginning to feel genuine affection. It wasn't a sentiment I could return, but it wasn't unwelcome.

The warmth in my chest remained until I reached my father's private chamber. Putting on the emotionless mask I always wore in front of the king, I stepped inside and made a cursory bow.

"You sent for me, your majesty?"

His eyes flicked up from the paper he was reading. "I have a call for you."

I raised a brow. He didn't usually summon me to his quarters to give me an assignment. In fact, he rarely gave me assignments at all, preferring to pawn them off on less important members of the court. My call to Annika's village had been the exception, an attempt to punish me with insignificance.

"Are you aware of the situation in England?" he asked, dropping the letter onto his lap.

"Which one?" I was familiar with the politics of all the major courts on the continent, but I hadn't heard of any situation that would cause a Catholic king to call a piper.

"Their lack of an heir. Queen Catherine lost another child this January." He fixed me with a stern look, as though this was somehow my fault. "Henry is growing desperate."

Desperate indeed, to seek us out. "I had heard about her loss, yes."

"England has the pope's ear. If you can bring Henry a son, it might improve the Church's stance on relations with Laute."

"I wasn't aware you desired the pope's approval." He'd spent enough time enumerating the faults of Christianity and the papacy.

"Don't be obtuse," he snapped. "What I think of Leo and his teachings is irrelevant. The fact is, he pulls the strings in over half the courts in Europe, and if we want to remain as we are, we need him to view us as, if not an ally, at least not an enemy."

"Of course. Forgive me." He was right; I was being obtuse. My father rarely let his personal opinions interfere with his politics. He'd make an alliance with the devil himself—if such a creature existed—if it brought him glory.

"You leave in three days. See that you're prepared."

I bowed my head, already making a mental list of what I would need. I'd bring my songbird, naturally. She wouldn't be pleased at being separated from her son, but it would only be for a couple months. She'd adjust. And perhaps the separation would allow her the freedom to surrender to her growing attraction to me.

Or perhaps I'd take the boy. After all, there was no reason not to. Annika would be more comfortable keeping him with her. As long as he didn't cause trouble, I had no objections.

As I turned to leave, the king spoke again. "And leave your pet. No distractions."

I gave a stiff nod and closed the door between us.

I walked down the hallway, toward my own quarters. I could think of several reasons my father would require me to leave Annika behind, and none of them pleased me. She could be a distraction, yes, but I doubted that was his primary purpose. On the few occasions he'd left our borders on diplomatic visits, he'd taken his mistresses. And I couldn't forget the last time I left a woman behind at court with my father. I couldn't forget Eva.

No, he wasn't trying to steal Annika away from me. Not like that, at least. The most reasonable assumption was that he wanted to tempt her into trying to flee. The presence of so many humans here at court grated on him, and if she tried to steal away with the children, he could have them all punished. Killed, even.

A knot of tension formed at the base of my skull. What was the use of my saving them if my father was just going to kill them anyway?

If Annika risked their safety by trying to escape, I'd chain her up. I couldn't take the risk of her getting them all killed, and she was foolish enough to run.

I'd have to ensure Teta watched her carefully in my absence. Perhaps Konrad, too—she'd developed a friendship with the merchant and his wife, and the more people watching her, the better.

FRIENDS AND ALLIES

ANNIKA

At Hall that evening, Loic met me at the door and took my arm with barely a glance. Rather than wandering through the room as he usually did, he walked directly to the dais, ignoring everyone around us. He sat down and draped his leg over the side of the chair, the picture of nonchalance.

I took my seat at his feet. After so many weeks, the position evoked no emotion, despite the crowd of people that could see me. He put a hand on the back of my neck, drawing lazy circles with his thumb.

The evening was interminably long. I sat stiff-backed and watched the petitioners come and go. Loic's hand dropped from my neck, and I risked a glance up at him. He stared out over the assembled pipers, his expression the usual one of boredom, but with a distance behind his eyes.

Why was he so distracted? Had something happened during the day? I didn't know whether to be worried at his preoccupation or pleased that he wasn't using the evening to humiliate me further.

When the king dismissed everyone, Loic stood and jerked his head at me to follow. He led me back to my room.

Falk was staying with Peter, as he did every week when I went to Hall, and my heart skipped a beat at the thought of being alone with Loic again. After our recent interactions, I wasn't sure I would be able to resist if he tempted me again.

He closed the door behind us and turned to me, his face void of emotion. "I've been called to England."

The words took a moment to sink in. "England?"

"King Henry and Queen Catherine are having difficulty conceiving an heir. I'm to assist in the matter."

"Assist how?" I knew pipers could control living things—and illnesses, for some reason—but to create life? That power was reserved for God Himself.

Wasn't it?

He frowned at me. "The same way I freed your village from the plague. If the queen has an illness in her womb, I'll draw it out. If the king has an illness in his loins—" I flushed at his casual use of the word "—I'll heal him."

"I see." I didn't understand how his magic worked, but I doubted I ever would.

A thought came to mind, sudden and unwelcome. What if he was telling me this because he intended to take me with him? I couldn't leave Falk, and he'd said he wouldn't allow us both beyond the borders of Laute at the same time. My stomach clenched.

"I can't leave Falk." I looked up at him with pleading eyes. I wasn't above begging. I couldn't bear to be separated from my son for so long. How far away was England?

His face tightened. "You'll remain here. I don't need the distraction of your presence."

"Oh." His words shouldn't feel like a rejection, but they did, even though I'd just told him I didn't want to leave. I *would* be a distraction. I didn't know the first thing about England; he'd have to explain my presence to the king, ensure I didn't do anything to offend the nobility... No, he was right to leave me behind. Which was what I'd wanted.

"In my absence, Teta will be responsible for your conduct." He fixed me with a firm look. "I expect you to obey her as you would me. If I learn you've taken advantage of her, tried to escape with the children, it will not go well for you."

I glared back at him. Hadn't I earned a modicum of trust after all these months? "I wouldn't do anything against her," I said.

"I expect I'll be back in two months. You won't be needed in Hall while I'm gone. In the meantime, stay away from my father and his men; they don't need to be bothered by your presence."

As if I was likely to seek out the Pied Piper. "I'm sure I'll find something to prevent me from being a distraction."

He nodded, missing the irony in my tone. "See that you do. I'll see you when I return." He paused, then opened his mouth as if to speak again. After a moment, he shook his head and left.

We didn't speak again before his trip. He was busy, I assumed, with packing and making preparations for the journey. Still, I'd expected he would at least tell me goodbye.

The first night he was gone, I found myself unable to sleep. After pacing in front of the low fire—the heat was unnecessary during the warm spring days, but still vital at night—I finally put on a robe and wandered down to the kitchens.

Hugo sat on a stool in the main kitchen, watching the dying flames in the enormous cooking fireplace. When I came into the room, he looked up and gave me an affectionate smile.

Two cups were out on the table. "I hope I'm not interrupting," I said.

"I had a feeling you might join me this evening." He waved at the cups. "I warmed some milk for us."

I grinned. "How did you know?"

"The prince left this morning." He shrugged. "I thought the excitement might have you up late. More freedom, yes?"

"One would think." I took a seat across from him and picked up my drink. Little brown flecks of cinnamon floated on top, and when I took a sip, I tasted honey. "But I don't see him during the day as it is. I doubt I'll notice his absence." It was a lie. I'd already caught myself glancing toward the mountain pass several times today. I shouldn't miss him, but we'd grown closer over the past few weeks. He'd softened toward me, even shown a hint of affection.

Until his cold manner last night, when he'd made it perfectly clear that I was nothing but a distraction to him.

"I'm glad he doesn't trouble you." Hugo took a sip of his own milk, then set it down. "Oh! I almost forgot." He glanced around the room and lowered his voice. "I've got a letter for you, from your friend."

Gisela? Or did he mean Brigid? My heart raced with anticipation as he took the paper from his pocket and handed it to me.

I unfolded it, and a second note fell out. I read the first.

Dear Annika,

I'm glad you've found a semblance of safety in the midst of the vipers' nest. I pray to all the saints you will remain safe until you can find a way to escape.

Enclosed is a letter from your sister. If you have any need, write to me again and I will do what I can for you. It is best not to write frequently, to minimize the risk of the demons discovering our communication. When you do write, you can send your letters through Hugo. He is an unlikely ally—though a piper, he lacks their pagan magic, and he does not support their demon king. You can trust him.

I cannot say much in case this letter is intercepted, but know that I am working to bring down the Pied Piper and his court. God willing, I and my allies will be successful, and you will be able to return home soon.

Burn this letter.

With fervent wishes for your safety,

Gisela.

She was Hugo's contact in Augsburg. And more importantly, she'd sent a letter from Brigid, as well. I scanned the second paper.

Annika,

I rejoice that you are with Falk, but I fear for you, trapped in that terrible place. Find a way out and come home soon, please. Dietrich and I married just a week after you left, as soon as Pater Huber allowed it.

We have sold your house, and we will keep the money safe until your return.

The woman who sent me your letter asked me to keep this short, so I will close by saying I pray for you daily. Be safe.

All my love,

Brigid.

Tears filled my eyes, and I pressed the letter to my chest. "Thank you," I whispered.

Hugo patted my arm. "You'll see them again soon."

I hoped he was right.

Audience with the King

Annika

The first month of Loic's absence passed without incident. I avoided the Pied Piper and most of the court, keeping to my room or the schoolroom as much as I did my best to keep the children out of the way. Konrad helped, taking the boys to help him with work while the girls stayed with me and Ilse and learned womanly skills.

After all my efforts to stay out of the way, it took me a moment to understand the two king's guards who found me in Ilse's sitting room one afternoon, overseeing the girls' sewing.

"King Edric wishes to speak to you." The guard who spoke was tall and stone-faced, his chestnut horns polished bright.

I stared at him. "Me? Now?" He gave a sharp nod, and I exchanged a bewildered look with Ilse.

Regardless of Loic's warning, I couldn't ignore a direct summons from the king. "Stay with Mrs. Bach," I told the children. "I'll be back soon." I stopped to correct one girl's grip, earning me a frown from the second guard.

I followed them out of the house, but they didn't turn toward the castle. They took the path out of the city, toward the woods that edged the valley.

"Where are we going?" I asked. Neither answered me.

Their silence didn't surprise me. I'd seen them both before—the king's guard was made up of about thirty men—but we'd never spoken. They were part of the faction at court who objected to my very existence. The hairs on my neck rose. Had I put myself in danger by following them?

No. They might hate me, but I was under the prince's protection. Besides, they'd come with a summons from the king. I doubted that the Pied Piper would take kindly to someone using his name in a deception.

But why would the Pied Piper be in the woods?

I shook myself as we reached the outermost trees. He was a king. Surely he had duties outside of the castle.

Then again, I'd never seen him leave the castle before.

We entered the shade of the trees. The afternoon sun dappled through the new leaves, and the fresh smell of late spring filled the air. I looked around, but the king was nowhere in sight.

"Where are we going?" I asked again.

They remained silent, continuing deeper into the woods. I stopped. "I'm not going any further until you tell me where we're going."

A man stepped out ahead of us. "To meet me," he said. His golden horns glinted in the sunlight. Alois, the son of the king's mistress. I shrank back from the loathing on his face. He pulled a black, turnip-shaped object from his pocket. Holes dotted the top of it. He raised it to his mouth, and my stomach plummeted.

He meant to enchant me.

The first note shattered the peaceful air. The metallic taste of magic filled my mouth, and I staggered back.

A crashing sound came from somewhere nearby. He wasn't enchanting me—he was enchanting an animal, something to attack me. Heart in my throat, I took off at a run, back toward the city.

The creature snorted behind me, too close for me to risk a glance back. It sounded like a boar. The song followed me, too, frantic and terrifying.

I put on an extra burst of speed, but still it came nearer. I was going to die, gored by the tusks of the massive beast.

If I could just make it to the city, someone—Konrad, Ilse, anyone—might be able to help. Might be able to call off the beast. But I had to get out of these woods first.

I should be out by now. Why wasn't I out? We hadn't gone deep into the trees.

If I was lost, I'd never survive.

My breath came in gasps. I leapt over a fallen log and kept running, skirts in my hands. Faster. Faster.

Still it gained on me.

My foot slipped, and I was falling off a ledge, off a cliff. Pain smashed through my arm, then my head. I landed on hard ground, and my vision blackened.

This was the end. I was dying. *Father, receive my spirit.*

A second tune reached me, low and sweet. Calming, like the music of angels. They were welcoming me home.

It's too soon. I wasn't ready to die. I couldn't leave Falk and the other children here alone. What would they do without me?

The first song, the boar-song, faltered. Somewhere above me, the snuffling and grunting of the boar faded. The song the angels played grew louder. I tried to lift my head, to look for them, but I couldn't.

Everything hurt. Would it stop soon?

The pain didn't stop, but the music did. I groaned. Why did the music stop?

Footsteps approached, and someone lifted me up in strong arms. An angel, come to take me to purgatory.

"What did they do to you?"

Loic's voice. Not an angel, then. A prince. He wasn't supposed to be here, was he? I started to open my eyes, but a wave of dizziness swept over me. I closed them tight again.

"Can you hear me, Annika?" His voice was concerned, almost desperate. That couldn't be right. "You're okay. You're going to be okay."

Strange. He sounded like he was trying to convince himself, not me.

Every step jostled my head, my arm. I gritted my teeth, trying not to moan.

"Your highness?" A voice came from nearby.

"Doctor," the prince snapped. "Now."

Everything was so loud. I tucked my head against Loic's chest.

We were inside now. I could hear the sound of boots on the stone floor. When he started climbing a set of stairs, the movement set a shot of pain through my shoulder. A whimper escaped.

"Sorry. I'm sorry." He shifted, and I clenched my teeth against the pain.

We went through a door, then another, and at last he stopped. He laid me gently on something soft. A bed?

"Look at me," he pleaded.

Pleaded? That wasn't right. Loic didn't beg. I tried to obey but only managed to open one eye.

His blurry face hovered close to mine. "Where does it hurt?"

Tears filled my open eye. "Everywhere," I sobbed, then gasped as another bolt of pain went through my shoulder.

The door opened, and someone rushed in.

"What happened?" Teta's voice.

Loic didn't turn around. "Where is the doctor?"

"Falk." what if they had gone after Falk, too? I struggled to sit up, but Loic pushed me back down by my good shoulder. "Where is Falk?"

"Lie still."

Teta appeared in my limited range of vision. "Falk? He's with Konrad."

"You've seen him?"

"Just ten minutes ago."

Falk was safe. I relaxed back onto the bed and closed my eye. Konrad would keep him safe.

"Where is the doctor?" Loic demanded again. His hands were at my waist. He tugged my skirt down below my hips, and I opened my eye again. "What—?"

He didn't respond as he bared my stomach. I tried to turn, to hide myself from his view, but he put a hand on my chest and held me down. With his other hand, he gingerly pressed around my stomach, testing. I gasped when he reached a sore spot.

Once he'd touched every part of my stomach, he raised my shirt higher, revealing my breasts. I reached to tug it back down, to cover myself, but he brushed my hand aside and felt his way up my chest, touching each rib.

My cheeks blazed by the time he pulled my shirt back over my bare skin. Next he took my left arm in his hands. He twisted my wrist, then bent it at the elbow. Then he did the same for the other arm—or tried. I let out a cry as he lifted it.

"I'll kill them." His voice was colder than I'd ever heard, his face set in stone. He pressed his fingers along the length of my arm until he reached the source of the pain. My shoulder.

The door opened again, and footsteps entered the room. Loic didn't look up from his examination.

Another face, this one unfamiliar, came into sight. A short black beard hid his mouth, and his dark eyes were crinkled with concern. The doctor, presumably.

"She has a dislocated shoulder," Loic told him. "Some slight bruising on her stomach. I hadn't gotten to her face or legs yet."

The doctor gestured for him to move out of the way. Loic took a seat next to my head, taking my uninjured hand in his. My heart fluttered despite the pain, and I rested my cheek against his leg.

The doctor continued where Loic's examination had left off. When he forced my swollen eye open, I gripped Loic's hand tight and gritted my teeth.

At last the doctor stood upright. "I need to get the joint back into place. Can you sit up for me?"

I started to nod, but thought better of it. "Yes."

Loic helped me into a sitting position, my legs over the side of the bed, and put his arm around my waist. The doctor sat across from me.

He lifted my arm, placing it on his own shoulder. I bit my tongue, but he smiled. "This won't hurt. Just take deep breaths."

I closed my eye, breathing as deeply as I could. He massaged the top of my shoulder, then the sides. After a minute, the throbbing pain eased. I let out a sigh.

He stopped massaging. "Better?"

"Much." I opened my eye again and gave a weak smile. "Thank you."

He stood and turned to Loic. "She'll need a sling for that arm. Other than that, rest is the best treatment. I'll leave something for the pain. Ice will help bring down the swelling on her face."

Loic nodded, his face grim. The doctor fitted a sling to my injured arm, then bowed and left.

As the pain in my shoulder had gone, exhaustion swept over me. My head felt thick, heavy. I wanted nothing more than to lie down and go to sleep, but Teta, who had been standing quietly in the corner, stepped toward the bed. "I'm so sorry. I should have been there."

Loic glared at her, releasing my hand to sign. *Yes, you should have.*

I reached for Teta. "It wasn't your fault."

She squeezed my hand. "Stay here and rest. Don't worry about the children. I'll take care of them."

Too exhausted to argue, I just smiled. She squeezed my hand again and left the room, avoiding the burning glare on Loic's face.

As the door closed behind her, he turned to me. "You should be sleeping."

"Mm." I didn't fight as he maneuvered me into a reclining position. I closed my good eye, relaxing back onto the pillow. Something brushed my forehead.

I forced myself to look. Loic was still sitting on the bed, his face screwed up in torment as he looked down at me.

"I'm sorry," he murmured.

I struggled to stay awake. This was important. "For what?"

"I shouldn't have left you here." He moved a stray hair out of my face. My headscarf was gone, probably lost somewhere in the woods. "It won't happen again."

"Wasn't your fault, either," I murmured. Darkness tugged at the corner of my vision. "Stay with me?"

Sleep consumed me before I could hear his response.

I woke slowly, aching all over. Voices, comforting and familiar, drifted nearby.

"It looks bad, but she'll be fine. She just needs rest." Loic's voice, gentler than usual.

"Who did it?" Falk.

I cracked my eye open to see the two of them standing at the foot of my bed. No, not my bed. This room was larger, the bed hung with curtains. Where was I?

"Dead men." The prince's voice held a promise of violence. A shudder went through me, unnoticed by them.

"Good." Falk stuffed a hand into his pocket, then shoved the other hand toward Loic. "Thank you. For saving her."

Loic hesitated a moment before he took the offered hand and shook it. "If—if it's alright with you, I'll keep her here while she recovers."

Did the prince just stutter? My fall must have damaged my mind. Loic didn't do that. He also didn't ask for permission, especially not from children.

"If you'll keep her safe, it's alright."

"I will."

I shifted, and they both turned.

"Mama!" Falk rushed to the bed and threw his arms around me. I gasped as he bumped my injured arm, and he pulled back. "Sorry. Loic—Prince Loic said you're going to be fine. You are, aren't you?"

I smiled as brightly as I could, ignoring the pulse of pain in my cheek. "I'm fine. Just a few bumps and bruises."

Behind him, Loic raised a brow but didn't contradict me. His gaze was fixed on my face, his eyes burning with some unnamed emotion.

I turned away, unsettled by the intensity of his stare, and scanned Falk. "You're okay?"

Falk frowned. "Of course I'm okay. Why wouldn't I be?"

"No reason." I ruffled his hair. "You've been good?"

"Yeah. Peter and I helped Mr. Bach *record inventory.*" He puffed out his chest. "He says I'm a natural. Then Teta came to get us, and we spent the rest of the day at his house."

"I'm glad." I glanced at Loic, who was still watching me with that strange expression. "What time is it?"

"Almost ten."

I'd slept for hours. I nudged Falk with my elbow. "Why aren't you in bed, *liebling?*" I asked, my tone light, teasing.

"Teta told him he could wait until you woke." Loic still hadn't moved.

Falk's face lit up with hope. "Can I stay with Peter until you're better?"

I nodded, then winced as pain shot through my head. "As long as you make sure to get enough sleep."

"We will!" He pressed a quick kiss to my cheek. "Night, Mama." He rushed out the door.

Loic closed the door behind him, then turned to me.

"Where am I?" I looked around. Anything to avoid his piercing stare. The room was ornately furnished, the walls hung with tapestries. A large fireplace sat unlit on one side of the room. On the table next to the bed, a lamp flickered, and next to it, a dagger and Loic's flute.

"My bedroom."

I flushed. I was in the prince's bed. "Thank you for saving me," I said. I struggled to rise. "I'll return to my own room now."

He was at my side in an instant, towering over me. "You'll stay where you are."

I froze, stunned by the fury on his face.

"What were you thinking?" he growled.

"I'm—sorry?" Was he angry with me for trying to get up?

"Did I not *specifically* tell you to avoid my father's men?"

I sat up, my cheeks heating with anger. "You think I did this on purpose?"

"I don't know. Did you?"

I gestured at my face, which I was fairly certain resembled a bloody piece of meat, and at my arm in its sling. "Why would I do this to myself?"

"Why were you out in the woods? Did it not occur to you that it wasn't safe?"

How dare he blame me for this? "Did it not occur to *you*—" I started, but my head throbbed. I doubled over, clutching it.

He sat down next to me. "Lie down."

Pompous, arrogant— I did as he bid, but only because my head hurt too much to stay upright. As I did, he shifted so I lay on his lap. I flushed and tried to pull away, but he took my head in his hands and rubbed my temples.

The pain eased immediately, and I let out an involuntary sigh of relief.

"Better?"

I glared at him as best I could through one eye. What had happened to the man who'd carried me out of the woods? Unless I'd imagined his gentleness, his words before I'd fallen asleep. With the way my head felt, it wasn't unlikely.

"In future, when I give you an order, I expect you to follow it. Stay away from my father and his men."

As if I'd be likely to make that mistake again. But— "Did the king give the order?" If he had, if he wanted to get rid of me...

"The men responsible are in the dungeon awaiting judgment. They won't harm you again."

That didn't answer my question, but the look on his face didn't invite discussion. "So why am I here instead of in my own room?"

"Because I obviously can't trust you with your own well-being. You'll stay with me until I'm satisfied that you're no longer a danger to yourself."

Not until I recovered? Either he was lying to Falk, or he was lying to me. I wasn't sure which version of him to believe. "I'll stay away from your father's men."

"Good." He maneuvered my head so it rested on the pillow.

I rolled over to face him. "So I can go?"

"Absolutely not."

He stepped out of the room, and I stared after him. Where was he going? If he thought I would stay here alone, he was wrong.

I was halfway out of bed when he returned, wearing nothing but a nightshirt. I froze, unable to look away. "What are you doing?"

"Going to bed."

"Here?" My voice rose a notch.

"It is my bed."

I tried to focus on his face, rather than the bare expanse of his legs, the finely honed muscles... I swallowed. "But you're not dressed."

"You didn't have to sleep in your clothes. Why should I?"

I glanced down at myself and saw I was dressed the same as him, in nothing but a long shirt. "Who—" I choked on the words, my whole body flaming with shame. "Who undressed me?"

He flashed me a grin. "Does it matter? Even if it was me, I've seen it all before."

I pulled the blankets up higher. He was mocking me. He wouldn't bother undressing me himself. He would have had a servant do it.

Then again, I wouldn't have expected him to carry me back to the castle on his own, either.

The bed dipped below his weight. I grabbed the pillow behind me and shoved it between us, piling the blankets on top. Anything to keep him at a distance.

He shifted, leaning over the wall I'd built. I kept my eye shut tight. The smell of him overwhelmed me, sweat and heat and spice. I held my breath as he lifted my head and placed a pillow beneath it.

Then he released me, and I could breathe again.

"What are you doing?" I whispered. I still didn't dare to open my eye.

"Going to sleep."

"You're not—" I couldn't put my fear into words. Not my hopes. I didn't want him. Lust was a sin. *Pater noster, qui es in coelis...*

He let out a loud breath. "No, songbird, I'm not going to take advantage of you. Not while your face resembles a raw cut of beef. Your virtue is safe with me." He rolled over. "Get some rest."

That wasn't likely. I'd slept half the day, and now there was a half-naked man lying next to me. A half-naked man who had kissed me more than once. Who I was fairly certain was attracted to me on some level.

I opened my eye and stared up at the ceiling. He'd doused the lamp. The room was dark, but I was still acutely aware of his presence.

It was going to be a long night.

DEAD MEN

LOIC

I t had been a long night.

Lying next to Annika in bed all night was an exercise in self-control. I hadn't lied when I told her her face resembled a cut of beef, but that didn't affect the rest of her body. In my absence she'd put on a little more weight, and her once sickly body was full and lush. Warmth radiated from her, and when I'd woken to her face on my chest it was all I could do not to take her then and there.

But I wanted her to come to me of her own accord, and not when she was injured.

The men who'd attacked her would pay for their crime. She was under my protection, and yet they'd lured her out of the city and attacked her, using our magic—*my* magic, the magic from my bloodline—to harm her.

My father had given up Alois and the guards. "This attack on the crown prince is no less than treason," he'd said. "It cannot be allowed to stand." He'd planned the attack, I had no doubt, but there was no proof. No way to confirm my suspicions. Even if the perpetrators confessed, he would claim they were trying to save their own skin.

If I had my way, they'd each experience every bit of what they put my songbird through, and then I'd flay them alive. But my father had been specific in his orders. I could execute them, but their execution was to be swift, straightforward. No torture or flaying.

He hadn't left me much freedom with which to punish them, but he'd given me enough. They would still suffer.

I stared at them, my face carefully impassive. All three were chained between two trees in the spot where I'd found her. She'd fallen off a ledge, and she'd been lying prone at the bottom when I caught up to her. The boar, still caught in Alois' spell, had been about to dive off and gore her.

If I'd been just a minute later, she would have been dead.

But I hadn't been. Now her attackers would die in her place.

The two guards kept their gazes fixed on the ground, but Alois glared up at me. He didn't seem to understand the severity of his situation. Did he expect the Pied Piper to save him? He was the scapegoat. If the king pardoned him, it would be tantamount to admitting involvement, something which my father would never do.

I'd brought the executioner with me. He stood behind them, waiting for my order.

"Do it," I said.

To their credit, the dead men didn't beg for their lives. The first guard closed his eyes, mouthing silent words. Then the executioner drove the dagger into his kidney and twisted, and he sagged against the chains, unable to speak through the pain. The second was equally stoic until the dagger hit his back.

As he watched his companions die, Alois' eyes grew wider. When the executioner grabbed him by the shoulder, he screamed. "Don't!"

"Don't?" I raised my brow at him. "Is that what Mrs. Brandt screamed when you lured her out here?"

"I didn't—"

"Didn't do anything? Is that what she told you? Did she beg you for her life, or was she too busy running?" I bent down until our faces were inches apart. "Be grateful the king put limits on my vengeance. If he hadn't, I'd peel your skin off strip by strip and leave you lying here for the animals to gnaw on."

"He ordered me to do it!" he cried. "The king! He said he wanted her dead!"

A muscle in my jaw twitched. It was one thing to know my father had planned this; it was another to hear the words said out loud.

Alois noticed my hesitation and seized on it. "He wanted it to look like she died trying to escape. He told me to lure her into the woods and summon a wild animal to kill her. It wasn't my idea! I didn't want to do it."

I knew it was a lie. He hadn't needed any encouragement to strike at me. Fury rose up, choking me. I stood and nodded at the executioner.

"Please, your highn—" The dagger twisted in his kidney, and his words cut off in a gasp.

I watched as his lifeblood drained onto the ground. His face contorted in agony, but in just a few short minutes, he fell still. It wasn't punishment enough for what he'd done to my songbird, and the true perpetrator remained free.

A hole formed in the bottom of my stomach as I turned back toward the castle. "Leave them there to rot."

ANNIKA

"How are you feeling?" Teta scanned me as though searching for more injuries. She and Ilse had come to see me this morning, leaving the children in Konrad's care.

Nauseous. Aching all over. My face felt as though the bore had succeeded in goring me. "Better," I lied. Mortification layered on top of the pain. It was bad enough to be confined to bed, but *this* bed? I was grateful Loic had been gone before I woke.

I had a vague memory of warm skin against my cheek in the night. I prayed I hadn't curled into him in my sleep. I'd never survive the humiliation, and I knew Loic wouldn't hesitate to bring it up. He thrived on embarrassing me.

Ilse looked around the room, slack-jawed. If she hadn't thought I was the prince's lover before, she certainly would now. I fought the urge to deny it; there was nothing I could say that would remedy the image of me Loic had created.

A thought came to my mind. The guards had said they came from the king. What if Loic knew how badly his father wanted me gone, and that was why he touched me so liberally in public and ignored me in private. Maybe he'd created this image to protect me, in his own strange way. The only way his father could respect.

It didn't explain why he'd insisted on sleeping naked with me, though.

My head ached from the strain of puzzling it out. I turned my attention back to my visitors. "How are the children?"

"They're fine." Ilse gave me a small smile. "Worried about you."

I wished I could see them, but I doubted Loic would approve of a dozen children parading through his quarters. I was surprised he'd even let Falk in. And considering the look on his face when I'd tried to get out of bed yesterday, he wasn't likely to let me go anywhere, either. "Tell them I'll come see them as soon as I can, but not to worry about me. I'll be better soon.

"Will you?" Teta asked, disbelieving. "You look like rats tried to eat your face."

I stuck my tongue out at her—the only thing I could do, since half my face was too swollen to glare properly.

Ilse raised her eyebrows at us, but Teta laughed. "I'm glad you're feeling better. The children weren't the only ones worried."

"I'm fine," I said again.

Teta's smile turned sly. "I didn't just mean us."

I frowned, instantly regretting it when a fresh jolt of pain shot through my cheek. "Loic was just worried he'd miss the chance to kill me himself."

Ilse shook her head, confused. "Why would the prince want to kill you?"

"She's joking," Teta said.

I hadn't been. "I think he was angrier with me for leaving the city than he was with the men who attacked me."

They exchanged a look.

"What?"

"It's nothing," Ilse said quickly.

Teta's lips formed a line. "I promise you, Loic was furious with the men that attacked you. He was angrier with *me* than he was with you."

"What did he do?"

"To me, nothing but yelling. To the men who attacked you... Less than they deserved."

A sense of foreboding tickled the back of my neck. "Just tell me."

Ilse was the first to answer. "He had them executed and left their bodies to rot outside the city."

"Oh." Bile filled my throat. Turning to the side, I emptied the limited contents of my stomach onto the ground.

Unfortunately, Loic chose that moment to return to the room. He eyed the dirty floor with distaste. *What did you do?* he signed at Teta.

She wanted to know what you did to her attackers. We told her.

I pulled the blankets up to my neck. "I'm sorry," I said.

"Out," Loic snapped. "And send someone to clean this up."

Ilse bowed, but Teta rolled her eyes as she stood. "Feel better, An-nika."

I gave them both a tight-lipped smile, and they left. Loic looked at me, his face unreadable.

"I'm sorry," I said again.

"Stop apologizing."

A cup of water sat on the bedside table. I picked it up and took a drink to rinse the foul taste from my mouth. "Did you..."

"Kill them?" His nostrils flared. "Yes."

Three men were dead because of me. Yes, they'd tried to kill me, but that didn't make it easier to know that I bore their blood on my head. I took another drink of water.

"You should be sleeping."

My head pounded too much for sleep to be a viable option. Besides, I had questions for him. Things on my mind. I couldn't focus on any of them.

A young woman came in to clean up the mess, and Loic took a seat across the room, next to the cold fireplace. He kept his gaze fixed on me. As the woman left, he said, "Bring some lunch for Mrs. Brandt."

I doubted I'd be able to eat it, but I knew better than to countermand the prince's orders. She bowed and left us alone again.

"How do you feel?"

"Better." My injured shoulder ached. I shifted it to a better position.

He narrowed his eyes. "I've told you before not to lie to me."

What did he want me to say? "My shoulder hurts, my head hurts, and I feel like I'm going to be sick every time I move."

"Better," he said. "After you eat, you can go back to sleep."

"I could hardly sleep last night. I doubt I'll be able to this morning."

He raised a brow. "You seemed to be sleeping just fine to me."

So I *had* curled up against him. My cheeks heated. "I would feel better in my own room."

"That's not up for discussion."

Fine. I changed subjects. "Why did you have them executed?"

"They touched what was mine. They needed to be made an example."

Bile rose in my throat, but I forced it back down. If he'd given some noble reason, like wanting to avenge me or some other such masculine nonsense, I might have felt less guilty, but his justification was so *petty*. He sounded like a child whose favorite toy had been taken. I hated it.

"Were you expecting a prettier answer?" He rose and came to the bed. "Were you hoping I'd speak of my affection for you, how my heart had broken when I saw you bleeding on the forest floor, and I'd vowed to have vengeance against those who had wronged you?" He knelt down next to me, and his voice dropped to a whisper. "You should know me better than that by now."

I turned my head away. "Why are you back already? You said you would be gone for two months."

"My work took less time than expected. Are you not pleased to see me?"

I had been. Now he was making it hard not to hate him. "I'm grateful that you saved me."

He brushed a hand against the uninjured side of my face. "As I said, they touched my property. I couldn't allow that to stand."

I didn't understand him. When he rescued me, his voice had sounded agonized, as though he couldn't bear to see me injured. As though he *cared*. And then he brought me back to his own room, held my hand while the doctor examined me, and slept next to me without touching me at all. Why did he say such hateful things? Calling me his pet, his property. It was like he wanted me to hate him. I understood why he acted like that in front of his father, but why did he treat me like his enemy when we were alone?

I didn't have the energy for his cruelty. "Just once," I said. "Just once, can you not be an ass?"

A shocked laugh burst from him.

"What?"

"I've never heard you talk like that. I think Teta's been a bad influence."

I hadn't meant to say it, but he could make a saint swear. "Please."

His face softened. "A temporary truce, then. Just for today."

"I am glad you're back."

His mouth twitched up at the corner. "Did you miss me?"

"I did," I admitted. And I had, despite myself. I paused. "Why did you come back early?" I didn't believe his story about his work being finished. He might have completed the task he was called for—he might have cured the English rulers of whatever illness prevented their conceiving an heir—but that didn't mean he had to return home immediately. If he wanted to form an alliance with England, staying longer would be to his advantage.

He hesitated, and for a moment I thought he was going to tell me the same story about his task being completed. Then he let out a long breath. "I missed you as well."

I offered him a small smile, ignoring the pain in my cheek, and he returned it. Maybe things could change between us.

A Man After God's Own Heart

Annika

"Absolutely not."

I tried to glare at Loic, though I was sure my swollen face dampened the effect. "You can't keep me locked in here."

"I can, and I will. You're not leaving my quarters."

I hadn't missed a Sunday meeting with Konrad and Ilse since I first met them. I wasn't about to let an injured face and a dislocated shoulder keep me from going. "Try to stop me." I stood, wrapping the blankets around my shoulders for modesty. I took a step forward and swayed.

Loic grabbed me by the waist. "You can't even stand upright."

"I'm fine." I didn't pull away, though. The room spun around me. "Just how long do you intend to keep me here?"

"Until you're healed."

"And when will that be? When the sling comes off? When my face looks normal again?" I pushed halfheartedly against his chest as my vision blurred. "You're never going to let me out of here. Admit it."

His eyes flashed. "You can't walk across the room, and you think I should let you back out into the castle? The last time I left you alone here, you nearly got yourself killed."

I couldn't help the tears that leaked onto my cheeks. In the three days since the attack, I'd cried over everything. The doctor told me the mood changes were normal for head injuries, and they would fade with time. I hoped he was right. All this crying exhausted me. "I just want to go for a little while," I whispered. "You could go with me."

He studied my face, then shook his head. "I'm not taking that risk. You're not leaving my quarters."

I let out a breath that sounded more like a sob. Hanging my head, I tried to turn back to the bed.

Loic placed a finger under my chin and drew my face up to look at him. "They'll have to come here."

"What?"

"I'll send word to Konrad. He can have his service here just as well as in his parlor, can't he?"

"Yes, but what about the children?" I looked around the bedroom. It was large enough to fit everyone, but it wouldn't be appropriate for them all to see me here, in the prince's bed.

"I'll allow you to move to the sitting room for the morning." He narrowed his eyes. *"If* you promise not to undertake any more foolish attempts to leave my quarters."

"Yes," I gasped. "Yes, of course."

An hour later, I was tucked securely into a chair by the fireplace as Konrad came into the sitting room. The children trailed behind him, followed by a waddling Ilse. She was due any day now, and it showed in her gait.

I'd expected Loic to leave the room during our meeting, but he took a seat in the corner. Konrad and Ilse shared a look as Konrad opened up his Bible.

"Saul was the anointed king of Israel," Konrad began, looking around at the children. "But he had lost God's favor. God sent the prophet Samuel to anoint a new king, David bar Jesse, the youngest of eight sons."

"Why the youngest?" Peter interrupted, frowning. "Shouldn't the oldest have become king?"

Konrad smiled. "Usually, yes. But usually it would have been the king's son who would inherit. The Lord chose David because he was a 'man after God's own heart.' Saul was cruel. He lusted for power. After Saul's wickedness, Israel needed a new king, one who could lead the people with justice and righteousness."

Until this week, we had been learning about the life of Christ. Why had he chosen to read about David this week?

My gaze flicked to Loic. He hadn't given any indication that he was listening, and Konrad hadn't so much as looked at him. Still, I wondered if Konrad had chosen the passage for him. King Edric, much like King Saul, was cruel and lusted for power. Did Konrad hope that Loic would see in David a model for himself and become, like the ancient king, *a man after God's own heart?*

I watched Loic throughout the rest of the meeting, as Konrad talked about Saul's mistreatment of David and the challenges David faced before becoming king. What did Loic think about all this?

He must have felt me watching him, because he looked up. His eyes met mine, and I flushed and looked away. Strange, that I could still be embarrassed after everything we'd been through.

When the clock struck the hour, Konrad closed the Bible. Ilse gathered the children. "Time to go, now. Mrs. Brandt needs her rest."

We normally sat together for hours discussing the passage. Loic must have been specific in his invitation, ensuring that they wouldn't overstay their welcome. I couldn't be upset about his limits, though. Sitting here for the full hour had tired me, another side effect of my head injury that the doctor had warned me about.

The girls took turns hugging me. Peter offered a solemn nod. "I pray you heal quickly, Mrs. Brandt," he said. Falk kissed my cheek, and the children trailed out after Konrad and Ilse.

"Thank you," I said to Loic as the door closed.

He looked at me, stone-faced. "I trust you feel adequately spiritual now."

He could be so frustrating at times. I opened my mouth to say so, but then he smirked.

He was teasing me.

"Really," I said. "This means a lot."

"Just so long as you don't expect to have them in here all hours of the day and night. They can come on Sunday mornings."

I stood, leaning heavily on the arm of the chair. "If I'm staying here until I'm healed, what will we do about Hall?"

"You won't be attending during your convalescence." He took my arm to help me back to the bedroom. "I don't want to advertise your injuries. Once the sling comes off, you can return."

I laid down in the bed, and Loic tucked the blankets around me. "Weeks away from Hall?" I murmured. "That almost makes my injuries worth it."

"Is my touch so repugnant?"

"No, it's not that." I paused for a moment. The barriers between us were crumbling. Now was my chance to tell him how I felt about the way he treated me. "It's the clothes. You let me wear what I want during the day, but as soon as the children are in bed, you parade me around in the most revealing dresses. It's humiliating."

A look of regret crossed his face, gone so soon I was sure I'd imagined it. "You've had a busy morning," he said. "Rest. Or there will be no more Sunday meetings."

CONVALESCENCE

"Your bath is ready, Mrs. Brandt," Silvia said as she gathered up my dirty laundry from the corner of the room. "Would you like help with it?"

"I'm sure I can manage. Thank you." No one had bathed me since I was a child. I'd come to appreciate the servant girl's assistance in most things, but bathing was one task I refused to give over to others.

I stepped into the bathroom and shrugged off my dressing gown. Pulling my injured arm from the sling, I sank into the steaming water. The heat soothed my stiff, aching muscles. Silvia had added dried flowers and salt to the bath; it made me feel a bit like I was sitting in a tub of soup, but she insisted it would help my recovery. I didn't know if that was true, but the water smelled good, at least.

I lay there soaking until the steam faded. The prince's bathroom was twice the size of mine, tiled with blue ceramic. A shelf next to the tub held various soaps, oils, and lotions. I reached for one and cried out as pain shot through my shoulder.

For a brief moment, I'd forgotten about my injuries. How was I going to wash my hair with only one hand?

I sank deeper into the water and closed my eyes, hoping the lavender and chamomile would hide most of my nudity. "Silvia?" I called out, feeling sheepish. The door opened. "I'm sorry to ask, but could you wash my hair for me?"

"Silvia isn't here," Loic said.

I jolted upright, sloshing water over the edge of the tub and making my shoulder throb. "You can't be in here!" I reached for a towel to cover myself.

"I can, actually." He leaned against the doorjamb and grinned at me. An unwelcome flutter of desire settled in my stomach. "I think you'll find there are very few places in Laute that I can't be."

"You know what I mean."

He crossed the room and knelt next to the tub.

"What are you doing?" My voice rose, and I clutched the towel to my chest.

"You said you needed your hair washed." He picked up a bottle of soap and poured some into his hands.

"Not by you!" The flutter of desire grew stronger, but I tamped it down. This was wrong. "Where's Silvia?"

"I believe she's doing laundry." He tugged me backward. "Relax, songbird. We have a truce, remember? I'm not trying to take advantage of you."

"No?" My voice came out in a squeak as he began massaging the soap into my scalp. It felt good. Too good. My thoughts slipped back to the dream I'd had in the bathtub, months ago. He'd washed my hair for me then, too.

Maybe that's all this was. A dream. A sinful, lustful dream. I closed my eyes tight. "It's not real," I murmured. "It's not real."

Loic laughed, a loud booming sound that shocked my eyes open. Not a dream, then. "Do you often imagine me joining you in the bath?"

I pursed my lips, holding the now-soaked towel tighter.

"Ah, yes." He poured water over my head, rinsing the soap out. "That dream you felt so guilty about."

"Don't you have better things to do than help me bathe?" I asked.

"Nothing quite so enjoyable." He grabbed a bottle of oil and began combing it through my hair. "You might be surprised to find that very few of my duties involve naked women."

"Few, or none?"

"Is that a note of jealousy I hear? Don't worry, songbird. I haven't been with another woman since you arrived at court."

"You mean you haven't been with *any* woman since I arrived at court," I said under my breath.

He heard me anyway. "I'd be happy to change that. All you have to do is ask."

I didn't want it. *Couldn't* want it. Lust was a sin. Adultery was a sin. But with every moment we spent together, I found him harder to resist.

His voice dropped to a low rumble. "Stop fighting this." He moved so our faces were level and took my chin in his hand. His thumb stroked my swollen cheek.

I couldn't breathe, but it didn't matter. His lips were on mine, stealing every bit of remaining breath in my lungs. His free arm drew me closer. Forbidden need rushed straight to my core.

He dropped his hand to my bottom and squeezed, and the touch brought me back into the moment. I was naked in the bathtub, kissing a man who wasn't my husband. A mortal sin.

I pulled back. "Stop," I gasped.

"Are you hurt?" He looked me over as I picked up the sodden towel to cover myself again. "Is it your shoulder?"

"I'm not hurt." I couldn't look into his eyes. What had I been thinking? I should have insisted he leave the moment he opened the door. I curled up into myself. "I think—I think I need to go back to my own room."

"We've already discussed that. You're not leaving my quarters until your safety can be assured."

If I stayed in his bed with him, I was going to put my soul in mortal peril. Tears filled my eyes. "Please, Loic. I have to."

He remained silent. When I risked a glance upward, he was scowling.

"Please," I whispered, though I knew it was pointless.

"The door between our rooms will remain unlocked at all times," he said finally. I looked up, unable to believe what I was hearing. "And someone will accompany you everywhere you go. If you're not with Teta or Ilse, you'll have one of my personal guards with you at all times. Do you understand?"

"Yes!"

He stood and held out a towel for me. "If I find you've put yourself in danger again, Annika, you won't leave my rooms again."

"Can I ask you something?" I asked Ilse the next day as we sat together. She was finishing some embroidery on the baby's gowns; I was rereading a page from *Le Morte d'Arthur* for what seemed like the hundredth time.

"Of course." She set aside her sewing, giving me her full attention. "What is it?"

"It's about sins." I chewed on my lip as I gathered my thoughts. "How do you know you're saved when you can't go to confession?"

Her face turned wistful, and she rested a hand on her belly. "I won't deny it's hard. I haven't been to confession since Konrad and I got married, and I haven't taken Communion in just as long. I want to see my baby baptized, but I don't know of a church that would even let us through the doors." She shook her head. "Sorry. The pregnancy has me feeling melancholy, but you didn't ask about that. You wanted to know you can still be sure you're saved."

"I just..." I shrugged. "I've done things here that I never expected to. Things that should send me straight to hell."

"Whenever I start to worry about our salvation, Konrad reminds me about St. Paul's letter to the Ephesians. 'But God hath quickened us together with Christ. For by grace are ye saved through faith; and that not of yourselves: it is the gift of God. Not of works, lest any man should boast.' We're not saved because of anything we do. We're saved by God's grace, through our faith." She leaned over and took my hand.

"You've been baptized, Annika. You have faith. No matter what sins you've committed, God forgives them all."

"Even lust? Even adultery?" Pater Huber had always preached that those were the worst sins.

"All of them." She smiled. "I'm not as knowledgeable about Scripture as Konrad. If you'd like, I can ask him to find some more passages for you."

"No, but thank you." She'd given me enough to think about.

PIED PIPER'S BIRTHDAY

Annika

I didn't see much of Loic after I moved back to my own room. Was he giving me space, or did he regret our indiscretion? Even Ilse's assurance that God forgave my sins did little to comfort me. I spent the next month in a foul mood, though whether that was caused by my guilt, my head injury, or the change in sleeping arrangements, I didn't know. I didn't have to sleep alone, but sharing a bed with Falk was a poor replacement for sharing one with the prince. More than once in the week after the attack, I'd woken in the middle of the night with Loic's arms around me and my head on his chest.

I missed him, ridiculous as the thought was. I missed the warmth of his arms around me and the softness of his kiss. I even missed his teasing. He lived just a few feet away from my rooms, but we felt miles apart.

The day after my sling came off, he strode into my room as if nothing had happened. Falk, sitting at the desk eating an apple, was the first to notice him. "Evening, your highness," he said. Ever since Loic had saved me from the boar attack, Falk considered him a hero.

"Good evening," I said, trying to ignore the flips in my stomach.

He sank into a chair across from me. "You're looking better."

Did he really think he could ignore me for weeks and then act like nothing had changed? Fine. I could do the same. "I really think you ought to learn to knock," I said, looking down at my book, a fascinating story of a man's journey through hell, purgatory, and paradise. I'd borrowed it from Konrad when I stopped by to visit Ilse and their newborn son, Hans. "It's a terrible habit, barging into someone's room."

"You're right." His eyes twinkled with mischief. "It would be a shame if I came in while you were changing or otherwise indisposed."

I flushed and shot a glance at Falk, who didn't seem to notice the undertone in the prince's words. Loic had seen me *indisposed* plenty of times. He'd been the cause for most of them. He'd even made me appear indisposed in public on multiple occasions, forcing me to parade around the throne room and sit at his feet in little more than a shift.

With my sling off, I'd have to return to those humiliating evenings. And while I was glad he seemed to be done ignoring me, I didn't know what would happen between us once we returned to Hall together.

Loic grabbed the book from my lap and turned it over to look at the cover. "Hall is canceled this week."

Sometimes it seemed as though he could read my mind. "It is?"

"It's my father's birthday. We'll have a ball instead."

I had noticed an increase in activity around the castle, but I hadn't known what it was for. "I hope you enjoy it," I said. I'd have to ensure the children were occupied elsewhere for the night.

He raised a brow, looking up from the book. "I said Hall was canceled. I didn't say you were free to do as you wished."

"Oh." I should have assumed he'd want to use the opportunity to reestablish our relationship before the court. "I don't have anything fitting to wear, and I can't dance." Not court dances, at least. The dances we did in the village weren't likely to be welcome in the castle.

"I'll have something sent up. As for dancing, I'm sure you'll manage."

I hadn't expected him to give in to my protests, but my stomach still formed knots. I wasn't ready for things to go back to the way they had been between us, the cold distance. "What about the children?"

He tossed the book onto the table next to me. "Konrad already agreed they could stay with him for the night."

Of course, Konrad and Ilse wouldn't be attending the ball. Ilse could hardly look away from baby Hans when I visited. There was no way she would leave him for a whole evening. I'd been the same way when Falk was born.

"Why can't we come, too?" Falk asked, coming to sit on the couch next to me. "At least me and Peter. We're the oldest."

"I have no objections," Loic said before I could stop him. "I'll see if I can arrange something for you to wear."

Falk made a face. He obviously hadn't thought about the clothing requirements of a ball. "Can't I just wear regular clothes?"

"I'm afraid not." Loic shrugged. "If you'd rather stay with Konrad, though, I'd appreciate you helping him. He's gotten behind in his work since his son was born, and the king and I rely on him for trade to and from Laute."

"You do?" Falk furrowed his brow. "Maybe I should help him instead. Since it's so important."

Loic's expression was serious. "Merchants are the backbone of any nation. Without them, the whole kingdom would fall apart."

Falk nodded. "I'll go."

"You should let Peter know, as well. I'm certain Konrad will need both of you to work hard tomorrow."

"Thank you," I murmured as Falk ran out of the room. If he saw the way Loic treated me in the king's presence, Falk would be devastated. He didn't need to see his mother treated as a whore.

Loic stood. "I assure you, my motives were entirely selfish." He leaned down, caging me into the chair with his arms. "I've been far too busy these past weeks. Tomorrow, I intend to have you all to myself."

A rush of sinful heat went through me at his words. That was another reason I didn't want the children present for my humiliation. I wasn't sure that shame would be my only response to the prince's treatment of me. They didn't need to see my descent into sin.

Loic brushed a breath of a kiss across my lips and straightened. He gave me a wicked smile. "Until tomorrow, songbird."

The following afternoon, Teta accompanied me back to my rooms, chattering excitedly about the ball that evening. "The whole city is coming. It's the biggest event in the valley."

I'll try to stay out of the way, I signed, my mouth twisted in a grimace.

Why? It's going to be amazing.

We'd reached my quarters. As I stepped inside, the response I'd been about to give her faded.

A dress stood in the middle of the room. Made of midnight blue silk and silver thread, it could have been sewn from the night sky. Unlike my dresses for Hall, it was full-skirted with several layers of petticoats. The sleeves were long and silver, ending in blue lace, and on a stand next to the dress was a matching headdress.

I stared, open-mouthed. *Did you do this?*

Teta shook her head. *Loic.*

I'd never had anything like it. Never *seen* anything like it. I brushed a hand against the fabric; it was cool and light, like water in a stream. *I can't—*

Teta cut me off. *If you say you can't wear it, I'll call someone to hold you down while I dress you myself.* She grinned. *It's perfect for you.*

My heart gave a nervous flutter. It would be rude not to accept it, after all the trouble he must have gone to get it for me. I touched the dress again. *It is perfect.*

Getting ready took longer than I expected. Dressing was a feat in itself, as the ornate ballgown consisted of more pieces than my usual clothing. Then I had to sit as Silvia plaited my hair so the headdress would fit.

I tried not to fidget. I hadn't thought about it, but the pipers' music was magic. I'd heard pipers play before without enchanting—nothing had happened at the king's dinner when I first arrived at court—but would the same hold true for this ball?

I cast a nervous glance at Teta, who sat nearby as another servant braided her hair into a complicated design around her horns. *The music won't...do anything to me, will it?*

Teta laughed. *No more than a glass of wine would. It's not the same as when we play to enchant something. We have to call out the magic when we play; it doesn't just happen. There's always a hint of magic in the air at something like this, but nothing dangerous.* She twisted her mouth and shrugged. *You'll see.*

Finally, Silvia announced that I was ready. She held up a mirror for me to look at myself.

The woman in the glass was unrecognizable. My cheeks were rosy, my brown eyes bright and lined with kohl. The headdress I wore had two high blue peaks, like horns covered over with fabric. A gauzy silver veil trailed from the back of the headdress. I looked like a piper, and the thought didn't horrify me. I'd never felt so elegant.

Tears filled my eyes. "Thank you," I managed to choke out.

Silvia gave a bow. "I'm glad you like it."

Teta grinned at me. *You're beautiful.*

You, too. Teta's dress was a rich yellow, lending warmth to her golden-brown skin. Her black hair spiraled around her horns in tight braids, and gold paint striped her horns.

She stood, and her wide skirt swayed with the movement. "Come on. We don't want to be late."

The castle was full of people, smiling as they chatted and sipped on drinks from slender golden goblets. We wove through the crowds, making our way to the ballroom, where strains of music grew louder.

A hint of magic accompanied the music, different from all the magic I'd felt before. It wasn't the low, intoxicating call Loic had used to cleanse my village from the plague, or his furious summoning of the children. It wasn't like the cajoling melody he'd used to enchant me, or the mournful tune he'd played the night I found him before his fire. And it was nothing like the frantic, terrifying boar-song of the man who'd attacked me.

This was...joy.

Pure, unrestrained joy.

We entered the ballroom, and the music picked me up and swept me across the floor. My worries disappeared. I spun and swirled between the other dancers, no longer afraid of knowing the proper steps. Everyone here danced to their own steps. Some had partners, but others, like me, danced alone. Laughter filled every face.

Minutes or hours later, I turned back to look for Teta. She stood near the wall, looking out over the dance floor. She saw me looking for her and grinned. *Enjoy,* she signed.

I smiled back and let the music carry me away once more. How long had it been since I'd felt this free? Since I'd been able to let go of my worries and just *be?*

Too long.

Strong arms caught me mid-spin, drawing me seamlessly into a new dance. I looked up to see hazel eyes crinkled with amusement.

Loic.

He smiled at me—a real smile, no sign of the smirk he usually wore. He was resplendent, dressed in a silver tunic with blue edging.

We complemented each other perfectly. Was he staking his claim, or did it mean something else?

"What do you think of the ball?" he asked, his voice barely audible over the music.

"It's incredible. Like a fairytale." It really was. I was living a fairytale. A simple village girl, swept into a magic world, transformed into a princess for a ball. A giggle escaped me.

Loic raised a brow. "Is something funny?"

"You're a fairytale prince." I giggled again. "I'm dancing with a fairytale prince."

"Have you been drinking, Mrs. Brandt?"

"No."

He considered me for a moment, then shook his head. "I would say I don't believe you, but I think you know better than to lie to me."

The song ended, and I let go of his hand, expecting him to release me. Instead, he guided me toward the balcony.

"You look warm," he said, by way of explanation.

I put a hand to my cheek. I was; my face felt flushed from the exertion of the dance and the crowded ballroom. Or was it his proximity?

A cool evening breeze played with my skirts as we stepped outside. It was later than I'd realized. How long had we been dancing? It was impossible to keep track of time with the music playing.

Behind us, in the ballroom, I heard the music start again.

We were alone out on the balcony. A strand of hair had worked its way from beneath my headdress. Loic tucked it behind my ear, and my breath caught.

"I wanted to thank you," I said, turning away. I leaned against the railing and looked out on the moonlit mountains surrounding us. "For the dress. You didn't have to do that."

He stepped behind me, so close I could feel the heat from his body. "Every pet deserves to be spoiled sometimes."

Pompous, arrogant, mule-headed— I spun around, nearly knocking heads with him. So much for our month-long truce. "Can't you ever just say something *nice?*"

He put a hand to his mouth, his shoulders shaking. He was *laughing* at me. I shoved away from the railing and balled up my fists. "No one wants to be treated like a pet."

"I can't help it." He dropped his hand to his side. "Your color rises so beautifully when you're angry."

"You absolute—" I couldn't finish my thought, because his lips crashed into mine.

He hadn't kissed me, really kissed me, in weeks, but there was no awkwardness, no hesitation. His tongue pressed at the seam of my lips, seeking entrance. I parted them, and he swept in, consuming me. I reached for his face, wanting him closer.

He pulled back. I nearly whimpered, but he wasn't finished. He tugged my head back and pressed a kiss to the hollow of my throat. "I'm tired of waiting, songbird," he whispered.

I was, too. I wanted him, even if it was wrong.

He trailed a finger down the front of my dress. "You look like temptation incarnate in this." He didn't give me an opportunity to respond before leaning down to kiss me again.

I raised my arms to wrap them around his neck, but a wave of dizziness swept over me.

Loic caught me before I could fall. "What's wrong?"

"It's nothing," I said, resting my head on his chest. "Just a little dizzy." And nauseous. I turned my head in case the contents of my stomach decided to make a reappearance.

"You overexerted yourself tonight."

"I'm fine."

"You should be in bed." He tucked his arm around my waist and guided me back into the ballroom.

I tried, unsuccessfully, to pull away. "The ball just started!"

He gave me a look that was half bewilderment, half amusement. "You've been here for almost two hours, songbird."

Had it been that long? "Oh."

He shook his head. "I'm taking you to bed. It's well past time."

My cheeks heated at the implication beneath his words, but I didn't object as he led me around the dance floor and out of the ballroom.

WARNING

LOIC

My father watched as we skirted the dance floor. I allowed myself a lascivious grin. Let the old man think I was taking my songbird back to my room for a night of debauchery. Undoubtedly that was the way it looked. Her headdress was askew, the front of her dress wrinkled from where she had been pressed up against me. She leaned against me, still dizzy, though to others she looked like someone who was leaving a ravishing or on her way to continue one.

If she hadn't been ill, she would have been. She'd fought her desires long enough, and she was finally ready to give in.

We stopped outside our rooms, and my songbird looked down at her feet, trying to hide the need on her face.

I had to kiss her again.

She let out a gasp as I pushed her against the wall. I wanted to devour her, consume her until there was nothing left, but I settled for a long, slow kiss.

Long before I was finished, she pushed me away and clapped a hand over her mouth.

"Annika?"

She held up her hand. "I'm fine," she said, stepping away. "Just—" She gagged.

I opened the door to her room and ushered her inside, despite her protests. "Time for bed, songbird."

"But—" She looked up at me with a confused frown.

I gave her a cocky grin. "Much as I would like to join you, I meant alone. I'd rather not take the chance of you vomiting on me mid-thrust."

She blushed, the redness spreading down her chest. How far down did it go? I wanted to find out, but I forced myself to take a step back. If I didn't leave now, I'd push her into the room and take her there on the floor, her illness be damned.

I placed a chaste kiss on the back of her hand and left her standing alone in the doorway to her room. I'd have to find some other way to relieve my tension tonight.

ANNIKA

I closed the door and sagged against it. What had I been thinking? I'd practically thrown myself at him.

I should be grateful. If it hadn't been for my increasing nausea, I would have done something I regretted. But I wished I had something to regret, rather than carrying this burning shame and unfulfilled desire.

I stepped out of my dress and tossed it on the floor, not wanting the reminder of my poor choices tonight. After a moment, guilt chased me—this dress was worth more money than I could imagine—and I picked it up and hung it neatly over the dressing screen.

Silvia had left a tray of bread and fruit on the table near the fireplace. I picked up a piece of bread and nibbled on it on my way into the bedroom. The nausea still rolling through me eased as I sat down on the bed.

After undoing the braids in my hair, I sank back onto the pillow with a groan. Something crinkled.

I frowned, reaching under the pillow. It was a piece of paper, folded in half, with a note inside in spidery handwriting.

Annika,

I cannot say much, for fear that this letter might be discovered, but I have to warn you: you must get out of Laute. You, your son, and any other humans there must find an escape by Michaelmas, or I cannot guarantee your safety.

When you escape, send word to me at the duke's castle in München.

God be with you,

Gisela.

I stared at the paper. What did she mean, we needed to go out? Had she heard something about an attack? Was Laute in danger?

A stone settled in my stomach. Once, I would have relished the thought of someone attacking the pipers. That was before, though. Before I'd made friends here. If someone attacked, Teta could be in danger. And Konrad and Ilse and baby Hans. Hugo, the kindly old cook, and Silvia, the servant who tended my rooms. Countless others would be affected as well, people whose only crime was being born piper.

And Loic. My feelings for him had changed. He might have rejected me tonight—which was good, I reminded myself once more—but that didn't change how I felt about him. It went beyond lust. I enjoyed spending time with him. I wanted to know his mind and heart. Every time he put up a wall between us, I wanted to break it down.

It helped that Falk had come to admire him. Loic treated my son like the man he was becoming, rather than the child he still was. I couldn't help but fall for him over that.

I put on my dressing robe and carried the letter out to the sitting room. I wasn't going to be able to sleep now. Taking a seat in the window, I looked out at the city below the castle. Konrad and Ilse's house was among those still lit; either Hans was keeping Ilse awake, or Peter and Falk had convinced Konrad to stay up late and teach them more about his business.

They were happy here in Laute. They thrived in a way they never would have the chance to at home. How was I supposed to give all this up?

The children would adjust again, I knew. They needed their families. But didn't they need the freedom they'd found here, too? Freedom from poverty, from the constant demands of survival.

Michaelmas was still three months away. Enough time that if I warned Loic, he'd be able to prepare a defense against...whatever this was. Would that make me a traitor to my people? I wasn't one of the pipers, no matter how happy I'd become here. I was human. If I warned the pipers of a potential attack, I might be causing human deaths.

But if I didn't warn them, I might be allowing the deaths of innocent pipers. Of my friends.

I didn't even know if I'd be able to get the children out, to say nothing of myself. My relationship with Loic was changing, but I didn't believe he trusted me yet. Not enough to allow me and the children to leave court together.

I let out a loud sigh and dropped the letter on my lap. It was an impossible situation. No matter what I did, someone was going to be hurt.

THREATS

ANNIKA

Too conflicted to face Loic, I busied myself as much as I could over the next few days, but he finally cornered me in my sitting room one evening.

"You've been avoiding me."

I looked up from the pair of pants I was mending. He stood in the doorway, arms crossed.

I prayed for my racing heart to slow as I met his eyes. "No, I haven't. I've been busy."

"Busy." He stared at me, face impassive. "With what?"

"Minding the children. Teaching. Mending." I held up the pants to show him.

"I see." His eyes narrowed, his mouth tightening into a scowl. "And the fact that I haven't seen you in almost a week has nothing to do with what happened the night of the ball?"

My mouth went dry. Had he found out about Gisela's letter?

He crossed the room and bent down, arms forming a cage on either side of me. "You're not regretting my touch, are you, songbird? Because that was just the beginning."

Heat crept down my neck. He didn't know about the letter. I squirmed back in my chair. "I wanted to give you space."

"You thought I needed space after such a small taste as that?"

I glared at him, my anxiety fading as my irritation grew. "I wasn't aware that I was a dish for you to taste."

His gaze turned predatory as he smiled. "Have you never been tasted? I hear songbird is a delicacy in some cultures."

"I—" My mouth snapped shut. Did he mean what I thought he meant? Did people really do that?

He traced a finger down my jawline. "I thought it would take more than that to leave you speechless."

I rolled my eyes, mustering my bravado. "I didn't think your vulgarity merited a response."

"Ah. I thought for a moment you didn't know what I meant." He stood and gave me an appraising look. "Shame. I would have been happy to demonstrate."

I swallowed hard at the implication but forced myself to turn back to my mending. "What are you doing here, your highness?"

"I'm trying to find out why you've been avoiding me." He took a seat on the edge of my chair, filling my nose with the sweet and spicy scent of him.

"I already told you, I wasn't." His presence was intoxicating. He needed to leave before I did something I would regret, like telling him everything.

"I see." He pulled the mending from my hands. I froze as he set it aside and bent down. "Then you won't mind if I..." He paused, his breath caressing my lips. I let out a sigh as he continued, "pick up where we left off?"

Blessed Virgin, guard me from temptation. But when his lips met mine, I didn't pull away.

His kiss was forceful and demanding. It crashed over me, sweeping me under a wave of desire. And saints preserve me, I kissed him back with the same intensity.

Loic was the first to pull back, but only for a second. He stood, lifted me by the waist, and wrapped my legs around him. Heat rushed through me as he kissed me again.

He carried me across the room, graceful even now. A warning bell tolled in the back of my mind; I shouldn't be allowing this. But the firm grip of his hands, the desperate claiming of his lips and tongue drowned out my better instincts.

He deposited me on the desk, surprisingly gentle, and stripped off his shirt.

He was beautiful. I reached a hand toward the spattering of dark hair on his bare chest. As I explored his torso, he closed his eyes, tilting his head back. The movement softened him, made him look kinder.

Then he opened his eyes and fixed that predatory gaze on me once more, and the moment was past.

"My turn, songbird." He slipped my headscarf off, trailing it down my neck and back.

My heart skipped a beat. "Your turn to what?"

"To see." He dropped the scarf on the ground and loosened my apron strings. "To touch." The garment fell to the floor, and he reached for the strings of my kirtle. "And I believe tasting was mentioned at one point."

Saints. He actually intended to do that. Was I going to let him? He wouldn't force me. I knew that now. There were some lines he wouldn't cross, and if I didn't want this, he wouldn't make me.

Did I want this?

Holy Mother, it was hard to think with his hands on me. I shouldn't want this. Right? There was something I needed to do, to say. Some reason I hadn't sought him out since the ball.

His hand found my breast. His lips brushed my neck, and I gasped. "Falk."

Loic straightened, frowning. "Do you often think about your son in moments like this?"

"I—" I cleared my throat and clutched the loose strings of my kirtle. "We shouldn't be doing this."

"According to whom?"

God. Scripture. The Church. He wouldn't understand those answers, though. He didn't care what God had to say about adultery and fornication.

"I have a son. *I* shouldn't be doing this."

He chuckled. "You have a son, and so you're obligated to be celibate for the rest of your life? I wasn't aware that was the custom these days."

"I—we—" I crossed my arms and glared at him. "It's not proper."

He leaned in until his breath tickled my neck. "You're right," he whispered. "The things I want to do to you are far from proper."

My heart thundered in my ears. "What if Falk found out?"

He stepped back, his face suddenly serious. "My apologies. You're right, of course. Would you like a moment to compose yourself?"

I frowned. Just like that, he was willing to stop? I'd known he wouldn't force me, but I hadn't expected him to give up so easily. I nodded, though. "I'll be right back." I crossed the room, giving him a curious glance before slipping into my bedroom.

I took a seat on the bed and reached for my medallion, which rested on my bedside table. *Pray for me, Blessed Mother of God, that I may be found worthy of the promises of Christ.*

I was as far from worthy as it was possible to be. Had Loic pressed any further, I would have given in, heedless of every reason I shouldn't.

I tamped down an irrational sense of rejection. It had been my idea to stop, after all. Just because he hadn't continued to push me didn't mean he didn't want me.

I shouldn't be worried about that, anyway. I should be focused on protecting the children from whatever Gisela had warned me about. It was one thing to make friends here, but I couldn't risk the children's safety by telling Loic about the attack. I had to find a way to get the children out of the castle by Michaelmas. And myself, preferably, but I didn't expect Loic would allow me out of the city with them. He wouldn't trust me that far. But perhaps if I could get him to send the children away for a few days, on an excursion... Yes, that was it. The Michaelmas services in Augsburg. Konrad could accompany them, and Pater Trost would make sure they were safe.

I adjusted my clothing and returned to the sitting room. Loic was still shirtless, leaning against the desk. He flipped disinterestedly through a book.

I froze, staring at the book in his hands. Was it the one I'd hidden the letter in? Stupid of me, I realized now, not to destroy the letter immediately. Why hadn't I?

Loic glanced up and set the book on the desk. "Feeling better?" he asked with a smirk.

No, he hadn't found it. He wouldn't be so calm if he had.

"Much, thank you." I took a seat on the couch. "I've been thinking. Michaelmas is coming soon."

"Oh?"

I glanced up. His eyes held vague amusement mingled with slight boredom. No cause for concern. "Seeing as there's no congregation here in Laute, I had thought you might allow the children to attend Mass in Augsburg. It would be good for them to be among humans again. Just for a brief visit," I added, seeing his face darken.

He stalked toward me, eyes narrowed. "Are you trying to circumvent our agreement, Annika?"

I swallowed hard. "Not at all. If you would prefer, I could stay here as...as surety that the children would return. Konrad can take them, and Pater Trost—he's the vicar at the church in Augsburg—he'd ensure that any other pipers you wanted to send receive fair treatment during their time in the city." At least, I hoped he would. Pater Trost had told me the pipers weren't demons, but I couldn't guarantee that he'd receive them well. Their presence in his congregation could threaten his standing with the pope. "It might be good for some of the piper children, as well," I went on. Anything to get as many innocents out of Laute as possible. "A chance to see some of the Bavarian culture, to learn about our beliefs and lifestyle."

Scowling, he scanned my eyes for something. My throat was dry, my heart racing as I waited for him to respond.

Finally he nodded. "You will stay. The children can go—for a week. No longer." He turned toward the door, then stopped and looked back at me. "And, Annika? If I find you've taken advantage of my lenience, I'll find the children again. And this time, you won't be treated as my guests."

I shivered as he closed the door behind him.

LOIC

She was plotting against me.

It shouldn't hurt. I'd stolen her child, behaved like a monster. I was the villain in her narrative, no matter how sweet and yielding her body was when I touched her.

I'd thought we were making progress, but I'd been wrong before.

As I'd been whispering in her ear, I'd caught sight of the letter sticking out of a book. I would have ignored it, but a niggling sensation told me it was important. I knew better than to ignore my instincts, so despite my raging lust, I'd given in to her half-hearted attempts to preserve her virtue. I'd read the letter while she was *composing herself*, and when I replaced it, I picked up a nearby book to see what her reaction would be.

The guilt that flashed across her face when she returned had told me all I needed to know. She'd received the letter, and she was hiding it from me.

Whether she was working with the woman who sent the letter or not, the result remained the same. I couldn't trust her, and we needed to prepare for an attack.

We couldn't evacuate; it wasn't worth the risk that the letter was a false lead. I could risk sending the children away. My father would be furious if the humans escaped, but I could face my father's wrath.

My little songbird, though, she would remain. If she was planning to betray me, I needed her where I could watch her, punish her if necessary. And if she wasn't, if she was—mostly—ignorant of her acquaintance's plans, I could still use her as a hostage.

I wasn't keeping her to protect her. No, I'd learned that lesson long ago. My own emotions weren't on the table.

I'd reached my father's study. Taking a deep breath, I steeled myself and knocked.

"Enter."

I stepped inside and bowed. My father sat at the desk, peering at a ledger. The golden crown he wore every day glinted in the white light that streamed through the window.

The king barely glanced at me. "What is it?"

"I have reason to believe there will be an attack made on the kingdom at the end of September."

His gaze flicked to me. "What reason?"

If he suspected Annika, he'd have her thrown in the dungeon and tortured until she confessed. Confession under duress was unreliable and would provide us with no advantage in case of an attack.

That was the reason I lied to my father. No other. "A contact in the Bavarian court. He couldn't get specifics beyond that—just that we should prepare for an attack of some sort by the end of September."

The king snorted. "Your contact is a waste, if that's all the information he could sniff out. Nothing on the type of attack? Numbers? Location?"

I shook my head.

He waved me out. "Double the sentries, and see that the guard is prepared for any eventuality." He turned back to his ledger. "And get better contacts. Your ignorance offends me."

"Yes, your majesty." I bowed and backed out of the room, keeping my face carefully neutral so my father couldn't see the effect of his words.

MICHAELMAS

ANNIKA

Tension filled the days leading up to Michaelmas. Loic was distant, busy, I assumed with some matter of state or other. Or maybe he was avoiding me after I'd pushed him away. Worry over Gisela's warning already gnawed at my stomach, and thinking about him didn't help.

On the twenty-eighth of September, I helped Konrad and Ilse pack the children, including a few piper children, into warm clothes. There weren't as many piper children as I had hoped, but I was glad for anyone we could get out. Three other pipers would be accompanying them, men Loic had chosen for protection and to ensure the children didn't escape. Konrad carried a letter from me to Pater Trost, giving a brief explanation of what had transpired since my arrival at Laute—leaving out my contact with Gisela—and asking him to extend his protection to the pipers and children while they were in Augsburg.

Fear tightened my chest as they drove off. I didn't know what was coming tomorrow, but if Gisela had been right, this could be the last time I saw my son. I couldn't even tell him goodbye properly; I had to swallow the tears and wave as if nothing was amiss.

They disappeared between the mountains, and I turned back to the castle, my throat thick. Loic stood at the top of the steps, watching me. I couldn't read his expression, and he didn't speak. We stared at each other for a moment, and then he turned and went back inside without a word.

The next morning, Michaelmas, dawned bright and clear but cold. A thin layer of from covered the ground outside, and inside, the servants had built fires in every room. I asked Teta to forgo our daily walk, claiming a headache, and we spent the morning inside. I did my best to act natural as I knitted a new pair of winter socks for Falk.

"What are you looking for?" Teta finally asked as I glanced out the window for the third time in as many minutes.

"Nothing." I bent my head back over my knitting.

"Worried about Falk?"

I gave her a sheepish smile, grateful for the excuse. "A little."

She set her book down and reached over to pat my leg. *He'll be fine,* she signed.

I nodded, though her words were little comfort. It wasn't Falk I was worried about.

The rest of the day passed without incident, and as I sat alone in my room before supper, trying and failing to focus on a book, a kernel of hope started to form in my breast. Maybe Gisela had been wrong. Maybe she'd misunderstood.

A thunderous blast tore through the air, shattering my thoughts. I jumped to my feet, heart in my throat. Was it cannonfire? How had they gotten cannons into the valley?

In the ringing silence, I rushed to the door and peered out. People ran through the corridor, terror on their faces. Some ran toward the source of the blast, others away.

I started to step into the hallway, but a second blast rang out, this one closer. The walls shook, and I staggered back.

They planned to take the whole castle down. Fear rooted me to the spot. Gisela was right. I should have gotten out. If they destroyed the castle, I might not even survive the destruction. And if I did, who might be waiting outside to kill anyone who crawled their way out of the rubble?

And how would Teta get out? She might not even know about the attack yet. She couldn't hear the blasts or the screams in the hall. She might have noticed the shuddering walls, but would she realize what danger she was in? The castle could come down around her before she even knew what was happening.

And if they destroyed the castle, Loic—

Panic was useless. I forced myself to step toward the door as another blast, this one further away again, hit the stone walls. I had to get out of the castle, out of the city. I could find shelter in the woods and wait for the attack to pass before escaping the valley.

I stopped only long enough to grab my cloak from its hook before making my way into the chaos of the hallways.

A fourth explosion, this one the closest yet, knocked me to the ground. As I staggered to my feet, I caught sight of a large crack in the wall next to me.

They really were going to bring the castle down.

Mouth dry, I tore down the hall. I couldn't get to the main doors—they'd be flooded with people desperate to get out—so I headed toward the kitchens. The door there led out into the gardens. I could get into the woods from there, escape to Augsburg and take Falk home.

My heart stuttered at the thought of leaving, but I had no choice. Whoever was attacking, they were going to destroy the castle and kill everyone inside. Falk had to be my priority. Falk and the other children.

Rushing down the steps, I heard the sound of clashing steel. The explosions had stopped, but a new sound rose over the noise of the battle. Clear, ringing music, soothing as a lullaby. My steps slowed, and the people rushing past me calmed momentarily, as well.

The music wasn't intended for us, though. It was targeted at whoever was attacking the castle, and after a moment, the panic in the corridor resumed.

The not-so-distant sound of battle didn't cease, despite the music. What could be attacking the pipers that would be unaffected by their magic? I shuddered and put on a burst of speed, turning a corner into an unoccupied hall.

Staggering footsteps sounded ahead of me. Desperate innocent or dangerous assailant? I tensed, but in a moment the familiar yellow-and-red of a guard's cloak appeared.

"Help... Please..." The guard staggered toward me, clutching his stomach.

Pity and fear warred within me. If I stopped, I risked being caught in the castle when—if—the intruders won. But this man had never done anything to hurt me. Could I live with letting him die to save myself?

"Please," he gasped again.

I squared my shoulders. Right or wrong, my choice was made. I couldn't abandon him, not when he'd asked for my help.

I met him in the middle of the corridor and caught him as he fell. I nearly collapsed under his weight, but I did my best to ease him to the ground.

"It's alright," I said, pulling his hands from the wound and instantly regretting it. His stomach was a mess of raw meat, oozing blood.

My knowledge about medicine was limited to what I'd learned working in my parents' apothecary, but I doubted he would survive this.

"It's alright," I repeated, more to myself than to him. "What's your name?"

He opened his mouth, but no sound came out. He twitched beneath my hand, and then he was gone.

I stood, trembling, and wiped my now-bloody hands on my apron. The sight made me nauseous. I'd seen death before, but not like this. Even Nikolaus's death, unexpected as it was, hadn't been violent. Pater Huber had come to give him Last Rites after he collapsed, and he'd passed in his sleep later that night.

"God receive his soul," I whispered, making the sign of the cross over the guard's body. There was nothing else I could do for him.

I leaned against the wall. How could humans be capable of such violence? I hadn't known that guard, but neither had his killer. How could people murder strangers?

The sound of clashing steel neared, but I couldn't bring myself to move. I'd done this. By failing to warn Loic about the attack, I was responsible for this man's death.

After a moment, the sound of battle moved away, then stopped altogether, replaced with the sound of running feet. Cheers rang out.

Was it over? Heart in my throat, I looked toward the sound. Who had won?

I didn't have to wait long to find out. A king's guard came running down the hall where I stood, a grin on his face. He stopped when he saw his comrade's body on the ground, and his smile faded.

"I'm sorry," I whispered. "There was nothing I could do."

He stared at me for a moment, then nodded. "It's over. They're gone." He ran past, leaving me alone once more.

I pressed my head against the wall, trembling. They'd beaten them back. Not as easily as they might have with my warning, but they'd managed nonetheless.

Not without casualties, though. I glanced at the body on the ground next to me. Who else might have been injured, killed in the attack? How many people I knew? How many innocents?

I swallowed hard. This was my fault. I didn't stop it from happening, but at least I could help now. I could help treat the wounded, help them deal with the consequences of my inaction.

LOIC

My father was dead.

I sat in his private quarters. My quarters, now. The room felt too large, the desk cluttered with the paperwork I so detested. His English bottle of aquavitae stood half-empty where he'd left it, the scent of alcohol and rye drifting up from the amber liquid.

I hadn't been with him when he died, not that it mattered. The end result was the same. The man who'd raised me, been endlessly disappointed in me, was dead. Now I was king.

I'd known immediately. The pied pattern on my skin had appeared the instant my father breathed his last, and I'd felt a rush of magic enter me.

Stupid of me, not to have sent a team of guards to protect the king today. An attack on Laute was an attack on the Pied Piper. He should have been the top priority. It was no wonder he'd always thought so little of me.

One of the attackers, a scraggly-haired mercenary, had almost managed to remove my head from my shoulders when the rush of the pipers' magic left me frozen. If not for Josef's quick thinking, I would be dead. He'd yanked me out of the way just in time.

What would Annika think of my new position?

The thought came from nowhere, and I frowned. Why did it matter what she thought? Like as not, she'd run away in the chaos of the attack, and I'd never see her again. But she could have been caught up in the fighting or captured by the humans as they fled. She could be injured, or worse.

Why did that thought make my heart clench?

I stood, pushing back the chair to my father's—my—desk. I was responsible for her. I should at least make sure she was uninjured. Not out of any particular sentiment, but because an injured pet was no use to me.

I waved away the guards who stood outside the study, but they followed me anyway and waited for me outside the door to her room. The sitting room was empty, the fire down to embers. A quill and paper waited on the desk; I glanced at it, but it was just plans for the children's lessons. She hadn't planned to leave, then, or didn't want it to appear as though she was leaving.

In the bedroom, I opened her wardrobe. The dresses she wore to Hall hung on one end, almost gaudy in their opulence next to the plain linen undershirts that took up most of the space. She'd be furious with me for invading her privacy if she found out I'd looked at her underthings. The corner of my mouth turned up at the thought. I loved the brightness of her eyes and the redness of her cheeks when she was angry.

I loved everything about her body. Her soft curves, the silken brown hair she tried to hide beneath those ridiculous scarves. Seeing her hair loose around her shoulders aroused thoughts in me that would mortify her. She was exquisite. My magnificent songbird.

If she'd left me, I'd find her again. Find her, and teach her the meaning of the word *pet*. She could sit in a cage all day and sing for me.

No, she knew better than to leave me. Despite her softening affections, she still feared me too much to flee. Perhaps she *had* been injured. Killed.

I wouldn't allow that. I'd bar her from the gates of heaven myself, if such a place existed, and damn the consequences.

I left her quarters, shadowed by my silent guards, and walked down to the throne room where a field hospital had been set up. If my songbird was injured, she'd be in here.

No one noticed me as I entered. The room was in chaos. The east wall, which had needed repair for years now, suffered a partial collapse under the force of the explosions. Several inhabitants of the castle had been caught beneath it.

Lady Helene sat on a cot, a bone protruding from her right arm. Silvia, the servant assigned to Annika, held the hand of a gasping old woman. On the dais, my father's body lay covered in a sheet.

Good. I wasn't ready to see it. Not yet.

Teta was the first to catch sight of me. *Do you need something?* she asked from across the room.

Annika. Have you seen her? Not because I was worried. Because I needed to know if she'd left me. If I had to send someone after her.

Teta pointed past me, toward the wounded, and a strange knot settled in my throat as I turned to look.

Annika stood next to Gerhard Klepper, one of the newest Delegates of the Pied Piper. The young man's left arm was a mangled mess of flesh and bone. My songbird sponged his wound, her lips moving in what I assumed were words of comfort, though I couldn't hear her from where I stood. Her headscarf was askew, and blood covered her apron.

I nodded my thanks to Teta as my stomach did a flip. From hunger, most likely. I hadn't eaten since before the attack, hours ago, and the onslaught of new magic had left me feeling strange.

I wasn't the only one feeling strange. My little songbird, who thought pipers were demons, was comforting my people and tending their wounds. I'd have thought it was a miracle, if I believed in miracles.

I shook my head. I needed to oversee the castle's defenses, fortify the castle, prepare the city for another attack. Instead I was standing here mooning over some...some...

Damn the woman. I couldn't even think straight. I turned away and caught Teta watching me with a barely-suppressed smile.

She can stay for another half hour, I signed, ignoring my friend's expression. *Then send her to bed.* Annika had no sense of self-preservation. If no one told her to rest, she'd work herself to death. I paused, then added to Teta, *The same for you. I'll need you ready to work tomorrow.*

Yes, Loic-Ass.

A rush of warmth went through me. Teta, at least, wouldn't treat me differently just because I was king.

I didn't let the warmth show on my face. *Back to work,* I ordered.

Yes, your majesty. She grinned, but it faded quickly. *I really am sorry. I know—*

I cut her off with a wave of my hand. I wasn't ready for sympathy. I didn't need sympathy. My father and I had hated each other, and his death was no great loss.

Teta's mouth twisted as it always did when I'd done something she didn't agree with, but she didn't press. She would let the matter rest for the night.

I had just a few more things to do, and then I could find a sanctuary until the morning.

I intended to make the most of it.

PIED PIPER

ANNIKA

It was near midnight when Teta finally sent me to bed. *On the king's orders,* she'd said, and it had taken me a moment to realize she meant Loic, not his father.

His father, who was dead.

Blood soaked my apron. I ripped off the garment and threw it on the ground. All evening, all night, I'd been with the injured. Bandaging their wounds, holding the hands of the dying. Despite our differences, it seemed humans and pipers bled and died the same. I was covered in the blood of those I'd once called demons.

My hands were clean, but I could still feel the blood. It settled into my skin, and I'd never be free of it. I'd hated these people, but they'd become my friends. Friends, and with Loic...something else. Something I couldn't name. Wouldn't name. Not now.

I had their blood on my hands.

I poured cold water into the washbasin and picked up the bar of soap. This was all my fault. If I'd warned them, if I'd said something to Loic, or to Teta, the king would still be alive. The guards and innocents who had died in the attack would still be alive. None of this would have happened.

My fault.

I scrubbed my hands.

All my fault.

I scrubbed harder.

"Annika."

I looked up into hazel eyes. Piper eyes. Loic.

My vision blurred with tears. He must hate me—or he would once he found out what I'd done. That I'd known something was coming, and I hadn't bothered to warn them.

My fault.

He pulled the soap from my hands and gently rinsed them in the basin. My skin was raw and red. How long had I been standing there, trying to scrub away an invisible layer of blood?

Loic took a soft towel from beside the basin and patted my hands dry. White spots marked his tawny skin, the sign of his new position. The Pied Piper.

He set the towel aside and pulled me into a tight embrace.

"I couldn't find you," he whispered. "I thought you'd left me. Then I worried you might be hurt. Dead."

Tears spilled over onto my cheeks. I should be. For what I'd done, I deserved to be dead.

He pulled back and scanned my face. "You're not hurt, are you?"

I shook my head, choking back a sob.

He brushed a hand over my cheek. "Shh, songbird. You're okay. I have you." He tried to draw me back into his arms, but I pulled away. I didn't deserve his gentleness.

"It's my fault." The words slipped past my lips, barely audible to my human ears.

"No, songbird." His voice was soft. So unlike him, to show this gentle side. Once he knew the truth, he'd never let anyone see this side of him again. He tried not to let himself be vulnerable, and I'd taken the freedom he gave me and used it to destroy his court. To destroy him. I'd gotten his *father* killed!

I had to tell him.

I took a step back, putting distance between us. I wouldn't be able to do this with his arms around me. "Yes, it is. It's all my fault." He opened his mouth to respond, but I held up a hand. "I knew this was coming. I knew someone was planning to attack, and instead of warning you, I..." The words caught in my throat as tears streamed down my face. "I should have warned you, but instead I made a sorry excuse to get Falk and the other children away from Laute, and I let it happen. I *let* them kill all those people." I covered my face with my hands and sank down onto the bathroom floor. "It's my fault they're dead. It's my fault your father's dead."

He didn't speak. I could feel his horror, his rage, hanging in the air between us. I couldn't bear to look up and see the betrayal on his face.

I swallowed the lump in my throat. "I know you have to punish me, but whatever you do, don't hurt Falk. He had nothing to do with this."

"Look at me, Annika."

I took a deep breath before doing as he ordered.

He wore a sad, almost wistful smile. There was no trace of the anger or betrayal I expected.

"Did you think I wouldn't know?" He knelt next to me and hooked a finger beneath my chin. "I found the letter. Why else would I have let the children go?"

My head spun. "You...knew?"

"I may have come to care for you, but I knew better than to trust you. My people have earned our reputation as monsters. I wouldn't blame you for hating us." His thumb brushed my bottom lip. "None of this was your fault."

He'd known. He'd known the attack was coming. He didn't blame me; he'd *expected* me to betray him. He'd been right not to trust me. And...he said he cared for me. Did he mean it? How could he care for me and not trust me?

How could I care for him and not warn him?

"You're quiet." He dropped his hand. "Are you angry with me?"

"What? No. I'm glad you found the letter." I twisted my hands in my skirt. "But why didn't you evacuate?"

"The entire city?" He shook his head. "Even if it was possible, I wouldn't have. Safer to stay here than to risk being vulnerable on the road. Your idea of a journey for the children dealt with my problem of protecting the most vulnerable members of the court, and I had time to prepare a stronger defense. If I hadn't known something was coming, things would have been much worse."

I swallowed. "I'm glad you didn't trust me, then."

"Are you?" He watched me, an odd note in his voice. "You don't wish they'd succeeded?"

Tears welled up in my eyes again. "No! I'm so sorry, Loic."

"Sorry for what?" I've already told you it wasn't your fault."

"For everything. For lying to you, for giving you reasons not to trust me. For hurting you."

He pulled me to my feet and led me into the bedroom. "How could you have hurt me? You did nothing I didn't expect you to do." When we reached the bed, he sat down next to me and pulled off my headscarf. As he combed his fingers through my hair, he went on. "At least until the attack started. I'd thought you might try to leave me, but instead you looked at my people, injured and dying, and you helped. You saved lives in my court, when I've given you every reason to want us all dead. And still you apologize."

He had no idea what I'd come to feel for him. That I'd spent the entire night thinking of him, terrified that he might have been hurt or killed in the attack. That my first thought hadn't been of my own safety, but of his. Despite all the obstacles between us, I'd come to feel something for him. Not love, perhaps—not yet—but something approaching it.

"What are you thinking?" he asked.

That I could love you. No, I wasn't ready for that. I cleared my throat and pulled away from his touch. "I was just thinking that I've taken up too much of your time. I'm sure you've got more important things to do."

His gaze darkened. "Are you telling me to leave?"

"I just thought..."

"That I was here out of duty? That I came to comfort you, regardless of my own needs and desires?" He shook his head. "I thought you knew me better by now. I only go where I want to be, and tonight, I want to be with you." He trailed a finger down my cheek, then my neck, stopping at my collar.

My heart thundered in my chest. "Shouldn't you be—"

He brushed his lips against mine, cutting me off. "Be what? Ruling the kingdom?" He skimmed his hands down my sides, and my skin pebbled. "That can wait until morning."

His touch was like fire. I leaned into it. "I looked for you. Among the wounded."

"Did you?" He nipped at my ear, sending a rush of heat through my body. "Were you hoping I'd be there? Or were you worried for me?"

Worried? Terrified. "I don't want to see you dead," I whispered.

"That's good." He pressed a kiss to my throat. "Because I intend to show you just how alive I am." He grabbed me by the waist and jerked me onto his lap.

"You are?" My voice came out in a squeak. I swallowed hard and spoke again. "I—" I didn't know what to say. He wanted me, wanted to take me to bed.

"You what?" he asked. "Do you want this?"

No. Yes. No. "I don't know."

Loic gave a sharp grin and loosened the strings of my skirt. "You don't know?" He slipped a hand beneath my shirt, caressing the curve of my breast. "It's a simple question. Do you want me, songbird?"

Something pulsed low in my abdomen. I felt a sudden need for him to touch me harder, to claim me. I fought the desire to squirm as he traced circles on my belly.

"You've not answered my question," he said after a moment. "Do you want me?"

When I still didn't answer, he pulled back. I whimpered, and he chuckled, the sound low and throaty. "Tell me, Annika."

It was all too much. My fears and guilt, his comfort and gentleness. The sound of my name on his lips. "Yes," I breathed. "I want you, Loic."

"Good." His voice was almost a growl as he pulled off my shirt. He knelt before me to remove my shoes and stockings, then pushed me down onto my back and pulled off my skirt.

He stared down at me with heavy-lidded eyes. I flushed and tried to cover myself, but he grabbed my wrists in one hand and pinned them above my head. "Not a chance, songbird. Don't hide from me." He punctuated the order with a bite to my breast, following it with a swirl of his tongue around my nipple. I shivered.

He trailed kisses over my breasts. I squirmed, but he held me in place, the soft touch of his clothes delightful and wrong against my bare skin.

Then he released my wrists and sat up on his knees, staring at me. What a sight I had to be, my cheeks red, my brown hair a mess. And the way he was looking at me, where he was looking... I tried to close my legs, but he grabbed my knees and held them apart.

"I thought I told you not to hide from me." He leaned in and inhaled—actually *sniffed* at my center. My blood turned molten. "So wet already. You're glistening, and I've barely touched you. I bet you taste divine. Shall I taste you, songbird?"

I wanted his touch. Needed it, even. But his mouth? I let out a sound that was half whimper, half moan.

He chuckled. "I'll take that as a yes." He bowed his head and dragged his tongue up my center.

I'd never felt anything like it before. My back arched as he licked me, drawing circles with his tongue around where my thighs met. Then he closed his mouth and sucked, sliding a finger inside me at the same time, and something exploded.

My body shook uncontrollably. As the shaking eased, he added a second finger to the first and curled them inside me, bringing me back to the peak. I gasped. "Loic, please." I couldn't think beyond his fingers, his tongue.

Finally he withdrew. I went limp, eyes closed as my tremors faded. I heard the whisper of fabric, and a moment later, something nudged between my legs.

I clenched my eyes tight as he filled me.

"Look at me."

I couldn't resist the command in his voice. I met his eyes, the pupils almost round in the dim light. Almost human. I couldn't fool myself into believing he was anything but a piper, though. His black horns formed dark shadows against the ceiling, and his face was a puzzle, new patches of white on his skin.

He wasn't just a piper; he was the Pied Piper. I was lying with the king of the pipers, and it was like nothing I'd ever experienced before. Pleasure bordered on pain. It was the temptation I'd desired and dreaded, and if it killed me, I wouldn't resist.

His bare chest pressed against my breasts as he leaned down to kiss me. I tasted something salty and musky on his lips—myself, I realized with a start. It wasn't unpleasant. His tongue swept into my mouth in languid strokes, matching the pace of our joining.

Some time later, he moved faster, harder, as his climax neared. I urged him on, pulling him into me with my legs around his waist. His face contorted with rapture, and he groaned my name as he came.

He withdrew and collapsed on the bed next to me. I curled into his chest and closed my eyes, but he pulled away. The bed creaked as he stood.

"Don't leave," I whispered.

Loic chuckled. "I wasn't." He took my hand and pulled me to my feet.

I stumbled after him in a haze. He led me back into the bathroom, where the bath had been filled with steaming water.

I frowned as he stepped into the tub. "When—?"

He shrugged, helping me in after him. "I ordered it before I came up. I thought you might need it after today."

The tub was plenty big enough for both of us. I nestled against him, letting the water soothe the aches of the day. "And you thought you'd join me?"

"What good is a pet you can't enjoy?" His tone was light, teasing.

I pulled back, suddenly shy. Had he enjoyed himself? I'd enjoyed myself. I hadn't known it could be like that for women. He seemed pleased, but I couldn't be sure.

I'd never worried about that before. With my husband, sex had been an obligation, done with the intent to procreate. We'd been unsuccessful apart from Falk, but that hadn't mattered. The Church cautioned against the sin of lust, and Nikolaus had been careful to ensure that we didn't fall into temptation.

Temptation.

Lust.

Sin.

The reality of my situation dawned on me. I'd lain with a man who wasn't my husband, and I'd *enjoyed* it.

I scrambled to my feet, reaching for a towel, a washcloth, anything to cover myself. My hands grasped the filthy apron I'd worn all day, and I held it tight to my chest. What had I done?

Loic looked up at me with a cocked brow. "Is something wrong, songbird?" He wiped a droplet from his cheek, where I'd splashed him in my haste to get away.

"This was a mistake."

He stood, and I turned my gaze toward the ground, trying not to notice his—saints, was that what it looked like? The only one I'd ever seen was Nikolaus's.

Oblivious to the turmoil in my thoughts, Loic stepped out of the tub. Water matted the dark hair on his chest, and his eyes were narrowed in that expression that had once terrified me. With lethal calm, he asked, "What was a mistake?"

"This." I gestured between us, looking at the walls, the ceiling, anything but him. "It's a sin. We shouldn't have done it."

"A sin." He stepped closer, and I backed away, clutching my makeshift covering tighter. "I'm afraid you'll have to be more specific. We did a great many things tonight." He caught me by the waist and pulled me close as I fought to keep my apron between us. "Did you mean this?" He drew me into a kiss, stealing my breath.

He wore a self-satisfied smile when he finally leaned back and looked into my dazed eyes. "Or did you mean this?" he continued, trailing his hand down my navel.

A shiver went through me. "This isn't... We shouldn't..."

He kissed me again, softer this time. "You worry too much." He took the blanket from my hands and tossed it onto the floor, then pulled me back into the tub. He sat down and drew me onto his lap, facing him.

I shouldn't want this. If I was good, if I was pure, I'd leave.

"You're still thinking about it. Stop thinking." He took my face in both his hands, his beautiful hazel eyes meeting mine. "Tonight, just for tonight, don't think. Just be with me."

Words couldn't describe how much I wanted that. I wanted *him*. Wanted to be with him, to forget about everything but his kiss, his touch, this moment.

His thumb brushed my cheek. "Please, Annika?"

It was easy to forget, with the walls he built around his heart, that inside he was just as fragile as anyone. Here with me, he'd dropped those walls. He'd given me the gift of his vulnerability, and I couldn't bring myself to reject it.

I leaned closer. "Just for tonight," I whispered against his lips.

"Just for tonight," he agreed.

REGROUPING

LOIC

My songbird was still asleep the next morning as I slipped out of her room and into my own to dress. It was far too early to be awake—I'd only slept an hour in total—but I had responsibilities.

Teta met me in the king's quarters—my quarters—a steaming mug waiting for me on the desk. I took a drink and made a face. Mint. I hated mint.

"You needed something to wake you up," she said.

I shot her a glare but choked down another swallow. The heat of it was welcome, if nothing else. The castle was frigid this morning, most likely due to the massive hole in the east wall and the fine layer of frost outside.

"Any more losses overnight?"

She nodded, her face grim. "Lord Pepin died an hour ago," she said, naming the nobleman who'd been with my father during the attack. "A couple of the guards may not make it through the day, but the rest should recover."

Three guards killed, plus two more injured to a point where they wouldn't return to their duties. And another dozen of my people dead from the collapse of the east wall.

Whoever did this would die an excruciating death. I just had to find out who it was—and how to kill them without embroiling my people in a war we couldn't win.

"All quiet?" I asked. I'd tripled the guards on duty around the castle and assigned them random patrols. Not that it would help much against a second attack, considering our weakened state, but I'd have to be a fool to leave us unguarded.

"All quiet," she confirmed. "I sent messengers to our contacts in München, but no response yet. Your advisors will be ready to meet with you in—" she glanced at the large clock on the mantle. "—ten minutes."

I sank into the chair, my head already pounding from stress and lack of sleep. "Any idea who it was?" The letter I'd found in Annika's room had seemed to implicate Bavaria, but I wanted Teta's opinion.

She didn't hesitate. "Wilhelm."

The duke of Bavaria, as I'd thought. "He's wanted our land for years," I conceded. "But would he risk war?"

"I doubt he'll make an outright claim. He just needs us weakened."

"And how did they manage to block our magic?" I frowned up at the ceiling. When I saw the mercenaries marching forward, unaffected by the song the Delegates played, dread had coursed through my blood. It still lingered there. Our people weren't safe. Annika wasn't safe. There was nothing I could do to protect them.

"Humans have been working on a way to do that for generations, Loic. It was bound to be successful at some point."

I ran a hand through my hair and let out a deep sigh. "How am I supposed to do this, Teta?" I hadn't planned on being king for years. Decades. Now overnight I'd been thrust into the role, with my kingdom under attack and more than a dozen of my people killed. My father had been a bastard, but at least he would have known what to do.

She took a seat on the desk, facing me. "Abdicate and go live in the forest?" I scowled, and she shrugged. "Or, if that doesn't work, do what all good kings do. Take counsel." She kicked the leg of my chair. "You're not doing this alone. You've got a whole team of advisors to help you." With a grin, she signed, *And a beautiful woman to comfort you.*

I scowled harder, ignoring the tension in my chest at the mention of Annika. I wished I was back in bed with her, rather than here worrying about the fate of my kingdom. Last night had been incredible. She'd been beautifully receptive to my touch, and the flush in her face when—

I cut off my thoughts before I could follow them to completion. I didn't need to go into the council meeting thinking of my songbird's arousal.

As though reading my thoughts, Teta smirked. *How is Annika? Not too tired, I hope.*

I rolled my eyes. "She was still asleep when I left." Was she awake yet? If so, she was undoubtedly already hard at work, trying to atone for the grievous sin of finding comfort in my arms.

The thought made me pause. She'd forgotten her guilt while I was with her, but this morning it would be back to plague her. I didn't know what she would consider sufficient atonement. Starving herself, most likely. As though she hadn't experienced enough of that in her life.

I reached for a sheet of paper and a pen.

Songbird, I wrote.

Knowing your tendency toward self-inflicted starvation, I thought it necessary to take precautions. I expect you to eat before you do anything else. There will be consequences should you disobey.

Teta watched me, still smirking, as I rang for Josef and handed him the note. "Deliver this to Mrs. Brandt's room. And take her something sweet to break her fast, and a large cup of milk. If she's not in her room, find her, and don't leave until she's finished eating." My songbird had a sweet tooth, I'd noticed. Despite the fasting she occasionally tried to subject herself to, she'd never yet managed to avoid the temptation of sugar.

As Josef left the room, I stood with a heavy sigh. "Well, then. Time to go *take counsel* with my advisors."

ANNIKA

That night, I returned from the infirmary to a dark, empty room. I shook off a nagging feeling of disappointment. I'd half-expected I'd find Loic waiting for me, but I should have known better. He was the king. He had responsibilities.

It was for the best. I was exhausted, and I'd managed to convince myself during the day that I wouldn't sleep with him again. I didn't expect that resolution to last long in his presence, but I could lie to myself.

I didn't bother lighting a candle as I stripped down to my long shirt and crawled into bed, shivering despite the small fire. I was nearly asleep when my bedroom door opened. I sat up, knots forming in my stomach.

"Did I wake you?" Loic asked, his face obscured by shadow.

"No."

"Good." He pulled off his jerkin and doublet and sat down at the foot of the bed to finish undressing.

My throat went dry. "What are you doing?"

"Going to bed." Wearing only his shirt, he turned down the covers and climbed into bed next to me. "Unless you have other plans?"

I flushed, grateful for the dark. "I mean, why are you in my room?" I shouldn't want him in bed with me. Shouldn't want his warmth. Shouldn't want *more* than his warmth.

He laid down and tucked his arm around me. "Ease of access."

I huffed and tried to pull away, but he held me tight.

"I'm joking, songbird. As much as I would like to enjoy you again..." He slid his hand between my legs and stroked me once to emphasize his point, making me gasp. "It's late, and we're both tired." He moved his hand back up to my stomach. "Go to sleep."

I closed my eyes and tried, but I couldn't get comfortable. As I rolled over for the third time, Loic sat up and frowned at me. "Are you incapable of obeying, or do you do it just to vex me?"

"I'm trying. It's just—it's been a long day."

"Yes," he said slowly. "That's why I told you to go to sleep."

"No, I mean..." I sat up. "I've got too many thoughts in my head to sleep."

He let out a loud sigh and sat up to light the candle. The small flame illuminated his face. "Is there a solution, or am I to be subjected to a sleepless night? Because if I'm going to be kept awake, I'd rather it be for something more enjoyable than your tossing and turning." He trailed a suggestive look down my body. "I'm not averse to being used as a distraction for your thoughts."

I clamped my thighs together against the rush of heat that filled my core. Shouldn't want it. I shouldn't want it. "How was your day?" I asked in an attempt to distract us both from the temptation.

"Long." He watched my mouth, desire written on his face.

I swallowed. "Did you find out anything about the attack?"

"Not yet." His eyes flicked to mine. "I have suspicions, but we're waiting on news from München." He raised a brow. "You never mentioned how you knew the woman who sent you that letter."

The heat in my core died at once. "She was a friend from Augsburg. She owns an apothecary." A thought crossed my mind, and I sat up straighter. "You're not going to do anything to her, are you? She just wanted to keep me safe. She didn't have anything to do with this."

"If she had nothing to do with it, then we won't touch her." His face was stony, and the candle cast an eerie light on it.

I didn't miss the implication: if she'd been involved in any way, nothing would stop him from avenging his people. But Gisela couldn't have done this. She had the motivation after a piper killed her husband and son, but a shopkeeper wouldn't have the means to hire a team of mercenaries.

But the duke would, and she'd said to send word to her at the duke's castle.

"How did you meet her?" Loic asked.

"She helped me to find you." I took his hand. "She didn't do this. She couldn't have."

"This was the same friend who gave you the protection against our magic?"

I frowned. I'd forgotten about the balls of fabric she'd given me, soaked in a potion to stop the pipers' magic. "Yes, but they didn't work."

He pulled his hand from mine. "She's had months to perfect her technique. Is it so unbelievable that she could have been the one to equip the men who attacked us? How else would she have known to warn you?"

"She's close to someone at the castle in München. She probably overheard something." I stood and reached for my robe, needing distance from him. "She didn't do this, Loic." I couldn't believe that someone who'd been kind to me could cause such devastation, no matter what losses she'd suffered.

He considered me, lips pressed together, and nodded. "You may be right." He pulled me back onto the bed.

I leaned my head against his chest as he wrapped his arms around me. "Thank you for listening."

He stroked my back but didn't respond. After a moment, he said, "You've handled the children's absence well."

"I'm glad they weren't here for this." Though I wished, desperately, that they were home safe with us now.

Home. Was that what Laute had become?

"But you still wish you were there with them."

I turned my head up to look at him. "I know you had to keep me here, but they're my kids. Of course I want to be with them."

He searched my eyes. "And if I'd let you go with them, would you have come back? Or would you have left me?"

A good question, and one I wasn't sure I could answer. "I don't know."

I could have sworn an expression of hurt flashed across his face. "And now?"

"No." I didn't have to consider it. "I couldn't leave you now." In the past two days, I'd realized what Laute and its people had become to me. What Loic had become to me. I couldn't imagine going back to my old life.

He rolled on top of me and captured my lips. "My sweet little songbird," he whispered. "You're finally mine." He pressed into me, and I moaned his name. Right or wrong, I didn't care anymore. I wanted him.

I expected him to take me then, but he pulled back, his expression turning serious. "You'll come back to me?"

I frowned, confused by the sudden change in his tone. "Am I going somewhere?"

"Just this once," he said. "Go to the children, and bring them back."

I stared at him. "You're letting me go?"

"I need them back here. It's not safe for my people outside the city, not after the attack."

His people. Warmth filled me. He thought of us, of me and the children, as his people.

He caressed my face, and his eyes narrowed. "And if I find you've lied to me and tried to run, I'll chain you to my bed and never let you leave."

I shivered at the threat in his words. Winding my arms around his neck, I said, "I couldn't leave you, Loic. Not anymore."

"Good." His mouth softened slightly. "You can leave in the morning."

"I'll hurry back."

TASTE OF FREEDOM

ANNIKA

My stomach twisted in knots as we neared the open city gate. Felix and Reimlin, my guards and companions, sat silent behind the horses. Loic hadn't been pleased at sending us with a wagon. We'd make better time with horses alone, he'd said, but I didn't know how to ride.

I couldn't believe he'd let me go. It was a sign of how much he'd come to trust me, that he was willing to let me go anywhere with just my word as bond.

As we entered the city, the pipers kept their hoods up to avoid drawing attention. They sat straight-backed, alert but undaunted by the city.

When I'd first come to Augsburg, I'd been overwhelmed by the sheer number of buildings, the magnificence of the cathedrals and the bustle of the streets as rich merchants and poor beggars mixed. Now, the city looked drab in the gray October light. Would anything ever compare to the opulence of Laute?

Pater Trost's *kirche* was in the middle of the city. We drove up just as midday Mass concluded. Ilse walked out, her horns covered in an angular red headdress—a gable hood, the piper noblewomen would have called it. She held baby Hans in her arms, and the rest of the children trailed behind her, all wearing hats of some kind so the piper children would be indistinguishable from the humans. The three guards Loic had sent with them stood at a distance; they seemed deep in conversation, but I knew they were alert to our movements.

"Mama!" Falk was the first to catch sight of me. He ran across the street and jumped up onto the back of the wagon as Felix, one of my companions, climbed down to speak with the other guards. "What are you doing here?"

"I'm supposed to bring you all back," I said, pulling him in for a hug.

Ilse and the rest of the children had reached us. "Nothing's wrong, I hope?" She frowned as she looked at Felix and Reimlin.

I climbed out of the wagon and helped Falk out. "There was an attack," I said, lowering my voice. "King Edric is dead."

Ilse gasped. "What happened?"

"I'll explain later. Loic—King Loic—asked me to bring you home."

"Is it not safe?" She clutched the baby to her chest. "Konrad won't be back until supper."

The oldest children wore worried expressions, while the younger ones ignored us. "I'm sure it's perfectly safe," I assured them. "The king just wants to cut your trip a little short. We can leave in the morning." I glanced at Reimlin, who nodded. Even if we didn't get back to the castle until the following afternoon, it would still be a full four days earlier than they'd planned. And staying for the night would give me the opportunity to attend confession and Mass. Perhaps I could even write to Brigid. Loic wouldn't have a problem with that now.

Pater Trost stepped out of the church. Catching sight of our group, he walked over. "Mrs. Brandt, I didn't know you would be here. It's good to see you again."

I smiled at the priest. "It was an unexpected visit. I'm not here for long."

"I hope you'll have time to come to confession before you leave?"

I glanced at Ilse, who said, "I had planned to take the children for a walk through the city. If it's—I mean—" She bit her lip and cast a nervous look up and down the street.

"Felix and the other guards can accompany you, Mrs. Bach," Reimlin said from the wagon street. "You will be safe. I can remain with Mrs. Brandt."

Pater Trost made the sign of the cross over Ilse and the children. "I will see you at Vespers, then."

I followed the priest into the church. Reimlin, at my side, looked warily around the empty sanctuary. When I opened the door of the confessional, the guard tried to follow me.

"I need privacy," I told him.

He frowned. "The prince—the king was specific in his orders, Mrs. Brandt. I'm not to let you out of my sight."

I should have known this tiny taste of freedom was too good to be true. I held the confessional door wide open. "You're not leaving me alone. Look. There's no way for me to go anywhere. If you sit down in one of the pews, you'll be able to see the door the whole time. Confession is private. I can't confess my sins with you breathing down my neck." Or with him reporting every word back to Loic. I needed to be free to tell Pater Trost about my hopes and fears without worrying how Loic would react. "You don't intend to sleep in the same room as me, do you? This is no different."

Reimlin took a few steps back and crossed his arms. He was far enough that he wouldn't overhear much. I sighed and closed the door between us.

A sense of peace washed over me in the darkness of the confessional. I closed my eyes and took a deep breath of the woody air. Crossing myself, I knelt and opened the screen between me and Pater Trost.

"Bless me, Father, for I have sinned. It has been nine months since my last confession."

"Proceed."

Where to begin? I'd committed so many sins since I last confessed. "I have failed to keep the Sabbath. I've kept hatred in my heart, and that hatred nearly got people killed. I've lied and betrayed, and...and I laid with a man outside the bonds of the marriage bed."

The priest was silent for a moment. Then he said, "You've had a busy few months since we last spoke, Mrs. Brandt. Why don't you tell me the whole story?"

The words rushed out of me. I told him of the Pied Piper's hatred of humans and the way Loic had claimed me. I told him about my fears that Loic would force himself on me and how he'd been kind in his own way. I told him how I'd feared and hated Loic, but over time, my loathing had turned to affection. When I got to the point of the attack on Laute, tears filled my eyes, but my heart was lighter than it had been in months.

"I know it was wrong to sleep with him, Father, but I was so scared I'd lost him, and he'd just been through so much…" My throat tightened, and I choked down a sob.

"You're in love with him, aren't you?" Pater Trost's voice was calm and collected, an anchor in the chaos of my emotions.

"I think I am. Is that a sin?"

"No." His voice seemed to hold a smile. "No, loving him isn't a sin."

"But I lay with him."

"And you have confessed. But you still desire him, don't you?"

My face heated, but I forced myself to answer. "I do." God help me, I did. Was I to be damned for all eternity?

"Saint Paul wrote to the Corinthians, *It is better to marry than to burn with passion.* And in his letters to Timothy he wrote, *I would have younger widows marry, bear children, and give the adversary no occasion for slander.*" He paused, and I could hear my breath, too loud in the small space. "You are young, Mrs. Brandt. What do you think the best course would be? How can you honor God where He has placed you?"

My skin felt too tight over my body. Was he suggesting… "I should marry him?"

"Are you asking me or telling me?" The priest gave a low chuckle. "It does seem to be the most logical solution. You care for him. If he feels the same—and I'm inclined to assume that he does—what could be more natural than marriage?"

My marriage to Nikolaus had been affectionate, but not passionate. With Loic, it would be different. Marriage with him would be full of excitement, of passion.

Pater Trost was still speaking. "You obviously care for his people, as well. I'm certain you would make a fitting queen."

Queen. The word clanged through my mind. If I married Loic, I wouldn't just be marrying the man. I'd be marrying the king. I'd be his queen. Could I handle that responsibility? Would he even want me to be his queen? Would his people want me?

"I've given you a lot to think about," the priest said. "There's no need to make a decision now. You can remain here for a while to think and pray, and I'll go introduce myself to your companion."

"What about my penance?"

"Say an Our Father."

I blinked several times. "Just one?"

"Christ already atoned for your sins," he said, "and it seems to me that you've done enough penance over the past few months. Say the Our Father and think on the promises of Christ." The wood creaked as he shifted. "Annika Brandt, I announce the grace of God to you, and in the stead and by the command of my Lord, Jesus Christ, I forgive you all of your sins. In the name of the Father, and of the Son, and of the Holy Spirit. Amen."

"Amen," I whispered. I heard the door to his side of the confessional open and close again, and a moment later, the murmur of voices. I took a deep breath, feeling at once freer and more confused than I had been before I'd entered.

Marrying Loic. The thought had never entered my mind, but now that it was there, I couldn't get rid of it. I was the last person he should want as queen—the last person he should want at all—but he cared for me. Did he care enough to marry me?

I could think and pray all day, but it wouldn't change anything. What I really needed was to talk to Loic, and I couldn't do that until

I returned to Laute. I crossed myself a final time and left the confessional.

Reimlin was frowning at the altar, looking ill at ease, while Pater Trost pointed to different symbols in the sanctuary. At the sound of the door, they both turned, and relief washed over Reimlin's face.

I hadn't thought how uncomfortable it would be for him to be in the house of a religion that called him a demon. Sour guilt filled my stomach. I should have been more considerate. I gave him a look that I hoped conveyed my regret.

"It was good to see you, Mrs. Brandt," Pater Trost said.

I smiled at him. "You as well, Father. Thank you." I bid him farewell and followed Reimlin out of the church.

Out in the cold autumn air, I turned to my guard. "I'm sorry," I said. "I should have realized how that must have made you feel."

"I go where you go. My personal feelings are irrelevant."

"Even so, it was insensitive of me. I apologize." I wasn't ashamed of my beliefs, but I was ashamed of the hatred displayed by others of my faith. I wished other Catholics could see the pipers for what they were: people in need of love.

"Shall we rejoin the others?" Reimlin asked.

"Actually, I have another stop I'd like to make, if that's alright."

He gestured for me to lead the way.

Gisela's shop looked the same as it had before I'd left for Laute. I didn't expect that she would be here, but I wanted to find out if she had left an address or if she would be returning.

As we reached the door, I glanced at Reimlin. "You might want to stay outside. The owner...has a history with the pipers." Even if she wasn't here, I didn't want to take the risk.

His mouth tightened, but he shook his head. "I go where you go," he said again. "They don't need to know who I am." He tucked his hood tighter around his face and pushed open the door.

A bell tinkled as we stepped into the shop. To my surprise, Gisela stood behind the counter, measuring out herbs with a wooden spoon. When she saw me, her spoon clattered to the counter.

"Annika! Thank God you're alright." She came out from behind the counter with her arms outstretched and wrapped me in a hug. "You got my message?"

I returned her embrace. "I did. Thank you."

"And your son is safe? And the other children?" She stepped back and looked me over. "When I didn't hear from you before Michaelmas, I was afraid you hadn't gotten out, but it was too late to stop it."

"The children got out, yes."

She caught sight of Reimlin and froze. His hood hid his face, but her eyes narrowed in suspicion. "You haven't introduced me to your companion."

"This is Reimlin. He's a friend."

Gisela pursed her lips. "Can we speak in private, Annika?"

I could tell by his stiff posture that he didn't like the idea, but I knew she wouldn't talk freely if she thought he could hear. "As long as we leave the door open." I gave her an apologetic smile. "He's a little protective, after..." I shrugged, letting her fill in the blank.

She scanned my face, then took my arm and half dragged me back to her sitting room. "Is everything okay? You got out, right?"

"Yes, everything is fine." I took her hand and squeezed it. "He's a friend, as I said. He's just trying to keep me safe."

"So you're home now."

"Yes." It wasn't a lie. Laute was my home now. I couldn't imagine being anywhere else.

"Good. I was worried my attack—"

"Your attack?"

"Yes, of course." She gave me an odd look. "Who did you think it was?"

"You hired the mercenaries?"

"Duke Wilhelm did." She glanced at the door, checking that Reimlin couldn't hear us. "He agreed to be my patron after I showed him I could block the pipers' magic."

The room was unbearably warm. I plucked at my collar. "You made it work, then?"

"Just recently." Her mouth turned down. "I'm sorry they weren't finished before you left."

"That's okay," I murmured, hardly listening. Gisela was the one who'd attacked the court. She was responsible for the Pied Piper's death. For all the deaths. My stomach churned at the memory of the throne room, filled with the bodies of the dead and dying.

"It wasn't a success, but it wasn't a complete failure. We killed the Pied Piper." She patted my shoulder. "They'll be in too much chaos to come after you."

A success. She considered the deaths of a dozen innocent people a success. I tucked my hands into my pockets to hide the shaking. "I hate to have to rush off, but I told Falk I'd be back by now. I just wanted to let you know I was okay."

"Of course. Thank you for coming."

I turned to go, but she grabbed my arm. "Annika, you know you can come to me, right? If you need help, I can protect you."

I smiled brightly despite my churning stomach. "Thank you, Gisela. I appreciate it." I had to get out of here before I was sick.

Forcing myself to move at a normal pace, I walked back into the main room of the store, where Mathis waited. He must have sensed

I needed the support, because he offered me his arm and led me out without a backward glance.

HOME

ANNIKA

The mass of emotions within me calmed as we drove out of the mountains and into Laute. The city spread out before us, unmarred by the attack. From here, the damaged castle wall wasn't visible.

Teta met us on the front steps of the castle. I'd expected Loic to greet us, but I should have known better. He was king. He had better things to do.

I was relieved not to see him right away. I hadn't yet decided how to broach the topic of marriage with him. Nor had I decided what to tell him about Gisela.

I hated what she'd done, but I understood why she did it. Under King Edric's rule, so many humans had been killed, including her husband and son. She didn't realize that most of the pipers weren't responsible for the atrocities the king commanded. She didn't know Loic wouldn't be a king like his father.

If I hadn't rushed out, I might have been able to explain it all to her.

Long trip? Teta signed as the wagons came to a stop.

I stretched. *Very.*

Loic-Ass is working with the guards. He said he'll see you tonight. She stumbled as Marta bowled into her.

"Teta!" the little girl said.

Teta grinned. "Did you miss me?"

She nodded, her braids swinging as she looked up at Teta. "The churches were almost as big as the castle!"

I smothered a laugh. Most of the children had never been to a city other than Laute. Small wonder they had spent the whole trip back chattering.

"Why don't you all get changed and meet us back in the schoolroom?" Teta told them, reaching out to ruffle Johann's hair. "Then you can tell me all about the city."

"Race you!" Peter shouted, bounding up the stairs. Falk gave a cry of annoyance and took off after him, and the rest of the children followed.

Teta turned to me. "You don't seem glad to be back."

"Just nervous."

"About what?"

"Loic and I haven't exactly had a chance to talk since..." I waved my hand around in a vague gesture. I hadn't told her what had happened between us, and I doubted Loic had either, but I was sure she knew anyway. She was astute. "I don't know what to expect."

She gave a sideways grin. "I wouldn't expect him to profess his undying love for you, if that's what you're worried about." My face fell, and she frowned. "Not that he doesn't care for you!"

"But he doesn't love me." I couldn't live in sin with him, but if he didn't want to marry me, I didn't know what other choice there was. I couldn't leave, not unless he let Falk and the other children go.

He could do that, though. Only the king could cancel the debt, but he was king now. If he loved me, wouldn't he free them?

"I think he's afraid of being in love again," she said.

"Again?"

Teta pursed her lips. "I shouldn't have said anything. It was a long time ago."

"What happened?"

"It's—" She sighed. "He was engaged, years ago. A love match, at least on his part. She was a lower-ranking member of the court. He found out she'd been sleeping with his father."

"No!"

She nodded. "He confronted her about it. He never told me what she said, but he was a wreck. He had her exiled. His father didn't bother to protect her. It's taken Loic years to trust again. You're the first woman he's been with since."

No wonder he was so closed off. My heart ached for him. If only there was some way I could show him I'd never hurt him like that. "I'm glad you told me."

"Don't say anything," she said. "It'll do more harm than good."

"I won't." But I would do everything I could to show him I loved him, and that he could love me back.

LOIC

My head pounded as I finally left the council chamber for the day. I'd known being king was exhausting, but I hadn't realized how draining it would be to spend the entire day with my father's—my—advisors. Most of them had been councilors before I was born, so they had the wisdom of age.

I rolled my eyes. The old men of my father's court were too set in their ways to be called wise. It was on their advice that my father had established the laws requiring us to take the lives of anyone who couldn't pay us. If I could, I'd have gotten rid of the entire council the instant my father died, but people were slow to change. If I overthrew the system, my court would collapse beneath me.

Fow now, I had to settle for small changes. With the execution of Alois and the death of Lord Pepin, two council seats remained open. I planned to appoint Teta to one; she was young, loyal to me, and didn't retain the same prejudices against humans as the rest of the council. But she was a woman, and it would be a fight to get her approved. And then there was the matter of the second seat. Several names came to mind. Konrad would be ideal, but would he be willing?

At least tonight I could put it all out of my mind and enjoy my songbird. I had hoped she would return immediately, rather than staying the night in Augsburg, but she was back now. Would she be waiting in my chambers or her own?

I hadn't yet moved to the king's chambers, but when I did, she would have to be moved to new rooms, as well. My father always kept a room for his mistresses off of his own chamber. I doubted Annika would accept that, though. She wouldn't consider it proper. I'd have to come up with an alternative.

The queen's chambers were empty.

My mind stuttered. No, I couldn't give those rooms to her. I'd thought to give them to another, a long time ago, and learned my lesson. Annika wouldn't want the queen's chambers, anyway. She had no interest in being queen. She was content with our relationship as it was.

"Your majesty!"

I fought the urge to groan as I turned to face the man who spoke. It was Reimlin, one of the guards I'd sent with my songbird into the city.

I didn't bother to hide the irritation in my voice. "What is it?"

He snapped to attention. "I wanted to apprise you of a discovery I made in Augsburg."

"Your debriefing can wait. Report to my chambers first thing in the morning." I turned away, dismissing him.

"Respectfully, your majesty, I don't believe this can wait."

I turned back to him and waved an impatient hand.

"While we were in the city, Mrs. Brandt made a stop at an apothecary. She and the woman went into another room, far enough that they didn't think I could hear them, but they talked about the attack on Laute." He waited for my reaction. When I didn't respond, he rushed on. "The woman mentioned that she'd warned Mrs. Brandt of the attack, and that she was responsible for the attackers' immunity to our magic."

So it had been Annika's witch friend. She undoubtedly felt betrayed. "Did they say anything else?"

"The woman said Duke Wilhelm hired the mercenaries. Mrs. Brandt didn't stay long after that."

More confirmation of Bavaria's involvement. Still, he was wasting my time. Annika could have told me all this herself. Unless he had reason to suspect she wouldn't tell me.

No, she wouldn't keep something like this from me. She had to know I'd find out, and she cared too much to keep secrets from me now.

I nodded to the guard. "You're dismissed." Without waiting for a response, I strode off in the direction of my songbird's rooms.

She sat on the couch near the fire, a book open on her lap. She wore a dressing gown over her long shirt, and her hair was loose, spread over her shoulders. She looked up as I came in, and an expression flashed across her face. Pity, or perhaps guilt. I frowned.

"I wasn't sure if you would come here or go to your own rooms," she said softly. "Falk is already in bed."

"Then I suppose we'll go to my room." I walked to the couch and extended a hand to help her to her feet.

She stood and threw her arms around my neck. Caught off guard, I stumbled before catching her. "Am I to take it that you missed me?"

She nodded, resting her head on my chest.

Her admission stirred up a strange feeling in me, and I leaned down to press a kiss to her lips. It hadn't even been two days, and yet she'd missed me. Was this what genuine affection looked like? Not someone thinking constantly about what they could get from the relationship, but a pure, simple desire to be with me.

I considered taking her then and there, but with Falk sleeping in the bedroom, I didn't want to risk being interrupted. I pulled her through the door adjoining our sitting rooms and bolted it behind us. Then I grabbed her face in my hands and kissed her again, harder this time. She responded with equal ferocity, moaning into my mouth.

I didn't want to wait. I tore the dressing robe off her and pushed her against the cold stone wall, sliding my hand between her legs. She was ready for me. I freed myself from my own clothes and was inside her in one smooth movement.

She wrapped her legs around me and drew me close, her eyes fixed on mine. I forced myself to go slow, pressing kisses to her face and neck until she was gasping my name. As she tightened around me, I moved faster, and my own release neared.

"Loic," she moaned. "I love you."

The words sent me over the edge, and I emptied myself into her, burning my head in the crook of her neck.

We stayed like that, clinging to each other, until our breathing slowed. I withdrew and placed her on her feet, then kissed her gently.

She didn't speak. I guided her into the bedroom and laid her down on the bed. The fire was already lit, driving away the dark and cold. I used a wet cloth to clean the evidence of our joining, and she watched me, her face shuttered.

Was she worried about how I would react to her declaration of love? Or did she feel guilty about what we'd done? She'd initiated it, but the woman felt guilty about everything. As to her confession, I didn't return the sentiment—it had been years since I was foolish enough to love anyone—but I appreciated hearing that she cared for me.

Unless she was lying. Eva had claimed to love me, as well.

I shook my head to clear the unwelcome thoughts. Annika was nothing like Eva. I stripped off my clothes and climbed into bed with her, pulling her back against me with my arm around her stomach.

"How was your journey?" I asked.

"Uneventful." Her voice was distant, distracted.

Uneventful? I would have thought her conversation with the witch counted as an *event*. "Did you see anyone while you were there?"

She turned to look at me, then glanced away. "Not really. I was only there for the day."

I narrowed my eyes. "No one?" Was she trying to protect the witch? She had to know I would find out.

"Well…" She sat up and twisted her hands together in her lap. A nervous habit, one she did when uncomfortable—or when hiding something. "I went to confession with Pater Trost."

I leaned on my elbow and quirked a brow. Was her priest involved in the attack as well?

She stared at her hands. "Loic, what are we?"

Was this an existential question? "I don't know what you mean."

"I love you, but I can't—" She sighed. "This is a sin. I can't keep doing this."

I sat up. "What do you mean?"

"Are you going to marry me?"

My jaw clenched. Why would she ask that?

She wrung her hands, looking up at the ceiling. "That came out wrong. I just—I want to be your wife. I want to be your queen."

She wanted to trap me into marriage. She wanted my title. I'd thought she was different, but she was just like Eva.

"I know you don't believe it, but what we're doing is a sin. I want to be with you, but I don't want to be damned for it."

It was a trick. It had to be. She couldn't honestly think I'd fall for it, could she?

When I didn't respond, she reached out to take my hand. I jerked away from her touch. I couldn't let her wiles cloud my judgment. "Did you do anything else while you were in Augsburg?" I asked, bitterness seeping into my voice. A test. If she loved me, she'd tell me about the witch.

"Why does that matter?"

She wasn't going to tell me. She said she wanted to be my queen, but she was protecting the witch who'd helped kill my people.

I stood, slipping on my old mask of indifference. "Why should I marry you? You're nothing special."

Hurt filled her face. "You don't mean that," she whispered.

"You don't honestly think you were the first woman I'd taken as mistress, do you?" I pulled on my robe. "You're good for a quick release, but you're far from noble. What could possibly possess me to make you my queen?"

"I know it's hard for you to trust, but you can trust me." Her eyes glistened with tears. Another weapon in her arsenal. "I'm not like her."

Someone had told her about Eva. Probably Teta. She was always sticking her nose where it didn't belong. "Not like who?"

"Like the woman you were going to marry. I wouldn't hurt you."

Liar. I stole her son. She'd carve out my heart and stomp on it if it meant she could go home. I'd almost fallen for her act, too. I'd almost believed she cared for me.

If she hadn't tried so hard, I might have been caught in her trap.

I put on the wicked smile I knew she hated. "Little songbird, you couldn't hurt me if you tried."

My words hit their mark. She flinched. She wasn't done trying, though. She reached out her hand again. I stared at it with cold eyes until she let it drop.

"I love you, Loic. I want to be yours."

I let out a humorless chuckle. "You are mine. You're my pet, my exotic little songbird. But no one marries a pet. A songbird can't be a queen."

A tear slipped out, cutting a path down her face.

"I'll give you a choice, though. You can stay here in my court, remain my little pet, and things can go on as they have been. Or you can go home. No questions asked, you can take your son and go back to your old life."

She wrapped her arms around her waist as more tears fell down her cheeks. "You know I can't just leave," she whispered. "The children need me."

"Take them, too. I'll cancel the debt." If she loved me, she wouldn't want to leave, but I knew she couldn't resist the temptation. It was everything she'd wanted since the first moment she set foot in Laute. "What will it be? Do you love me enough to leave things as they are, or will you fly away now that I've opened your cage?"

"You know that's no choice." Her voice was thick, her face red and splotchy. She was a better liar than I'd thought. "We can't go on like this."

As I'd expected. The instant I gave her the chance, she was ready to flee from me. If I'd been foolish enough to fall for her lies, the realization might have hurt.

"Then you can leave in the morning. I'll send someone to escort you out of the valley." I left her alone in my bed. I wouldn't sleep here tonight. I'd sleep in the king's chambers, where I belonged.

ALONE

ANNIKA

I didn't know how long I lay there alone in his bed, but at last I forced myself to my feet. Stumbling out of the room, I found my dressing gown on the floor where he'd dropped it. I pulled it on, not bothering to fasten it as I left the room.

Teta. I needed Teta. She could fix this.

I let myself into her quarters without knocking—it wasn't as though she could hear me. Despite the late hour, she was still at her desk, writing something in the lamplight. Her desk faced the door, and she looked up as I entered.

What's wrong? She rushed to me and wrapped an arm around my shoulders. Guiding me to a seat, she asked, *Are you hurt?*

I shook my head, crying too hard to answer. She offered me a handkerchief, and I wiped my streaming eyes as she rang for a servant.

"Bring a bottle of spiced wine," she told the girl who came. Then she took a seat next to me and pulled my head down onto her shoulder. "Should I go get Loic?" she asked as she rubbed my back.

I cried harder, shaking my head again.

She pulled back and looked into my eyes. "Did he do something to you?"

I opened my mouth to respond, but no words came out. *He wants me to leave,* I signed.

"He what?"

The servant returned with a bottle and two cups. I could feel her questioning eyes on me as she poured us each a cup, but Teta waved her out of the room.

I took a large gulp of the drink, barely tasting it, and closed my eyes to calm myself. "He told me to go home in the morning. He's sending the children with me."

"You must have misunderstood. Is he letting the children go home?"

"No, he—" I choked on the words. Lifting my cup, I drained it in another swallow. Teta refilled it. "He doesn't want me anymore."

"I don't believe that. What did he say?"

"I told him I'd missed him while I was gone, and that I loved him. I told him I would never hurt him like she did, and I wanted to be his wife."

"Oh, Annika." Teta wrapped me in a hug, and I clung to her. "He's just scared."

I shook my head. He wasn't scared. He was trying to hurt me. I'd pushed him too far, asked for too much. He didn't want me.

"Listen to me." She took me by the shoulders and looked into my eyes. "Loic's father took everything he ever loved. Now whenever anyone gets too close, he pushes them away. I know you're hurt right now, but he cares for you."

"You didn't see the look on his face," I whispered. The coldness in his eyes had burned through my soul.

"He's a bull-headed ass, but he doesn't want you to leave. I'll talk to him. We'll fix this."

Could she? She knew him better than anyone, but the Loic I knew wasn't inclined to fits of passion. He didn't change his mind on a whim. Still, if anyone could fix things between us, it would be Teta. *Thank you,* I signed.

She pressed a kiss to my forehead. "Stay here and get some sleep. Things will be better in the morning."

LOIC

The door to my bedroom slammed open. "What were you thinking?"

My guard followed Teta into the room. "I'm sorry, your highness. She insisted."

As if my head didn't ache enough. Looking down at the incomprehensible pile of paperwork before me, I pinched the bridge of my nose. At least I hadn't bothered going to bed yet. "Leave us."

He backed out of the room and closed the door. Teta stormed across the room, hands on her hips. "Do you have any idea what you're doing?"

I waved at the papers. "I'm working. Or trying to."

"Annika is on my couch right now, sobbing her eyes out. She seems to think you're banishing her from Laute."

So, when she'd failed to get her way, she'd gone running to Teta. It was almost too predictable. "Quite the opposite. I gave her the choice to stay or go. She chose the latter." As though none of our time together had meant anything to her. As though she hadn't been begging me to marry her moments before she decided to leave.

"Only after you did everything you could to make her hate you."

"Why would I need to make her hate me?" Annika didn't need more reasons to hate me. I'd stolen her son, forced her to act as my whore, and let my father nearly kill her. I should have known she'd never care for me after all that, but I'd let myself believe the pretty lies.

"Stop that," Teta snapped.

I set down the paper in my hand and frowned at her. "Stop what?"

"Stop acting like this. Annika Brandt is the best thing that's ever happened to you, and you're going to let her walk out of here like you don't even care."

How dare she act like she knew what was best for me? She knew nothing of my life. I kept my voice and expression calm despite the rage seething beneath the surface. "Feel free to leave your opinion wherever it's wanted, Teta."

"Oh, drop the court act. Your father's not here."

"No," I agreed. "He's not. He's dead, and I have a kingdom to defend. So if you've finished lecturing me—"

"Lecturing you? I haven't even started lecturing you. Until Annika got here, I hadn't seen a genuine smile on your face in years. And you want to throw that away for what? Because you're scared to feel a little affection?"

"You think I care for that whore?"

"Take that back," she seethed.

"No." I refused to feel guilty for my words. Annika Brandt had played my whore willingly, and then she'd used her position to manipulate me.

"Fine." She threw up her hands. "You want to be miserable? Be miserable. Keep pushing everyone away. But don't blame me when you wake up one day and you're all alone."

I didn't move as she turned on her heel and stormed back out of the room. I didn't care. I couldn't. Every time I opened myself up to anyone, they betrayed me, and I couldn't leave Laute vulnerable.

LEAVING

ANNIKA

My eyes were dry and raw when I woke at dawn on Teta's couch. I sat up and looked around. She sat in a chair nearby, and I didn't have to ask how her conversation with Loic had gone. I could see the answer in her face.

I'm sorry, she signed.

I swallowed hard. "I'll go tell the children to pack." I paused. They'd come to Laute with nothing but the clothes they wore. They'd been given new things, but would they be allowed to take them? I doubted Loic would let them leave with anything. The way he'd spoken to me, I wouldn't be surprised if he threw us out with nothing at all. My stomach twisted at the memory of the cruel smile on his face before he'd walked out.

"I already had the servants pack for them," Teta said. "There will be a wagon waiting for you at the front steps at noon."

I only had a few hours to say goodbye to the place that had become my home. "Do the children know yet?"

She shook her head. "I thought you'd want to tell them yourself."

They would be glad to be going home. I tried to find a shred of joy in myself. I'd see Brigid and Dietrich, and I'd been gone long enough, a new niece or nephew might be waiting for me.

I missed my sister, but I couldn't bring myself to be excited about returning to the tiny village I'd left behind.

I returned to the rooms I shared with Falk, studiously avoiding looking in the direction of Loic's rooms. Once dressed, I went into the bedroom and shook my son awake.

He pulled the covers over his head. "Five more minutes."

"You need to wake up." I pulled the covers back down. "We're going home."

He sat up and blinked at me. "Home?"

"The village. Back to Tante Brigid." I smiled, tucking my heartbreak firmly away. There was no need for my grief to taint the children's happiness.

"But we just got back." He frowned in confusion. "We're going on another trip already?"

"Not a trip. We're going home to stay."

His frown deepened. "We're leaving Laute? Why?"

"It's time. Past time."

"What about Loic?"

I ignored the thud of my heart at the mention of his name. "King Loic has agreed to let us go home."

Falk threw off the blankets and climbed out of bed. "I'm going to go talk to him."

"No, you're not. We have enough to do, and the king is a busy man." I didn't want Falk subjected to the sudden cruelty of the man I'd come to love. He didn't need to be caught in the middle of this.

"He wouldn't just send us away," Falk insisted. "He wouldn't do that."

My heart, already breaking, shattered at the hurt on my son's face. I brushed his hair back. "He knows it's best for us to be with our own people. It doesn't have anything to do with you."

He turned an accusing look on me. "What did you do, then?" Not waiting for my answer, he rushed out the door, nearly bowling Teta over in his haste.

He didn't take it well? she signed.

I shook my head. *He wants to talk to Loic.*

I'll talk to him. She gave me a sad smile. *You can go to the others.*

The rest of the children had mixed reactions to the news. Little Johann had only vague memories of his parents, having been only two when they were taken. "I stay!" he cried when he finally understood we were leaving.

His sister Marta put an arm around his shoulders. "Maybe we can come back and visit everyone," she said. "But Mama and Papa miss us. Don't you want to see them?"

Peter was more enthusiastic. "My father will be glad to have an extra hand in the business." His father was a merchant, handling the bulk of the trading for the village. The skills he'd learned from Konrad would serve him well back home.

I tried to smile. It would be good for them all to be back with their families. I just prayed they wouldn't be returning to a life of hard work and poverty.

Too soon, Teta was helping me button coats and wrap scarves around the children's necks. We walked to the front doors of the castle, and I reached for Falk's hand. He pulled away. He hadn't been able to speak with Loic, and he refused to look at me.

Outside, a crowd waited at the foot of the castle steps. Konrad and Ilse were there, with chubby baby Hans in his mother's arms. People of all ages smiled up at us, from friends of the children to pipers I'd befriended after the attack. Hugo, the sweet old cook, stepped forward as we descended the steps and pressed a warm, heavy bundle into my hands.

"Some lebkuchen for the journey," he said, his blue eyes twinkling. "As long as you promise to share with the children."

I held the bundle to my nose and sniffed the sweet and spicy aroma of my favorite cookies. My eyes prickled. "I promise."

I tried not to cry as the children shared hugs and tears with their friends. Konrad stopped Peter and Falk to shake their hands. "You'll be fine businessmen," he said, and the boys' chests nearly burst with pride.

Ilse hugged me, tears in her own eyes. "God's blessings, Annika. We'll miss you."

I swallowed the lump in my throat. "I'll miss you too. I wish I could stay to see this one grow up." I tapped Hans's nose with my finger. "You'll come visit?"

"Of course we will." Konrad took my hand and pressed a heavy purse into it. Coins clinked in the bag.

"I can't take this," I said, trying to hand it back.

"You'll take it, or I'll subject you to a three-hour sermon on gratitude." He grinned at me. "Take it, and go with God."

I clenched my fist. The pain of my nails digging into my palm served as an anchor against the tears. "Thank you, Konrad."

Teta waited by the wagon. She hugged each child and helped them up into their seats. Finally, she turned to me.

I'll miss you, Annika. She smiled, but her eyes glistened.

I'll miss you, too, Teta. I threw my arms around her neck.

She squeezed me tight, then pulled back. "I'll write as soon as he comes to his senses."

That wouldn't happen, but I appreciated her optimism. "You'll come visit, too?"

"As soon as I can." She hugged me again.

I climbed into the wagon, and the driver made a clicking sound at the horses. We started off. I put my arm around Johann and took one last look at my home. On the highest balcony, I saw familiar dark horns silhouetted against the gray October sky. Loic.

His face was too far to see. Did he regret sending me away? Or did he wish he'd never let me stay to begin with?

I couldn't watch him any longer. If I did, I'd lose all resolve, and I'd throw myself at his feet and beg him to let me stay. So I turned ahead and left my heart fading in the distance behind me.

THE VILLAGE

ANNIKA

Nothing had changed.

As we reached the outskirts of the village, the late afternoon sun showed a familiar scene. The street was quiet, smoke rising from the chimneys as people prepared their suppers. The once-comforting sight left me feeling empty inside.

The nearest barn door was ajar. Inside, Hans Weiss had just finished milking his goat. At the sound of our approaching wagon, he came to the door, milk bucket in hand, and peered out with a curious expression. His eyes landed on his children, and the bucket crashed to the ground.

"Papa!" Marta scrambled out of her seat. I called for the driver to stop. The wheels had barely stopped turning before she jumped off back of the wagon and ran to her father, her sister only steps behind her. Their brother Johann, asleep with his head on my lap, sat up and looked around blearily.

The shouts drew others onto the street. In moments, we were surrounded. The wagon emptied as parents reunited with their children. Hans Weiss pulled a bewildered Johann from my arms and pressed kisses to the boy's head as his daughters clung to his legs. Peter shook hands with his grandfather, the head of the town council, as though he were an adult returning from business, but he couldn't hide the grin that spread across his face. Tears filled every eye, and everyone wanted to hug me or kiss my hand.

Murmurs of, "Bless you, Annika," and "You're a Godsend, Mrs. Brandt," echoed in my ears. I tried to smile and return the embraces, but what I wanted more than anything was to be alone. I slipped my hand into my pocket and clutched my medallion. *St. Anne, pray for me.*

"Tante Brigid!" Falk's shout rose over the babble of the crowd. I turned to see my sister approaching. Her hair was braided in a married woman's coronet—she'd forgotten her headscarf—and her belly was large and round. Dietrich walked with her, an arm around her waist.

I ran to her and threw my arms around her neck, and a deluge of tears burst from me. She held me tight, rocking back and forth. Behind me, I could hear someone speaking to the crowd, but I couldn't understand the words.

When we finally pulled apart, the street was nearly empty. Brigid hugged Falk as I wiped my eyes. Dietrich stepped up next to me, his hands in his pockets.

"We'll have a council meeting next week, once everyone's had a chance to settle in," he said. "Let's go home. Is there anything I can carry, Annika?"

I looked around for our wagon driver, but he had disappeared along with the wagon, leaving our trunks in the middle of the street.

I'd hoped to thank him for returning us safely, but he must have left in the middle of the confusion. It was for the best; I didn't know how the villagers would respond to a piper, even one who was returning their children. I wished he hadn't left so quickly. His absence felt like the severing of one more thread that tied me to Laute.

I pointed to my trunk, and Dietrich picked it up. Falk took his own pack, and we walked down the street toward Brigid's home.

The house was a small farm on the other side of the village. It was a standard farmhouse, a byre-dwelling, with the barn attached to the house. The smell of stew filled the air as we stepped into the kitchen. Brigid took off her cloak and hung it on a hook, then rushed over to the fire and stirred the pot.

"I thought it might have burned," she said, "but I think it's okay."

My stomach rumbled, and I flushed.

My sister grinned. "I'm just going to add a little more to it. It'll be done soon."

"Come with me, Falk. I'll show you where to put your trunk." Dietrich jerked his head toward a door on the other side of the room, and Falk followed him through it.

Brigid poured a pitcher of water into the stew and tossed in some small vegetables. "We don't have an extra bed, but there's a straw tick mattress in the stables that you can sleep on until we get something more permanent."

I took a seat in one of the two chairs at the table and looked around the house. The door Dietrich and Falk had gone through led to the barn, and across from it was the door to the bedroom. It was larger than the home Brigid and I had grown up in, but the entire house would have fit into my sitting room at court.

"I forgot to congratulate you," I said loudly, trying to drown out my thoughts.

Brigid blushed and placed a hand on her stomach. "I tried to talk Dietrich into waiting until you returned, but he insisted."

"I'm glad he did. You'd kept him waiting long enough," I teased.

She rolled her eyes. "He wanted to marry me the day you left. Pater Huber made us wait a whole month so the banns could be read."

I rolled my eyes as well. The banns were used to ensure there was no reason a couple shouldn't be married—that they weren't too closely related or already married to someone else. In most cases, it was a good practice, but given the special circumstances and the fact that Dietrich and Brigid had known each other since childhood, an exception could have been made. Not that Pater Huber, our village priest, would ever consider deviating from routine.

Changing the subject, I nodded toward her belly. "When are you due?"

"Two months." She looked down, rubbing her hand in a circle. "I haven't told Dietrich, but I think it's a boy."

I reached over and pressed a hand to her stomach. "Is he moving?"

"A little." She prodded near my hand, and I felt a kick in response.

"He's a strong one." An ache opened up in my chest. Not jealousy, but something like it. I would have loved another child, but Nikolaus and I had struggled to conceive. After we'd been blessed with Falk, I'd prayed for more children, hoping to give Falk siblings, but it seemed I wouldn't be granted that blessing.

Dietrich and Falk returned to the kitchen, each holding a stool. They set them at the table as Brigid took the pot from the fire and ladled out four bowls of thin stew. She took a loaf of bread from the shelf next to the stove and cut it into four pieces.

Dietrich folded his hands and prayed. "Benedic, Domine, nos et haec tua dona quae de tua largitate sumus sumpturi, per Christum Dominum nostrum. Amen."

"Amen," I whispered. It wasn't like praying with Konrad and Ilse. Konrad always prayed so we could understand. *Latin is for Mass,* he would say. *God can understand us no matter what language we speak. Besides, if we wanted to pray in God's language, we'd be speaking Hebrew. Christ was a Jew, after all.*

A pang of homesickness hit me, and I took a large bite of stew to wash it down. It was thin and bland, though I knew that if I'd tasted it before Laute, I would have thought it was delicious. My time among the pipers had made me spoiled and greedy. I swallowed and forced myself to take another bite.

"So, you talked the pipers into letting them go." Dietrich dipped his bread into the stew. "How did you manage that?"

"They didn't let us go," Falk said, picking at his bread. "Loic kicked us out."

"Falk!"

"What?" He shrugged. "It's true. I heard the servants talking about it while they were packing."

Brigid looked between us. "Who's Loic?"

"The new Pied Piper," I said, as Falk said, "Mama's paramour."

Dietrich choked on the bite he'd just taken. "Her what?"

My face grew red. "He's not my—He's—Do you even know what that word means?"

"That's what the servants called you." Falk scrunched his nose. "It means you're in love."

Dietrich and Brigid stared at me. I closed my eyes and took a deep breath. "That's not what it means, and I don't want to hear you using that word again." I would have enough difficulty adjusting back to life in the village without my son telling everyone the Pied Piper was my lover. Even if it had been true. Opening my eyes again, I said, "There were some misconceptions about the nature of my relationship with King Loic while I was in Laute."

Brigid raised a brow in the exact same expression our mother used to make when she knew we were lying. "The new Pied Piper."

"King Edric, the old king, was killed last week." I wanted to be relieved at the slight change in topic, but I knew better. She wouldn't question me in front of Falk, but she'd have her answers eventually, no matter what my thoughts on the matter. She was unstoppable when she wanted something. "His son, Loic, took over."

"Was killed?" Dietrich asked. "By who?"

"The court was attacked."

Brigid's spoon lay forgotten in her bowl, her wide eyes fixed on me. "You weren't in any danger, were you?"

I waved away her concerns. "I was fine, and the children weren't there."

"Where were they?"

Falk perked up a bit. "Mr. Bach took us to Augsburg for Michael-mas."

Brigid gave me a questioning glance. "Mr. Bach is a Christian living in Laute," I explained. She wouldn't understand if I said he was a piper. "He's a merchant, and he taught Falk and Peter some of his trade."

"Did you learn much?" Dietrich asked Falk.

His chest puffed with pride. "He said I'm a natural."

Dietrich grinned. "Excellent. Maybe you can go to town with me next time I head to market. I could use an extra hand."

Warmth filled me. Despite his distress at having to leave, Falk wouldn't struggle to readjust to the village. He would miss Laute and his friends there, but he was resilient. And with the money Konrad had given me, he wouldn't have to work to keep us from starvation. He could learn a trade, or perhaps even go to school. I hadn't had the chance to count the money, but I'd looked in the purse. It was a veritable fortune in our village. It would be pocket change to a piper, but for me and Falk, it could change our lives. Not in the way I'd hoped for them to be changed, but we wouldn't have to live in poverty.

After we finished eating, Dietrich rose and stretched. "I'm off to bed. I've got to be up early with the sheep." He walked past Falk and patted his back. "If you like, you could come with me. I could use an extra man."

Falk nodded, putting on a serious face that did nothing to mask his excitement.

"I'll wake you when I get up."

As Dietrich disappeared into the bedroom, Falk stood and stretched as well. "I'm off to bed, too, then. Night, Mama. Tante Brigid." He nodded to both of us and strode out the door to the barn, his hands in his own pockets in imitation of his new uncle.

I glanced at Brigid, expecting to see her suppressing laughter at Falk's swaggering walk, but she frowned at me.

"What?"

"Did he—" She shook her head. Taking two of the bowls to the washtub, she wiped them clean.

I picked up the remaining bowls. "What?"

She took them from me and stared down at them. "Did he force you to be his mistress?"

Force me to— "Loic? No!" It shouldn't bother me, considering he'd let all of Laute believe that was what he'd done, but I hated to have her think badly of him. Even if he wasn't mine. "He's not like that."

"So you did it deliberately, to get the children back." She nodded as she washed out the other bowls. "I know it's a sin, but I'm glad you brought them home. Was he the one who took them?"

"No! I didn't—I mean, yes, he was the one—" She wouldn't understand. She was going to think I'd lost my mind. Still, I had to tell her. I couldn't let her think I'd used him like that. "Brigid, I'm in love with him."

The bowl she held fell into the tub. She stared at me.

I fidgeted under her stare. After a full minute of silence, I said, "Brigid?"

She blinked. "Have you lost your ever-loving mind?" She sank into a chair, dishes forgotten. "You fell in love with the demon that stole Falk?"

"He's not a demon," I snapped. Brigid flinched back, and I sighed. "I'm sorry. I just..." The pit in my chest threatened to swallow me. Tears leaked onto my cheeks as I sat down. "He never wanted to take them, Brigid. He's nothing like Mama's stories. He's kind and caring, and he's—he's—" A sob overtook me. "He doesn't want me."

Sympathy and confusion battled on her face. She passed me a rag, and I wiped my eyes, taking deep breaths to calm myself.

"What happened to you?" she asked.

As simply as I could, I told her everything. How Loic had risked his father's wrath to save our village. How he'd allowed the court to believe I was his mistress while still maintaining my virtue. How I'd realized I cared for him on the night his father died.

"I thought he felt the same, but when I came back with the children and told him how I felt, he told me to leave." I wiped the tears from my eyes, but they kept coming. "He was so desperate to get rid of me, he told me I could take the children home."

Brigid brought her chair next to mine and pulled me into a hug. "He doesn't know what he's missing. You would have made an excellent queen."

"I didn't even *want* to be queen." I hiccuped. "I just wanted to be with him."

She rubbed my back. "I'm sorry it happened like this."

I leaned into her embrace, and we stayed like that until my tears finally dried.

HERO

ANNIKA

My head ached when I woke the next morning. Falk was already gone, leaving the mattress cold. I missed Laute, and not just because of Loic. I would have given anything for the soft bed I'd left behind. Every part of me hurt after spending the night on the hard, scratchy mattress. How had I lived with beds like this for so many years?

I twisted the kinks from my neck as I dressed and went to the kitchen. It was warmer than the barn, and Brigid stood at the table, kneading dough for the day's bread.

"Morning. There's porridge in the pot and beer on the shelf." She nodded toward the stove.

Serving myself breakfast, I took a seat on a stool and balanced my bowl on my lap to keep out of Brigid's way. "You should have woken me."

"You needed the rest." She looked up at me and grinned. "Besides, I think the town might draw and quarter me if I upset their new saint."

I paused with my spoon halfway to my mouth. "Saint?"

"Oh yes." She placed the dough in a wooden bowl, then set it on the shelf to rise. "It's only an hour past dawn, and I've already had three people asking to speak to you." A knock sounded at the door, and she sighed. "Make that four." She wiped her hands on her apron and opened it.

Mathys Kiefer, the weaver who'd taken over my husband's practice, stood there. "Good morning, Brigid. Mrs. Brandt."

"Good morning, Mathys." Brigid stood back to let him into the house. "What can we do for you?"

"I just wanted to stop by and pay my respects to Mrs. Brandt." He took off his hat and pressed it to his chest. "What you did, bringing those children back—you're a hero."

Something unpleasant shifted in my stomach. "I'm not a hero, Mr. Kiefer, but I appreciate your kind words."

"I won't argue with a woman, but I believe we'll have to agree to disagree on that." He smiled, though his eyes held a touch of sadness. He'd lost his wife and infant daughter to the plague just days before the council called Loic. I wondered if he blamed them for not calling a piper sooner, or if he wished they hadn't made the call at all.

Brigid cleared her throat. "Can I get you something to drink, Mathys?"

"No, thank you. I've got work to do. I'll see you both at Mass on Sunday?" He looked expectantly at me, and I nodded. "Until then." He gave us each a brief bow and turned to go, then paused. "And Mrs. Brandt, if there's anything I can do to ease your return, please don't hesitate to ask."

I shifted in my seat, uncomfortable with the attention. "Thank you."

The door closed behind him, and Brigid gave me a pointed look. "See? You're a hero. Mrs. Weiss was already here with a basket full of vegetables from their garden. Don't start," she said when I opened my mouth to speak. "I already told her we wouldn't take it, but don't be surprised if she tries again. She said she opened her children's bags last night and found a bag of coins in each of them. She's convinced you're a miracle-worker."

"But I'm not a saint!" Konrad and Ilse must have put the money in the bags, or perhaps Teta. Even after we left them, our friends were still caring for us.

She raised her hands. "You don't have to convince me. I know you're no saint. I still remember the time you tipped Mama's rising bread dough onto the floor and blamed me for it."

I let out a laugh despite myself. "If I remember right, you had gotten me into trouble a week before for letting a goat into the shop."

She opened her eyes wide in feigned innocence. "I would never." Then she laughed. "My point stands. I know you're not a saint." She shrugged and turned back to the table. "Give it a few days. They'll get used to you again, and the worshiping will stop."

I spent the next few days hiding in Brigid's house, doing my best to avoid the constant stream of well-wishers. Mrs. Weiss stopped by twice a day to kiss my hands and thank me profusely for returning her children. All my protestations served to further convince her of my sainthood, as proof of my humility.

I prayed my fame would fade quickly.

On Sunday, I couldn't hide anymore. Hoping to attract the least amount of attention possible, I dug through my trunk for the simplest dress I could find. The fabric was much finer than anyone in the village owned, but at least it was dyed a modest brown, rather than the sumptuous reds, greens, and blues so popular in Laute.

As I walked through the church doors, I could feel everyone's eyes on me. Pater Huber, standing at the altar, frowned down at me. I hurried into the pew and bowed my head.

The start of the service sent a wave of relief through me. At least now I could lose myself in the familiar cadence of Mass.

When Pater Huber stepped up into the pulpit for the sermon, my sense of relief disappeared. The look of judgment he wore was aimed at me. "'God resisteth the proud, but giveth grace to the humble.'" He stared out at us, face twisted in fury. "Pride has wormed its way into our congregation. There are those among you that flaunt your wealth, your ill-gotten gains. Do you not know, sinner, that in death your riches will be taken from you? 'For when he dieth he shall carry nothing away.'"

His beady eyes pierced my soul. Was he talking about me? I'd spent every hour since my return hiding in Brigid's house. He couldn't think I'd been trying to flaunt the belongings I'd brought back from Laute.

"But pride and vanity are not the worst sins the Enemy has sent among us!" he went on. "Fornicators and adulteresses, liars and idolaters. Those who would sell their souls for earthly gain. And what do you do?" He looked out over the congregation, and my cheeks burned. Brigid took my hand and squeezed it. "You embrace them! As though the blessings of God are not enough for you. When God takes all from you as He took from Job, do you trust Him? Or do you kiss the feet of whatever false prophet promises a return to abundance?"

Each word he spoke hammered into my head. I wanted to stand up and scream that I was innocent of these things he was accusing me of, but I couldn't. I'd committed so many sins in my time away, and I'd spent the days since my return wishing to be back in Laute. Was it really Loic and my friends I missed, or did I long for the overabundance of the piper court?

I bowed my head as Pater Huber's words rolled over me. "These evils must not be allowed to stand. For the sake of your souls, your children's souls, you must expel these sins. Put away your vanity, you evildoers, and repent!"

He went on and on. By the time the service ended, I wished the floor would open up and swallow me. Brigid took my hand and pulled me toward the door.

"How dare he?" she hissed in my ear. "As though you didn't go through hell to bring them home. Don't listen to him, Annika. He doesn't know what he's talking about."

But he was the priest. Ordained. Chosen by God. How could he not know what he was talking about? I bit my tongue to keep from crying. What would Konrad say about all this? He hadn't criticized me for being Loic's mistress. We'd talked about sin and the need for repentance, but he'd always emphasized God's forgiveness. I never left a Sunday meeting in Laute bogged down with guilt and shame.

"Mrs. Brandt!" Pater Huber's voice boomed over the chatter of the exiting congregation, and I cringed. I turned to see his black robes billowing as he walked toward us.

"Good morning, Pater Huber." I felt like a child all over again, about to be scolded for fidgeting during Mass.

"You haven't been to Confession since you returned. I assume I'll see you this afternoon?" He raised a stern brow. "It has been nine months since you've confessed, after all."

I twisted my hands in my skirts. "I attended Confession just last week, actually."

He looked skeptical. "Oh? And where was that? I don't suppose there are many confessors at the demon court."

"In Augsburg, with Pater Trost at the Church of St. Thomas the Apostle."

"Hm. I hope he gave you an adequate penance. He has a reputation for frivolity."

I made a noncommittal sound. If I told him my only penance for nine months of sins had been a single Our Father, he'd be appalled.

"Pater!" Mathys Kiefer stepped between us and shook the priest's hand. "That was quite the zealous sermon. Was your beer a little sour this morning?" He laughed heartily, and Pater Huber's face pinched up. "Oh!" The weaver looked around and saw me and Brigid standing behind him. "So sorry, Mrs. Brandt, Brigid. I didn't see you there. How are you this morning?"

Brigid shot him a grateful look. "We're well, thank you, Mathys."

"I hope I'll see you all at the town meeting this week." He grinned at Pater Huber. "I'm certain our man of God won't miss it. The entire town will be there."

"I hardly think it's appropriate—" the priest began, but Mathys slapped him on the back.

"Nonsense!" he said. "After this past year, haven't we earned a little celebration? Christ's first miracle was turning water to wine, after all."

"If you'll excuse me. I see someone I need to speak with." Pater Huber bustled off, his lips pressed tight together.

"Thank you, Mathys," Brigid said.

"It's no problem. You've had enough stress lately; you don't need him adding more to it." He smiled at me. "Both of you."

"Thank you," I murmured. The guilt still gnawed at my stomach, but I felt better knowing my sister and Mathys Kiefer, at least, didn't think I'd corrupted myself completely.

"May I walk you home, Mrs. Brandt?"

I glanced at Brigid, who nodded. "Dietrich will stand around talking for the next hour. You go on ahead. I'll stay here and wait for him and Falk."

"Thank you, Mr. Kiefer."

He offered me his arm, and I took it. Threading expertly through the crowd, he managed to guide me out of the small *kirche* without anyone accosting us.

"I'm sorry you had to listen to that sermon," the weaver said out on the quieter street.

I stared at the rocky ground beneath our feet. "He all but called me damned."

"He's wrong. Besides, Mrs. Weiss thinks you're a saint. That has to count for something."

"I did what any mother would."

"And yet you're the only one who did it. I think you're selling yourself short, Mrs. Brandt."

"Everyone's making me out to be a hero or a monster," I said, my voice small. "It wasn't like that. I just wanted to save my son."

"I understand."

"Don't you resent me? Or the council?" I asked. "If they'd called a piper sooner..."

He shrugged. "It's hard to celebrate after everything I lost, but I can't begrudge them their happiness." He was silent for a moment. "What about you?"

I'd lost my love, my friends, and my home in one fell swoop, but he didn't know that. All he knew was that I'd saved my son.

"Your husband?" he prompted.

"Oh." Right. "It's been a long time. Not that I don't miss him, but..."

"I understand. I thought you might be angry with me for taking his position."

I had been, briefly, but that part of my life seemed like ages ago. "Not at all. You had a family to take care of, and I couldn't keep up with the work."

He gave a wry chuckle. "It's hard to do on your own. If I could afford an apprentice, I'd hire one. Without my wife, I don't know how I'm going to keep afloat."

"I'm sure you'll manage."

We'd reached Brigid's house. "Thank you for letting me walk you home," he said. "I'll see you at council this week?"

Brigid wouldn't let me miss it. "Yes, I'll see you then."

AN OFFER

ANNIKA

Walking to the inn the night of the town council was like walking back in time. Everyone was out, and I knew every face I nodded greetings as people I'd known my whole life smiled and waved at me. Apparently Pater Huber's sermon hadn't damaged my reputation irreparably.

The inn was packed full, the atmosphere as cheery as Christmas. Someone had moved the tables to the sides of the room, clearing the floor to fit everyone. In the corner, the inn owner had opened a barrel of beer and was passing out mugs. It wasn't a meeting so much as a celebration of the children's return.

Falk caught sight of Peter and ran off after him. I tried to squeeze into the back of the room with Brigid and Dietrich, but I had no luck. Elmar Beck, the council head, saw me and called over the babble of voices.

"Ladies and gentlemen, she has arrived!" He caught me by the arm and drew me toward the front of the room. I cringed as he raised his mug. "A toast! To the woman who entered the demon court and brought back our children: our hero, Annika Brandt!"

"To Annika!" they cheered.

My face flamed, and I ducked my head.

"Whore," someone hissed among the cheers.

I looked up, scanning the room for the source. No one else seemed to have heard it.

"Enjoy yourselves!" Elmar said. He handed me a mug of beer and added, "You can't know how grateful we are, Mrs. Brandt. The town is forever in your debt."

I lifted the mug to my mouth to hide my grimace. No one was in my debt. The only reason I'd managed to bring the children back was because Loic had tired of me. I gulped down my drink, the sour taste a distraction from my thoughts.

Elmar waved to someone across the room. "Excuse me, Mrs. Brandt." He wandered off, leaving me alone in the crowd.

In the corner, the baker had taken out a drum, and Hans Weiss put a flute to his lips. People cleared the floor in preparation for a dance.

The music that began was energetic but uninspired. I couldn't help but compare it to the pipers' ball, where the music had been pure emotion. Then, I'd felt entirely free, but here, even among the dancers that twirled across the floor, there was an undercurrent of something unpleasant. Some fear, some anger, some worry for the future.

Brigid popped up at my elbow. "Are you going to stare at your cup all night?"

"If I have to. Thanks for the rescue, by the way," I said, my voice dripping with irony.

She shrugged. "What was I supposed to do? I told you they'd turned you into a hero."

"Some warning would have been nice."

"I was as caught off guard as you. I thought we were coming to listen to you talk about how you'd managed to free them, or what to do now that you're back." She nodded at Mrs. Weiss walking toward us with single-minded intent, Johann on her hip. "Your greatest admirer is coming."

"Not again," I groaned. I'd already seen the woman today, and her praise grew more effusive every time I saw her. "Ward her off, Brigid. Please."

"Fine, but you owe me."

"Anything!" I ducked around a corner just before Mrs. Weiss reached us.

Mrs. Wagner, an elderly widow, stood in the corner nearest me. She and Pater Huber scowled out at the gathering, oblivious to my presence. "It's tainted," she was saying. "The earnings of sin. I don't care how badly they need the money. They can't use it."

"Exactly right," the priest agreed. "Using a whore's wages to provide for one's children is tantamount to whoring oneself. I've counseled the families to give the money to the Church."

Whore's wages? They had to be talking about the money we'd brought with us from Laute, but it wasn't payment. Loic hadn't paid me to be his mistress.

Didn't he? a voice in my head whispered. *The money came from Konrad and Ilse, but everything else came from him. You left home in rags, and you came back with a trunk full of fine clothes and books. How is that any different from a courtesan?*

"Mrs. Brandt?"

Mathys Kiefer stood in front of me. I blinked at him. "I'm sorry?"

"I'd asked you for a dance."

"Oh. Um, yes. Thank you." Anything to get away from the conversation I desperately wished I hadn't overheard.

"You looked like something had upset you," he said as he drew me into the movements of a dance. "Is it the celebration?"

"It did catch me by surprise, but no. As I said on Sunday, I don't resent them for celebrating."

"Then it's the dancing you object to." He grinned at me. "Only one dance, then, and I'll release you."

I forced a laugh. I didn't object to dancing—but I did object to the memories it brought up. Mathys Kiefer didn't hold me as tightly or look at me as hungrily as Loic, but I couldn't help thinking of him.

The dance ended, and Mathys stepped back. "Shall I send you back to the wolves?" he asked.

Pater Huber, standing on the edge of the dance floor, had caught sight of me. I knew that if he had the opportunity, he'd spend the rest of the night lecturing me. I took Mathys's hand again. "I'd prefer you didn't, actually."

He laughed. "Maybe some fresh air, then, since you don't seem fond of dancing." He put my hand on his arm and guided me to the door.

We stopped just outside, in a pool of light streaming from the window. The air was cold, frost just beginning to form on the ground. I shivered and tucked my shawl tighter around my shoulders.

"How are you adjusting to your return?" he asked.

"It's been hard, but we're getting there." At least, I hoped we were. Falk enjoyed shepherding with his uncle, but he had no spare time like he'd had back in Laute. He came home in time for supper and went to bed as soon as he finished eating. The schedule was too rigorous for a ten-year-old boy.

Mathys leaned against the wall of the inn. "Will you stay with your sister long?"

"We haven't talked about it. They're not in any hurry for us to leave."

"I'm sure they aren't. Your boy has been a world of help to Dietrich this week, and Brigid will want the extra hands around with the baby coming. Still, I expect you'll want your own space eventually."

"Probably." But moving out of Brigid's house felt too permanent. Like I was shutting the door on the possibility of returning to Laute. I wouldn't return; I knew that, but I couldn't help clinging to that last vestige of hope.

"I hope you haven't had trouble since Pater Huber's sermon on Sunday."

"No, of course not." Nothing but horrible comments.

"Good. I'd worried certain people might take it as a license to spew hate."

"Mrs. Wagner would like to, I'm sure, but I've managed to avoid her for the most part." I'd seen the vicious old woman glaring at me across the sanctuary on Sunday.

He let out a laugh that fogged in the autumn air. "Mrs. Wagner isn't happy without a reason to complain. Still, I hate that anyone dares to criticize you after what you went through for us. You're an admirable woman."

"I was beginning to like you, Mr. Kiefer, but then you had to ruin it by praising me." I gave him a wry smile. "I told you the other day, I've done nothing worth admiring."

"I suppose we'll have to resolve ourselves to disagreement on that matter."

"I suppose we will."

The sound of music filled the silence between us. Mathys cleared his throat. "This may be unexpected, but..."

When he didn't continue, I frowned. "Yes?"

He tucked his thumbs into his pocket. "We've both lost a lot over the past few years. I know we can't replace what we lost, but perhaps we can find a way forward together."

"I don't understand."

He smiled. "I'm sorry. I'm not being clear." He took my hand in both of his. "I loved my wife, but you're a strong woman. I admire and respect you. Mrs. Brandt—Annika—will you do me the honor of becoming my wife?"

"I—" I froze. In an instant, I could see my whole life before me. A marriage of convenience and mutual respect, just as my first had been. Decades of colorless existence. The undercurrent of fear and worry in the village worming its way into every aspect of my life. No passion. No joy.

No pipers.

No Loic.

"There's no need to answer right away," Mathys said, patting my hand. "I'm sure you have a lot to think about. Take a month or so to settle back into life here. Talk to your sister and your son."

The door to the inn opened, and Brigid stepped out. "Annika? Are you out here?"

"And speaking of," he said. "She's here, Brigid." He gave me a slight bow and dropped my hand. "Until later, Annika."

TRAITOR

Loic

I stared at the man quivering on his knees before my throne. I'd finally found him. The pathetic worm working with our enemies.

My father's cold voice came from my mouth. "What do you have to say for yourself?"

"Please, your majesty." He pressed his face to the ground. "It was a mistake. I didn't know—"

"A mistake?" I stood. "You conspired with foreigners, you delivered their messages, and you allowed them into our valley. Your actions caused the deaths of more than a dozen people, and you call it a mistake?"

"I didn't understand. I thought—I thought she only meant to kill the king—I—" Sobs engulfed his words.

Hugo. I'd seen the man before, many times. He was a cook, and though he'd worked in the castle for years, I hadn't known his name until he formed a particular friendship with my songbird.

No, not my songbird. The conniving harlot who'd pretended to be mine so she could take advantage of my position. She'd probably been working with him from the beginning.

She was beyond my reach now, but I could still punish him.

"You admit your guilt?" I asked. I could execute him without a direct confession, but such action would agitate my advisors.

"Yes, yes," he babbled. "Forgive me, your majesty. I only meant to—"

I cut him off. "For your crimes against the people of Laute and the late King Edric, I sentence you to be boiled alive." A murmur ran through the assembled crowd, but I ignored it. "Take him back to the dungeon."

"Please, no! Have mercy!" His screams echoed as the guards dragged him from the room.

Mercy. There was no place for mercy in my life. Not anymore.

As his screams faded, I took my seat on the throne once more. I looked out at my subjects and waited for their muttering to stop.

"This is what happens to those who betray my people." I looked around the room. No one would meet my eyes. My father would be proud; he'd done his best to instill in me that it was better to be feared than to be loved, and I'd finally achieved it. I was feared, and never again would I make the mistake of seeking love. "I make you this vow: no matter what power they have, those who seek to harm my people will face the same fate."

The room was silent. I waved a hand. "Dismissed." Not waiting for them to depart, I rose and strode out of the hall. My guard—after my father's death, I never went anywhere without at least one—followed me.

An additional sound of footsteps sounded in the hall. I glanced back to see Teta, her face grim.

Don't you think that was a little extreme?

Go away, I signed over my shoulder.

She caught me by the arm and turned me to face her. "You know, when I call you Loic-Ass, it's supposed to be an affectionate nickname, not a description."

"I think you've allowed our childhood connection to give you ideas above your station." I removed her hand from my arm. "You become too familiar."

"And you 'become' insufferable." She put her hands on her hips. "I don't know why you're acting like this, but ever since Annika left—"

I struck her cheek.

She reached up to touch where I'd smacked her, staring at me with wide eyes. My guard's eyes widened as well, though he stared fixedly at the wall.

I shouldn't have done that. I didn't even know why I reacted so vehemently to her mention of my—of Annika. She wouldn't let it go now.

I braced myself for the inevitable tirade, but she turned on her heel and walked away.

I stared after her, unsure how to take her lack of response. Maybe she'd realized how out of line she was and decided to leave before she caused more trouble for herself. It didn't sound like the Teta I knew, but I'd changed since my father's death. Was it so unbelievable to think that she might have changed as well?

I walked down the hall to the king's quarters. I hadn't returned to my old rooms since I began sleeping alone; I conducted all my business from here, so it made little sense to sleep elsewhere. The proximity to the council room alone saved me time.

The fact that I'd moved rooms had nothing to do with the fact that my old room still smelled of her. I hadn't set foot in her old rooms since she left, but I imagined the smell was even stronger there. And the memories—

I shook my head to clear it.

The castle was quiet now that she'd left. An unexpected benefit. No piper children lived in the castle, and with the human children gone, it was silent as a grave.

It wasn't *too* quiet, or too empty. That would imply that I missed the noise, which I didn't. I had enough to do without worrying about them scurrying underfoot, and having the traitorous woman gone was a reward in itself.

No, the emptiness around me—inside me—was a relief.

STRANGER AT HOME

ANNIKA

"Have you thought about what answer you'll give to Mathys?" Brigid asked over the quilt she was piecing together.

It had been two weeks since his proposal, and I still hadn't made a decision. I hadn't even told Falk about it. "I don't know."

"It's a good match." She put the needle between her teeth and snipped off a bit of thread. "You've been a weaver's wife before, so you'll settle in quickly. He's a good man."

I stared at the tiny gown I was sewing for the baby, barely seeing it. "He is a good man." With the money from Konrad, I didn't *need* to marry, but it would be easier than trying to get by on my own. Marrying Mathys would give me a certain amount of respectability, and with Pater Huber's poorly-disguised sermons about my wrongdoings, that respectability could protect me. It could protect Falk.

And it wasn't as though anyone else wanted me.

"I know he doesn't match up to your piper king, but he's safe," Brigid went on, rethreading her needle. "You could use 'safe.' I've heard rumors since you got back…" She trailed off.

"What?" I looked up at her, frowning.

She shrugged. "People are saying you came back different."

"Different how? Who?"

"I don't know. Just different." She frowned at me. "It's not just Pater Huber and Mrs. Wagner, either. Mr. Beck mentioned it to Dietrich the other day, and Hans Weiss told his wife to stop coming around here."

"I'd wondered why she hadn't made her daily pilgrimage the past few days."

"They're right, though. You did come back different."

They were right. In the stories our mother had told us, when someone went to the piper land, they always came back changed. They moved and spoke differently. Their eyes had a far-away look, and they acted as if human food was ash in their mouths.

After my months in Laute, I knew why people came back changed. Living among the wealth of the pipers made returning to village life almost painful.

"You know how people around here react to things that are different," she said when I didn't answer. "Haven't you been listening to Pater Huber's sermons?"

"Pater Huber delights in spewing hatred to anyone who will listen," I snapped.

She raised a brow. "He's a man of God, no matter how little we might like him. I know you care for some of the pipers, but that doesn't give you the right to go against everything the Church teaches."

"Did it ever occur to you that the Church might be wrong?" I set aside the gown; I hadn't made a single stitch since the conversation began. "There's a priest in Augsburg, Pater Trost, who told me the pipers aren't demons at all. He says they're human, like us."

Brigid sighed. "I don't want to argue with you, Ani. I just want you to realize how dangerous things could become. You've got a lot of supporters here, but you made some enemies, too. Some people think you made a deal with the pipers yourself, or that you sold your soul to them to get the children back."

I scoffed. If I'd tried to sell him my soul, Loic would have laughed himself hoarse.

A pang went through me at the thought of his name, and I shook myself. "I didn't sell my soul."

"Obviously," she said. "I'm just worried for you. People have been wary since you came back. If you settle down, the rumors will stop. I think you should say yes."

Say yes to Mathys's proposal, and confine myself to a lifetime as a weaver's wife in an impoverished village. Marry a man who didn't love me, who I could never love because I'd already fallen for someone else.

Before I could answer, someone knocked. "I'll get it," I said, grasping at the chance to leave the conversation.

I opened the door, but no one was there. I looked around and saw a dead dog on the doorstep, a noose around its neck. Bile rose in my throat.

"Annika?" Brigid came up behind me.

I whirled around, closing the door to keep her from seeing. She didn't need the stress in her condition.

"You're white as a sheet," she said. "What's wrong?"

"Nothing."

She reached past me and yanked the door open—she'd always been stronger than me. Glancing down at the poor creature, she pursed her lips. "As I said, you've made enemies."

"I'm sure it was just a misguided prank." I grabbed a large rag. "I'll go bury it."

Closing the door behind me, I wrapped the mangy creature in the cloth and picked it up. Despite what I'd told Brigid, I knew this was no prank. It was a threat.

"Good morning, Annika!"

I spun around to see Mathys coming up the street, several bolts of cloth in his arms.

"Is everything alright?" He frowned. "You look ill."

"Yes, I'm fine."

"You're shaking." He set the bolts down and reached out a hand. "What's wrong?"

"Just a mistake, I'm sure. It's nothing."

"It doesn't look like nothing." He pulled the cloth from the dog's head and quirked a brow. "Yours?"

"No. I...I found it. On the doorstep."

His gaze darkened as he saw the noose around its neck. "Do you know who did it?"

"I'm sure it was an accident."

He frowned at me and pulled the bundle from my arms. "You're smarter than that. Go inside. Is Dietrich home?"

I shook my head. "He and Falk are out with the sheep."

"I'll bury the dog. Lock the door, and don't open it for anyone else."

I darted a glance up the street. "You don't think—"

"They might be waiting to get you alone." He nudged me toward the door. "Go wait with your sister."

Brigid and I sat in silence. What was there to say? I'd known these people my whole life. The idea that one of them would threaten me, would kill a helpless animal just to frighten me... I couldn't imagine who would do such a thing.

At last, Mathys's knock broke through the tension. "It's me," he said through the door. I let him in, and he nodded a greeting to us both. He took my hand. "You're alright?"

"Is Falk safe? Should someone go get him?" I looked up into his face. His blue eyes crinkled with concern.

"I'm sure he's fine. Dietrich is with him, and this wasn't about him. It was about you."

"I told you people were upset," Brigid said.

I shot her a glare. "Not helping."

Mathys guided me to a seat. "Your sister's right. I've heard—" He cut himself off and shook his head.

"You've heard what?"

"Let's just say not everyone shares Mrs. Weiss's opinion on your sainthood. I heard a couple men in the inn last night make some rather crude remarks about how you managed to get the children free from the pipers." His face pinched in disgust. "I disabused them of the notion, but I doubt they're the only ones."

I stared at the ground. It wasn't as though their opinion of me was wrong. If I hadn't slept with Loic, if I hadn't offered to marry him, none of us would be here. The children would still be living at court, and I would still be Loic's *pet songbird*. If this was how people treated me based on rumors, what would they do if they knew the truth?

"I was just telling her the same thing," Brigid said. She folded up her quilt and set it aside. "This isn't going to blow over. She needs protection, and I don't think it's the kind Dietrich and I can offer." She gave me a pointed look, and I flushed.

"They're idiots if they think you'd sell yourself to the people who stole your son," Mathys said. "You're a good woman—better than most of this town. They shouldn't have called a piper in the first place, and then when they paid the price, they didn't have the courage to fight for their children." He shook his head. "Idiots, as I said."

"Idiots or not, it doesn't change what's happening." Brigid pursed her lips. "They don't see you as part of the community anymore. They need to see that you're still one of them. One of us."

Mathys took a seat next to me. "I know you can protect yourself—you went into the pipers' court alone, for Chrissake!—but just because you can doesn't mean you should have to. You need someone to help you. Your boy needs a father to guide him. I need someone to help me run the shop." He took my hand again. "Marry me, Annika."

My chest tightened. What they were saying made sense. If the town saw me as separate from them, as changed, marrying someone who was respected in the community would change that. And Falk did need someone to look up to. My first marriage had been one of convenience. Why not my second?

I opened my mouth, then closed it again. After a moment, I said, "Can I give you my answer in the morning?"

His face fell slightly, but he squeezed my hand. "Of course."

All night, I tossed and turned on the straw mattress, listening to the sound of the nearby sheep. Falk slept soundly, oblivious to my turmoil. At last, I rose and went to sit in the kitchen. I poured myself a cup of beer and stirred up the fire. Taking a seat next to the stove, I looked into the flames.

If I married Mathys, Falk would be safe. I wouldn't be happy, but maybe I could convince myself to be content. I wasn't sure I *could* be happy anywhere but in Laute, among my friends. Did I want too much? Maybe, like the people in my mother's stories, my time among the pipers had changed me so that I could no longer be content anywhere else.

But my parents had wanted more for me. They'd worked hard so I could change my lot in life. I was literate, and I had enough money to settle somewhere else. I didn't have to stay in this village, where people left dead dogs on my doorstep and spread rumors behind my back.

And as kind as Mathys had been to me, I couldn't marry him. Not because of my feelings for Loic, but because I couldn't stay trapped here. Brigid had managed to form a comfortable life for herself, married to the man she loved, but I wanted more. I wanted to help people, not to be trapped by the small-minded fears of the villagers.

The money I had was enough to give us a new start in Augsburg. I could—could start a shop that was welcoming to pipers, where they didn't have to hide themselves. It wouldn't do much against the reckless hatred against them, but it could be a step in the right direction. Maybe someday our cultures wouldn't have to be at odds.

And maybe that tiny connection to Laute would fill the aching in my heart.

By the time the rest of the house woke, my mind was calm. As Falk, Dietrich, Brigid, and I sat at the table eating breakfast, Mathys knocked at the door.

I stood, smoothed my skirts, and let him in. "Good morning, Mr. Kiefer."

He raised a brow at the formality but gave me a slight bow. "Good morning, Mrs. Brandt."

"Shall we take a walk?" I grabbed my cloak.

He followed me back outside in silence, and we turned down the street. "Have you thought about my offer?" he said after a minute.

"I have." I stopped walking and looked into his eyes. "Mathys—I'm grateful, but I can't marry you."

He smiled sadly. "I had a feeling you would say that."

"It's nothing to do with you. I just..." I looked at the quiet houses around us, smoke rising from the chimneys. "They're right." I waved a hand. "All of them. I've changed. I can't go back to the way my life used to be and act like none of this ever happened. I need to get away from here."

"I understand."

"I'm sorry." I regretted the sadness on his face, but I couldn't find the same feeling in myself. I'd made the right choice.

"There's nothing to be sorry for." He glanced back at Brigid's house. "I suppose I should return you to your family."

We walked back in silence. At the door, he took my hand and pressed a kiss to it. "I wish you all the best, Mrs. Brandt."

THE PIPER'S PRICE

Loic

"**I**s there any other business?" I cast a lazy glance around the table at my advisors. Teta still wouldn't meet my eyes. Even though I'd had her assigned to the council, ever since I hit her, she'd refused to speak to me outside of her official duties.

"A French noblewoman requests a Delegate of the Pied Piper." Lord Gero, a member of my father's council before mine, produced a letter. "Apparently her husband was wounded in the battle at Marignano. She's hoping a Delegate can hasten his healing."

I was loath to send more of my subjects outside of Laute so soon after the attack, but our Delegates were the only reason the pipers had survived this long. If we refused to answer calls, the other nations on the continent would be at our throats within the year.

"Send two, but get approval from King Francis first. We need him on our side." If we sent a Delegate into his land without his permission, he could use it as a pretext to attack us. Vulnerable as we were right now, I wouldn't take that chance.

"Should we double the price, as well?" Lord Gero asked. He was always anxious to grow the kingdom's treasury. "Since we're sending two."

"Whatever you think is best." None of this truly mattered. We didn't need the money, and the humans didn't need our services. If Laute vanished off the map, no one would miss us. And we had enough gold in our treasury to buy all of France three times over.

Teta scowled, looking into my eyes for the first time in days. "Why charge more? We're providing the same service no matter how many Delegates we send, and we don't need the money."

"Because I commanded it," I hissed, daring her to contradict me.

"And if the family can't pay?" she asked.

The rest of the council was silent, waiting for my response. Would I be the king my father was? Or would I show weakness by offering the humans mercy?

"The law is clear," I said. I heard my father's voice beneath every word. "A life taken for every life saved."

She shook her head. *I thought you wanted to be better than him,* she signed.

I pretended as though I didn't see. "If there's no other business, you're all dismissed."

A New Beginning

Annika

We'd planned to leave within the week, but my nephew was born the day after I rejected Mathys's proposal. As I helped Brigid adjust to life with baby Dieter, I sent word to Pater Trost, and by the time we finally left for Augsburg a fortnight later, the priest had secured us a small house and found Falk a school to attend.

"You'll come visit as soon as we're settled," I told Brigid, taking the baby from her arms and holding him close to my cheek.

"And you'll come to stay with us for Christmas." She wrapped me in a hug, squishing her son between us. "Stay safe, Annika."

Falk kicked the wagon wheel. "Why do we have to go?"

"You'll be back before you know it," Brigid said, ruffling his hair.

"Besides," Dietrich chimed in, "you need a good education. How else are you going to teach your cousin to be a businessman like you?"

That mollified him, but the wrinkle of frustration on his brow didn't vanish. He shook Dietrich's hand and submitted to Brigid's kiss before climbing into the wagon. I hugged them all one last time and climbed up next to him.

I felt nothing but relief as the village faded into the background behind us. Falk wasn't in the mood to talk, and I didn't want to force him, so we sat in silence. Three times in the past year, he'd been forced to leave his home and friends behind. Hopefully Augsburg would be different. A new beginning, for both of us.

We reached the house late that afternoon. Small and white, it was positioned just a block away from Pater Trost's church and two streets from the school Falk would be attending. We carried our trunks inside. It was simply furnished and no bigger than our house in the village. Compared to our rooms in Laute, it was miniscule, but at least here no one was going to drive us away. And no one would leave dead animals on the doorstep.

"What do you think?"

"It's small," Falk said.

I took a seat on the bed. "It's no smaller than home."

"The whole house would fit into our bedroom in the castle." He flopped down onto the bed next to me and crossed his arms. "Why can't we go back?"

I ruffled his hair. "Things just didn't work out."

He shoved my hand away. "Did you do something to Loic? Is that why we can't go back?"

"That's enough." I fixed him with a stern look. "King Loic was more than generous in sending us home." He could have done much worse, like forcing me to leave while keeping the children. He might have grown tired of me, but at least he cared enough to give me back my son.

Filled with a rush of gratitude toward Loic, I pulled Falk into a hug. "We're going to make a new home here. A happy one."

He wriggled out of my embrace. "I thought he liked us," he grumbled.

"Him sending us home had nothing to do with how he feels about you. He thought—thinks—you're wonderful. He just wanted to do what's best for everyone." Loic hadn't been thinking of what was best for everyone when he sent us away, but Falk needed assurance more than truth right now. And I did think that Loic had genuinely cared for my son.

Then again, I'd thought he cared for me, too.

"I have another surprise," I said, hoping to cheer him up. "How do you feel about being a shopkeeper?"

He gave me a wary look. "What do you mean?"

"One of Pater Trost's congregants was selling an apothecary." Gisela, after moving to München, had decided to sell her shop in Augsburg. She'd hired a man to conduct the business for her, and I'd bought it without any contact with my one-time ally. "Did you learn enough from Konrad that you can help me run it?" He would be at school during the day, but in the evenings, he would help me run the shop. Eventually, I hoped it would become his.

"You bought it?"

"I did."

He shrugged. "I guess it'll be okay, then." But he couldn't quite hide the glint of excitement in his eye.

This would be good for us. We could be happy here.

Gisela was an organized shopkeeper—almost compulsively so—and had left notes on her suppliers, customers, products, and anything else I might have needed to know about the business. I worked from the moment I rose until the moment I fell asleep, using the excuse of work to keep me from dwelling on the emptiness inside me. I missed having someone to confide in. My whole life, Brigid had been my confidant, and when I reached Laute, I'd found Teta and Ilse as well. Now I was truly alone, and I missed that companionship as much as I missed Loic. Perhaps even more.

A week in, it had snowed, and the shop was empty. Taking advantage of the quiet morning, I was cleaning the shelves behind the counter, trying to familiarize myself with some of the more exotic stock we hadn't had in my parents' apothecary. A small jar containing a white root was labeled *ginseng,* which Gisela's notes listed as *beneficial for sugar sickness.* Another jar, this one containing tiny brown seeds, was labeled *fennel, for digestive troubles.*

I opened the jar of fennel. The scent was strong, reminding me vaguely of the licorice root my parents would give us for coughs. Closing the jar, I went to set it back on the shelf when I caught sight of a small door hidden behind where the jar had been. Frowning, I set the fennel aside and pulled on the ring-shaped handle.

It opened to reveal a dusty cupboard full of jars and bottles. Extra supplies for the shop? I took out a small clay vial.

Incendiary potion: Handle with care.

Not supplies for the shop. Potions. She'd been experimenting with magic, and judging by the success of the attack on Laute, she'd been successful.

I rifled through the cupboard, reading every label.

Explosive: Handle with care.

For combating musical enchantment.

Topical poison: Do not touch.

She had a whole cupboard full of supplies for waging war. Was that why she had moved to München, to outfit the duke for war against Laute? Judging by the dust in this cupboard, she'd forgotten about it when she packed for her move.

The bell above the door tinkled, and I slammed the cupboard shut. The fewer people that knew about this, the better.

I turned to see a hooded woman, her face completely in shadow. "Good morning," I said, praying for my racing heart to calm. "Is there something I can help you with?"

"Nice place you have here." She removed her hood.

"Teta!" I ran across the shop and threw my arms around her. "Why are you here? Is something wrong?"

"Slow down!" She laughed, pulling back. "I can't understand you when you talk into my shoulder."

Sorry, I signed as I released her. *Come, sit down!* I flipped the sign in the window to read *closed* and led her to the sitting room behind the shop. I poured us each a cup of beer. She took a drink from hers and wrinkled her nose.

"Sorry. That's all I have." I laughed, feeling lighter than I had in weeks. "I missed you."

"I missed you, too." She set her cup aside. "You seem to be doing well."

I shrugged, and my smile faded. "We're adjusting. Falk is in school, and the shop keeps me busy. But what brings you here? Did you come to visit?" It seemed unlikely that Loic would allow it so soon after the attack, but she must have been able to convince him.

"No. I came to bring you home."

Home. My heart skipped a beat. "He changed his mind?"

She rolled her eyes. "I'm changing it for him."

The bubble of hope in my chest popped. "You can't change his mind for him."

"You don't understand. He's changed since you left. He's angry all the time. He lashes out at everyone, and he's withdrawn—even more than usual, I mean. He *hit* me a month ago. We haven't spoken since."

My eyebrows rose. No matter how angry he was, I'd never seen Loic hit anyone. Especially not Teta.

She went on. "He needs you. You soften him. You humanize him. He should never have sent you away."

"But he did. He doesn't want me anymore."

She let out a dry laugh. "If you believe that, you're an even bigger idiot than he is. I told you the day you left, he was scared. He pursued you, and the instant you indicated you might have some real feelings for him, he ran the other way."

"How do you know he won't send me away again?"

"Tell him to get his head out of his ass."

"Yes, that sounds safe." I snorted. "You're the only one who can get away with talking to him like that, and you know it."

"You stood up to him plenty while you were there, and you're still alive." She grinned. "Come back with me. You can kiss and make up. He'll soften up again, you'll be among friends, and we can all live happily ever after."

"It sounds lovely, but—"

"But what? Do you love him or not?"

I did. Saints, I did. He was the reason I couldn't go back to my old life. Why I was stuck here in the city, doing whatever I could to keep busy and drown out the emptiness in my heart. "You know I do," I said softly.

"Then I don't see what the problem is. You're a fighter, Annika. Why won't you fight for him?"

I threw up my hands. "He sent me away, Teta!"

"And you left!" She let out a long-suffering sigh. "I swear, playing emissary between the two of you has been the most exhausting experience of my life."

I decided not to point out that her position as emissary was self-appointed.

"Please, Annika. I'm begging you. For his sake. For your sake. Whatever it takes to get through to you. Come back. Come *home*. Fix things between the two of you. I know you can live without him, but he can't live without you."

I shook my head. "You're wrong." He could live without me. "I can't live without him."

A grin spread across her face. "So you'll come."

I might regret opening my wounded heart back up to him, but I had to know if Teta was right. "I will."

ABANDONED

LOIC

I scowled at the empty chair across from me. What could possibly have possessed Teta to leave? If she came back, I'd throw her in the dungeon for a week. It was akin to treason for one of my advisors to leave without notice. Without authorization.

One of my councilors was droning on. I turned to the man who had spoken. "Are you implying that we should attack Bavaria? Do you *want* to bring every court on the continent down on us?"

"What about England?" another asked. "Henry might be willing to consider an alliance, now that his wife is expecting an heir."

My magic had helped him conceive that heir, but until his son was born, Henry wouldn't view Laute as friends. Possibly not even then. The king of England was arrogant and more likely to credit his own virility than to thank me for my magic.

"Even if he did, that would make England and Laute against all the might of Europe. Henry is no fool. He won't take that risk, no matter what favors we did for him."

The first man crossed his arms. "Then what do we do? We can't sit around waiting for the duke to send another proxy attack."

"What do I pay you for?" I stood and glared around the table. "I ask you for solutions, and you bring me half-cocked suicide plans and more problems!" I picked up the stack of papers before me and threw them in the air. "Out! Come back when you have answers."

My advisors scrambled for the door. Cowards, all of them. Teta wouldn't have run. She'd have thrown the papers back in my face, then told me to sit down and stop throwing a tantrum.

The old Teta would have, at least. The Teta who'd emerged after my father left hadn't spoken to me for a month, except to answer a direct question. And now I'd finally pushed her too far, and she'd left me.

Good for her. If the rest of my advisors had their way, Laute wouldn't last much longer. Better for her to be gone when the surrounding kingdoms descended and swallowed us whole. Maybe she'd find Annika, and the two of them could settle into a happy life without me, far away from the mess of my court.

Good riddance to both of them.

I sighed, straightening the gold band on my head. Time for Hall, where my subjects tripped over themselves to curry favor. The weekly sessions were tedious but necessary to maintain the order of the court.

The evening began as usual. Requests for mediation between bick-ering neighbors, offers of gifts calculated to gain the Pied Piper's no-tice. I half-dozed through it all, speaking only when I had to.

Movement appeared along the edge of the throne room. A late-comer, most likely, pushing toward the throne in hopes that I might notice him. I rolled my eyes.

The newcomer reached the center of the room, and I sat up straight on the throne. The back of my neck prickled. The man had a cloth over his face, a mask of some sort, fashioned to cover his mouth and nose. His eyes, narrowed in anger, met mine. He pulled a ball from his pocket and threw it onto the ground.

It shattered, releasing a cloud of purple smoke into the air.

I jumped to my feet as my guards darted forward. Another at-tack—this one also orchestrated by Annika's witch, I assumed. As soon as the tendrils of smoke reached my guards, the men collapsed.

Screams rang through the room. Members of my court ran for the doors, tripping over one another in their haste.

I took a step forward and stumbled. No. I was too late. I wouldn't make it out.

The room grew hazy as despair swallowed me whole. This was it. The end of Laute. The end of my people. I'd failed them all.

I'd known the court would fall, but I hadn't realized how soon that would be.

At least Annika wasn't here for this. Teta must have gone to her. She'd keep her safe. They'd keep each other safe.

My songbird's face was the last thing on my mind before darkness took me.

ANNIKA

"What do you mean, I can't go?"

Falk had been thrilled when he came home for supper and found Teta waiting with me. His excitement was fading fast now that I'd told him I was going back to Laute without him, for the moment.

"Loic and I have some things to work through first," I said. "I'll be back in a couple days." I didn't know how Loic would respond to my sudden reappearance, and I didn't want to bring my son into the middle of it.

"And then I can go back with you, right?"

"I hope so."

Teta shot me a glare. "Of course you can. Your mom just needs to go put Loic-Ass in his place, and then you can come home." She put an arm around his shoulders. "Who else is going to help me cause mischief in the castle?"

He looked up at her, mouth pinched in suspicion. "Promise?"

"I promise."

At least they were optimistic. It was bad enough that I was setting myself up for another heartbreak, but I hated doing it to Falk. He'd already been devastated when we left. If this didn't work out, he would never forgive me.

I'd packed while we were waiting for Falk to come home. Once we finished eating, I kissed him goodbye and sent him to the *kirche* with a note for Pater Trost, asking the priest to keep an eye out for him. I planned to be gone no longer than two days, no matter how things went with Loic. Hopefully when I returned, it would be to close the shop and take my son back to Laute.

It was late by the time Teta and I reached Laute. A fine layer of snow had fallen during the journey, and the full moon lit up the pine-covered mountains.

It felt like coming home.

Despite the comfort of the familiar scene, knots filled my stomach, growing tighter as we drove into the valley. The city, spread before us, looked the same. Smoke rose from the chimneys, and candlelight danced in the windows. It took me a moment to realize what was missing.

The guards.

Even before the attack, the pass into the valley had been guarded. After King Edric was killed, Loic had doubled the guard, but I saw no sign of anyone. Did Loic care so little for himself and his people that he'd stopped protecting them?

No, that wasn't like him. Something was wrong. I glanced at Teta and found her face tight with worry as well.

Was it still guarded when you left? I signed, unwilling to break the silence.

Yes.

At least I'd left Falk behind. *Should we turn around? Come back with help?*

Help from who? She waved at the city below us. *We're pipers.*

She was right. Few people, if any, would be willing to lend aid to the pipers. If something had happened, our only help could come from within Laute.

We reached the castle and clambered down from the wagon without bothering to tie off the horses. No one guarded the doors. Inside, all was quiet. My heart pounded as we walked through empty halls. Where was everyone? Had there been an attack?

Maybe Loic had evacuated. Yes, that had to be what he'd done. He'd left and taken the court with him, gone someplace safer, someplace where Gisela and the duke couldn't find him.

But then why did the city still look occupied?

I reached out to tap Teta's shoulder, but she held up a hand. I froze.

She pointed to the ground by the doors to the throne room. Something lay on the floor there. A—was it a hand?

She motioned for me to remain silent. Dread pooled in my stomach as she crept toward the doors.

Looking inside, she let out a guttural cry of horror.

"What? What is it?" I grabbed her as she collapsed into a heap. Teta clung to me, and I looked over her shoulder.

Bodies filled the room. The king's guards lay dead before the throne, their cloaks of red and yellow coated with blood. Their swords lay next to them, unbloodied.

"They didn't fight," I breathed. Why hadn't they fought?

The rest of the court was scattered through the room, most having collapsed in the process of fleeing—a broken bottle? Those that I could see had gruesome wounds on their necks or abdomens, as though whoever had killed them had wanted to be sure they were dead.

This had to be Gisela's doing. She'd found some way to incapacitate a whole room, leaving them prone so her mercenaries could kill them.

I tore myself from Teta's grasp and scrambled toward the throne. Where was Loic? He had to be here. He couldn't be here.

I grabbed a body on the steps of the dais and turned it over. The limbs were cool, stiff with death.

Not him.

I let out a sob of relief as I crawled toward the next body.

Not him.

The next—not him. But this one I knew. Reimlin, the guard who'd accompanied me in Augsburg. He wasn't in his guard uniform, so he hadn't been on duty when he died. He'd come to petition Loic for something, or perhaps just to observe Hall. He hadn't known he was going to die here.

Tears streamed down my face, blurring my sight.

Across the room, Teta was doing the same as me, checking each body for a familiar face. Searching for Loic.

At last, we met by the doors.

He's not here, I signed.

Then he's alive. Despite the tear tracks, Teta's face was set with resolve. *Maybe he escaped.*

I shook my head. *He would have come back.*

Then where is he?

She took him. Gisela. For what nefarious purpose, I didn't know. But it was the only thing that made sense.

The witch?

I nodded, looking around at the scattered bodies. *It hasn't been long. A couple hours at most.* The metallic smell of blood was thick in the air, but not the stench of decay. I hadn't seen much death, but I'd seen enough to know what it looked like.

Teta closed her eyes. *I have to get out of here.*

I took her hand, and we walked away from the grisly scene. Hopefully we'd find better news in the city.

THE WITCH

LOIC

My father had been right all along. I was an idiot. Enough of an idiot to allow myself to be captured. My entire court was probably dead, too.

I'd woken in chains, bound by wrists and ankles to the wall in a room lit by a single torch. The shackles bit into my skin; whoever had bound me hadn't been concerned with my comfort. My head pounded, and an acrid taste filled my dry mouth, the after-effects of the potion that had incapacitated everyone at Hall. I couldn't feel the familiar weight of my flute around my neck, so any hope of enchanting my captors was gone.

The Last Pied Piper. That was what I'd be known as. If anyone knew me at all. Those of my people that survived would be scattered. And when I died—I knew better than to hope I'd make it out of here alive—what would happen to their magic? As the Pied Piper, I was the source of all the pipers' magic, of our ability to enchant and entrance with music. If I died without an heir, would the magic pass to a distant relative, or would it die with me?

I looked around the dim room, searching for a sign of who had taken me. Bavaria was responsible, I was sure, but had Wilhelm come for me directly, or was he working through someone else as he had before? I was inclined to believe the latter, given my surroundings.

The room was long and narrow, with an empty table in the center. A shelf of jars and clay vials stood against one wall, and several horrible instruments hung next to them. It didn't appear to be a room in a castle: not as gruesome as a dungeon, and still too rustic to serve any other purpose. A proxy abduction, then, carried out by someone in Bavaria's employ.

My suspicions were confirmed when the door opposite me opened and a young woman walked in. She was dressed in black apart from the white scarf around her head. The witch, I presumed. Gisela Volk, the woman responsible for the deaths of so many of my people. Responsible for more than the deaths in her first attack, unless I was mistaken. She couldn't have stolen me without help, and I doubted that her accomplices had left all the people in the throne room alive after incapacitating them. She wouldn't have wanted to risk pursuit when they awoke.

The thought made me sick. Nearly fifty of my people dead. More, if she'd managed to do the same to the rest of the castle as she had in the throne room. She must have, or someone would have heard the screams and come to investigate. If any of my guards had been left alive, they would have come after her.

How many of my people had this witch killed?

She didn't speak but scanned me head to toe as she approached.

"Shall I call you Gisela, or just Witch?" I sneered at her.

She took my chin in her hand. I jerked back. When she grabbed me again, I snapped at her fingers with my teeth. She snatched her hand back in time, but my respite was temporary. She went to the door and spoke to someone outside, then returned with a bulky, stone-faced guard.

He took my head in both hands, holding me firmly as she looked into my eyes. "No residual effects from the sedative." She pulled an apron off the hook on the wall and tied it around her waist. "Move him to the table. I'll start immediately."

So she planned to torture me before she killed me. Whatever information she was seeking, she'd chosen the wrong source. I wouldn't give her anything.

The witch looked over the wall of torture instruments as the guard unlocked the chains around my wrists. He forced me to my feet, my ankles still shackled together, and shoved me toward the table in the center of the room. I stumbled but managed to keep my feet.

A step away from the table, I jerked my head back. It collided with his nose in a sickening crunch. Not waiting for his reaction, I moved toward the open door. The shackles gave me just enough range to move at a near run. The witch let out a shriek, and thundering footsteps followed me as I reached the hallway.

I barely had time to note the door at the end of the hall before a large hand caught me by the collar. I fought, but the guard was stronger. He dragged me back to the room, blood dripping from his nose. Good. I hoped I had broken it. He glared at me as he bound first my arms, then my legs to the table.

"Running won't do you any good," the witch said, coming toward me with a small but wicked knife in hand. "No one in this city will help a piper."

I clenched my teeth in anticipation of the pain. I wouldn't scream. Wouldn't give her the satisfaction.

I'd witnessed enough torture to know my resolution would fall to pieces before long, but that didn't stop me from making it.

She pressed the tip of the knife into my arm, right above my elbow. I flinched as she carved a narrow slice of skin from my arm. A stinging pain followed. It seemed my fate was to be a slow flaying. I'd suffered worse wounds training with the castle guards. Was she incompetent as a torturer, or did she have ulterior motives for skinning me?

She picked up the piece she'd removed and turned away.

What was she doing with it? I strained my neck, trying to see, but the guard's large body blocked my view. Glass clinked, and a moment later she returned to remove a matching slice of skin from the other arm.

She needed my skin for some spell or potion; that was the only explanation that made any sense. Maybe that was how she'd managed to block our magic, by using piper bodies against us. Now she wanted to use the Pied Piper's body for ingredients.

Once she'd removed her carvings from my arms, she bound my wounds with a thick layer of linen.

"Why are you doing this?" I couldn't help but ask.

She pursed her lips. Her eyes held nothing but hatred as they met mine. "Because you killed my husband and child. You stole my friend's son, and when she tried to get him back, you held her captive as well. You've tormented people across the continent for years." She wiped her hands on her apron. "You're all monsters, and I'm going to end your reign of terror."

That hadn't been what I'd meant, but her answer was interesting nonetheless. We'd held her friend captive. She had to mean Annika. I forced out a laugh.

"You find that amusing?" Her nostrils flared. "Which part, pray, is funny? The hundreds of murders your people have committed? Or the children you've stolen or killed?"

I tried to sit up, but my chains held me tight. I settled for smirking at the witch. A dangerous move, considering she still held the knife, but if I angered her enough, she might kill me quickly. "Which friend was it that I supposedly held captive? That brown-haired little slip of a thing? She was a wonder. So tender, so willing." I licked my lips, watching her eyes flash. Speaking of Annika tore something open in my chest, but I had to convince the witch to kill me. If I lived, I could be used against my people. "Do you know she begged me to keep her? But by then she had grown boring. I moved on to more interesting conquests." I scanned her black-clad body. "Perhaps you'd like to take her place."

Her eyes cast daggers at me, and her chest rose and fell as she struggled to contain her fury. After a moment, she drew a small clay vial from her pocket. She uncorked it, and a wisp of purple smoke rose into the air.

The same potion she'd used to incapacitate my court. I held my breath, but it didn't matter. She waved the vial under my nose. Darkness grew at the edges of my vision.

"A shame," I murmured, fighting unconsciousness. "You might have made an interesting pet."

ANNIKA

The rest of the city was untouched, thank God. Teta and I stayed with Ilse while Konrad and a group of men went up to the castle. Baby Hans dozed in a cradle next to his mother's chair. I held my spiced wine and stared into the fire.

"You didn't hear anything?" Teta asked.

"Nothing until you knocked." Ilse said. "You're sure there were no survivors?"

"We didn't search the whole castle, but I doubt it. Anyone who survived would have raised the alarm."

Ilse shook her head, staring down at the baby. "And they have the king."

I shuddered, and Teta grabbed my hand. *We'll find him*, she signed.

I just hope we're not too late, I signed back. Aloud, I said, "We're going after him."

"There's no one to go with you." Ilse picked up Hans and held him tight to her chest. "Everyone skilled with magic or weapons lived in the castle."

"It wouldn't make a difference. Force won't do us any good here." If Gisela was under the duke's protection, taking armed men to attack her could embroil Laute in an unwinnable war. Loic wouldn't thank me for that. "I might have something else that can help, though." Gisela's forgotten stash of potions had to have something we could use. We couldn't storm the gates of München, but with the blessing of St. Jude, Teta and I might be able to rescue Loic undetected.

"Whatever you're going to do, you can't do it tonight." Ilse stood. "Get some rest. We'll all think clearer in the morning."

We went to our separate bedrooms, but even the warm, soft mattress couldn't lull me to sleep. The horrors I'd seen in the castle kept playing in my mind, alternating with visions of what Gisela might be doing to Loic. Was she torturing him? Had she turned him over to the duke for a reward? Had they already killed him and displayed his body in the streets as some grotesque war prize?

I couldn't think that. Loic was alive. He had to be.

My one comfort in all this was that Falk hadn't been here to witness it. I'd been right to leave him behind. He didn't need those images in his mind.

I slept fitfully. Long before dawn, I crept into Teta's room. She sat on the bed, arms wrapped around her knees, staring out the window.

Can't sleep? she asked.

I sat down on the bed next to her. *No. You?*

I should have been there.

If you'd stayed, you'd be dead like everyone else.

She wiped unshed tears from her eyes. *I didn't tell him I was leaving. He probably thought I'd abandoned him.*

He knows you'd never do that. You can explain everything when we find him.

Neither of us said what we were both thinking: *If we find him.*

I stood. *There's no sense in sitting here all night. The sooner we go, the sooner this will all be over.*

Downstairs, Konrad was awake. "I thought you'd be up soon," he said. "Ilse said you're going after him."

I nodded, my stomach twisting in knots. "We are."

"You know where he is?"

"München, I hope."

"That's a big city. How will you find him?"

Despair clawed at the back of my throat. How *would* we find him? And if we did, would we even be able to help him escape? Or would we all end up in a Munich dungeon awaiting execution?

"Prayer," I said finally. He nodded in understanding. Only a miracle from heaven would make us successful, but we had to try.

"There's a wagon waiting. If there's anything else we can do..."

"Keep the valley safe," Teta said.

"And pray," I added. "Thank you, Konrad."

"God go with you."

We reached the shop early that morning. Falk was already at school, and the shop was dark and silent.

"Supplies first," I told Teta. "Before we leave town, we'll stop by the school and tell Falk what's going on."

She followed me inside, and I began to fill a bag with the potions Gisela left behind.

A tinkle from the bell over the door announced the arrival of a customer.

"I'm sorry," I said without looking up. "We're closed."

"Annika?"

I turned around to see Gisela standing at the door.

JEZEBEL

ANNIKA

My heart leapt to my throat. "Gisela!" I shifted, trying to shield both Teta and the open cupboard from view. *The witch,* I signed behind my back. "What are you doing here?"

She stopped in front of the counter and gave me a half-smile. "I was in the area and thought I'd see how you were adjusting. You're closed today?"

"Yes." I clutched the bag of potions tight. "A family emergency."

"I'm sorry to hear that. I hope nothing's wrong with your son?"

"No, Falk is fine. He's at school."

"Ah." She glanced over my shoulder at Teta. "You haven't introduced me to your friend."

I had to get her out of here. "I'm sorry, but there's really not time. We're expected."

Gisela's smile disappeared. "Annika," she whispered, "is that a piper?"

Sweat beaded on my neck. "What? Why would you—"

"Are you in danger?" She reached across the counter and grabbed my wrist, keeping her voice low. "I can help you."

"She's a friend." I pulled from her grip as Teta stepped around the counter into my line of sight.

What do I do? she signed.

Gisela's eyes flashed, and she took a step back. "I hoped he was lying. Surely it was nothing but a demon's ravings, calculated to infuriate me. But no, you've actually come to care for the creatures."

My stomach formed a knot. "Loic? You have him?"

"You even call him by a name. Have they enchanted you? Is that it?"

Tears filled my eyes. "Tell me you haven't hurt him."

Teta looked between the two of us. With her face still hidden by her hood, I knew she couldn't understand us.

She has Loic, I signed.

"Is he hurt?" Teta yanked down her hood. "If you hurt him—" She cut herself off, shaking with fury.

Gisela's nostrils flared at the sight of Teta's pointed ears and black horns. She turned to me. "You harlot. You *Jezebel.* You've whored yourself to them completely, haven't you?"

I jerked my chin up. "I am no one's whore."

She let out a bark of humorless laughter. "And yet the way you protect that beast says otherwise. Did they promise to share their wealth with you? You must know they're lying." Her gaze softened.

"Please, Annika. Don't let yourself be dragged to hell with this unholy alliance."

"They didn't promise me anything. They're not what you think. Loic, the man you took—"

"He's not a man. He's a demon!"

Is, not was. I glanced at Teta. *He's still alive.* She let out a sigh of relief.

To Gisela, I said, "Whatever you call him, he wasn't the one who killed your family. He's not responsible for any of the crimes the pipers have committed. He wants to change them, wants to be better."

"Is that what he told you?" She scoffed. "A cat doesn't stop mousing. He's not capable of change. None of them are."

"Please, just let him go. I need him."

She gasped, looking at my stomach. "You're not carrying his child, are you?"

"Wh—no!" I wrapped my arms around myself as though to protect the imagined child. "He didn't—we didn't—"

She considered me for a moment. "Good. If you were, I'd have to kill you with the rest of them."

I flinched at the threat. I wasn't carrying Loic's child, but if I had been, I would have fought until my very last breath to protect it. No matter what Loic's feelings toward me were, I would never have let this witch take our child.

"Be grateful I didn't come armed, Annika. I'll leave your companion untouched. But let your new friends know: any pipers that cross my path in future have forfeited their lives."

It was a declaration of war. "They're not what you think they are," I said. "You don't have to do this."

"When you went after your son, I thought you intended to save him from the evil of the pipers. But you don't even see their evil, do you?

You wouldn't resist if they took him again." She spat at me. "You don't deserve to be a mother."

I squared my shoulders. "Get out, and take your hateful rhetoric with you."

We stared at each other for a moment, and then she turned on her heel and left.

Teta took my hand. "He's still alive," I said, needing to hear the words out loud.

"Should we follow her?"

"She'll be watching for us." I turned back to the cupboard and continued filling the bag with potions. I wasn't leaving on what was likely a suicide mission without telling my son goodbye. "We already know she'll be in München. Stick to the original plan."

Once we'd finished packing all the potions we could find, we hurried to Falk's school. It wasn't quite midday; he wouldn't be done for hours, but we didn't have time to waste.

The schoolmaster frowned when he caught sight of me in the door to the classroom. "Continue on," he told the students. "I'll be back in a moment."

He stepped outside with me and closed the door. "Is something wrong, Mrs. Brandt?"

"No—well, yes," I said. "I need to speak with Falk."

He furrowed his brow. "I'm sorry, but Falk isn't here. He left a few minutes ago."

"Left?" Why would he have left? "Where was he going?"

"To you, I thought. The woman who took him said you'd sent her. Falk didn't seem surprised, so I assumed it was alright."

My chest tightened. "Who was she? Did she give a name?"

"I didn't catch a name, no. She was young, dressed in all black. A widow, I think."

Gisela. I clenched my fists, trembling with fear and anger.

I'd kill her.

IMPRISONMENT

LOIC

After the witch took her bits of my skin, she left me shackled to the wall, alone but for the stone-faced guard. He came to feed me once a day, a hunk of stale bread or a bowl of cold, watery soup. He ignored everything I said, whether I bribed or threatened or attempted harmless conversation. When he refused to tell me his name, I called him Cretin, which he ignored as well. He was probably too stupid to understand what it meant.

The pinch in my stomach and the stinging pain on my arms were a welcome distraction from my thoughts as I tried not to dwell on the fate of my people. If I had been a praying man, I would have prayed for their safety, but I knew better than to trust any god with my people. We were universally reviled, and no supernatural being would save us from those who hated us.

My songbird would likely have a different perspective. She would tell me about ancient Israel, how the small kingdom was surrounded by enemies but still survived with the protection of her god. She'd tell me about the Israelite king, David, who faced countless trials and overcame them all with her god's strength. If I allowed her to continue, she would tell me I was like David, my people like the Israelites.

My songbird was naive, but I couldn't fault her zeal.

I wondered how her village had responded to her return. Had they lauded her bravery for going into the demon court and bringing back the children? Or did they fear the woman who could go into the pipers' lands and come out unharmed?

I allowed myself a grin at the thought. If they believed a castle full of demons would stand between my songbird and the people she loved, they were wrong.

My grin faded. She wasn't my songbird. She'd never really been mine.

It was three days before the witch returned. As she walked into the room after her absence, closely followed by Cretin, I smirked at her. "I knew you couldn't stay away."

She pursed her lips and went to the wall containing her supplies. Considering for a moment, she selected a large glass jar and a jagged saw.

My pulse leapt at the sight of the wicked instrument, sharp enough to cut through bone, but I maintained my amused expression. "I wondered when you'd come back to play with me. I hope you have something more interesting planned for today. The last time was so uneventful. Unless you've changed your mind and decided to become my pet?"

She jerked her head toward the center of the room, and Cretin removed me from the wall and bound me to the table. I didn't bother to fight; after three days in the same position, with minimal food, I knew I didn't have the strength to get away.

"Still not willing to surrender to me?" I let out a long-suffering sigh. "Fine. We can play your way. What's it to be today? Shall you take more skin this time, or are we moving on to something new? I must ask that you allow me to keep my tongue. It's one of my favorite features."

She had donned her apron while Cretin moved me to the table. She tucked the jar in a large pocket. "How did you do it?"

"Do what?"

"Convince her you weren't evil." She scowled at me. "After everything you've done, not just to her, but to hundreds of people, she should have been able to see what you really are, but she still believes your lies."

Annika. My heart clenched, and I gripped my shackles to ground myself. The witch had seen her, spoken to her. It took everything in me not to react.

"I'm afraid I don't know who you mean," I said coolly. If she meant to use Annika against me, it wouldn't work.

"Your *pet,*" she snapped. "Annika Brandt. She thinks you're some sort of paragon. Incapable of evil. Idiotic woman."

A sharp pain twisted in my chest. Despite all I'd done, all the ways I'd hurt her, she still didn't believe I was evil. She'd defended me to the witch, possibly even broken ties with her over me.

I couldn't allow myself to think like that. I'd worked hard to stamp out all sentiment, and hoping that Annika cared for me was the worst weakness of all. It was another means of torture, more clever than pain, but still a lie.

"I suspect it's because you gave her back her son," she said, taking the saw and walking around the table. "That matter has been rectified, though."

She stopped at my head as the words sank in. Had she done something to Falk? My nostrils flared. If she'd hurt the boy, I'd kill her myself. Or whatever was left of her after Annika finished taking her apart.

The witch pointed with the saw, and Cretin took my head in his hands, holding me with a too-tight grip. The witch, opposite him, grabbed one of my horns.

She was going to cut it off.

I thrashed, but Cretin held me firm. The pain was like nothing I'd ever felt. I screamed, fighting my bindings, as she sawed through the bone. My vision turned red, red like the blood that poured from the top of my head. I'd never survive this.

She sawed for what felt like hours, but at last it stopped. Bone clattered against glass, and a burning, scarlet oblivion claimed me.

ESCAPE PLAN

FALK

I should have known not to go with the woman. She'd come to school and said Mama sent her, and I hadn't even bothered to question her. I'd thought she was a piper from Laute, coming to fetch me so I could go home with Mama and Loic. I hadn't noticed her eyes were wrong until we left the city, and by then it was too late. Stupid, really. Loic would never have made that mistake.

Mrs. Volk had captured Loic, too. I'd heard her talking about him to the mountain of muscles that guarded the door at the end of the hall. That had to be where they were keeping the prince—no, he was king now. I kept forgetting that. She was probably torturing him for information about the pipers. And she'd taken me because she knew what Mama and I meant to Loic. If he didn't tell her what she wanted to know, she'd probably start torturing me to force him to give up.

I looked around the small room where she kept me. The bed was hard, the blanket itchy. The bedside table held a candle and a cross. I wasn't scared of the witch, but I was bored. Even school was better than this.

Mama would come for us soon. She wouldn't let Mrs. Volk hurt us. But how would she find us? I didn't have any idea where we were. And even if she did come for us, she'd need help. Loic and I had to escape.

I crept toward the door and peered out. The guard stood in front of Loic's door, frowning with his arms crossed. He looked like one of the gargoyles on top of the churches in Augsburg. He wasn't much smarter than a stone gargoyle, either. Which made my plan easier to execute.

I threw the door open and skipped out. "Oh!" I stopped, acting surprised to see the guard standing there in the hall. "I thought you left."

"What?" he grunted.

"Mrs. Volk said you were supposed to help her at the smithy today." I hoped the smithy was far enough away that it would keep him busy. "Did you forget?"

"The smithy?" He looked confused. My plan was working.

"She said she needed new shackles for the prisoner. You're supposed to carry them for her."

"She did?" He scratched his head and looked at the door.

"She won't be happy if you're late," I said. "I can go instead."

He glared at me. "You're not supposed to leave the house."

"Fine." I shrugged like I didn't care. "You'll be the one in trouble. Not me." I looked around. "Do you have anything to eat? I'm hungry."

"I'm not your nurse," he snapped. "Find your own food."

I shrugged again. "Okay." I skipped off in the direction of the kitchen. As I closed the door behind me, I heard the front door open and close.

It worked! I pumped my fist in the air. I didn't want to rush out, though, in case he came back for something.

I looked out the kitchen window. We were outside the city wall but near the gate, overlooking the river. If Mama figured out we were in München, she'd pass right by the house to get into the city. Maybe I could leave her some sort of sign.

I grabbed a knife from above the stove and used it to tear a strip of fabric off of my shirt. Tying the cloth to the sill, I hung it down outside the window. Mama would see it on her way into the city. If we hadn't escaped by then, she'd come and rescue us.

LOIC

When I awoke to throbbing pain and darkness, I was once again bound to the wall. My head felt as though it had been split in two—which it had. I raised my hand, chains clinking, and touched the side of my head, feeling for the stump of my once-beautiful horn. Someone had bound it in linen while I was unconscious.

What was she doing with the pieces she collected from my body? If she was trying to create more potions to block our magic, she didn't need me for that. Another piper, someone easier to get to, would have sufficed. Whatever she was doing, it required the Pied Piper.

Was she trying to destroy our magic?

It shouldn't be possible, but I hadn't thought that blocking our magic was possible, either. Her spells were effective in a way nothing else had ever been against piper music. If anyone would be able to destroy our magic, it would be this witch.

The thought was devastating. Our magic was the only thing between us and ruin. Without it, the nations around Laute would swarm in and destroy us. My people were vulnerable enough; without that final defense, we would be destroyed, and there was nothing I could do.

Once again, the witch left me alone with my thoughts in the aftermath of her brutality. Only the throb of my missing horn could distract me from my pool of dread. Every twitch and pang I felt made me wonder if she'd managed it yet. Her success would spell my imminent death, and not long after that, my people would be wiped out as well.

On the second day of my isolation, a scuffling came from the direction of the door. I didn't bother to look. Every movement of my head sent pain through me, and I had no desire to see whatever vermin had decided to take up residence in my spacious cell.

The door cracked open. "Loic?"

I jerked my head toward the whisper, and a searing pain shot through me. Falk. In the aftermath of the witch's latest visit, I'd forgotten her comment about the boy.

"Falk? What are you doing here?"

His face split in a grin. He closed the door quietly behind him and crept across the room. "Are you hurt? I'm sorry I couldn't get here sooner. The guard never leaves you alone."

"Does your mother know you're here?"

"I think so. I can't stay long, though. She'll be looking for me." He held out a bundle. "I brought you some food."

She would be looking for him. "Your mother? She's here?" The treacherous little—

"What? No. Mrs. Volk." He pressed the food into my hand. "Did she hurt you?" His eyes locked on my bandaged stump of a horn.

"I'm fine." I set the bundle of food next to me, ignoring it. It was a trap, some cruel trick Annika and the witch were playing on me. They'd tried to make me believe Annika still cared for me, when in reality she'd been working with the witch all along. Now they'd sent the boy to try and break me.

And they called me the monster.

"Why are you here?" I bit out.

"She—Mrs. Volk—met me at school and told me Mama had sent her. We came here to München, but she's kept me locked in the house ever since. Don't worry, though. I'm sure Mama is looking for us."

I frowned, fighting against the wave of relief threatening to crash over me. She wasn't working with the witch. The witch had stolen the boy. Unless he was lying, but... I looked into his face and saw nothing but sincerity. He was a child, and not a particularly effective liar.

So the witch had made an enemy of my songbird. I almost pitied her.

Almost.

"I put a sign out for Mama, so she'll know we were here," he went on. "Every day after dinner, Mrs. Volk leaves. I think she's reporting to whoever she works for. The guard doesn't leave, but I can distract him for long enough that we can get out."

"Has she hurt you? Mistreated you?" There was no need for him to risk himself on a half-cocked escape plan. The witch seemed to be treating him well for the moment, but I held no doubts that if she felt threatened, she'd turn on Falk in an instant.

A sound came from another part of the house, and he glanced at the door. "I have to go. Be ready. I'll get the keys from the guard tomorrow morning. We'll leave as soon as Mrs. Volk goes out. Then you and Mama can fix whatever happened between you, and we can be a family." He crept back across the room, peeked out the door, and slipped through it.

A family. The idea was laughable. I would make a terrible father, possibly worse than I'd been as a king. Falk deserved better. And Annika—was it possible that I'd misjudged her? Maybe she really did believe we had to marry to be together. A foolish concept, but if she thought that was the only way she could be with me, if she genuinely cared for me...

Those thoughts would lead to madness. I shook my head, then groaned at the fresh wave of pain. I would never see Annika again. As long as Falk didn't raise the witch's ire, he would be fine until Annika came for him. I would die alone, but they would be safe.

She left me alone for the night, but the next morning, the witch returned with Cretin. She put on her apron—I'd begun to hate the sight of the white fabric on her black dress—as he dragged me to the table and strapped me down. Once I was secured, she waved for him to leave. The door closed behind him, and the witch selected several vials from the shelf.

"Alone at last." I sighed. "I wondered when your friend would give us privacy. Shall we play some more?"

She glared at me. "I'd expect someone as close to death as you to talk less."

I shrugged as best I could in the chains. "As I told you before, my tongue is my favorite feature."

"When I'm finished with you, you won't have enough features left to choose a favorite from." She pulled a small book from her pocket and set it next to my head. "I couldn't find any traces of magic in your hair, skin, skin, or horn, and as I don't want to kill you prematurely, I suppose I'll have to start working with the raw material."

I'd been correct; she was trying to remove my magic, or at least to find the source of it. I didn't doubt that with enough time she would succeed.

"Will this take long? I have afternoon plans." I grinned at her.

"The only one you should be making plans with is your Master, the devil. You'll be seeing him soon. Now, where shall we begin?" Considering me for a moment, she uncorked a vial and held it up. "Perhaps your favorite feature."

She grabbed my chin, and before I could move, poured the potion into my mouth.

It tasted like smoke and fire. She released me, and I coughed, trying to expel the foul liquid. It remained on my tongue, burning a hole through the muscle. My stomach heaved, and I retched on the table next to my head. It did nothing to ease the pain.

The witch snatched her book back just in time. Opening it, she watched me dispassionately. I spat bile at her, but she stepped back and wrote something down.

"Can you speak?" she asked.

I didn't want to give her anything she wanted, but I feared she had taken my voice. I opened my mouth. "I...can."

She frowned. Evidently that wasn't the answer she wanted.

The burning sensation in my mouth had faded slightly. I moved my tongue around, feeling for the whole left behind, but found nothing. She hadn't damaged me irreversibly.

She made a final mark in her book and set it down near my feet, where I couldn't damage it with vomit. I tried to kick it to spite her, but my bonds were too tight.

"Ears next, I suppose." She picked up another bottle and uncorked it.

Even if she didn't manage to remove my magic, she could still deafen me, pouring her spells into my ears. I writhed against the chains, but turning one side of my head away exposed the other.

She poured the potion into my ear, and something erupted.

MÜNCHEN

ANNIKA

She had my son.

I'd been angry before, devastated at the havoc she'd wrought on the pipers, but now that she'd taken Falk, I was livid.

She'd chosen the wrong child. Harming me and my friends was bad enough, but my son was off limits. I'd faced people I once thought were demons in order to save him. She and her duke wouldn't stand in my way. I'd save Falk and Loic, and I'd stop her. Whatever it took.

Teta and I drove through the countryside in silence, absorbed in our own thoughts and worries. I barely noticed the scenery, the snow-covered trees and breathtaking mountains, so like the ones that surrounded Laute.

München was in sight when Teta let out a loud groan and doubled over.

"What is it?" I asked, forgetting she couldn't hear me. I put an arm around her, looking frantically around as she clutched her head. Were we under attack? I didn't see anyone nearby, but maybe they were hidden. I grabbed the reins, ready to leave at the first sign of movement.

"I'm fine," she said. "I—oh!" She groaned again, rocking back and forth. "I think—I think it's Loic."

My stomach dropped. What was Gisela doing to him? My chin quivered as I held her close. If Gisela had killed him, her death would be long and painful.

Teta finally recovered enough to sit up and look at me. Tears filled her eyes.

Is he dead? I signed, afraid to speak the word out loud.

I don't think so. I've never felt anything like it. She looked up at the city before us. *I think he's hurt. Or the magic is hurt.* She rubbed her hand along the edge of her ear, then drew her hood tighter around her face. *We have to find him. Now.*

We crossed the bridge and approached the city gate. Where did we go from here? It wasn't as though we could march up to the duke's residence and demand to see Gisela. Was she even staying with the duke? Just because he supported her didn't mean he was housing her. *Blessed Michael, defend us,* I prayed. I looked around, fighting against the rising wave of despair.

A piece of blue fabric fluttered from the window of a nearby farmhouse. Familiar fabric. My heart skipped a beat, and I drew the horses to a stop.

"What is it?" Teta asked.

That's Falk's shirt.

"Are you sure?"

Yes. But was it a trap laid by Gisela, or a sign left for us by Falk? We'd have to take the chance. *Let's go.*

LOIC

If I'd thought my head hurt before, it was nothing compared to now.

The witch had been ecstatic after pouring the potion into my ear. Whatever reaction she'd been hoping for, she'd found it. She'd examined me thoroughly, peering and poking at different points on my head. Finally she'd poured another potion into the other ear, causing a second agonizing eruption, and left me alone.

My head ached and my ears rang, but more than that, there was a hole in my chest, a bone-deep emptiness that filled me with dread. I looked at my arms. The piebald spots were still there, the symbols of the Pied Piper, but I felt different.

I didn't need the witch's confirmation to know she'd taken my magic. She'd ensured my people's doom. Now all she needed was some proof that it had affected the other pipers before she killed me.

Death would be a welcome reprieve.

I lay staring at the rafters, awaiting my doom. Movement flickered in the corner of my vision, though no sound accompanied it. I turned my head to look my killer in the eye.

It wasn't the witch, though. Falk's mouth moved, but no sound came out.

I wouldn't be responsible for his death as well. "Go away, boy," I said. My voice sounded hollow and distant.

His mouth moved silently again. Had the witch taken my hearing with my magic? Damn her. Not that I would need hearing when I became food for the worms.

"Go away," I said again. "You're going to get yourself killed, and your mother will flay us all alive." Not an exaggeration. For all her innocence, Annika would tear heaven itself apart for her son.

Let's go, he signed. *Quiet.*

I lifted my hand as high as I could to reply. *Who taught you to sign?*

He shook his head and pulled a key from his pocket. Unlocking my chains, he reached to help me to my feet.

"I can stand on my own, thank you." I was shaky, weak from pain and lack of food, but I sat up, then stood.

He said something else that I couldn't hear, and he froze, horror dawning on his face.

I turned to the door and saw the witch.

Ice ran through me. I pushed Falk behind me. She could kill me, but he had to get out. He couldn't die for me.

She said something I couldn't understand. Damn me. Why hadn't I learned to read lips like Teta. It would have been a useful skill—more useful than signing.

The witch's lip curled in distaste as she spoke again.

Distract her. Draw her attention. "How long will the effects of your potion last?" I asked, pushing Falk further behind me. *Get out,* I signed behind my back.

She laughed and spoke again. I thought I saw her mouth form the word *forever.*

No matter. I wouldn't survive long enough for it to make a difference. Not without weapons or magic. I just needed to keep her distracted long enough for Falk to get out. But the boy wasn't moving. Why wasn't he leaving?

He stepped in front of me, and the witch looked to the door, shouting something. Calling for Cretin, most likely.

My suspicions were confirmed when the brainless guard stepped into the room. I fought as he grabbed me, but he overpowered me with ease and chained me to the wall.

"Run!" I yelled at Falk. He darted toward the door, but the witch blocked his way. Cretin caught him by the waist and picked him up, carrying him to the table where I'd been bound.

"Leave him alone!" I thrashed against the manacles, but there was nothing I could do as Cretin strapped the boy to the table.

The witch said something to Cretin, and he walked over to me, raising a large hand. He hit me atop the head, and I saw stars.

EXORCISM

ANNIKA

The fabric hung from a kitchen window. I peered inside, but it was empty. We inched around the house and looked inside each window. Nothing. Either the house was abandoned, or they were in a windowless room. We stopped in front of the door.

Do you hear anything? Teta asked.

I pressed my ear to the door, straining for the slightest sound. All was silent.

Then I heard a shout from inside. *Loic.*

She tested the door. Unlocked. *Hold your breath.* Pulling a vial from her pocket, she threw the door open and chucked it inside. She slammed the door shut as purple smoke erupted.

After a minute, we dared to open the door again. The hallway was empty; our potion hadn't drawn anyone out. I held up a hand for Teta to wait.

I hear water.

Water?

Splashing.

Loic screamed again. Heart in my throat, I took off running toward the sound.

"Annika!" Teta's harsh whisper stopped me in my tracks. *Rushing in won't help anyone.* She pushed the door open a crack. *See what's happening first.*

Loic hung on the far wall, chained by his wrists and ankles. His face twisted in fear and anger as he stared at the center of the room.

I followed his gaze to the table, and my heart stopped.

Falk lay prone on the table, his head hanging off the edge. A bulky man with a flat nose held him by the collar and dunked his head into a bucket of water. Gisela stood over him, a cross in one hand and a Bible in the other. Smoke from a bowl of incense filled the air, choking me.

"...Prince of the heavenly host," Gisela intoned, "remove from this child all influences of the Evil One. Free him from the bonds of temptation, and cast this demon and his ilk back into the abyss with their Master." The big man pulled Falk's head out of the water and dunked him again.

"You're killing him!" I screamed, rushing into the room.

She turned, eyes wide with shock. "I'm *saving* him." She stepped in front of the table, blocking me from my son.

"Let them go." My voice shook as I looked from Falk's unconscious body to Loic's agonized face. His eyes wouldn't focus, and one of his horns was broken off, white bandages covering the stump that remained. Teta crept around the edge of the room, toward Loic, while Gisesla and the guard were focused on me.

"Your son's soul is in immortal peril, but still you worry about the demon." Venom filled her words. "As I told you before, you don't deserve to be a mother."

I took a step closer, reaching a hand toward my son, but she didn't move.

"You're killing him," I said again. My voice cracked.

Her face held no trace of sympathy. "Better to die saved than to live damned." She turned back to him, raising the cross once more.

I pulled a potion from my pocket, but the guard barreled into me before I could throw it.

"Annika!" Loic shouted as I hit the floor. The vial shattered.

A faint shimmer rose from the broken potion. I held my breath, but the guard wasn't quick enough. He took a deep breath of the fumes, and his eyes rolled back in his head. He collapsed in a heap.

Struggling not to inhale the potion, I scrambled to my feet. Its range wasn't far. I took a step away and could breathe freely.

I reached for another potion. I didn't care what it was—fire, poison, anything—as long as it would hurt her.

LOIC

My songbird was here.

I could have wept. She was here. To save—to save—

I struggled to focus on the scene before me. Fog filled my head, but I fought my bonds anyway. I had to help, had to get her and Falk out. Cretin lay on the ground, unmoving, but the witch was still a danger.

Teta's face filled my vision. I blinked, but the sight remained. She spoke. I couldn't hear her.

Loic. The key.

Signs. I understood signs. The key.

Do you know where the key is?

Why was my head so thick, my thoughts so slow to come?

The key. Teta needed the key to my chains. I blinked, looking around. I'd seen the key. Falk must have dropped it when he—when he— Something.

There. I pointed, and Teta turned to look.

The witch was distracted by my songbird. My songbird, whose face was full of torment. Tears streaked her face.

I should go to her, comfort her. I tried to reach out my hands, but they wouldn't move.

Chains. Right.

Teta unlocked my shackles. My hands fell to my sides, needles running through them

We have to go, she signed.

Not without Annika. Not without Falk.

But Falk wasn't moving. *Is he alive?*

The witch whipped around to look at us, but Annika threw something at her. It missed, sailing harmlessly past the witch's head to shatter against the wall. Green sparks erupted from it.

Annika threw potion after potion at the witch, who dodged again and again. Teta took my arm, trying to pull me away from the scene, but I couldn't leave. Not without them. The potions exploded all around us, hitting the walls and the floor and releasing sparks and smoke of various colors.

ANNIKA

Gisela stepped over an oily puddle of potion. "All that time with the demons, and you can't even wield my magic."

I didn't bother to reply. I'd run out of potions, but there were weapons on the wall. I grabbed a jagged saw.

She pulled a small black jar from her apron. "The wicked will be thrown into the lake of fire, Annika. You will burn with the demons you love." She threw the jar at me.

I slammed into her as the jar hit the wall behind me. A roar of heat and light filled the room. I ignored it as I pressed the saw against her neck.

"The only one who will burn," I whispered, "is you." The teeth of the saw bit into her neck, and warm blood rushed over my hands.

LOIC

Flames filled the room. I couldn't breathe, couldn't see anything. Where was Annika? I put out a hand in front of me, feeling for something, someone. I groped around until I found the table, and on top of it, Falk's body, drenched with holy water and smaller than he'd ever seemed before. I put a hand on his chest. It rose and fell, faint but steady. He was alive.

But the key. Where was the key?

A hand touched my shoulder, and the key dangled in front of my face. Teta. I grabbed it from her hand and unlocked the boy.

We need to get out of here, she signed.

Where's Annika? I scooped up the boy and looked around. Through the haze of smoke and fire, I saw her rise, staring down at the witch.

"Annika!" I shouted. She flinched, and her eyes met mine. "Let's go!"

The flames were growing higher. If we didn't make it out soon, we wouldn't be able to leave. I shoved Falk into Teta's hands and pushed

them toward the door. Dropping to my knees, I crawled toward Annika.

She jerked back when I grabbed her leg, but I pulled her down to
me. "Falk is safe," I yelled. "Come with me."

I half-dragged her toward the exit. We made it outside just before
the roof caved in.

Annika collapsed on the ground, coughing. "Falk?" she asked. I
couldn't hear the word, but I knew what she was saying.

I gathered her into my arms. "He's here. He'll be okay."

She let out a shuddering breath and relaxed into my touch. She'd
come back for me. She'd saved me. Risked her life for me. How could
I ever have doubted her?

She rested her head on my chest, and her whole body shook with
sobs I couldn't hear.

"It's over," I said, clinging to her, needing to reassure myself that
she was safe, whole. "We're going to be alright."

THE PIPERS

LOIC

The fire drew people toward us. Men carried buckets of water, dumping them onto the burning building, as women and children gawked at the spectacle.

We need to leave, I signed, *before someone notices us.*

Teta deposited Falk into his mother's arms. She pulled up her hood. *I'll bring the wagon. Meet me at the bridge.*

I shepherded Annika toward the bridge out of the city, where Teta waited. Falk had woken, and Annika helped him into a sitting position in the back of the wagon. She peered into his eyes and checked him for injuries. Her mouth moved rapidly as she spoke.

A pit opened in my chest. I might never hear her voice again. The last time we'd spoken, I'd said things I didn't mean. I'd hurt her. The last words she'd spoken to me had been devastated, heartbroken, because of me. And now I might never hear her voice again.

If the witch wasn't already dead, I'd kill her myself.

But Annika was safe, and Falk and Teta. That was what mattered. I climbed up onto the wagon seat next to Teta, and she handed me a pile of clothes. *You should put on something clean. You reek.*

Is it gone? she asked as we drove across the bridge. *Your magic?*

I shrugged. I wasn't sure I was ready to face that possibility, but Teta always had a knack for making me face things head-on. *Probably. I haven't had a chance to test it yet.*

She touched her head. *I felt it happen.*

That didn't bode well. I clenched my teeth. If she'd felt it, so had all the other pipers. It was only a matter of time before word got out to the rest of the world. Our magic was gone, the one thing standing between us and our destruction.

My father had been right. I was a failure. The destruction of Laute. The last Pied Piper.

Teta waved her hand in my face. *Stop.*

Stop what?

What you're thinking. It wasn't your fault.

I scowled at her. *I hadn't realized you could read minds. It might have come in handy during council meetings.*

She grinned. *There's the Loic-Ass I love.*

Love. I didn't deserve it. My scowl deepened, and she punched my shoulder

I said stop.

Annika put a hand on each of our backs, drawing our attention. *What's wrong?*

Teta shook her head. *Just Loic-Ass being his usual gloomy self.*

Annika looked up into my eyes. Her face was soot-covered and splotchy, her lip still trembling. The sight sent another crack through my shriveled heart. I couldn't look away.

She opened her mouth, then closed it again. Then she turned back around and sat next to her son. She wrapped her arms around him and rested her cheek on his head. For once, he didn't fight the affection. He could see how badly she needed it, how frightened she had been. And maybe he needed the assurance as well. He was just a child, after all.

I'd nearly gotten her son killed. If I hadn't taunted the witch about Annika, Falk would never have been taken. I was a damned fool. She deserved better.

Teta and I spent the next several hours discussing the state of Laute and what to do from here. We avoided the topic of her disappearance. If she'd left me for good, I didn't want to know. For now, she was here, and I would need all the help I could get if we were going to survive this. We could deal with her defection tomorrow. In a month. Never.

More surprising was her silence on the topic of Annika. My songbird had fallen asleep in the back of the wagon, along with Falk, but still Teta didn't press me about what had happened between us or what the future held. She must have realized it wasn't her business. It would be a first for her, but these were unprecedented times.

At last the familiar mountain peaks of home came into view. I let out a deep sigh as the lengthening shadows reached us.

Home. Safety, at least for tonight.

Annika and Falk woke as we entered the pass. It was strange, entering the familiar place without one of my senses. I missed the howl of the wind and the clatter of horses' hooves against the stones. The scent of pine and snow filled my nose. The frigid air wrapped around me, welcoming me home, but it felt wrong. Incomplete.

As though she'd sensed my discomfort, Annika's gentle touch ran over my hair. I turned to look at her, and she snatched her hand away.

Was she worried about my reaction, or embarrassed by her own? I wanted to grab her hand back, but she stiffened, eyes fixed on something at the end of the pass.

ANNIKA

A voice called through the darkness. "Who goes there?"

I froze, dropping my hand to my side. Teta couldn't hear him, and if Falk was right, Gisela had taken Loic's hearing as well. The speaker was too far to see. Was it a friend guarding the pass, or someone who'd returned to finish off the pipers?

We'd have to take the chance. I cleared my throat. "Your king, returning from his captivity, along with his companions."

"Why doesn't he speak for himself?"

I tapped Loic on the shoulder. I could barely see him, but I signed near his face. *Tell them to stand down.*

"Stand down!" he called, louder than necessary. "Your king commands it!"

A light flared ahead of us, and a face I didn't know came into view. "Your majesty! Where have you been?"

With the light, Teta could see the man's face. "Do you think now is the time to interrogate him?" she snapped. "It's freezing out here, and he's injured. Your questions can wait."

"Lady Teta! Yes, of course. Right this way." He turned as though to lead us into the valley.

"We can find our own way," she said. "Don't leave your post."

He scrambled out of the way as she drove past. The mountains opened up, and we entered the valley. Home. I took a deep breath and sank back down next to Falk. We were safe.

Konrad met us on the castle steps. "Your majesty, we're so glad you're back safe."

Loic nodded, glancing at Teta and then me as he stood. He couldn't understand anything. I signed Konrad's words for him, feeling as though it was my fault. If we'd been faster, we might have gotten to him in time to save his hearing.

"Unfortunately, the people who took me didn't leave me undamaged," Loic said, his voice too loud. "They took one of my horns, as you can see, but they also managed to take my hearing. I'm hopeful that the effect is temporary, but until it fades, Lady Teta and Mrs. Brandt can act as my interpreters."

Warmth spread through me. He trusted me, at least enough to let me do this for him.

"Of course, your majesty." Konrad bowed. "After the...events of your disappearance, we've been using my house as a central meeting point. People are uncomfortable being in the castle." He waited while Teta translated.

"We'll go there, then." Loic climbed out of the wagon. He stumbled, and my heart stuttered.

"Maybe we should—" I cut myself off. If Loic wanted to take the wagon, he would take it. He didn't want to be seen as weak in front of his people. They needed someone strong to lead them now.

I went to him and took his arm. If he was going to walk, he could at least have someone to lean on.

Konrad's house was packed full of pipers, all talking at once. Ilse met us at the door. "Annika!" she gasped, throwing her arms around me.

It wasn't until she let go that she noticed Loic. "Your majesty!" She swept a bow. "I'm sorry, I'm—"

He waved her off, not waiting for me to translate. As strong and confident as ever, he strode past her into the house. He tucked his hands into his pockets, giving off a casual air, but I knew he did it to keep everyone from seeing how they shook.

Falk, Teta, and I followed behind him. He stopped in the sitting room, next to the fire, and waved a hand for silence.

"I'm sure you've all been wondering where I've been," he said. His voice was loud, but if I hadn't known about his hearing, I would have assumed he was just trying to make himself heard throughout the house. "Did I abandon you in your greatest hour of need? Was I captured? Killed?

"I did not abandon you, and you can see I wasn't killed. Our enemies, those who perpetrated the attack in which my father was killed, took me captive. This past week, they used me for vicious experiments, trying to remove my magic, and in turn, yours."

A murmur went through the room. He took a deep breath and looked around. "I fear they succeeded."

Someone in the back of the room spoke. "I tried to play a tune this afternoon to call the sheep back in. They never responded."

"Is that what the pain was this morning?" another asked.

A panicked voice rose up. "Are we defenseless?"

Teta couldn't see the speakers, and I couldn't sign fast enough to keep up. I cast a frantic look at Loic, who raised his hand again.

"Peace," he said. "There's no need to panic. We don't know for sure that the magic is gone." He paused. "A test. Does anyone have a flute?"

One was produced, and Loic put it to his lips. I held my breath as he met my eyes and began to play.

The song was filled with sorrow and regret. The loss of his hearing hadn't affected his ability to play in the slightest. He kept his gaze fixed on me and poured out a tune of remorse and repentance. For me? For his people? I didn't know, but it made me want to weep.

But I didn't sense any magic. Didn't taste the tang of metal or feel the heaviness in my bones.

She'd done it. She'd taken their magic.

Tears dripped down my cheeks as the song came to an end. He passed the flute back to its owner and closed his eyes, taking a deep breath. Then he opened them and addressed the room once more.

"It would seem our enemies were successful."

Everyone began talking at once. He spoke over them. "As I am no longer your Pied Piper, I will not decide your future for you." Sorrow filled his face. "I won't deny it—we are vulnerable. All the powers of the continent will want to come for us once they find out what we've lost. Staying here, in this valley, we could hold them off for a time, but not indefinitely. We could seek a new home, but I can give you no guarantee that we'll find one." He sighed. "Or we can disperse."

Disperse? Did he mean to disband Laute? What good would that do?

Konrad was the first to speak. He stepped in front of Loic. "You may not be my Pied Piper, but you are my king. I would follow you to the ends of the earth, but I fear there will be no safe place for our people. Not together, not in these numbers." He looked around the room. The people in the house represented only a small fraction of the pipers Loic ruled. "If you allow it, I will take my wife and son and leave. We will live among the humans."

THE END

ANNIKA

This was the end of Laute.

The discussions went on all night. Teta finally convinced Loic to sit down, and Ilse found him some food. He sat, attention fixed on whoever was speaking, though he couldn't hear the words. Occasionally, he would take a bite, chewing thoughtfully as he considered his response.

By the time morning came, I was dozing in my chair. Falk had long since disappeared in search of a bed, and most of the pipers had left for their own homes. Still Loic showed no sign of exhaustion.

It was only when Konrad shooed the last of them out that Loic finally sagged back in his seat, a hand over his face.

My heart broke for him. His kingdom was crumbling beneath him, and despite all he'd suffered, he had to be strong.

After a long moment, during which I thought he might have fallen asleep, he sighed and stood. He nodded to Teta, Konrad, and Ilse—the only ones who remained. Then he extended a hand to me.

"To bed, songbird." The words were an order, but I saw the vulnerability behind his eyes. He needed me.

I couldn't refuse him.

We found a guest room upstairs. I was so tired I could hardly walk, but when we reached the room, a strange, hazy energy took over.

Loic stripped off his borrowed shirt, then took a seat on the bed and removed his boots. His eyes followed me as I poured water into the washbasin and scrubbed away the worst of the soot and blood.

"Come," he said finally. He helped me pull off my filthy clothes, leaving me in nothing but my long shirt.

"I would kiss you," he said, lying back on the pillow and tucking me into his chest, "but I don't know if I could stop." He closed his eyes, and in an instant his breathing was slow and even.

It was enough. For now, being together, being safe, that was enough.

When I woke, neither of us had moved. The dim light of sunrise or sunset came through the curtains.

I tilted my head up to look at him. It was the first opportunity I'd had to really consider him since we'd left München. He hadn't yet shaved his beard, and the week of growth gave him an almost feral look.

I liked it.

He had a bandage on each of his arms above the elbows, and a cut on his cheekbone, as if someone had struck his face. I raised my hand to trace it.

"I don't recall giving you leave to touch me," he said. His eyes cracked open.

I smiled, brushing my hand over his cheek. *I don't recall asking for it,* I signed.

He gave me that familiar smirk, but it faded, and he sat up.

"Forgive me," he said. "I've put you in a compromising position again."

I frowned, sitting up as well. I was a mess, desperately in need of a bath, with my shirt wrinkled from sleep, but I didn't care. *What are you talking about?*

He stood and turned away from me. A fresh set of clothes had been laid out for each of us. He pulled on the shirt, irrespective of the layer of grime that covered his skin. "I thank you for your assistance. It was kind of you to free me when you came for your son."

Was he trying to tell me he didn't want me? Tears pricked at my eyes. I'd thought we could move past it. I loved him—why else would I have saved him? But maybe he didn't want me after all.

After a moment, he turned back to me. He saw my face and stopped. "Why are you crying?"

"Don't you—" He couldn't hear me. *You don't want me?*

He was the picture of confusion. "What?"

I came back for you.

"But Falk—"

Teta and I were already coming when we found out she had Falk. I bit the inside of my cheek to stop from crying. I'd cried enough. *Did you really think I'd leave you to her?*

"Thank you for that."

He didn't understand what I was saying. *I love you, Loic.*

There was a chair next to the bed. He sank into it. "I—what?"

I repeated it. *I love you.* "I love you." Once the words were out, I couldn't stop saying them, signing them.

He watched my hands and my mouth as though he couldn't believe what I was saying. "I'm not a king. I'm nothing."

I threw my hands up in the air. "You complete and utter idiot!" I took a deep breath. *I don't care about that. I never did. I love you, and I never wanted to leave. I'm yours, Loic. For better or worse.*

"'For better or worse.'" His eyes darkened, and he scowled at me. "Are you still trying to trap me into marriage? You think I would make you my equal?"

Something cracked inside me. I didn't have to listen to him insult me and break my heart again. I stood, ready to run out the door, but he grabbed my chin in his hand and forced me to meet his eyes.

"I can't make you my equal, songbird. You're not my equal, and you never will be."

Hadn't I proven myself to him again and again? Why did he have to drive everyone away? I tried to jerk from his grasp, but he held me firm.

"You're so far above me, it would be cruel to let you believe you're my equal." He let go of my face and went to his knees before me.

I stopped breathing.

"But I'd rather be cruel than let you leave me again, so I'll do whatever it takes." He took my hand in both of his. "Stay with me, Annika. Be my queen."

"I—" I choked on the words. *Are you asking me to marry you?*

"No, I'm not asking you. I'm telling you. Be my queen. Be the mercy to my justice, the kindness to my cruelty. I'm the king of a broken kingdom, but whatever remains, it's yours."

It was all I'd ever dreamed of and never dared to picture.

His eyes narrowed. "You haven't answered me."

I didn't know I was supposed to respond. He hadn't asked a question, after all. And what could I say to the fulfillment of all my dreams?

"Don't play with me." He pressed a kiss to my hand. "Marry me, Annika."

Joy rose inside me, bubbling up into a laugh. "Yes. Yes, Loic, I'll marry you."

EPILOGUE: LAUTE REBORN

ANNIKA

Loic stood against the rail of the ship, watching the land fade behind us. The sunlight shone on his dark hair, glinting off his remaining horn.

Falk's shout of excitement came from the front of the ship, where he was learning to sail. He wanted to be a pirate prince, he said. He'd taken to his new title with relish, as soon as he'd discovered he didn't have to learn statecraft or wear a crown everywhere.

Just this moment he looked as un-prince-like as it was possible to be. He was bare-chested, his hair tousled by the wind, and he ran after one of the crew, doing his best to help. Teta watched from nearby, grinning at him.

I shook my head and stepped up beside Loic, wrapping my arm around his waist.

He turned from the shore to look down at me. "Hello, my queen." *What are you thinking?*

He smiled ruefully. "I'm thinking this will be a long journey."

Do you regret it? I searched his face. He was always so guarded, impossible to read. Even now. Even from his wife.

But he was learning to open up to me. He shook his head. "Not leaving. I'm not looking forward to spending the next several months in that tiny cabin, but I don't regret leaving Laute."

I rested my head on his shoulder. *We're not leaving Laute. We're taking it with us.* I waved at the two ships accompanying us. Only a fraction of the pipers had agreed to come with us; the rest had decided to take their chances in Bavaria and the surrounding lands.

He gave me a crooked smile. "If this is Laute, it's fallen far."

No, it hasn't. I pressed a kiss to his cheek. *We still have our king. You make us the grandest people on earth.*

"I thought I told you never to lie to me, songbird." At my frown, he tucked a finger under my chin and lowered his voice. "The king doesn't make a people great. The queen does."

He leaned in to kiss me, but I pulled back. *What about the prince?*

He glanced toward Falk, who was climbing a rail at the front of the ship. "He's every bit his mother's son," he said with a smile.

I moved his hand to rest on my stomach. *Or princess?*

His face went blank.

Was he displeased? In the weeks since we'd rescued him, we hadn't had time to discuss having more children. Conceiving Falk had been such a struggle, I hadn't even known if I would be able to bear more children.

He searched my eyes. "Are you—"

"Pregnant?" I nodded, my chest tight. *Are you upset?*

"Upset?" He took my face in his hands. "Songbird, seeing you as a mother has been the greatest joy of my life. I don't deserve it, but I'm honored to father your children."

I love you, Loic.

"I love you, Annika."

My eyelids fluttered closed as he leaned in, and our lips met. I didn't know what the future would hold, but with him at my side, I could face anything.

THE END

AUTHOR'S NOTE

If you're looking for more of the pipers, stay tuned for my next fairytale retelling, *Wings of Living Flame,* coming March 2025. In the meantime, enter a world of vampires and witches, and demon hunters with my *Trials and Temptations* series. Book 2 releases September 2024.

To keep up to date with all my future releases, follow me on Instagram @dakotah.gumm.author or on my website, dakotahgumm.com.

Acknowledgements

As usual, I couldn't write what I do without my God and Savior who gave me life. Annika's story is close to my heart and follows my own faith journey over the past few years. Reader, I hope you found something between these pages to touch your own heart.

This book was written for my husband, my pied piper, who even in our darkest moments never made me feel anything less than worthy. Andrew, thank you for your undying love and support.

The people responsible for putting this book in the world are innumerable. My alpha and beta readers: Madeleine Miles, Sarah Logan, Harmony Marquardt, Faye Knightly, Heather Carter, Elizabeth Myrva, Janna Rice, Kelly Keith, Courtney Taylor, Coy Haddock, and Zara J Black. The artists who made this story come to life: Paula and the other lovely folks at Majikah Perfumery, who worked with me to create the Piper's Muse perfume; Cherron, for creating the first art of Loic; and Michelle Hermes, for giving Annika a face.

To my friends and family who have always supported me: thank you. To name you all would require more page space than I have here, but you know who you are.

And to those who tried to stop me—get rekt.